FOR RUTH BRIDGET

Sometimes I like my clients, sometimes I don't. I try to convince myself that I do an adequate job either way. But sometimes I wonder. I wasn't fond of Miles Stewart, M.D., whom I had just defended in the Wayne County Circuit Court. We were in a courtroom located high up in the towering City-County Building, a governmental sky-scraper overlooking the sports-minded City of Detroit. Detroiters love all sports, especially contact sports, like mayhem. Here mayhem has been raised to a contest of Olympic proportions. Mayhem is a sport where scorekeeping is easy. Corpses, number of stitches, or artful location of bullet wounds count for points, but you truly win only if you survive. Lately, in Detroit, there had been a lot of losers.

Stewart, who had been reading a medical journal, put it down and walked to where I was sitting. His steps echoed in the nearly empty courtroom.

"They've been out a very long time," he said. "I presume that's a good sign."

"You never really know," I replied. "Juries tend to take murder cases somewhat seriously. Even in Detroit. It's been a long trial, and this is only the second day of deliberations. But common wisdom does say that the longer a jury is out the better it is for the defendant."

"I have a difficult time thinking of myself that way, as the defendant."

I studied him for a moment, wondering if at last he might be exhibiting some sign of human vulnerability. He had maintained an icy cool throughout the trial, almost a detachment. Although I had kept him off the witness stand, I knew the jurors had watched him. They had eyes. They had seen the obvious arrogance.

Dr. Stewart was tall, well over six feet, and athletically lean. He was almost sixty, but looked forty. His silky ginger hair, groomed as carefully as a television anchorman's, held no trace of gray. His alabaster skin was smooth and unwrinkled. His features would have been pleasant if it weren't for his eyes. They were two little green stones, cold and without emotion. He seldom blinked. The total effect suggested a reptilian quality.

"Do you still think I'll be convicted?" He smiled, but as usual the expression was more imperious than friendly.

"We'll see. Maybe we'll get lucky. You never know."

"And if not, if we're not lucky, what happens then?"

"It's all been arranged, Doctor. This is a front-page case, so there will be quite a fuss no matter which way it goes. Should the jury come back with a verdict of guilty, you'll be taken into custody, handcuffs and all, chiefly for the benefit of the photographers. The court officers will hold you in an office behind the courtroom for an hour and then you'll be released. The judge has agreed to continue bail."

"Does this sort of thing happen often?"

"What?"

"Where both sides come together like this to orchestrate a theatrical charade for the benefit of the great unwashed." The words held the suggestion of a sneer. His reptilian eyes watched for a reaction. "Or is this how the legal system really works?"

I restrained myself. I had often had to practice such restraint during the course of our lawyer-client relationship. It seemed to please him when he could provoke an angry response. I paused and then spoke in a carefully measured tone. "I have no idea about medicine, but the law lends itself to compromise, real as well as for show. I worked out this arrangement to save you a night in jail. The prosecutor knows you would eventually get out on bond, pending appeal, no matter how vigorously he objected. He just wants his triumphant moment in the camera's eye if you're convicted. I admit it's for show, but this way no one is inconvenienced, especially you."

"How thoughtful." His words dripped with contempt. He turned away from me, no longer interested.

Boredom permeated the almost empty courtroom. A few newspeople sat around talking. A court officer, his face slack, his eyelids heavy, was losing his fight against sleep.

My client walked to a courtroom window and looked down on the city below.

The press had tagged him Doctor Death. His face caught the outside light, lending shadow and texture to his angular features, accentuating his unusual eyes and producing an effect that suggested something sinister. It was the way villains in the old horror pictures were lighted, just before they bit someone in the throat. There wasn't a discernible trace of human concern or care in that face. The prosecutor had called him an executioner. At the moment, he looked exactly that.

If a sulfuric mist had suddenly swirled up about him, it

wouldn't have seemed at all out of place.

Despite a certain oily charm, a facile quality he could call forth when it suited him, I hadn't liked Miles Stewart even the first time we had met. That very negative reaction had grown with each day we had spent together.

The case against him wasn't legally strong, mostly just a weak web of circumstances and suspicions. But the judge had purposely allowed the prosecutor to enter grossly inadmissible evidence against my client. Judge Gallagher, who didn't like doctors and especially doctors accused of killing their patients, had his own ethical idea about how the case should come out. The trial was drawing national attention, and legal or not, the judge wanted to send a public message. A warning to all doctors. And it was a very, very public warning. It was that kind of public case, the kind tabloid editors dream about, the kind that produced wonderful headlines like TYCOON CONTRACTS FOR OWN MURDER.

The tycoon, Francis X. Milliard, had been just that, a financial wizard who had gobbled up half the manufacturing companies in America. Milliard, the father of three grown sons, had divorced his socialite wife and then stepped out of the closet and into the leather bars. But he had danced with the wrong partner and had contracted AIDS, although his publicity people had artfully concealed his condition, even at the last.

Despite his billions, Milliard couldn't buy a cure for the deadly disease that had been slowly killing him. No amount of money could buy that. But the prosecutor said Milliard did have sufficient funds to acquire the sinister services of Dr. Miles Stewart, purchasing a happy little injection and a quick, painless way out of a bad situation.

The right-to-die people rallied to the cause of Dr. Stewart, calling him a pathfinder, an angel. The other side did everything but put a bounty on him.

The officer assigned to shepherd the jury came hurrying into the courtroom. His excited whisper had the force of a shout. "They got a verdict!"

Boredom evaporated instantly.

Within minutes every seat in the courtroom was filled. The jury came trudging in slowly, as if they had done something wrong and expected trouble. They looked solemn, mournful. They awkwardly formed a ring before the judge.

"Have you reached a verdict," the court clerk spoke the formal question, "and if so, who will speak for you?"

"We have, and I shall speak," the rotund little woman who was a computer programmer answered. Her words had a distinct tremor, and she continued in an unnaturally loud voice. "We find the defendant guilty as charged, guilty of second-degree murder."

No trial lawyer likes to lose, but I had expected the verdict. During the trial, old Judge Gallagher had committed more errors than a blind shortstop.

I would take the case up to the court of appeals and I would win there. They would order a retrial, a fair one.

But the jury case was a public loss, and I had to face the press and television cameras out in the hallway. They didn't like my client any more than I did, so their questions seemed unusually vicious.

After that ordeal I made sure my original deal was carried out. It was, and Doctor Death was eventually spirited away to freedom, on bond, far from the prying eyes of the camera crews.

It all took more time than I had anticipated, but finally I was finished, although I was beginning to experience the tiring drain of an emotional cool down. In the old days I would have sucked up some quick liquid energy at the nearest saloon. That seemed so long ago now.

I set about gathering up my court papers and possessions for the hour-long drive back to Pickeral Point.

Pickeral Point is a small Michigan city approximately

forty miles northeast of Detroit. It is a river city. I moved there after my trouble. That's all behind me now, I hope, but I still live in Pickeral Point, and my office is there, although I'm doing Detroit trial work once again.

"Hey, Charley!"

I had been alone in the deserted courtroom. I turned to see who had come in.

At first I didn't recognize him. I hadn't seen him for six or seven years.

"It's me. Mickey Monk." He grinned, exhibiting the familiar crooked smile. It was a beguiling choirboy grin, the kind that belonged on a fresh innocent face. But the face I was looking at wasn't innocent or fresh. It was puffy, and the skin color resembled something you might see on ice in a fish market. Fleshy bags hung below cornflower blue eyes. Only the eyes and the smile looked healthy.

"How are you, Mickey? It's been a while."

We shook hands. His was warm and sweaty.

"Jesus, I hear the jury jammed it up Doctor Death's ass. Too bad."

"It won't stick. The court of appeals will overturn it."

"You got the fix in?"

I laughed. "I don't need a fix. This thing will practically appeal itself."

I took a closer look at him. Mickey, a lawyer too, and I were old drinking buddies, brothers at the bar in more ways than one. We were about the same age, with the big five-oh looming just down the road for us both. He had put on weight, a lot of weight. His clothes, expensive but wrinkled, strained against thigh and belly.

"Let's go grab a drink, Charley."

I shook my head. "I don't drink anymore."

He nodded slowly. "I heard that. Was it tough? Quitting, I mean?"

"Depends on how you define tough. Why? Are you

interested in giving it up?"

He laughed, his puffy cheeks shaking from the effort. "Hell, no. If I stopped drinking, the national economy of Scotland would collapse. How about coming with me while I get a quick one?"

"I try to avoid saloons these days."

"Hell, Charley, you got your law license back. You're doing okay again. Relax, enjoy life a bit. One snort won't kill you."

"I'll pass, Mickey. Thanks anyway."

He ran a meaty hand through his thinning blond hair. "I gotta confess I didn't just happen by. I heard you were up here so I came looking for you."

"You've found me. What's up?"

"I'd talk better if I had a drink."

I remember the need I saw in his eyes. My eyes used to look that way, too, the need bordering on pain. In those days I was never very long between drinks.

"Okay, where do you want to go?"

He brightened. "Mulrooney's, of course."

Mulrooney's, one of the oldest bars in the city, was the traditional watering hole for circuit court lawyers, judges, and clerks. I thought I probably held some kind of record there for number of consecutive times drunk.

"Anyplace but Mulrooney's," I said.

He looked disappointed. "Well, there's a nice bar over at the Westin Hotel. And it's close."

"Let's go."

During the trip over I noticed even the short walk tended to wind him and his puffy face began to glisten with sweat. Mickey filled me in on his life as we walked. His second wife was talking divorce, and his kids were in perpetual trouble of various kinds. He was in a downtown Detroit office with three other personal injury lawyers. Business was up and down, mostly down.

I told him of my little one-man office located above an

insurance agency and looking out on the St. Clair River. He wasn't impressed. And I told him about my daughter, although I didn't tell him she was a recovering alcoholic just like her dear old dad. I did tell him, brag would be the better word, that she was an honor student at the University of Pennsylvania and thinking about going on to law school. He remembered my third wife, who had divorced me years ago. He had some unkind things to say about her. I didn't object. They were all true.

By the time we got to the bar we were all caught up on personal history.

Mickey ordered a double scotch, straight up, and gulped it down, then ordered another. Sometimes it bothers me to watch people drink. Sometimes it doesn't. This time I wasn't bothered. I sipped my Coke and waited for him to tell me what had prompted him to search me out.

"Are you going to handle the Doctor Death appeal yourself?" he asked. "I mean, prepare and brief it yourself and then argue the case?"

I nodded.

He worked a bit slower on the second drink. "As I remember, you got some friends over there on the court of appeals, right?"

"I do, but that won't count for a hell of a lot. I know a couple of the judges there. So do you."

"Not as well as you do," he said quickly.

"What's your point, Mickey?"

"You know what I do, right?"

"Sure."

"I'm a personal injury lawyer," he said, staring at the ice cubes in his glass. "I used to be pretty good, or at least I thought I was. Made money, too. It's tougher now, Charley. No-fault this, no-fault that. It's hard to make an honest buck anymore. At least it is for someone like me who handles mostly small stuff. Quantity, not quality, that's what pays my rent, you know?"

"So?"

"I finally got my teeth into something good, real good. Big bucks, you know? But it's on appeal. I've handled appeals before but not many, and none that were really big. I don't think I want to do this one all on my own."

"The town is full of appellate experts, Mickey. Hire someone to help you."

He shrugged and signaled for another drink. "I know those guys. Paperwork men, nothing more. I need someone who has a wire in over there."

"I don't have a wire in, if that's what you mean. No one does, as far as I know."

He laughed, but it had a mocking sound. "You been away from the action around here, Charley. Things have changed."

"Like what?"

"There's a whisper that a judge or two over there is up for sale."

"Which ones?"

"I don't know. It's just a rumor, but I think it's probably true. It's one of those things you hear a lot. You know the old wheeze, where there's smoke there's fire."

"There's always that kind of rumor floating around, no matter what court it is. You know that, Mickey."

"What about Judge Newark in Recorder's Court? Would you call that a rumor?"

I laughed. "No matter what they may say about him he's still on the bench. I understand the grand jury came close a few times, but they couldn't nail him."

Mickey looked around to make sure no one could hear what he was about to say. Then he spoke in a near whisper. "I know how he does it."

"Oh?"

"Remember Sid Williams?"

A memory flashed in my mind, a picture of a sleazy little

lawyer with bulging eyes and the world's worst toupee. Sid was a fixture in Recorder's Court. He had no law office but practiced out of a bondsman's storefront. "I remember Sid."

"He's Judge Newark's partner."

"C'mon! Newark wouldn't have anything to do with a slime like Sid."

"You wouldn't think it, would you? Maybe that's why it works so well." Monk sipped his drink. "Sure you won't have one of these, Charley?"

"No. Go on. Tell me about Sid and the judge."

He flashed that boyish grin, then chuckled. "Suppose you got a criminal case in front of Judge Newark. Say, for instance, you got a client charged with sale and possession of narcotics. He's got a record, and they got a good case on him. He's looking at twenty years. The prosecutor won't go for a lesser plea and your man is desperate. What do you do?"

"Try it."

Monk nodded. "You do, but you waive a jury so that Newark will make the ultimate decision. But before you try it, you quick find Sid Williams. Only you don't discuss that case, not a word, nothing. But you hire Sid to be your cocounsel on another case. It doesn't matter what case, civil, criminal, whatever. You pay Sid maybe four thousand dollars, then you go to trial before Newark."

"And you win."

"No. You lose. That's the neat part. You lose, but the judge finds your man guilty of a lesser offense. And he does some time too, but not much, maybe six months. Nobody complains. The prosecutor and the police aren't happy, maybe, but they're satisfied. The fucking dope dealer is ecstatic. You get the four grand from him, plus a bonus. You're a hero, the judge looks good, and there's no way to trace anything. Even if you were trying to make a case and were wearing a wire it wouldn't do any good. You and Sid never talk about the matter up before Newark."

"Slick."

Monk nodded. "Like sheet ice. From what I understand Sid gets maybe a third and the rest goes to the judge. Cash, of course. I don't know how they arrange the money transfer between them, Sid and the judge, but it's probably just as neat as the fix itself."

"If you know about it, Mickey, you can bet other people do, and then it's no secret. That's the danger in those kinds of arrangements."

"Hey, it's not common knowledge, I just happened to stumble onto the thing. I had a burglar in front of Newark for B & E nighttime. A lawyer, one of the regulars over in Recorder's, tipped me. I paid Sid the fee, just like he said, and my man got found guilty of daytime. Got three months. Jesus, he had a record that would stretch from here to Florida. I never seen anybody so happy as him when he got sentenced."

"That's something I wouldn't talk about, Mickey, or do, for that matter."

"Get real. It's all part of life. Anyway, like it or not, I had to do what was best for my client. Hey, things like that happen."

"And you think something similar might be going on over in the court of appeals?"

"I hear talk. Nothing concrete, like I said, but it's possible."

"I'm not a Sid Williams, if that's what you're getting at."

He looked hurt. "Jesus, Charley, I know that. But you got friends on that court. I just thought you might have heard something. Anyway, that's not the reason I wanted to talk to you."

"What is?"

"I would like you to handle this big appeal I got over there."

"What's it about?"

"It's a product liability case. The defendant is Ford, although it's really about a recreational vehicle made by another company. Ford bought that company and with it all the claims pending against it. Anyway, my man is driving this big hog of a self-propelled mobile home when the damn thing accelerates suddenly, like a fucking rocket, and he slams into a tree. Fractured just about every bone in his body, including his neck. He's paralyzed. About the only thing that works is his mouth."

"Did Ford make a settlement offer?"

"They just laughed at me."

"Product liability cases are tough to win."

He nodded. "You're telling me. Nobody else would even touch the damn thing. Christ, the damages are terrific. The guy's a plumber and made good money. He's thirty-five, so he had a lot of work years left in him."

"Damages don't count if you can't show the company was liable. It sounds like the old story, Mickey, good damages, bad liability."

"I dug up some other incidents involving the same make and model of recreational vehicle. Sudden acceleration, exactly the same, injuries too, but none as bad as my man's. The company had notice the product was dangerous but did nothing about it. I really put some work into the damn case. Cash, too."

"It sounds like you got a little carried away?"

He sighed. "More than that. I went out and borrowed heavy money to pay for expert witnesses. You know, engineers who could testify about the vehicle and why it did what it did. They made tests and that sort of thing. Counting everything, I'm out forty grand. All money that I don't have."

"Does the client have it?"

"He's in worse financial shape than I am. He and his family are living on Social Security disability. They live with his wife's folks."

I shook my head in sympathy. All lawyers gamble now and then, but what Mickey had done was equal to trying to fill an inside straight. No matter how you looked at it, that kind of gamble just wasn't smart.

"And you want me to handle the appeal?"

He grinned. "Yeah."

"And just maybe you'd like to tag me with part of those expenses you ran up?"

He pretended mock surprise. "God, what a good thought, Charley. Would you do that?"

"Of course not."

Mickey signaled for another drink. It was now starting to bother me. The scotch had begun to look inviting.

"Here's the deal, Charley. You take over the appeal. I did all the trial work and invested all that dough. I even did the appellate brief. It won't cost you a penny. Whatever I get, you get twenty percent of that. I figure that's fair."

"Twenty percent of nothing isn't very much."

"It could be. In this case, it could really turn out to be a lot."

"Still dreaming, Mickey? What makes you think you'll win in the court of appeals if you lost the trial?"

"I didn't lose," he said, and this time there was no smile.

"What do you mean?"

"The jury came back with a verdict for just under five million."

"Jesus!"

"Ford is the one appealing the case."

"Settle with them."

He shook his head. "They still think they'll win. They offered peanuts. The outfit they took over doesn't make recreational vehicles anymore, so they aren't afraid of adverse publicity. They are what you might call smug and extremely confident."

He smiled, almost wistfully. "I got the case on a third. So, if the appeals court upholds the verdict, I get a fee of a little more than a million and a half. Twenty percent of that, Charley, ain't what you'd call chicken feed. Will you take the case?"

"Why don't you do it? You've been there before."

"I'm too nervous. I got too much riding on this. If it's lost, I'm ruined, honest-to-god ruined. Christ, I think I'd burst into tears right there in the appeals court, or faint. I need someone who can be cool about the whole thing. How about it?"

I could see the fear in his eyes. He had bet everything he had, money, honor, future. The case didn't sound like a winner. Appellate courts look with hard eyes on such cases. Still, to say no to him would be like running over a puppy.

"Okay, Mickey. I'll do it."

"This calls for a drink, Charley."

"Not for me. I have to go." I gave him my card. "Send me the file."

I patted his shoulder and started for the door.

"Thanks." The word was practically whispered. But I didn't know if he was talking to me or to God.

SOME MEN HURRY home to loving wives, some to not-so-loving wives, and some, with wary care, to other men's wives. I was fresh out of wives, at least at the moment, so I drove back to my office in Pickeral Point. I didn't even hurry.

I seemed to have gone through a platoon of secretaries since I occupied the office over the marine insurance company. I even drafted my daughter, Lisa, as secretary, before she went off to college.

It's an easy job, really, working for me. I'm a trial

lawyer, mostly criminal cases, so paperwork is at a minimum, at least in comparison to some lawyers. I like to think I'm easy to get along with. Of course, some of my clients, I admit, would scare Dracula, but they are generally on their best behavior when visiting my office. Murderers, robbers, and muggers, when not engaged in their employment, as Gilbert and Sullivan observed, can be as courteous and civilized as other people.

Mildred Fenton, the woman presently occupying the secretary position, had much to recommend her. She's efficient, organized, and intelligent, although completely lacking a sense of humor. She's never late and always leaves precisely at five o'clock. She doesn't approve of small talk. Her telephone manner is polite, albeit cool. She's been married to her husband for twenty years. Like many married people who have lived together for a long time, they have come to resemble each other. Like her husband, she's tall, straight up and down, and plain. She wears no makeup and her mousy brown hair is pulled back in a tight knot behind her head. Even a sailor who had been at sea for a very long time wouldn't consider Mrs. Mildred Fenton an attractive love object.

Which is a plus, since her presence doesn't provoke in me distracting carnal thoughts. She doesn't smoke, or drink, another plus for me, obviously, and she has no children. I suspect she doesn't approve of some other things as well.

To her friends she is Milly. To me she is Mrs. Fenton. We both feel comfortable with that formal arrangement.

I arrived back at my office just a few minutes after five, so Mrs. Fenton had already gone.

As usual, she left a carefully typed note, almost a diary of what had happened during the day, plus telephone messages received.

The mail, stacked in a compulsively neat pile, awaited me on my uncluttered desk. I like the desk cluttered but

Mrs. Fenton does not.

My office may not look like much, filled with ancient furniture that had been in place and inherited when I took over from a long-dead lawyer. But it has one stunning attribute that many modern, classy law offices lack.

You can't beat the view.

I sat in my lopsided chair and swiveled around so I could look out the big picture window.

The wide St. Clair River was calm. Canada, on the other side of the river, seemed a world away, although the distance was just over a half mile. The river is one of the main connectors between the Great Lakes. Chicago, Detroit, Cleveland, even Toronto are easy ports of call for ships of many nations.

I watched as a huge oceangoing boat approached and then glided past my window, so close it seemed as if I could open the window and touch its enormous gray hull. It was like watching a metal mountain majestically sliding by.

From its markings, the ship was Swedish, and since it was heading north, I presumed it was on its way around Lake Huron, toward Lake Michigan and Chicago.

There was something so final and invincible about its sure swift passage. Like fate, there didn't seem any way it could possibly be stopped.

I watched until it was out of sight, enjoying the sense of tranquillity passing ships seem to evoke in me, then I turned in the chair and attacked the mail.

Mrs. Fenton had opened each letter, separating those that held checks, just a few, from those that contained bills, many more. The checks weren't for large amounts, nor were the bills.

I had a letter from a client who was in Jackson Prison, Michigan's largest penal institution. It was a chatty letter. Things had been going well, it seemed. It apparently didn't bother him that he would still have six or seven more years to spend behind the walls. His letters had become quite regular. I presumed he had no one else to write to except the lawyer who had gotten his murder charge knocked down to second degree with the prospect, at least, of eventual freedom. He was grateful, which is often unusual in those circumstances. He didn't write to his wife because she was the reason he was in. He had killed her, chopped her up and buried her in various places around his farm. As always, it was a cheerful letter.

My telephone rang. Mrs. Fenton had set the answering machine, so I didn't pick it up. Most of the telephone messages she had left me were from media people looking for a new angle to write about Doctor Death. I thought it was another newsperson and I didn't feel like rehashing the case again.

After three rings, the machine buzzed, transmitted its recorded message. Then the caller responded, his words metallic in amplification, into the turning tape.

I recognized the voice immediately. I had been listening to that voice for a week.

"This is Miles Stewart." Even speaking into an answering machine, he sounded frostily arrogant. "I'm at my apartment but don't call me here, since I'm not answering the phone. It's been nothing but one damned reporter after another. I shall call you again in an hour. It is now—"

I grabbed the phone at my desk.

"I'm here," I said. "What's up?"

"So, you're not answering the phone either." He made it sound as if he had discovered me in something shameful, something on a par with dope dealing or sex with animals.

"I just came in the door."

I was answered by a disbelieving chuckle. "Of course."

"What is it you want?" I snapped, regretting it

instantly. He liked getting that kind of response.

The chuckle turned a trifle triumphant. "A bit touchy, are we? Well, I suppose that's natural, seeing how you lost the case."

I wasn't going to go for the bait a second time. "What is it you want, Doctor?" I tried to sound pleasantly cool.

I could sense his disappointment. "Two things," he said. "First, I'm on bond. Do I have to stay here? In my apartment?"

"I arranged that you could travel to other states, but you can't go overseas. That's the only restriction. If you do leave the state, you must notify the court of where you can be reached. Why?"

"I have an invitation to spend a week up north."

"It might do you some good to get away for a while. Do a little fishing, something like that."

"Fishing is for idiots," he replied. "This is just social. Mrs. Cynthia Wilcox has invited me. She has a place up on Lake Huron. Rustic, but quite elegant inside, I'm told. She will send a car for me."

"Wilcox, as in the widow of Poindexter Wilcox?"

He paused, then spoke. "A family friend."

"A rich friend," I said. "A very rich friend."

"Yes, she is that, isn't she?"

I thought of why he was called Doctor Death.

"Have you ever been up there before?"

"No."

"Is Mrs. Wilcox sick, by any chance?"

I was answered by a soft chuckle. "Not that I know of."

"Look, I'm going to be frank. If she happens to have a terminal condition and passes away in her sleep while you're up there, no appeal on earth is going to help you. You will have effectively proven everything the prosecutor alleged. Understand?"

That chuckle was becoming like fingernails on a blackboard. "You told the jury I was innocent."

"I told the jury the prosecutor hadn't proved his case. There's a big difference. If there is a repeat of the other times, Doctor, no one is going to be able to help you."

The chuckle faded and his voice became more businesslike. "This appeals process, what again are we talking about, in terms of time?"

"Depends on a lot of variables. Weeks, sometimes. Mostly several months."

"So, we're talking what? A year? Two years?"

"Doctor, there are no guarantees, but right now I'd estimate that from start to finish we're talking about something less than a year. Maybe even six months."

At first I thought he hadn't heard me, then he spoke. "Lawyers wouldn't last five minutes in an operating room. Six months? You people lack precision. What a way to run a business."

I didn't want to argue with him. He liked it too much. "If you decide to spend more than a week with Mrs. Wilcox, let me know. It's understood that you will let the court know where you are."

I suddenly realized I was talking to myself.

Doctor Death had hung up.

2

Marylou lay on the pillow, her blond hair spread about her like fine netting. She smoked her cigarette as if it were a required part of some religious ceremony. Her eyes were fixed upon the ceiling of my bedroom.

She had modestly pulled the sheet up to just below her chin.

The bedside lamp bathed her in soft light. She was beautiful, the kind of beauty seen on the screen or television. Full lips, high cheekbones, firm chin, and eyes so darkly blue they seemed unreal. And with body to match, a thirty-year-old body, but one that a teenager would envy.

She had been the queen of morning television in Dallas, and then Cleveland, and then a number of places, but never quite queen again. All the jobs had been on a descending scale. Now she was doing radio work on a small jazz station in Detroit. A fondness for vodka had greased the downward slide.

We were typical, a standard relationship called the AA romance. Recovering alcoholics tend to feel comfortable with their own. All human needs remain with us, they are there, but they're tinted by the never-ending fight against the inner demon. It saves a lot of explaining if your companion has the same set of problems. It promotes a kind of romance that is, at best, only temporary.

"Do you love me, Charley?"

"Of course."

She smiled, still staring at the ceiling. "A hard question, an easy answer."

"Oh, not all that easy. I can think of a dozen women I wouldn't say that to."

She turned, put out the cigarette, then snuggled down even deeper into the sheet.

"Do you remember that audition I did last month in Tampa?"

"Sure. You came back tanned."

"I didn't think they liked me."

"So?"

"They called."

"So?"

She looked at me with those penetrating eyes. "What about us, Charley? You and me? Is this just another shipboard romance, or do we have a future?"

She had never asked before, but I knew she had thought about it. So had I, although we had only been together for a few months.

"It's a little early to tell, don't you think?" I asked. "Why the question? Is it about Tampa?"

"Tampa has something to do with it, yes. But I don't think it's the real issue."

"And what's the real issue?"

"Commitment."

"In time, maybe …"

She laughed softly. I thought the laugh sounded sad.

"You've already answered," she said. "You're not ready, Charley, and you probably never will be. At least, not with me."

"I'm a three-time loser, Marylou. I don't have exactly a great track record as a family man. Three wives, three divorces, one kid. Every one of us an alcoholic, even my daughter, Lisa. Marrying me would be like getting a last-minute ticket on the *Titanic*."

She sighed. "I'm not worried about that, Charley, not at all. That's not the big problem."

"What is?"

She paused a moment, then answered. "You're a romantic."

"So?"

"Have you noticed? Most alcoholics seem to be."

"I don't follow."

She rolled over and took another cigarette from the pack on the bedstand. She lit it and watched the smoke curl toward the ceiling.

"It's true, Charley. At least it is in your case. You see the world through romantic eyes. You want things to be the way you think they should be. You try to make things come out that way, although they usually don't. That's the problem, Charley."

"I'm a lawyer, Marylou. We have to look at things realistically."

She smiled. "Facts maybe, but not anything else. You're the kind of guy who used to ride out with a shield and lance, Charley, looking for dragons."

"Or windmills?"

"Romantics can't tell the difference. That's the problem."

"So what's this business about Tampa? To be realistic for a moment."

"They've offered me a new morning show. The station

is an affiliate of a network, and they say I might have a shot at something national eventually. It's my big chance, Charley. Maybe my last chance."

"What are they talking about in terms of money and a contract?"

"They're offering a two-year contract. The money's good, about triple what I'm making. If I succeed, that's only the beginning."

"Do you want me to look at the contract?"

She paused again. "I've already agreed."

I felt a sinking sensation. "When do you leave?"

This pause seemed longer.

"Tomorrow."

"Tomorrow!"

"My roommate will arrange for my stuff to be sent down when I find a permanent place."

"Jesus!"

"This was a nice interlude for both of us, but we both knew it wouldn't last, Charley."

"Maybe you did."

She inhaled deeply, then expelled the smoke slowly. "We both knew," she said, not looking at me.

I watched as she got up and dressed.

She was so beautiful, I felt close to tears. She came to the bed and kissed me softly on the cheek.

"Suppose I said I wanted to get married? Would that have changed things?" I asked.

"You wouldn't have said it."

"Why not?"

"There are just too many goddamned windmills around. That's why."

And then she was gone.

THERE IS AN ARMED guard at the law school now, a stern-eyed black woman, squat and heavy, who scrutinized me and then my law alumni card as if she were a border agent and I were a spy. She insisted on additional proof, my driver's license, complete with awful photo, and my bar association card. Even then, I thought she was going to refuse admittance.

Finally, as if against her better judgment, she reluctantly allowed me to pass. I walked in with a group of serious-looking students who were hotly debating some obscure point of probate law among themselves. Some of them glanced at me, as if assessing whether I might possibly be someone of importance. Apparently I wasn't, since I was given no more than a perfunctory up-and-down.

They continued on as I stopped in the vaulted room they now called the Atrium, an artfully high enclosure of glass and rising beams.

It occupied the space that had once held the dental clinic. The law school and the dental school had shared the building when I had been a student. In my mind, I seemed to hear the echo of long-ago screams from poor patients providing the young students with live practice. In the old days, we had to pass by the clinic to get to class. It had seemed more Dickens than dental.

The dental school, now part of the rival University of Detroit, had been moved years before to much more elaborate quarters. I wondered if they still offered the free work.

St. Benedict University had been founded at the turn of the century by the Benedictine Order as a challenge to the academic supremacy of the Jesuits and their University of Detroit. But the Jesuits had won out, slowly but surely, eventually gobbling up, one by one, all the Benedictine colleges, everything except the law school, and that too would be gone soon, given economic reality. Merger talks were already under way, with plans to unite the two Catholic law schools located only half a mile apart in the decaying dangerous downtown section of Detroit.

But until that time, it was still St. Benedict, a kind of mother ship for thousands of its graduates. It had once been the law school for working students, Catholic mostly, the sons and daughters of immigrants, living their parents' dream. St. Benedict's was the first step up on the ladder to something better. If the University of Michigan was Tiffany's, then St. Benedict would be a kind of working-class, academic K Mart.

Still, the boys and girls of St. Benedict, those who got through, did all right. Half the judges in the state were St. Benedict products.

So was Jacques Mease, the famous graduate who had gone on to become a bank financier and who had amassed a billion-dollar fortune. He had paid for the new Atrium and it had borne his name until his indictment and conviction. The brass plate had been removed after that. Mease had done his time, only a year, and had paid an enormous fine, a fine that left him with only a hundred million on which to skimp by. According to the magazines, Mease, poor devil, now lived a quiet life on his estate on the Caribbean island he owned, consumed, no doubt, with remorse. In any event, he was no longer interested in making big donations to his former law school.

But before it stopped, his money had helped fund in part St. Benedict's excellent law library, which was why I had driven in from Pickeral Point. Doctor Death's appeal had to be prepared, which meant hours of searching law books to build a foundation for the arguments I would toss at the court in written form first, and later verbally.

Most lawyers at some time in their lives have near-death experiences with court-imposed deadlines. Everybody tends to put things off, but lawyers make a religion of it. At least they do until they come too close one day. From then on, stark terror inspires convertlike diligence.

I had had that happen. More than once. Those past

experiences had been so close that now I watch the calendar like a heart monitor. Doctor Death and I would both be finished if I missed getting the appeal in on time. I had to do the research now.

Plus, this time, I also needed to do some serious reading on the product liability case. Mickey Monk had written the brief surprisingly well, but I had to know every facet of that subject when it came time to argue that case before the three-judge panel. Being an appellate judge is boring work. So it's like therapy for them when they get the opportunity to tear some poor underprepared lawyer to shreds. They then attack, like lions ripping apart a limping antelope. Which is all right, if you aren't the antelope.

University law libraries are pretty standard. Entrance is gained by passing muster at a long counter presided over by working students, who use their time there both to study and earn minimum-wage money. The law books are contained in endless stacks, like soldiers on parade. The stacks are marked so you can search for what you are interested in by state, or court, or even journal.

Rows of long desks serve as book platforms for the students. It never changes. The students peer earnestly at the pages of opened law books, puzzlement and confusion gluing their eyebrows into perpetually frustrated frowns.

No one talks, and everyone moves quietly. Like a church.

I flashed my alumni card, which was my ticket to browse. The privilege was part of the yearly alumni dues and worth every penny.

No one glanced at me as I staked out the end of a long table as my temporary headquarters, placing my worn briefcase like a claiming flag.

I was about to search the stacks for product liability

cases when I noticed a young woman looking, staring would be a better word, directly at me.

Most of the students were dressed casually, most coming from or going to the jobs that supported their studies, but my watcher was attired in a well-tailored, expensive business suit, the feminine equivalent of a power suit. She was pretty enough naturally so she didn't need much makeup. Her hair, a soft brown, had been cut by someone who knew what he was doing and probably charged enormously for that skill. Her eyes were blue, I could see that even at a distance.

I smiled. She didn't.

She hesitated and then walked over. She probably played a lot of tennis, or something equally healthy. She possessed an easy grace, the kind that athletes seem to have.

The closer she got, the better she looked.

"Mr. Sloan," she asked. "Charles Sloan?"

"Yes."

Two students looked up in irritation. But when they saw her they quickly dived back into their books.

"Would you step out in the hall for a moment?"

I nodded, and followed her past the long desk and out through the library doors.

"You don't remember me," she said. "Of course, there's no reason why you should. I'm Caitlin Palmer."

When I failed to indicate recognition, she added, "Judge Palmer's daughter."

I suppose I showed my real surprise. She allowed a small smile. "The last time you saw me was at least twenty years ago. I was about ten years old then. Father had you and your wife over for dinner."

"They called you Cat." I remembered a proper little girl who showed a quick intelligence, but a little girl with bad skin and a weight problem. Things had certainly changed.

"Are you a student here?" I asked.

"Not exactly. I'm the assistant dean."

"I didn't know."

"This is my first year. It's like coming home. I used to come here often with my father."

"I remember. How is your dad? I haven't seen him in a long time, probably a year or two."

"He never changes. He lives for the court and that damn boat of his." She studied me. "You've changed, Mr. Sloan. Older, but more distinguished, I think."

"Please call me Charley, everyone does." I wondered what she meant by distinguished. The fancy tailor-made suits and the gold Rolexes were long gone. I wore off-the-rack now. I hadn't grown or shrunk, I was still average height. Average weight, average everything. I thought myself a little more rugged-looking now, especially around my blue eyes. I wondered if she was referring to the little bits of gray sneaking into my average brown hair just above my average ears. Her eyes gave no clue.

"What brings you here, Charley?"

"A little research for a case on appeal."

"Doctor Death?"

I smiled. "Among others."

"I've more or less followed your career. I'm glad things are going well for you again."

"Thanks. What about you? Do they still call you Cat?"

The small smile dimmed a bit. "Yes, but never here."

"Okay, Dean Palmer, tell me about yourself."

The smile came back, but was still tentative. "Nothing much to tell, really. I'm Daddy's girl, the only child, as you know. I had to go into the law, whether I liked it or not. Luckily, I like it. I came out of Yale, did some clerking for the federal court and then spent a year with a New York law firm. I decided practice wasn't for me, so I followed the teaching track. I worked my way up to a full professorship in Chicago and then came here when this job opened. That's my history in a nutshell."

"Married? Children?"

"No. What about you? You have children, as I recall."

"One, a daughter. She's a student at the University of Pennsylvania."

"I remember your wife," she said. "I thought she was the most beautiful woman I had ever seen. You brought her to dinner one night."

"That was my first wife. Two followed after that."

She smiled a bit more. "Are you a Mormon?"

"Nope. I made it a practice to get a divorce each time."

"And now?"

"Single once more."

She paused for a moment and then proceeded on a new tack. "Do you think you'll have a chance with Doctor Death on appeal?"

"Ordinarily, I take a wary view, but this time I'm willing to bet serious money that it'll be reversed."

"Oh?" An inquiring eyebrow raised slowly. "Why?"

"Judge Gallagher was personally appalled by the good doctor. He let in everything except the allegation that my client shot Lincoln. He would have let that in too, if the prosecutor had asked. For instance, he let a woman testify that she heard that my client engaged in mercy killing. Just a rumor, nothing more, but he let it in."

"You objected, I take it?"

"Oh yeah, but it became more of a lynching than a trial."

"If the case comes before my father, will he disqualify himself?"

"Because he knows me? No. Your father knows most of the lawyers in this state, … Dean Palmer."

The little smile returned. "You may call me Cat, if you like. But not in front of my students."

"You got them properly terrified, I presume?"

"Terror? No. But a bit of firmness never hurt, Charley, especially since a number of students here are around my own age, or older. The job requires some respect. I can't afford to be a Rodney Dangerfield around this place."

"Can I buy you a coffee? I presume they still have a machine in the student lounge."

She shook her head. "I'll take a rain check. I have a million things to do. I'm teaching criminal law, in addition to my other duties. Our criminal law man walked off the first week of the semester."

"Your dad's old course. He was my professor."

"You taught it, too. I remember that."

"Long ago. That time when your father was sick."

"Did you like doing it?"

"Teaching? Not very much, frankly. How about you?"

She nodded. "I do, a lot." She looked at her watch. "Well, I do have to go. It's been nice seeing you again, Charley."

"When you get home, remember me to your father."

"I don't live at home. But I get invited out on the boat from time to time. I'll pass along your hello."

She turned and walked away. It was pleasant to watch. She wasn't a pudgy little girl anymore.

When I returned to the library, the students behind the desk seemed to view me with new respect. I wondered if Cat Palmer, the quiet little girl I remembered, might have grown up and become a tyrant. If so, she was the best-looking tyrant I had ever seen.

Her father, Judge Frank Palmer, had been my criminal law professor. He had taken an interest in me, even arranging for a clerkship with a judge who was a friend of his. And later, when disbarment seemed certain for me, he had quietly stepped in and helped save my license. I had been suspended for a year, but without his behind-the-scenes help, I would have had my license jerked forever.

He had done so much for me, it seemed unworthy and ungrateful that I was now having lustful thoughts about his daughter. Natural, maybe, but ungrateful nonetheless.

I went back to the library and began my reading on the latest product liability cases. I read, but my mind really wasn't on it.

RECOVERING ALCOHOLICS GET lonesome just like everyone else, only sometimes it seems even worse for us. Until you stop you don't realize how much of modern social life is built around drinking.

For some, bars and saloons become second homes, a substitute for the rich man's private club, a place to see friends, kill time, laugh a little. Even a brief visit to relatives or friends calls for a beer or something alcoholic as a form of greeting. Beer at the ballpark, a flask at the football game, it's almost universal, a liquid bond that cheers the head and warms the heart, a tribal rite.

Nothing wrong with that, as long as you can handle it.

For people like myself, those who can't handle it, the world becomes a rather closed-in place when you give it up. So you learn to compensate. You hang around with people like yourself, friends you've made at AA meetings, people who won't insist that you drink with them, people who share the common problem. Instead of bars you find new places to gather. Now with Marylou gone, the loneliness seemed more acute.

One of my regular stops had been Goldman's Marina, a small place on the river just a mile up from my office in Pickeral Point.

Herb Goldman is one of those people who doesn't look rich but is. But his marina was different. It looked run-down and was. Herb believed no wood was old until it splintered underfoot. Walking out on any of his boat docks was an adventure, sometimes a dangerous adventure. He provided moorings for nearly a hundred boats, none over thirty feet. The place smelled of gasoline, boat oil, and the river. To boat people, those pungent fumes were far more fragrant than the rarest perfume.

Herb also reeked of gas and boat oil. His worn work clothes, stained with the ghosts of a thousand dabs of oil and hull paint, hung on him like gray rags. Herb, who was fifty, looked much older. His hair, what remained, was a white grizzle around his ears and the back of his head, and looked more like an early frost. Herb's skin was the texture of alligator and burned black by fifty summer suns. His dark features, a wide flared nose, and deep-set eyes, were almost simian. He had a set of bottom teeth but seldom wore them, using them just to eat. He now kept the teeth in his shirt pocket. He used to keep them in his back trouser pocket, but one day he skidded on a slippery dock, fell, and in effect bit himself. Thereafter he parked them in his shirt. His large hands were gnarled and the color of engine oil. He stared out at the world through murky yellow eyes, eyes permanently squinted and suspicious.

Unless you knew better, Herb looked like a boat bum, the kind of guy who hung around the yards and performed whatever jobs other people didn't want to do.

But he was rich and sitting on even more.

Hungry developers eyed his run-down marina, riverfront land, seeing it as a gold mine for condos, and worth perhaps a million or two. Herb didn't need the money. He was a magician of motors and the court of last resort for anything that sucked gas and floated. Boaters sometimes flew him to their yachts overseas just so he could make a diagnosis. They paid for his services through their golden noses.

Herb had managed to hold on to most of the money he had amassed over the years. And that made him a most unusual ex-drunk. Most of us, myself included, had done quite the opposite.

I drove my Chrysler into Herb's cinder-covered parking lot. People sometimes complained it was rough on their tires, but when they did, Herb merely suggested they move their boat and business to some other place. Few did.

The Chrysler was new and I was conscious of the ripping sound below as I slowly rolled over the rough cinders. I had tried to talk Herb into at least paving the place with cheap asphalt. But no asphalt was cheap enough.

I went looking for him.

It was just the beginning of May, so most of the boats were still out of the water. A few people were working on their hulls. I looked for Herb in the big storage hangar but found only a huge cruiser riding in the deep well, its motor coverings off, but no Herb. He wasn't in his littered office either, so I went out to the nearly empty docks.

Herb was standing at the end of a very short dock. His oily deck shoes toed the end that now consisted of scorched and splintered wood.

"Hey, Herb. What happened?"

He turned, looking more mournful than ever. "Drunks," he said, as if that explained everything. He stepped by me, returning to the shore.

"I was going to call you, as a matter of fact," he said. "It happened only a couple of hours ago."

"What happened?"

He ignored the question. I followed him up to his office. Inside he extracted a can of soda from a battered cooler.

"Want one?"

"Sure."

He grabbed another and flipped it to me.

He took a long drink from the can, then wiped his mouth with the back of his hand.

"They came in here just before noon."

"Who did?"

"The drunks. A man and a woman. They come in an old thirty-three-foot Wexler. You know the boat?"

"No."

"God, but that Wexler outfit could make boats. They been out of business for twenty years now. But, until then, they were the best. They refused to convert to fiberglass and that was the end of them. This boat was a Wexler, thirty-three feet, handmade, all gorgeous wood. Some of them Wexlers are worth a fortune now. This one wasn't well kept, you could see that right off. Goddamned sin to have a boat like that and not keep it up."

He took another long drag at the can. "Anyway, they come in and tied up. I thought they wanted gas, so I go out there to tell them to pull over to the gas dock. They were looking for a bar, that's all. I guess they thought we'd have one here. I told them the nearest was O'Hara's down the road. They walked there. Staggered might be a better word."

He sighed. "They were gone a couple of hours. I was working in the shed, but I happened to see them come back. Hear them would be more accurate. The two of them were going at each other, with some choice words that even I hadn't heard before.

"I thought there might be trouble so I came out. They cursed all the way to their boat, then got on."

He shook his head. "Jesus, Charley, I heard the asshole hit the engine without using the blower first. I didn't even get a chance to shout a warning. The damn thing blew up like the Fourth of July. Those old boats, they have a way of building up those gasoline fumes. It was a goddamn good thing the dock there was empty or they would have blown up everything within fifty feet."

"Were they killed?" I asked.

Herb shook his head. "No way. God looks after drunks, otherwise you and I wouldn't even be here, would we?"

He finished the can, then, like a member of the Pistons, shot it into a far wastebasket. "The woman ended up about fifty feet out in the river. He landed in the water between two docks. They both looked like toasted marshmallows, although the doctors tell me the burns aren't serious. The fucking boat no longer exists, just toothpicks mostly."

Herb sighed. "They were talking about suing me as the ambulance was taking them away." He looked at me with those cloudy yellow eyes. "Can they?"

"Anybody who has the filing fee can sue anyone else," I said. "The question is, can they collect?"

"Can they?"

"Anybody besides you see him start the motor without hitting the blower?"

He nodded. "Old Snodgrass. That guy is here more than I am. He sands that hull of his so much it's paper thin. It's his hobby. I think he really hates having to put the boat in the water. He just likes working on it. He says he saw it, same as me."

"You didn't give them gas, or service them in any way?"

"Just let them tie up."

"Did you think they were so drunk they couldn't handle a boat?"

"No. They had been drinking, that was obvious. But they seemed okay as far as running a car or a boat. At least, they did to me."

"How about the people up at O'Hara's?"

"I called them. They say they looked all right. Of course, they would anyway. They don't want to get sued either. Why?"

"The only way they can collect is to show you had some kind of duty toward them and neglected it, or you did something you shouldn't have, something that caused the explosion."

"He caused the explosion. Even a baboon knows enough to run the blower and disperse the gas fumes before hitting the ignition."

"Then, if everything is as you say, you have nothing to worry about."

"Do you think I'd lie?"

"Hey, we all color things to put a good light on ourselves. I do, Herb. You do. Lawyers know that, so we take everything with a grain of salt."

"No wonder everybody hates you fuckers."

"Yeah. But everybody loves us when they need us."

"This guy is really pissed off. I think he'll end up suing, even if he can't win. You ever own a boat, Charley?"

I smiled. "I owned a lot of things before I drank them away. A Rolls, even my own airplane. But never a boat. Why?"

"It's different. It becomes like a religion with some people, the center of their lives. Like dope, I suppose."

"Or like booze?"

He nodded. "Yeah, like that. They can't think of anything else. I think the Wexler, even if he didn't take good care of it, might have been like that to this guy. His whole damn world blew up on him. It doesn't matter that it was his fault or that he was lucky to come out of it with a few hairs burned off, or that his wife will look like a walnut for a couple of weeks. The beautiful handcrafted Wexler is gone. He's going to raise some hell."

"Let him. You have nothing to worry about."

"We'll see. Women, boats, no matter what, if you love something enough it makes you crazy."

I finished my soda and flipped the can. Only I missed. I walked over and stuffed it into the wastebasket.

"You going?"

"I've got things to do."

"Okay. You owe me sixty-five cents for the pop."

"Nice of you. What about my legal advice?"

"Hey, I can get that free in any bar in town. There's always a drunken lawyer or two around who wants to show off. On the other hand, the soda pop has value."

"Put it on my tab."

He grinned, showing the missing teeth. "What the hell, I'm a softy. We'll call it even."

I left. It wasn't the first sixty-five-cent fee I had earned. Sometimes my advice went for even less.

Out in the boatyard I detected the faint odor of burnt wood, an aftereffect of the explosion. It mixed in well with all the other aromas.

I saw a man working with a sander on a hull of an old boat that sat on wooden supports. I presumed he was Snodgrass. I waved, but his concentration was total and he didn't see me.

He was making a kind of love with that sander, not sexual, nothing like that, more the kind of love that Michelangelo might have put into that famous ceiling. Every brushstroke a caress.

I wondered what Snodgrass would do for the object of his love. From the look of satisfied rapture, probably anything.

For some reason, I felt more lonely than before.

BACK AT MY APARTMENT the little red light on my answering machine was blinking. Each blink in the series represented a recorded call and message. Any voice, even a recorded one, was welcome in my present mood.

I filled a Manhattan glass with ice and diet ginger ale. It looked like the real thing and I sipped it as if it were. Then I sat down by the phone and pushed the button to summon the genie of the tape.

The first call was my insurance man reminding me that a premium would be due in a few days and asking me to come in to reconstruct my insurance package. Fat chance. He had already talked me into more coverage than I could ever need.

The second call was from Mrs. Emily Proder. Mrs. Proder had slipped in the local supermarket and fractured her wrist. It was the most exciting thing that had happened to her in her seventy years. I was suing the store on her behalf, and I had carefully explained it might be months, perhaps years before we got a settlement or judgment. That had been a week ago. She called every day. If she missed me at the office she called my apartment. She was one of the reasons I was considering getting an unlisted number again. A hungry lawyer looks for every advantage to bring in business, a listed phone is one. A successful attorney always makes sure his home number is unlisted. I was slowly becoming successful again, so I was rethinking the telephone situation.

The third recorded message was different.

"Mr. Sloan, my name is Rebecca Harris. You know me, I think. I'm a waitress at the Pickeral Point Inn. I go by the name of Becky there." She had paused. Her voice sounded strained, not an uncommon thing for people who need to call lawyers after business hours.

"I need to see you," she continued. She gave the phone number. I jotted it down on the pad I kept by the phone.

All the waitresses at the inn tended to look alike. Harry Sims, the manager who did the hiring there, liked older blondes, women who had once been beauties and who, while still pretty, had the tested look of old cars, worn some but carefully maintained. The attitude of the inn's waitresses, apparently by policy, was friendly but not familiar, at least that was the attitude I saw on the rare occasions I went there to eat.

I tried to conjure up a Becky.

I thought I knew which one she was. If I was correct, Becky was a tall woman who, while trim, had a sturdy look to her, the kind for whom toting a heavy tray isn't much of a chore. The one I was thinking of seemed tough and wore her blond hair pulled back into a stylish pony-tail.

Like most ex-drunks I have a soft spot for waitresses. For most of us, they, along with bartenders, constituted the major social contact of our lives, a kind of extended family. Waitresses dealt with all kinds of people, good and bad, and seemed, generally, to be tolerant of drunks. Which was a nice quality if you happened to be a drunk.

I dialed the number. It rang several times and then I heard a blip and a recorded message. It was the same voice, but the prerecorded tone was untroubled and rather bouncy.

The little bleep sounded and I spoke. "This is Charley Sloan, Ms. Harris. If you're unable to get back to me tonight, I'll be at my office tomorrow morning. You can reach me there. Thank you."

I hung up.

I smiled. Just have your machine call my machine and set up an appointment. It was a wonderful age in which to be alive.

I sipped my drink and pretended.

3

Mrs. Fenton, my secretary, was at the office when I arrived. Every morning at nine o'clock precisely she appeared. I always got the impression when I arrived later that she felt I was late, even though I was the boss. She never said anything. The disapproval was in her expression.

"I made an appointment for you. A Rebecca Harris. She'll be here in a few minutes."

"Did she say what her trouble is?"

Mrs. Fenton frowned. "I never ask. You know that."

"Sometimes they volunteer things."

"She didn't."

Much to my annoyance, Mrs. Fenton had once again straightened up my desk. Everything was in perfect square piles. The problem was I didn't know what was in which pile. I had spoken to her and politely asked her to curb her neatness compulsion, at least as far as my desk was concerned, but it did no good.

I fished out a yellow pad so I would have something to make notes on when Rebecca Harris arrived.

Big corporations, when they have legal problems, seek out the big law firms that specialize in big firms and big bucks. People come to a lawyer like me when the old man has blackened their eye and they want out of marriage, or when the bills are choking them to death and they're thinking about bankruptcy. Some have been injured in an accident, some fired by a boss they consider biased or unfair. Some want to make a will or attack one made by a dead relative. There are as many reasons as human beings. Many, if not most, of the people who come looking for me do so because some cop or prosecutor has voiced the suspicion they have done something the law considers bad, bad enough to spend some time in prison. Fear, anger, or greed, and sometimes a mix of all three, are the root reasons people come to a lawyer like me.

I wondered what reason propelled Rebecca Harris. I didn't have long to ponder.

Mrs. Fenton ushered her into my office and then shut the door discreetly behind her.

I did recognize her, although she looked very different dressed in something besides the black dress uniform all the waitresses at the inn wore. She had on well-cut slacks and a black sweater. A puffy silk scarf covered her throat. She carried a black raincoat. She was the one I thought she was, hair pulled back and all.

Her hand was warm but her grip tentative as I directed her to a chair in front of my desk.

"Do you remember me?" she asked.

"Yes. It's good to see you again. May I call you Becky?" She nodded.

"How may I help you, Becky?"

"I'm not sure that you can."

"Tell me your problem and we'll see."

"It's, well, embarrassing."

I tried to look reassuring. "Everything you tell me is confidential. Just relax and tell me the problem."

She studied me for a moment, as if trying to make a decision and then she finally spoke. "I've been raped," she said without any evident emotion.

"Have you been to the police?"

"Yes. The sheriff's office here."

"And?"

"They said they'd do an investigation."

"Becky, you had better tell me what happened, from the very beginning."

"Do you mind if I smoke?"

"No."

She pulled a cigarette from her purse and lit it, expelling a large cloud of white smoke. I noticed that her hands trembled slightly. "I'm trying to stop," she said. "But I'm just too nervous to think about that now."

"Understandable. Go on."

"Do you know Howard Wordley?"

"The car dealer?"

She nodded. "He did it."

I didn't laugh, although just the visual picture of Howard Wordley as a rapist was hilarious. He owned Wordley's World of World Class Cars, a dealership that handled all imported luxury cars, plus a few upscale Japanese models. I had met him a few times at civic functions. Wordley I thought was approaching seventy, a short stout little man with a jaunty bantam cock swagger and little beady eyes, eyes that seemed predatory. He resembled a bowling ball with legs, and he wore his white hair cut short, military style. Becky was a half-foot taller.

She inhaled deeply on the cigarette and continued. "It happened the night before last."

"Where?"

"In the parking lot behind the inn."

"Your car?"

She shook her head. "His car."

"Go on."

"He was going to drive me home. When I got in his car he wanted to make love. I didn't. He started to get rough and I tried to get out. He tore my uniform and hit me."

"He's not very big," I said softly.

She didn't seem offended. "That's true, but he's surprisingly strong."

"Go on."

"I tried to fight him but he grabbed my throat. I couldn't breathe. I passed out. I suppose it was only for a moment. When I came to, he was on top of me. Finishing off, if you understand."

I nodded. "Did you call the police then?"

"No. He told me it wouldn't do any good. He thought **it was** funny. He let me out and one of the other girls **drove** me home."

"And you then called the police?"

She shook her head. "Not then. I did yesterday, when I woke up. They came to my house. They took me to the hospital. It was all very embarrassing. Humiliating, really."

"Did they talk to Wordley?"

"I don't know. They said they would."

"How was it that you came to get in his car that night?"

She shrugged. "He often picks me up after work."

"Boyfriend?"

She drew on the cigarette before answering. "I'm forty-eight years old, Mr. Sloan. I've been married three times. Nothing to show for any of it, no money, no children. As you probably know, there aren't many available men up here in Pickeral Point, at least not for single ladies my age."

She crushed out the cigarette. "Howard is married. He never meant to leave his wife, I knew that. He was, how shall I say it, just someone to pass the time with."

"Did you ever sleep with him?"

She nodded slowly. "Yes."

"Often?"

"I've been seeing Howard for approximately three months. I have slept with him." She paused. "At first he used to take me to a place just past Port Huron, a nice little beach motel and restaurant. It was nice, dinner, drinks and then the motel."

"And then?"

She sighed. "The dinner and drinks were eliminated. The motel, too. He just wanted me to service him occasionally in the parking lot."

"Did you?"

She looked away and nodded.

"And this time you said no."

"I have that right, I believe."

"You do."

"I wonder," she replied.

"What do you want me to do, Becky? Sue Wordley?"

She shook her head. "No."

"What then?"

She looked as if she might cry, but then she got back in control. "I just want justice," she said in a near whisper. "Howard is a big man up here, an important man. I just don't want him to think he can get away with doing something like that to me."

"The sheriff's office is professional. I'm sure you have nothing to worry about. If they think they have a case, they'll prosecute. But cases like this are extremely difficult to prove. It boils down to one person's word against the other. Without more, there's no real way they can show a crime really happened."

"Like what?"

"Becky, without a witness who heard screams, or proof of a weapon, it's difficult to prove something like this. If there had been injuries, then it might be something else."

"Like this," she asked as she gingerly pulled the silk scarf away from her throat. Her exposed skin was as indigo as spoiled meat, streaked with yellowish red. The flesh was puffy and swollen. It looked as if someone had tried to twist her head off.

"Jesus!"

"I said he was strong. The doctors told me I was lucky he didn't fracture my neck. Or break my ribs. My chest is all black and blue. They took X rays at the hospital but nothing was broken. It hurts to turn my head, or even breathe."

"Who did you talk to at the sheriff's?"

"A detective Maguire and a woman, I think she's a detective, too, her name is Gillis."

"I know them both. They're both very competent. Sue Gillis handles sex crimes. You're in good hands. You don't need me."

"Howard's lawyer called and demanded that I drop the whole thing."

"Who is the lawyer?"

"Victor Trembly. Do you know him?"

Trembly, a criminal lawyer with offices in Port Huron, had a reputation slightly more murky than my own. His was earned.

"I know him."

"I'm afraid, Mr. Sloan."

"You don't need to be, Becky. The court will handle everything."

"I don't trust the courts, to be frank."

I smiled. "Sometimes it pays to be wary, but I think you're safe enough in this case. They're pretty honest up here. The courts are really the foundation of our government. If the foundation is rotten, the whole house comes falling down."

It sounded good and I meant most of it.

"I'll tell you what, Becky. I'll call Sue Gillis and see if there's any special problems. I don't think there will be. If Trembly calls again, refer him to the cops or to me."

"What do I owe you?" she asked. "I don't have much money."

"The phone call to the police will be gratis. If I have to do something more than that, we'll work something out. Okay?"

She carefully replaced the scarf and stood up. "I appreciate this very much. Just talking to you makes me feel better."

I walked her to the door.

"You have nothing to worry about," I said.

I hoped I was right.

THE DAY SPED BY without my accomplishing much. I dictated some letters, made some calls, and saw a man who was having trouble with his teenage son. What he needed was a social worker, not a lawyer, so I gave him the name of the person to call.

I had promised Becky Harris I would call and check on her case. The promise was made merely to make her feel better, but it was a promise.

I called the sheriff's office and asked for Sue Gillis. Sue was a cute little thing who looked very young but was almost forty. She looked more like a school cheerleader than a very experienced cop. She had started life as a registered nurse but had switched careers and gone into police work, beginning as a patrol officer in Pontiac, Michigan. After that she had come up to Pickeral Point and worked as a detective.

She was quiet, and smart. Her schoolgirl looks fooled a

lot of people. And they certainly fooled the guy who tried to rob a local drugstore while she was inside shopping. He wouldn't drop his gun so she blew his brains all over the foot powder display.

From that point on, no one gave Sue Gillis a hard time.

She had been the investigating officer on several cases where I had defended people charged with sex crimes. She was quick to laugh but she could be as tenacious as a bulldog chewing on a postman.

"Mrs. Gillis," she answered as she came on the line.

"It's Charley Sloan, Sue. How are you?"

"Fine, Charley. What's up?"

"I'm calling on behalf of a client."

"Which one? It's been a busy day. I have two child molesters and a dick waver. Give me the name."

"None of the above. This concerns Howard Wordley."

"I thought Trembly was representing him."

"He is. Wordley's victim is my client."

"Rebecca Harris?"

"Is there more than one Wordley victim?"

She chuckled. "Not today. What's your interest?"

"Informal mostly. Becky Harris came to see me. She's worried that Wordley might walk away on this."

"The investigation's in progress," she said quickly, maybe too quickly.

"C'mon, Sue, is there a problem here? Did you see her neck?"

There was a pause. "Yes. We took photos. The doctors say she could have been killed."

"So?"

"I shouldn't be talking to you, Charley."

Suddenly I was interested. "Why not?"

"You know the rules."

"Look, tell me off-the-record, okay? You know me, Sue, I'm not going to go off half-cocked."

"What did she tell you?"

"Also off-the-record?"

"Sure."

"I didn't go into it very deeply, Sue. She said she started seeing Wordley a couple of months ago. They used to go to a motel for a little sweaty love until Wordley decided he didn't want to waste time and money and asked her to service him in the inn's parking lot. Apparently she did until the other night, and when she refused he grabbed her throat and forced the issue."

"That's about what she told me, too," she said.

"Well?"

"We took a statement from Wordley. Trembly was there. Wordley says he's been paying for it."

"Bull."

She laughed again. "It's been known to happen. Not everyone is as handsome and attractive as you, Charley."

"I can't, or won't argue that, Sue, but it's obvious Wordley is lying."

"Why?"

"They've been having an affair."

"He says not. He says he's paid for everything he's gotten."

"Then how come the near strangulation?"

"He said he had sex with her and gave her twenty bucks. He said she wanted more and when he refused she went nuts and tried to stab him. He says he had to fight her off."

"Well, I suppose there isn't a hell of a lot he could say. Probably Trembly cooked up that story for him. It sounds like something he'd think up."

"Maybe."

"Sue, you got serious injuries to the woman. And he admits having sex with her. The injuries substantiate her version. So what's the problem?"

She paused and then spoke in a softer voice. "Well,

Becky Harris has a past conviction for accosting and soliciting."

"What?"

She sighed. "In Cleveland, about ten years ago."

"Did you ask her about it?"

"I called her after we ran her prints. She said she had some trouble in Cleveland. She tried to deny the conviction, but finally she admitted it."

"Damn it."

She laughed. "So, now you can see our little problem, can you?"

"That conviction is older than some of the judges up here. Besides, a woman's past sex life isn't admissible."

"Charley, it is when it's germane to the defense. He says she was hustling. He can bring it in to support his defense that she was charging for services rendered. She's the complainant, she has to take the stand. A jury would bounce her without blinking an eye, and you know it."

"How about dropping the rape business and go for assault."

"Same story, same defense. He might plead to it, but I doubt it. Trembly wouldn't let him. Not under these circumstances."

"Sue, he damn near killed the woman. You can't let him just walk away."

"Charley, if he was your client you'd be howling to have the charge dropped."

She did have a point. "So, what do I tell her?"

"The truth. We're digging into the secret life of Howard Wordley, as you can imagine. If this is part of a dangerous pattern, that could change things. We'll let her know what the prosecutor finally decides."

"And when will that be?"

"A week, maybe less. I want to check the motel records and a few other things before we go to the prosecutor."

"So, what's your position going to be?"

She sighed. "I can't get the sight of that woman's throat out of my mind. I'll recommend prosecution, even if I don't think we can really nail him. I'm fair, but not that fair. A few more pounds of pressure and this would have been a murder."

"Keep me advised, okay?"

"It's odd to find you on our side, Charley. It's disorienting. I'll let you know what I can."

"Thanks, Sue."

I hung up.

We had had a change in prosecuting attorneys for Kerry County. Mark Evola, the former prosecutor, had jumped at the chance for appointment as a circuit judge. He believed, because I had beaten him in the Harwell murder trial, that I had ruined all his chances for other political offices. He was now one of the county's three circuit judges. However, he was up for election in the fall, so he always made it a point to smile at me. But only with his teeth, his eyes never smiled. He would eventually try to stick it to me. I knew that. He knew I knew.

It was now only a matter of time.

The new prosecutor, named to Evola's old job, would also have to run for election in the fall. Until then he was playing everything so safe that nothing even slightly controversial was being considered for official action. The charge of rape against the town's leading auto dealer would be controversial.

Becky didn't have a chance.

MICKEY MONK CALLED a few minutes after three. He sounded drunk.

"We got a court date. Jesus! I didn't expect it so soon." His voice was so strained it sounded like he was about to scream. I wondered if he was tipsy or just plain terrified.

"What's the date, Mickey?"

"The twenty-fifth of May. Too fucking soon."

"We have three weeks before we argue. That's plenty. All the pleadings are in. What are you worried about?"

"Charley, you know what I got riding on this thing. If you don't win this, my ass is grass. My creditors are getting edgy as it is."

"Relax, Mickey. We'll give it our best shot."

"You know those guys you read about on death row, the ones waiting for the date with the executioner?"

"Yeah?"

"I know exactly how they feel."

"This is a hell of a lot different, Mickey."

"Maybe for you, but not for me. I think maybe a quick death would be preferable to what will happen to me if you lose it."

He paused and then spoke, this time in a calmer voice. "I think you should meet my client."

"Why?"

"I think it's important that you see the poor son of a bitch for yourself. It might help when you argue the thing."

"Can you bring him up here to my office?"

"I can't, Charley. He's a fucking vegetable, damn near. Look, you set the day and we'll drive out to his place."

"I don't think it's necessary."

"Maybe not for you, but it is for him. His future rides on this too. It's one thing to tell about someone you've only seen on paper. It's better when you really know the problem, when you've seen it firsthand."

"I'm pretty busy, Mickey."

"We're all busy, but this is important. I'm asking as a special favor, Charley."

I sighed. "Okay. When do you want to go?"

"Next week, Monday. Is that good?"

I flipped through my desk calendar. I had a few things

to do but nothing that couldn't be put off. Mickey sounded as if he was coming apart. I could afford to lose a day, if for no reason other than charitable concern for a brother lawyer.

"Okay," I said.

"I'll drive up there and pick you up."

Mickey, I knew, couldn't exist the day without drinking. It would be inconvenient, but safer, if I did the driving.

"I'll pick you up in front of your office building. What time?"

"Ten o'clock okay? It's about an hour's drive from here. We can see the guy and then have lunch. Sort of make a day of it. Like old times."

"Ten o'clock," I said and hung up.

I had a bad feeling about the case, although I didn't really know why.

I marked the date and time on the calendar.

I spent the rest of the day preparing for some motions I had the next day in circuit court. The matters weren't earthshaking. I wanted a client's temporary alimony reduced. My client was getting desperate, and poor. He didn't mind a bit of desperation, but without relief he soon would be sleeping in his car. The judge had been divorced twice and I thought we had a fair chance, on empathy if nothing else.

The second motion was to reduce another client's bond. He was a nice quiet little man unless you said something to him in a bar. He didn't need much, maybe just a request to pass an ashtray. Little or not, he regularly inflicted great damage to flesh and property. He was going to trial on his third assault charge, having smashed one nose and broken three bar stools before being subdued. Without booze he was a mild family man who worked as an accounting clerk. Add alcohol and he was transformed into a hundred-and-thirty-pound hurricane. Bail had been set at $100,000 by the judge who had let him out on probation the last time. He would lose his job if he didn't get out. His wife and children would suffer.

But, despite that, I was just going through the motions. The judge's patience had run out, and my man had as much chance of getting out of jail as I did of winning the lottery.

My preparation for both cases was merely to recheck the pleadings and review what I was going to say.

That done, I would dine at my usual greasy spoon restaurant and then drive into Detroit, an hour away, for the weekly meeting of my club. The club was what we called the folks who regularly came to the Thursday night AA meeting in the basement of St. Jude's Church.

It was not so different from any other club. We have kind of a ritual, the reading, usually of the Twelve Steps. We know and like one another, more or less. And we have a common interest—staying sober. The only thing missing is dues.

Mrs. Fenton made her usual quiet departure precisely at five o'clock and I was left alone.

The phone rang almost as soon as she had closed the door behind her. I could hear her walking down the outside steps. She was not rushing back, so I picked it up on the fourth ring.

"Charley Sloan," I said.

"Please hold for Victor Trembly," an officious woman demanded.

I waited as she patched me into recorded music. I was about to hang up when he finally came on the line.

"Charley, how are you!" The greeting was as enthusiastic as it was insincere.

"Never better, Victor. What can I do for you?"

"I was told by the police that you have some connection with Rebecca Harris."

"The same connection you have with Howard Wordley. I'm Ms. Harris's lawyer."

"To what purpose?"

"Why do most people hire lawyers, Victor? To sue the living shit out of someone, right? Maybe that's the purpose, maybe not. What business is it of yours?"

Even his chuckle was arrogant. "Charley, the bitch is a hustler, a cheap lying hustler. You never used to represent hookers. How come?"

"I represent this one, whatever she is. You called me, remember, what's on your mind?"

"I want the woman to drop the charges against my client."

"Who wouldn't? Sexual criminal conduct or rape, it's still something that doesn't look too good on the old résumé. Wordley damn near killed her, you know that? Nothing's going to get dropped, Victor."

"Are you thinking about a civil action?"

"Maybe. Why?"

"She's lying and we can prove it, but rather than drag my client through that, we might come to an agreement."

"Victor, are you into obstruction of justice now? Everybody says that, but I never believed it. Shame, Victor, shame."

He laughed, but it had a nasty sound. "Look, Charley, we are two lawyers discussing ways to solve a legal problem. We aren't buying her off. Nothing like that. This is strictly a legal matter, that's all it is."

"As far as I know, Victor, she isn't interested in money."

He snorted. "Hey, she's a woman, right? That's all they're interested in, when you cut away all the bullshit."

"Happily married, are you, Victor?"

"Ecstatic," he snapped. "Look, I'm not trying to do anything illegal here. Discuss this with her. If she plans to sue, we may settle just to get rid of this thing."

"And the criminal charge?"

"There'd be no point in it, would there, not if she's settled everything for money. Talk to her, Charley. If she's
reasonable we might be able to do something."

"Define reasonable."

He snickered. It was an ugly sound. "Call me after you
talk to her, Charley. Maybe we can work on a definition."

He hung up and all I had was the dial tone. No more
music. I felt like I needed a bath.

If she asked for money now it would be extortion, and
Trembly knew that. It would be a perfect defense to both
a criminal and civil action. I was insulted that he thought
I was stupid enough to dance right into his obvious
little net.

I needed a drink.

It was nice to have the AA meeting to go to.

There, everybody needed a drink.

4

On Monday, as promised, I picked Mickey Monk up in front of his office building. He eased his bulk into the front seat and looked around. "Jesus, Charley, this is nice but it isn't exactly your old Rolls, is it?" I pulled out into the slow-moving traffic and headed for the expressway. "Like everything else, my not-so-old Rolls got sucked up. Booze and my ex-wives were the vacuum cleaners."

He grunted. "I got lucky with my first wife. She was humping the doctor she finally married. She wanted the divorce worse than I did. She didn't ask for a cent. This one, the second Mrs. Monk, has the soul of a pirate. But that's what keeps me married. If I gave her the chance for divorce she'd take everything but my balls and get a mortgage on them. Hey, you do know where we're going, right?"

"Just past Ann Arbor. You're the one who gave me the directions."

"It's about an hour, depending on how fast you drive." He sighed. "This is a treat for me. I can sit back and watch the scenery."

I could sniff the alcohol on his breath. Things were bottoming out for Mickey. People who needed a drink in the morning, to start the heart, or whatever excuse they used, were in serious trouble.

I could speak from experience.

For the first part of the ride, Mickey couldn't shut up and kept rambling on, obviously nervous. I nodded or grunted as my sole contributions to the conversation.

About the time we drove past the entrance to the sprawling Metropolitan Airport, he was winding down. Finally, he shut up completely.

I glanced over to see if he might be napping, but he wasn't. He was staring out at the passing flat farmland and gently chewing his bottom lip. If Mickey didn't get a grip on himself he would have no lip by the time the case was finally decided.

We left the interstate and I found myself speeding along a deserted farm road just past the college town of Ann Arbor.

"There it is, that little place up there on the left," Mickey said, pointing.

You couldn't call it a farm, it wasn't big enough, just a small frame house and a few ramshackle sheds. A trailer was parked behind the house. I noticed that an electric line ran from the house to the trailer.

I pulled into a rutted driveway and parked behind a rusting pickup truck.

"His wife's parents live in the house," Mickey said. "He lives in the trailer."

"He's got a wife and kids? The trailer doesn't look big enough for all of them."

"They live in the house, with her parents."

"Sounds crowded."

"It is."

A small dog came running toward the car. He stopped a few feet away and barked. He didn't really want to go to the trouble of barking but knew it was expected of him. You could tell it was for show, his heart really wasn't in it.

He stopped the noise as we climbed out of the car. He came slowly toward us, pretending suspicion, although his tail was wagging enthusiastically.

Mickey made some soothing sounds, and the little dog instantly submitted to being petted.

The dog was our only reception committee.

I followed Mickey as he walked around the side of the house, headed toward the trailer.

"Did you call and tell them we were coming?" I asked.

"They know."

The trailer was set back about forty feet from the rear of the house. A rough walkway between them had been constructed of wooden pallets, and a homemade wooden ramp had been built up to the trailer's door. The trailer was an old metal model with rounded corners to make it less wind resistant. It looked like something left over from a low-budget science fiction movie, a dented space capsule or an alien pod. I wondered if we would all be able to fit inside.

As we started up the wooden incline of the ramp, the trailer door opened.

A woman stepped out. She was thin and wrapped in a cheap housedress. Her skinny legs sprouted from oversize gym shoes, the kind of ankle-high, thick-soled sneakers basketball players sell on television. She wasn't ugly nor was she pretty, just plain. Her hair was cut short, almost mannish. She wore glasses. The thick lenses tended to enlarge her eyes.

And those eyes had a hard, almost hostile look.

"Hello, Mildred," Mickey said as he approached. "This is Charley Sloan."

She looked me up and down. It was the kind of look a woman might give a fish that doesn't look too fresh.

She didn't extend her hand, merely nodded and stepped back through the trailer door. "Come in," she said. Her tone indicated our intrusion would be tolerated, but only that.

I hadn't expected the odor. The trailer reeked with the unpleasant aroma of an outhouse.

"It needs cleaning," she said, "but I just haven't had the time."

The trailer wobbled a bit as we stepped in. The interior was dark, and it took a minute for my eyes to adjust.

I almost wished they hadn't.

He was propped up in a kind of high-backed wheelchair. His hands were secured to the arms of the wheelchair by bandages, as were his matchstick legs, which stuck out on a kind of extended ledge from the chair. His head was held in place by a band affixed to the chair's high back.

The flickering light from a small television placed on a shelf in front of him danced eerily across his thin features. I noticed that the picture was fuzzy. The volume was set so low it was barely audible.

"How are you doing, Will?" Mickey asked without realizing just how inappropriate the greeting was in the circumstances. "This is Mr. Sloan. He's going to argue your case in the appeals court."

"Howdy," he said and tried to smile, but the attempt failed.

I had seen the photographs and the videotape of him that Mickey had used at the trial, but even with that advance warning I wasn't prepared.

He looked like a skeleton, his cheekbones almost jutting through his taut skin. He was thirty-five but he looked ninety. His hair was unkempt, and whoever had shaved him had missed a few spots.

"Jesus, Will," his wife said in a nasty whining voice, "did you poop your pants again?" She made an exaggerated sniffing gesture.

"I don't know, Milly," he said quietly, his thin voice echoing through a sea of misery. "I can't feel anything, you know that."

"Are you going to be long?" she asked Mickey.

"No, I don't think so."

"I'll wait to change him then." She turned and left the trailer.

"I'm sorry," Will McHugh said. "I have no control over anything. She changes me a couple of times a day. I wear diapers." He tried to smile and make a joke of it, but once again he failed.

"Don't worry about it, Will," Mickey said, clearing some clutter off a small padded bench. He sat down and I sat next to him. McHugh's eyes followed us. The bench was a snug fit. The whole trailer was a snug fit. It seemed uncomfortably warm. Then I noticed the gleam of an electric heater directly behind the wheelchair.

"Mr. Monk says you're a specialist in these kinds of appeals," Will McHugh said to me. It sounded as if he was unaccustomed to speaking aloud.

"I do that kind of work," I replied.

"Will we win?"

"We have a very good chance," I said. As I spoke the words I saw alarm in Mickey Monk's eyes.

"Only a chance? My God." McHugh's eyes seemed suddenly to fill with tears.

"Much more than that," I added quickly, as much for my morale as his. "Let me ask a few questions about the accident. I've read your testimony at the trial, but I'd like to go over a few things." I didn't really need to, but it seemed the thing to do.

"All right," he said softly.

"Before the accident, did you ever have trouble with your vehicle?"

It was like talking to two disembodied eyes. He couldn't nod or gesture. Only his eyes and voice could communicate.

"I didn't have it long, just a month or so. There was no trouble, no warning. It was working perfectly."

"Were you the only one who drove it?"

He sighed. "Yeah. My wife can drive, but it was too big for her. She was afraid of it." He paused. "I should have been too."

"You had never heard or been told that they were having sudden acceleration problems with that model?"

"Hell, no. Nobody said anything."

"The sudden acceleration never happened before to you?"

"Never. I was coming from a bar, as you probably know. I had a few beers. I wasn't drunk. They say I was, but I wasn't. The blood work at the hospital showed that."

"It did. Go on."

His eyes seemed to lose their focus as he remembered. "I wasn't going fast, really. Maybe thirty-five, maybe forty. Suddenly it started going much faster without me doing a thing. It was as if someone had jammed the accelerator down to the floor. It was like something in a bad dream, you know? I had no control. I hit the brake, but it didn't do anything except scare me that I might tip the damn thing over. I didn't think to shut the engine off." He stopped, then spoke in a calmer voice. "After that, nothing. I woke up in the hospital." A tear formed, then trickled down the side of his gaunt face. "Like this."

I wanted to get out of the hot, smelly trailer.

"Okay," I said. "I just wanted to talk to you a bit before the case came up. Sort of get a feeling for it, you know? I'll do my very best for you."

His eyes returned to the television set. "It's really not for me, the money," he said quietly. "It's more for the wife. This is no life for her. With the money they can put me in a nice place. Not a nursing home, not the kind with old people. I wouldn't want to go there. But a nice place, with people like myself. They could take care of me."

"Your wife doesn't mind, Will," Mickey said. "She loves you."

"This is God's punishment on me," he said, as if talking to the television. "I was on my way to commit sin that day. It's a terrible punishment, but I suppose it's fair as far as I'm concerned. My wife, she didn't do anything. It's not fair to her. With a little money she and the kids could get a place of their own, a nice place."

He paused again, this time longer. "She has to do everything now, feed me, wash me, change me. It's no life for her, and I know she hates me for what I've done. I don't blame her."

"Don't worry, Will," Mickey said. "We'll do the worrying for you."

"They have a visiting nurse who stops by and does the things Milly can't do. But the rest …"

Mickey stood up and patted Will McHugh's leg, forgetting that he could not feel the gesture. "Everything is going to be just fine," he said.

"He's right," I added, feeling like a fraud. It was a choice between cruel truth and mercy. I chose mercy.

"We'll win," I said. "I promise you."

I wasn't sure he even heard me. His attention was completely directed at the fuzzy picture on the screen. It was as if he had escaped into the flickering picture; it was the only escape open to him anymore.

Outside, the air seemed like cool perfume. I gulped it in.

Mildred McHugh had been watching. She came quickly out of the house.

"Are you all done?" she asked Mickey.

"Yeah."

"Good. I'll go change him. He can't feel anything, but it makes me feel better. Anything else you want?"

Mickey shook his head. "No."

"When is the appeal hearing again?"

"In a couple of weeks."

"Do we have to be there?"

"No," Mickey answered. "Just the lawyers."

She nodded. "Just as well. It's hell trying to arrange things to move him."

She looked at me through those thick lenses. "If you lose I believe I will kill myself." She said it without any humor, emotion, or even threat. It was said as a quiet fact. She marched off toward the trailer.

I followed Mickey back to the car and climbed in.

"Let's go," Mickey said. "I can use a drink."

"So can I. That's why we won't be stopping for one." I backed out of the driveway. "Mickey, why the hell did you insist on bringing me here? It was a wasted trip."

He snorted. "No, it wasn't wasted. When you're standing up there and talking to those three black-robed assholes you'll remember this. You'll remember that poor bastard, and you'll do a better job because of it."

I didn't reply, just shoved the accelerator down and sped away.

Mickey didn't say anything more for a while, then he turned to me. "Do you remember that movie, *The Fly?*"

"Yeah."

"Will McHugh reminds me of that movie. He's trapped in his own kind of web, saying 'help me—help me,' that's how I think of him."

"They helped the 'fly' in that movie by squashing him, do you remember that?"

Mickey nodded. "Mercy can be manifested in any number of ways," he said softly.

We drove silently for a while and then he spoke again. "God, I hope we win this thing."

Mickey was dying, or said he was, so I took pity on him, and we stopped for lunch at a restaurant just past the airport. I had a corned beef sandwich and coffee. Mickey ordered a ham sandwich that he didn't touch and four manhattans. By the fourth, he was becoming more like his old self. Not jolly exactly, but not deeply depressed either.

We talked about the case.

"Any idea who you'll draw?" he asked.

"I won't know that until next week."

He sipped his drink. "That's the key, Charley. Any way you can maneuver who you'll get?"

I shook my head. "It's been tried by better men than me. Unsuccessfully, as far as I know."

"You sure?"

"The judges sometimes try to angle for a case they want to hear. They're not supposed to, but it's done. It's like a game. Unless one of them is really interested, it really isn't worth the effort. It's an in-house thing."

"Do you think one of your friends over there might take pity and do something for us?"

I laughed. "I don't have those kind of friends, Mickey. Besides, no one I know would try something like that. It's all risk and no reward."

"I told you what I heard, about the reward part."

"Yeah, you did. But as far as I know, everything is on the up and up over there. Those appellate judges are in a fishbowl, they can't really screw around with things much. They all watch each other like hawks. You've got liberals, you've got conservatives, you got all points of political view on that court. Everybody is touchy about their own judicial philosophy. Nobody can go into business for themselves, at least not easily. Too many eyes are always watching. Also, you might be able to fix one judge, but not three."

"I wonder."

"When I hear who we've got, I'll give you a call."

He nodded, then looked away. "You wouldn't mind if I didn't go there when you argue, would you?"

"No. Why?"

"This goddamn case is driving me bats. It's just too important to even think about. I don't think I could bear just sitting there and listen to those judges shoot questions at you. Unless you really need me, I'd like to stay away."

"The whole thing will only last an hour, Mickey."

"An hour can be a long time if your nuts are on fire. Mine are, Charley. Will you need me?"

I shook my head. "No. You did the work on the brief. You did your part, Mickey."

"Good."

He finished the drink. "You told Will McHugh that we'll win. Did you mean it?"

"No. We have a good chance, but that's all. If I were betting, to be frank, I'd say we were even money, no more."

"Shit."

"You disagree?"

He sighed. "That's the problem. I don't."

Mickey walked out to the car ahead of me. He walked slowly, his head down, hands in his pockets, moving a bit awkwardly, like an old man who had no place to go but knew he had to keep moving or die.

Suddenly the uneasy feeling I had felt about the case escalated to pure dread, a sense that I was staring into an unspecified but certain doom. As in the old stories about cursed seamen, it seemed for a moment to me as if I might have agreed to sail on some kind of death ship.

The sensation was not unlike the sudden sweaty anxiety that jolts you awake from a half-remembered nightmare.

I would have liked to get off this ship, but I had signed on.

Mickey was waiting in the car, staring silently at something only he could see. I wondered if he might be thinking the same thing.

I started the car and we drove back to Detroit.

I WAS INVITED to meet with the prosecuting attorney. Summoned was more like it. His secretary, a new woman whom I didn't know and who sounded so stuffy that I felt I was better off that way, had frostily informed me that the subject to be discussed was my client Becky Harris.

The prosecutor was new. Judge Collins had slumped over dead during a particularly boring trial. It came as a surprise, especially to Judge Collins. In Michigan when a judge quits, gets convicted, or dies, the governor appoints someone to fill the term. The new judge has to run but election is almost a certainty, and without scandal the job becomes lifetime, at least de facto. Even before the mortuary wagon carted Judge Collins away, local lawyers went after the vacancy like starving cats diving for a fat fish. When the dust cleared, my old courtroom opponent, Mark Evola, the county prosecutor, had his big teeth firmly in the belly of the fish, and the governor appointed him.

That, of course, left the prosecutor's job open, a position to be filled by appointment, by law, by the county's three circuit judges. But each judge had a different candidate, and they couldn't agree. The delay in selecting someone became politically embarrassing. Finally, they decided that none of their personal favorites could win so they appointed an outsider, a lawyer none of them really wanted, but who would at least keep the chair warm until someone more suitable could beat him in the election.

Their selection, P. Daniel Parkman, a local probate lawyer who didn't know very much about criminal law or politics, was as vulnerable as a one-winged duck in a fox pen. Lawyers were already lining up to try and defeat him, a fact that did not escape the notice of P. Daniel Parkman. He was being as careful as a nearsighted man in a mine field.

I had met Parkman socially. His predecessor had been a backslapping politician who never met a voter he didn't like. Parkman, on the other hand, was short, stout, and scowling, and looked more like a grouchy loan manager than someone running for office. He was young for the job, just a few years past thirty, but thinning hair and a paunch made him appear much older. He sported a little scraggly mustache that looked more like a chocolate milk stain across his stern upper lip.

Sue Gillis, everybody's badge-toting cheerleader, was waiting for me when I got to the prosecutor's office. We didn't even get a chance to gab but were ushered immediately in to see Parkman.

That hadn't changed, except the walls seemed obscenely bare. The many framed photos of Evola with politicians had been removed.

Parkman, seated behind the big desk, didn't stand but waved us to two chairs in front of his desk. He frowned at us, and I wondered if he thought he had our votes tied up.

I shook hands with him before I sat down. He seemed reluctant even to touch another human.

"What's your connection with the Harris woman?" he said, growling at me.

"A client."

He nodded slowly, as if I had just said something puzzling or profound, but he wasn't sure which.

Then he spoke again. "I trust you know, Sloan, that the prosecutor's office is not a private collection agency?"

"Are you thinking of going into that business?"

His scowl deepened. "You know what I mean."

"I'm afraid I don't."

"Your client and you are using this office to squeeze Howard Wordley for money."

"Oh? Who says?"

"Victor Trembly."

I glanced at Sue Gillis. Whatever she was thinking was concealed behind her placid schoolgirl face. But I thought I saw amusement in her eyes.

I looked then at Parkman. "That, to put it bluntly, is horseshit. Trembly is defending Wordley. That's his idea of terrific pretrial tactics."

"There's nothing to defend," Parkman said. "We haven't charged anyone with a crime. Yet."

"Did you see Becky Harris's throat?"

He nodded. "I saw the photos."

"The flesh is even worse. The doctors who treated her say she came within an inch of getting strangled. You don't think she did that herself, do you?"

"She's got a record as a whore," he snapped. "God knows what she'd do."

"Trembly called me," I said. "He wanted to talk about the case and a possible settlement. I thought he might pull something like this so I refused. The guy has a reputation for being a sleaze."

"Like yours?" Parkman's smile was an accusing grimace. "Judge Evola told me to watch out for you."

"He's still pissed because I ended his political career by knocking his ass off in the courtroom."

"There's no need to be vulgar," Parkman said, nodding toward Sue Gillis. "I presume your client will pursue this matter in civil court."

"That's possible. At the moment she's pursuing it in

criminal court, or trying to. Are you going to recommend a warrant in this case, or not?"

He shrugged. "She has a record as a prostitute. Mr. Wordley's story is quite believable. It was self-defense, as I see it. I do not intend to go forward, not without stronger evidence."

I sat back and studied him for a moment. "I do admire your courage. Not many elected officials would have the kind of guts you have. As soon as all this hits the newspapers, every woman in the county will be up here after your scalp. But, as they say, duty is its own reward."

"What do you mean, newspapers?"

"I will have to bring a civil action if no warrant is issued. I'll try to keep it out of the newspapers, but you know how they are, always checking new lawsuits and the like. Everyone in the media seems to be going in for the tabloid approach lately. Sex, rape, rich car dealer, you know how it is. I shudder when I think of that woman's throat being shown in color photographs. Front-page stuff. God, I hate that kind of sensational exploitation."

"You wouldn't dare do something like that," he said. "The woman is a whore!"

"One little conviction a long time ago in a city far, far away. A mistake. She pleaded guilty because she didn't know any better. A victim. Like now."

I thought he was turning pale.

"Of course, if you were a coward and issued a warrant you could avoid all that bad publicity. But I know you wouldn't think of taking the easy way out. My heroes have always been politicians who did the right thing, even though it cost them their jobs."

"I didn't say I wasn't going to recommend a warrant."

"Oh?"

"I'm just not sure what charge to bring."

I nodded, as if agreeing. "When might you decide?"

He tried to smile. "Oh, these things take time. A week or two."

"I had better go ahead then and bring a civil action. I wouldn't want to let those terrible injuries fade away before the news photographers could shoot them."

"Tomorrow," he snapped. "I want to talk to my staff. I'll take action tomorrow."

"Good. Just so it isn't a slap on the wrist. Let me know. If the charge is substantial, I'll recommend to my client that we not bring a civil action just now."

He looked like he might cry. "That's all," he said.

"Have a nice day," I said.

Sue Gillis walked me out. "That was mean, Charley. The poor bastard is afraid of his own shadow. Were you a school yard bully when you were young?"

"I only picked on small kids. Cripples, if possible. I like to play things safe."

She laughed and waved good-bye.

When I got back to my office, Mrs. Fenton handed me a telephone message from Becky Harris.

I wanted to tell her the news, maybe brag a little, so I called immediately.

She answered on the first ring.

"Hi, Becky. Charley Sloan. How are you doing?"

"Very good, much better," she said brightly.

"Good. I just came back from a meeting with the prosecutor, Becky. Tomorrow—"

"That's what I wanted to talk to you about."

"Yeah, anyway, tomorrow they will recommend that Wordley be arrested."

"Oh no!"

"No?"

"Can you stop it? Howard and I have talked things over. He was very sweet."

"*Sweet?*"

"He's been under so much stress. After he explained things, I understood everything."

"Like nearly getting goddamned murdered?"

"It wasn't that bad. Anyway, Howard feels just terrible about everything. He's going to make it up to me. I think he just might leave his wife. He hinted that he was thinking about it."

I sighed. "Did he offer money?"

"No." She sounded offended. "He bcught me a beautiful diamond ring, a really big one. He didn't say so, but I think he intends it as a kind of an engagement ring."

"What about the quick sex in the parking lot? Are you going back to that again?"

"Howard explained. His business has been in trouble. That's all it was, just stress. I understand now. Everything is going to be just fine."

"And the criminal charge?"

"I don't want to bring a charge. Can you take care of that?"

"Becky, after today, I don't think they would believe me. I tell you what, you call Sue Gillis. Remember her?"

"Yes."

"Call her and tell her you don't want to prosecute."

"All right." She paused, then spoke. "Mr. Sloan, how much do I owe you?"

I thought of the enemy I had just made in the county's top law office. What was that worth? And I hated the thought of Victor Trembly laughing at me.

"Nothing, Becky, you owe me nothing, it's just something to be chalked up to experience."

"By me?"

"No. Me."

I hung up.

MOST OF US LIVE our lives according to the dictates of routine, some more than others, some less. I was no exception. I had been routinely devoting my Thursday afternoons to St. Benedict's law library. The McHugh case was getting closer by the day, and I needed to anticipate anything that might be asked by the judges. In addition, although my brief was in, I needed to study the law concerning the issues in Dr. Stewart's case. Almost daily, courts across the country were issuing opinions in cases with issues similar to Doctor Death's. Some were favorable and supported our position, some were flat-out disastrous. I had to know each and every one so I could use the language in support or be prepared to defend against it. The prosecutor's answering brief was due, and when it came in I wanted to write a quick reply and get the case set for hearing.

So on every Thursday, unless I was caught up in court, I drove into Detroit, worked the afternoon at the law library, then caught a quick dinner so I could make the regular weekly meeting of the club in the basement beneath St. Jude's Church.

It was a rather tranquil way to live, and Thursday was fast becoming my favorite day of the week.

I was in the school's law library reading a North Dakota case almost identical to the McHugh facts. It was a new decision, just in. Part of it hurt us, but part of it helped. I was lost in complete concentration when I felt a strong grip on my shoulder. Like a vise. So strong I was immediately at the edge of pain.

I turned and looked up.

"Charley Sloan. What a pleasant surprise." The words seemed to echo in the quiet library.

"Hello, Judge." His fingers bit even deeper into the flesh around my shoulder.

Students glanced up at the disturbance and frowned their disapproval.

"Got a minute, Charley?" he asked.

I marked the page for the North Dakota case and followed him out of the library.

He wore a tailored, gray pinstriped suit in place of a toga, but he looked the way I thought Roman senators probably had. Tall, wide-shouldered, and powerful, he had the fleshy build of a football player. Everything about him was big, muscular. His snow white hair was brushed back so smoothly that it resembled a white helmet until it curled regally around his expensive collar. His florid features could have graced a Roman coin. Although he was nearing sixty, his manner was youthfully energetic, his walk was two points away from a strut.

Judge Jeffrey Mallow.

Judge was a title of courtesy. He had resigned from the court of appeals to go into private practice. To make a little money, he had told the newspapers at the time. But his career off the bench had been stormy.

"Coffee, Charley?"

He put his big arm around my shoulders and led me toward the student lounge down the hallway.

"Damn, I love this place, don't you?" His deep baritone voice was unnaturally loud in the quiet hall. "They're going to surrender to the goddamned Jesuits and close this place down. Perhaps by the end of this school year. It breaks my heart."

He gripped me as if he thought I might try to escape. It was awkward to try to walk in step with him but there was no alternative.

"This place was the dream of our fathers, wasn't it?" The question was rhetorical. "Without this place you and I wouldn't have had much of a prayer, would we?"

I said nothing, mostly because I didn't get the chance.

"Were you one of my students, Charley?"

"No. You taught procedure here after I graduated."

He nodded and guided us through the door into the lounge. The few students there glanced up, probably wondering who we were and what we were doing there.

He released me. "What do you take, Charley? Cream? Sugar?"

"Black."

He nodded and played the coffee machine until he came up with two steaming cups.

"How about over there?" It was in the form of a question but it was really a command. We took a small table well away from everyone else.

"So, how's it feel to be back in harness, Charley?"

He talked as if we were old friends. We weren't. He had been chief judge of the appellate court when I had clerked for Judge O'Dowd. Mallow had ignored me then. And he hadn't shown any great interest later when I had appeared before appellate panels he had been on.

Our only other contact had been at St. Benedict alumni meetings. Before I had disgraced myself, I had been quite active in support of the school. We had talked a few times then, or to be more accurate, I had listened.

In any event, we were not buddies under any construction. I wondered what he wanted from me now. I presumed he was about to work me for some kind of financial contribution to a school activity.

I sipped the metallic-tasting coffee and waited.

He didn't touch his coffee but studied me, as if he were about to pass sentence.

Finally, he spoke. "I've been following your career since"—he paused—"since your suspension. Apparently you're beginning to do quite well again."

It was time to poor-mouth a little in case this was leading into a serious solicitation for some St. Benedict cause. It would help keep the request on a reasonable dollar level.

"I've had a few front-page cases lately, but financially there's been more smoke than fire. I do all right. I support myself, but that's about it."

He smiled as if he didn't believe a word. "That chap,

Doctor Death, must be paying you a pretty penny. He could end up in prison for life. He has money. I hope you're getting your share, Charley."

"A good fee. It balances out some of the stuff that doesn't pay or that I do for free."

"Free?"

"It happens."

"I hear you have an extremely juicy product liability case coming up on appeal," he said, studying his coffee but still not drinking.

I nodded. "The damages are substantial. A young man paralyzed for life. The company's liability is the big issue."

"What was the jury award, something around five million?"

"Yes." I wondered how he knew it was my case. My name wasn't in the newspapers, only on the amended appearance filed as cocounsel.

"I presume the fee is at least a third of the award?"

I nodded.

He smiled slowly. "Well, if you win, Charley, you'll be a millionaire. Thinking about retirement, by any chance?"

I shook my head. "It's not my case. I'm just arguing the appeal. I'm being paid for that."

"I'm curious. How much?"

I resented the question but I answered. "A percentage of the fee, if any. Twenty percent."

He nodded. I could see he was doing mental arithmetic. "Perhaps not enough to retire on, but substantial nevertheless."

"If we win."

The smile got wider. "Life's little problems. Everything else going well?"

I presumed he was asking if I was still off the stuff. "Yes."

"I'm proud of you, Charley. We all are."

"Thanks. How about you, Judge?" It was a delicate subject. He had been in the newspapers a lot, and none of it good.

"A minor setback here and there. I left Brookins Stanley, as you probably know. The damned newspapers have treated it like some banana republic war. My former partners are suing me, but they'll never win."

He made a wry face. "And I have that other suit against me, the one brought by the widow of that chap who worked for me up on my farm, the one who fell into the reaping machine. You'd think the reporters had nothing else to write about but me. That's another lawsuit I have no fear of losing. The woman doesn't stand a chance. The man caused his own death. The case should have been thrown out. And I think in time it will be. I don't even own that accursed farm anymore."

"What are you doing now?"

For the first time he sipped the coffee, almost as if trying to avoid answering. He looked at the cup. "God, but this stuff is awful. They must not clean that machine very often." He pushed the cup away from him. "I was on my own for a while," he said quietly. "Now I share offices with Thomas Slatmore. Do you know him?"

I nodded. I did. Thomas Slatmore had an odious reputation, a lawyer who slithered into courtrooms. He had narrowly escaped indictments in several corruption scandals. I was surprised and I supposed it showed.

"Thomas isn't such a bad fellow," he said. "Charming, actually, but the kind of man who seems to attract a bad press. We're not partners, we just share an office. It's working out quite well."

I wondered if that were really true.

"Do you come back to the school often, Charley?"

"Not usually. But I'm doing some research on that product liability case. I'm here on Thursday afternoons lately."

He stood up. "I'm frequently here myself. Perhaps we'll run into each other again."

He didn't offer his hand, but merely smiled down at me. "We talk of you often, Frank Palmer and myself. He's quite interested in what you do."

"I'm flattered."

"I understand he'll be on the panel assigned to your case."

Before I could comment, Mallow turned and walked briskly from the lounge.

I wondered if getting Judge Palmer might be good or bad. But chiefly I wondered how Judge Jeffrey Mallow knew so much about the case.

It occurred to me that he might be trying to muscle his way into the McHugh case, maybe even try to take over the whole thing.

My coffee was almost cold, but I finished it anyway.

It left a bad taste in my mouth.

Like a lot of things.

5

His son had asked me to represent him, although over the phone *fils* did not sound overly enthusiastic about *père*.

I went to the jail, and after the usual two-step with the bored guards—they love to practice officiousness whenever the chance presents itself—I was finally allowed to see my new client, albeit through glass and over microphones.

I knew him. Everyone in Pickeral Point knew him.

Without his wearing his usual uniform I hardly recognized him. His customary mode of dress consisted of a perfectly pressed dark suit, starched white shirt, and sensible tie. It was the uniform of a banker, which suited him perfectly, since that was his occupation.

But now, as he sat across from me in the interview room, blinking at me from the other side of the glass, he didn't look like a banker. The wrinkled white shirt was disheveled and stained. And, if he had been wearing one, his necktie had been confiscated. Despite everything he sat ramrod straight. In his sixties, a tall, heavy man, he looked as out of place as a hamburger in a vegetarian restaurant.

His perfectly groomed gray hair was no longer perfectly groomed. Uncombed, it sprayed out from his skull like a mop that had accidentally encountered an electric socket, making him look like a white version of Don King.

A one-day gray stubble frosted his fleshy jaw. His banker's expression was the same, however: dignified and just a tad suspicious. But the usually cold eyes were different. They had that same shocked look that accident victims do upon awakening in an emergency room. There was some minor swelling under one eye, and his lower lip had been cut slightly.

Vincent Villar was the vice president and chief loan officer of the Pickeral Point Bank, a small bank that had grown large holding mortgages on most of the homes and businesses in our river community.

I had first met Vincent Villar when I had come up to Pickeral Point after getting my law license back. I had wanted a small loan, unsecured, since I owned nothing of value after my troubles. His mouth had been sympathetic but not his eyes. He had gently but firmly turned me down. I didn't resent it. Given the circumstances then, I would have done the same thing if our positions had been reversed.

Now, in a way, they were.

"Your son asked me to represent you, Mr. Villar."

"I don't want a lawyer." His was a no-nonsense voice that had turned down a thousand would-be borrowers. "I'm guilty, and I intend to plead that way."

"Indecent exposure is a misdemeanor, but sometimes

things can be worked out. I'm not promising anything, but sometimes, with treatment, an arrangement can be made so that a conviction doesn't even become part of the record."

"I know."

"Has this happened before to you?"

"Yes." The word was spoken with cold finality, as if closing the subject for all times. "I appreciate your coming here, Mr. Sloan. But I won't be needing your services. Please send me a bill for your time."

"You'll be going before the judge this morning, Mr. Villar. Obviously, things at that point become public. I don't think you want that. Let me talk to the police and the prosecutor. Maybe I can work something out."

"No."

It was a simple, one-word sentence, ending the conversation. He got up stiffly, as if in pain, and the deputy escorted him back to the holding cells.

One of the convenient things about Pickeral Point is that everything governmental is close by. For a lawyer that's a nice perk. I walked over to the sheriff's office and looked up Sue Gillis.

She was on the phone when I got there, but she nodded a greeting and pointed toward a chair at the side of her desk.

The phone call was obviously official; she was using her ministry-of-fear voice. It sounded incongruous coming from her cheerleader lips in her cheerleader face. Even her ponytail seemed suddenly businesslike. Her words were polite, there was a hard edge to her tone. Apparently a witness was a little reluctant to come and testify. When Detective Gillis finished, I got the impression that the reluctance was a thing of the past.

She put down the phone and grinned at me. "We're out early this morning, Charley? What's up?"

"Do you have Vincent Villar as a customer?"

Her smile grew less broad. "Yes. Indecent exposure. I was about to go over to the court and introduce him to the justice system. Is he your client?"

"That's problematical. His son asked me to represent him. I went over to the jail to see him, but he says he doesn't want a lawyer and is determined to plead guilty."

"Isn't that sweet of him. If only there were more criminals like that, the world would be a better place."

"What's his story, Sue?"

"He's guilty, if that's what you mean."

"Tell me about it."

She giggled. "It sounds like something out of a farce but it's all true enough. You know the Kerry County Park?"

I nodded. Calling it a park was stretching things a bit. It was a vast weed-filled hunk of land with a few scruffy bushes and some rusty swing sets.

She continued. "The complaining witnesses, two young ladies, were engaged in a twilight jog around the park when a man, later identified as your client, popped out of the bushes. He wore a shirt and a ski mask and nothing much else besides his shoes. He was, as we like to say in court, fully erect. He said nothing, just stood there and let his swollen appendage do the talking.

"Unfortunately for Mr. Villar, the two young women, cute little things both, are gym teachers at our local high school. Also, between you and me, I think they have seen one or two of those things up close before. In any event, they were not frightened, and certainly they weren't impressed. They jumped poor Mr. Villar and gave him what we in police work like to call a sound thrashing. They used his ski mask as a kind of impromptu handcuff and led him forth, sans pants, to the street, where they flagged down a passing scout car."

"And I presume they were outraged."

She shook her head. "Not really. I think they enjoyed

striking a blow for aggressive feminism. Also, they are teachers, and a lot of kids use that excuse for a park. They don't want him waving his dingus at children."

"It was probably just a one-time episode."

Sue Gillis smiled, but there was a sadness in it. "I'm afraid not, Charley. We've had reports about an exposer in the park before. Mr. Villar meets the descriptions. Ski mask, too. I think your man feels the need to wave that thing every few months or so."

"You know the type, Sue. Almost all exposers are the same. They're not dangerous usually, just sick."

"I agree, but that doesn't lessen the shock to some little girl skipping through the park, does it?"

"Does he have a record?"

"Nothing shows, but I talked to him. He says he's been caught before. In Chicago. They let him go, providing he would agree to treatment."

"Did he get treatment?"

"He says he did. Maybe he did, maybe he didn't. Anyway, he's been quite active for the last several months, therapy or no therapy."

"If treatment helps, that's what he needs, not jail."

One cute little eyebrow shot up. "Jail? Charley, c'mon. You know better. Since he has no record, the most he'll get is a fine and probation. He doesn't have to worry about jail, at least not this time."

"Jail is nothing compared to what will actually happen to him. He's the town's banker, Sue. A conviction will ruin him. He'll be fired for starters. This is a small community. He won't be able to go to the grocery without seeing the looks and hearing the whispers. He'll have to move."

She smirked, but pleasantly. "What would you like, counselor? Shall we give him the ski mask back and provide him with a map of the local schools?"

"How about just holding the charge in abeyance until he gets treatment?"

"The schoolteachers may not like that, nor the judge."

"I'll talk to the teachers, and the judge. If they don't go along, that's it. How about it?"

"How do you define treatment, Charley?"

"Hospital to start, then whatever the doctors think is right after that, okay?"

"It's not my decision."

"Let's start with the complaining witnesses."

She sighed. "The world would be such a better place without lawyers."

"No it wouldn't. It just seems that way."

"Come on, Charley," she said as she got up. "Let's see what you can do."

THE SCHOOLTEACHERS WERE EASY. I think they felt a little guilty about roughing up the portly old banker, pervert or not. In any event, they seemed relieved, even enthusiastic, about the proposed compromise.

It was the judge who turned out to be trouble. The Honorable Thomas J. Mulhern had all the signs of a hangover. Not an unusual situation for him, but this one was apparently so bad he wanted the world somehow to share the pain.

I liked Tommy Mulhern, as he did me, but I was talking to the hangover more than him, and things got tense.

Finally, he agreed to put the case over for six months, but only on the provision that Villar get serious, intense treatment.

It took a while to arrange that. I called my friend and fellow recovering drunk Robert J. Williams, M.D., a board certified psychiatrist, and explained the situation. Fortunately, Bob Williams is the chief of psychiatry at one of the local hospitals, and he used his muscle to arrange for Villar's immediate admittance.

I was doing just great as a problem solver, but the biggest problem turned out to be my reluctant client.

VINCENT VILLAR STILL hadn't yet combed his hair when he was released. He got all his property back, sans ski mask, and I escorted him out to the jail's lobby where his son awaited him.

The son, an accountant with a Detroit firm, was a carbon copy of his father, except his hair was dark and his waist thin. But the aloof expression was the same, and the eyes. In fact, the son's eyes sparked with something deeper. Whether it was anger or hatred I couldn't tell.

"Do I go to court now?" Villar asked.

"The case has been put over for six months," I said. "The court wants you to be seen by doctors. If they feel you can be helped, the case will be dismissed."

The elder Villar's head jerked up as if he had been hit. "I don't want that! I want to plead guilty and get this over with once and for all."

"Mr. Sloan is doing what's best for you," his son said. The words were spoken from between clenched teeth.

His father glared at him and then at me. "You have no right to interfere," he rasped.

"Your son and I are going to take you to the hospital now so the doctors can talk to you," I said. "Believe me, this is the best way."

He jerked away from me, his eyes on the wild side. "No. I need to do what must be done."

"Oh, Jesus," his son exploded, "haven't you done enough? Ma's back home crying her eyes out. What the holy hell's the matter with you?"

"Get away from me," his father said, then headed for the door.

The deputy who manned the glass cage looked down at me, silently inquiring if I needed help.

I shook my head.

I followed Villar out into the parking lot. His son was somewhere behind us.

"I can understand how you feel," I said, trying to catch up, "but in a few days you'll be very glad ..."

He started to run. At first it seemed funny, this gray-haired fat man dodging between parked cars, running awkwardly but surprisingly fast.

I started after him and I heard his son's disgusted shout.

A woman pulling out in her Mazda blocked my pursuit for a moment while Villar seemed to pick up speed flying through the rows of parked cars like racelines. I felt foolish trying to catch him and I suppose I really hadn't committed myself to an all-out run. I wasn't exactly the picture of athletic grace myself.

Then I saw where he was headed.

My legs, unaccustomed to such exercise, began to feel leaden. I looked around. Villar's son was far behind, running but not fast.

It was like a nightmare. Suddenly I realized what Villar intended to do, and there was no way I could stop him.

Traffic wasn't supposed to move fast on River Street, the main artery of the town, but everyone usually ignored the twenty-five-miles-per-hour speed limit, at least during the workday. Cars and trucks were whizzing by at forty or better.

A big refrigerator truck was coming at a good clip; Villar ran out right into its path.

The son shouted. I suppose I did too.

There seemed to be no noise, everything happening like an old silent film, as if in slow motion.

The driver saw him and tried to brake and swerve. Villar faced him and held out his arms, as if preparing for crucifixion. His mouth was open, but there was no sound; his eyes were fixed on the truck.

Then there was noise. The truck brakes shrieked and the big vehicle shook convulsively.

The driver was good, very good: the truck was almost stopped when it hit Vincent Villar.

Bouncing off the grill, he stumbled backward, sitting down hard on the pavement.

The driver was out of the truck, screaming obscenities, his body shaking with a mixture of anger and fear.

Villar just blinked up at him, appearing not to be injured, just surprised.

A crowd gathered and the police came. I arranged for an ambulance to take Villar to the hospital where they were already waiting for him. Villar began to cry as we waited. His son held him, talking quietly, this time without rage or hatred.

As for the truck driver, he was still shaking with emotion.

"What the fuck was he trying to do," he snapped loudly at me, "kill himself?"

I NEEDED A DRINK, BADLY, but instead I walked the hundred feet over to the river boardwalk. I gripped the steel safety rail and waited, watching the water until the feeling passed.

My concentration on the dark flowing waters was so intense that I didn't realize she was there until she spoke.

"You're not thinking of jumping, by any chance?"

Sue Gillis had taken a position next to mine, looking out at the river.

"No. I don't feel like a swim at the moment."

"I saw what happened from my window," she said. "For an elderly gentleman, Villar moves pretty well. He looked like a fat O. J. Simpson running through an airport. You didn't have a chance of catching him."

"I was gaining there, at the end."

She smirked. "A word of advice, Charley. If you're thinking of going out for the track team, don't."

"Thanks for your support. You have the knack of making old men feel young."

"You're not old." She studied the water. "It's my fault, really. I should have guessed what he had in mind." She looked at me. "It's a pattern of behavior, the offer of a quick plea, anything to get out and destroy the creature that can't be controlled. Everybody in police work, especially vice, knows that danger. I don't know why I didn't spot it this time."

"Well, it didn't work, whatever Villar intended. All he got for his trouble was a bruised behind."

"I feel sorry for some of them, the ones like Villar who can't help themselves. You can understand the suicidal feelings. The shame must be overwhelming. Maybe not long lasting, but strong enough at first that self-destruction must seem the only answer."

I looked at her. "You sound more like a social worker than a cop."

She smiled. "Maybe. Of course, I never let pity interfere with my duty, counselor."

"So why are you here? The social worker side? Or the cop side?"

"You did a very nice thing back there, Charley. You really tried to save that old man. I was impressed. I thought someone should tell you."

"As you say, my speed leaves something to be desired, but I thank you for the good thought. I have in my time performed even greater exploits. If you have time I could buy you lunch and bore you silly with past glories."

"You want to take me to lunch?"

"That's the idea. How about it?"

She hesitated. "Well, I do have to eat, don't I? How

about we go dutch, that way no one can say it was some kind of bribe."

"Jesus, if cops can be fixed for sandwiches I've wasted my entire life. So, I pay or the deal's off."

"I have to go back to the office and get my purse. Where shall I meet you?"

"How about the inn?"

"Give me five minutes."

BECKY HARRIS WASN'T ON DUTY, which was a plus, since she would have perhaps haunted both of us. The waitress serving the table assigned to me was a Becky clone, a woman nearing fifty, handsome but with that touch of sadness a life of hard experience brings.

I ordered an iced tea and waited for Sue Gillis.

It should have been just a mundane lunch between a lawyer and a cop, a chance for both to form an informal network, a business lunch, nothing more.

But I felt like a pimply teenager out on a first date, and marveled at the feeling.

She came bouncing into the place, her movements and manner as youthful as any high school girl.

I was worried that long-latent pimples might pop out momentarily.

"Sorry to be late, Charley," she said, sitting down, "but I had to take care of a few loose ends. What is that?"

"Iced tea."

"It looks good."

"It doesn't rival bourbon but it's not bad."

"You don't drink, I understand?"

I nodded. "There is an ugly rumor going around that I almost ruined my career, my life, whatever, by booze. The ugly rumor is quite true, Sue. But I am what we in the program call a recovering alcoholic. I go to meetings, and, knock wood, I get through each day without taking a drink."

"It sounds pretty grim."

"Not really. It was in the beginning. But you kind of get into a rhythm after a while. But someone like me can never let their guard down. We're all just one drink away from destruction."

"God, you are a smooth talker, Charley. I bet with a sure-fire line like that the women are all over you, right?"

"It is a burden, I admit."

She picked up a menu and studied it.

"Curiosity is a two-way street, Sue. We've done business for a while now, rapist here, window peeper there, and everyone always calls you Mrs. Gillis. I presume there is a Mr. Gillis?"

She put the menu down. "There was."

"Divorced, I take it?"

She shook her head. "I'm a widow."

"Children?"

"No."

"Recent widow?"

"You certainly are nosy."

"Hey, I'm not going to fork over good money for a lousy chicken salad sandwich unless I know all."

One small eyebrow went up like a railroad crossing arm. "You drive a hard bargain."

"We have ways of making you talk."

She sighed, a theatrical sound. "Oh well, in that case." She stopped and took a roll from the basket, tore it in two but didn't eat. "This is all pretty boring, frankly."

"Bore me. I love it."

"I was a nurse. I had a degree from Mercy and went to work at Pontiac General. I met a wonderful man, two years older than me, an engineer. He worked for General Motors. It was one of those magical things, frankly. We met in a singles saloon, and three months later we got married. My parents were ecstatic, so were his. Could grandchildren be far behind?"

She still fingered the roll as she talked, but she was looking out the window at the river.

"It was like out of the movies, as far as I was concerned. We had candlelight suppers, the whole romantic ball game. We did all the silly things people do before their lives shake down into dull routine."

She was looking at the river but she wasn't seeing anything. "Then one morning he came out of the shower. He told me he had a small lump under the arm."

She paused for a moment, then continued. "I thought it was nothing. And that was good enough for him, since I was after all a nurse. But to be safe, I told him, we should have it checked."

"And?"

"It wasn't nothing. It was cancer. We were hurled into the center of a nightmare, with surgeries, pain, medication, the whole ugly thing. He went fast, at least that was a blessing of sorts. Six months from lump to end."

Her iced tea had been delivered, and she took a long sip. "After that I couldn't bring myself to work in another hospital. I got a job as a cop and ended up here."

"Jesus, I'm sorry."

"About me ending up here?" She laughed.

"No. You know what I mean."

"Life is funny. Not hilarious, maybe, but funny. Being a cop helps you cope. You realize you're just along for the ride. It can be smooth or it can get choppy, but you basically have no real control, the ride takes you where it wants to go."

"Fatalist?"

"More or less, I suppose I am. Most cops are."

The waitress took our orders. Sue had the perch and I ordered the special, brook trout. Fish was always a big item at the inn, since the river itself suggests the menu.

"Okay," she said, "you've sat through my life story. It seems only fair that you get your turn."

"You probably know much of it, since a lot of it is public record."

She smiled. "Let's hear your version."

I finished the iced tea. "I worked my way through St. Benedict's law school in Detroit. Then, I got a job clerking for an appellate judge, and then, later, I got hired as an assistant prosecutor in Wayne County. Mostly, I did City of Detroit felony trials."

"Were you any good?" Her eyes danced with merriment.

I pretended annoyance. "Madam, I was so damn good felons stood up in open court and confessed."

"Maybe you were just boring and they wanted to get it over with. Ever think of that?"

"It never entered my mind. I left the prosecutor and opened my own office. I hope this will impress you. I ended up with an entire floor on the Buhl Building, a dozen partners, and a platoon of associates. I was, to put it mildly, making a fortune."

"Married?"

"Several times. Three, if you like precise figures. One child, a girl, now a student at the University of Pennsylvania."

"So? What happened? How did you get to our restful shores?"

I took a roll, pulled it apart but also didn't eat. "I began drinking when I was, I think, fourteen. There was always plenty of the stuff around the house. Mom and Dad, God bless them, were full-fledged alcoholics. I had an enormous capacity, at least then. But at some time, down the road, my tolerance level dropped. I became the classic drunken bum, money or no money. And I drove my automobile into lots of things and places, including one hospital."

She listened, but said nothing.

"I ended up in a number of tanks, so-called, and finally I got with the program. In the process, the wives, the fortune, even the kid, until lately, were all gone. They suspended me from practice for a year. I sold real estate and other things. I wasn't very good at it. When I got my license back I moved up here and did nickel-and-dime stuff to survive."

"Until the Harwell case," she prompted.

"Yes. After that, things have brightened somewhat."

"Girlfriends, Charley?"

"A few. The last one just jumped ship and moved to Tampa."

"So, and this is important to all women like me, you're free?"

"I suppose so."

The waitress brought our meals.

I picked at mine, my mind full of thoughts and perhaps a speculation or two.

I noticed that she pushed around her perch as well.

"Do you like country and western music?"

I nodded.

"Merle Haggard is giving a concert a week from Saturday at Pine Knob. I have a couple of tickets. Would you like to go?"

"Sure. I'd like that very much."

"Do you know where I live?"

"No."

She took out a notepad, wrote down her address, and handed it to me.

"Pick me up about seven, okay? It's about an hour's drive to Pine Knob from here."

"I know."

The waitress came back and looked at our plates and then at us. "Not hungry today?"

We both nodded.

"How about coffee, or dessert?"

"Just coffee for me," she said.

I nodded my agreement, and the waitress left.

It was one of those awkward silences. Both of us found places on the river to look at. Finally I spoke.

"What was your husband's name?"

She paused for a very long time, then she spoke.

"Charley." She said it softly.

6

The McHugh case was coming up and so was my anxiety. I kept remembering Will McHugh, tied eternally to his wheelchair, and the memory of his pleading eyes haunted me.

All lawyers know it's imperative that an attorney not become emotionally involved in any case, at least not so much that it interferes with judgment. I tried to put out of my mind the fate of Will McHugh if I lost.

It was becoming tougher by the day as the court date came closer.

I was back at St. Benedict with enough law books in front of me to build a pretty good fort. They all were opened to product liability cases of various kinds. My notepad was almost filled and I had lost track of time.

"I wondered who was hiding behind all these books."

I looked up and saw Caitlin Palmer smiling down at

me. "Want to take a break?" she asked. "It looks as if you could use one."

I nodded and followed her out to the hall.

"Coffee, Charley?"

"Sounds good."

We made the usual small talk on our way to the student lounge. I poured two cups and then joined her at a table.

She seemed a little more feminine this time. The business suit had been replaced by a good silk blouse and a skirt, fashionably tight, that demurely clutched each seductive curve.

I sipped the coffee. Some things never change. The law school coffee was a constant. It was terrible.

Caitlin didn't taste the coffee. She smiled again. "I'm having an informal get-together Saturday night, Charley. Mostly faculty people from here. I was wondering if you'd like to come?"

"Sure."

"I've borrowed my father's boat. We can't take it out. He only trusts me so far. But it's moored at the yacht club, and it's sort of a pretty place to hold a party."

"Cat," I said, "your father's on the panel that's scheduled to hear the product liability case I told you about. I don't think it'd be such a good idea for him and me to meet socially, not at this point."

She smiled even wider. "That's no problem, Charley. Dad's going to be in Reno at a judicial conference. He's the main speaker. So, if he's your excuse to say no, you just lost it."

"Still, it might not look so good. He might feel …"

She held up her hand. "Charley, I'm an adult woman. I'm throwing a party on my father's boat. I doubt even the longest-nosed prude in the bar association would think there was any impropriety. Please say you'll come."

"Shall I bring a date?"

The smile flickered. "I rather hoped you'd be my date."

"Oh?"

"Is that a problem? Is there someone, Charley?"

"Not at the moment, no." I thought of Sue Gillis, but one casual lunch didn't seem like much of a binding commitment.

She stood up. "Then it's settled. It's at the Fountain Yacht Club. I'll leave your name at the gate so you'll have no trouble. The boat's named the *Sirocco II,* not very original, but Father never did have a wild imagination. Seven o'clock, Saturday?"

"You got it. I look forward to it."

She left me there.

Thinking about her.

And her father.

Suddenly, I wished I hadn't agreed quite so fast.

I GOT TO THE OFFICE EARLY for a change, an event that seemed to surprise my secretary. It was Friday, motion day in our circuit, and I had a few motions to argue. I gathered up the files I'd need and was preparing to leave when Miles Stewart, M.D., made a personal appearance, unannounced and with his usual air of supreme arrogance.

"It's customary to make an appointment," I said as Mrs. Fenton ushered him in.

"I was in the neighborhood." He said it as if no other explanation was necessary.

"I have to go to court now," I said calmly, remembering how much it pleased him to rile me. "What is it you want?"

"What's the situation as far as my appeal?"

"Nothing's changed. It is progressing, and almost all the briefs are in. I'm waiting for a reply from the prosecutor. When I answer that, the case will be ready for hearing. Then, depending on the docket, the court will give us a date."

He frowned. "I've been talking to some people. Informed people. They say it should all happen much more quickly than this."

"Knowledgeable people, I take it?"

He smiled, all teeth and superiority. "Very."

"Good. Have them take over the case. Now I have to go."

"You should try to develop more patience." His eyes glittered. "I didn't say I was dissatisfied, did I?"

"It sounds that way."

"It isn't. Despite the trial's outcome, I still have confidence in you."

"How nice. Now I do have to go."

"Nobody died, by the way."

"Pardon me?"

"You seemed worried that someone might pass away while I was being entertained up north. No one did."

"Good. Now you'll have to excuse me." I shoved the files into my briefcase.

"I have another invitation."

"Where?"

"Key West."

"A sick industrialist, by any chance?"

"An old friend. Since you seem to be in a hurry, I'll leave the number where I can be reached with your harridan out there."

"Good-bye, Doctor."

As I raced down the steps, I wondered what the real purpose had been of his unexpected visit. He was always working some angle.

But I had other things to think about.

Doctor Death would have to move to the back burner for a while.

■ ■ ■

SPRING HAD COME TO BELLE ISLE. Cars were moving slowly over the bridge, the only connection between the city and its two-mile-long island park. The procession was bumper to bumper, a line of vehicles, some with families, some with hot-eyed kids, all moving toward the island, that sylvan escape from the grim realities of the City of Detroit.

A police car had positioned itself at the foot of the bridge, a silent reminder that some of those grim realities came over the bridge with the traffic.

Belle Isle had once been the jewel in the crown of Detroit. The island, a half mile wide, sat in the Detroit River like a green boat. On one side was Detroit, on the other Canada. The city had bought it as a park and hired Frederick Law Olmsted, the man who had designed New York's Central Park, to do the same with the island.

He had done an outstanding job, creating a place with pools, streams, forests, ball parks, all a quarter mile away by a free bridge.

But the park had become like a woman who sits in the shadows at the end of a dim bar. At first she looks spectacular, like she did once, but as you approach, you see the flaws. She hasn't aged well, and she hasn't kept herself up the way she used to. She's still pretty, with help, but no longer truly beautiful. The island was like that. Benches needed painting, the roadways needed new pavement, the grass needed cutting. The old riding stable was closed and boarded up. The poverty on the city side had stolen quietly over the bridge and squatted down in what had once been splendor. Even the small herd of tame deer, begging for handouts at the roadside, looked moth-eaten.

But poverty had been stopped at the small bridge to the Fountain Yacht Club. Money still lived there in a guarded enclave, and everything was just as wonderful and glistening as it had been in the roaring twenties, when the place had been built on a landfill just off the main island.

There are three yacht clubs on Belle Isle. The oldest, nearest the big bridge, is city owned now, and it is crumbling just like the island. The one in the middle, the Detroit Yacht Club, is well kept, but even there the future seems uncertain, a bit like an elegant British cricket club in Kenya just before Her Majesty abandoned the place. The music at the yacht club is still pleasant and the gin is cold, but rumblings are heard and the servants are no longer quite so civil.

The Fountain Yacht Club, however, still holds forth as a bastion of the old values: money, privilege, and greed. No longer does the Fountain, as Detroiters call it, bar Jews and Negroes. If they have money, lots of it, and believe in privilege and greed, they are welcomed as equals.

I once belonged to the Fountain, in other times, when I had money, lots of it, and saw no fault in privilege or greed, more or less. I had been thrown out, sans ceremony, when I could no longer pay my bar bill or the dues. In those days, there were very few places that I wasn't eventually thrown out of.

As I drove over the cute little bridge toward the cute little guard post, I hoped they wouldn't remember.

Berlin was no longer divided, but the Fountain had its own Iron Curtain, complete with border guards, men who wore guns and looked as if they would welcome the chance to use them.

I rolled down my window as the guard came out of the small post building and glared at me as if I owed him money.

"I'm a guest of Miss Caitlin Palmer," I said, trying to sound as friendly as I could.

For a minute I wondered if he had heard me, then he spoke.

"Name?"

"Charles Sloan," I said, hoping they had no current list of former deadbeats.

He studied the papers he had on a clipboard. He did it very slowly and carefully, as if a mistake might be fatal. Finally he spotted my name.

He looked up and forced a practiced smile, formal, without warmth. "Very good, Mr. Sloan," he said. "Just follow the drive along to the parking area marked visitors. Miss Palmer asks that you join her on the boat *Sirocco II*. It's the last one out on Main Dock. Everything's marked. You can't miss it."

I nodded my appreciation, rolled up the window, and drove along the well-remembered hedge-lined path.

The main building of the yacht club looked like the country palace of an English Tudor lord, all yellow stucco and dark wood. Inside, that Tudor effect had been maintained, even in the club's main dining room. The main building housed an enormous bar, an Olympic-size indoor swimming pool, club rooms devoted to various interests—mostly nautical—a library, and a great room, complete with a fireplace that could easily roast several cows, and had enough room to seat five hundred well-padded people.

Mostly, members used only the bar.

It was not yet eight o'clock, but it was Saturday night and the parking lots were almost full. Valets parked the members' cars. Aliens, like myself, found our own way.

I located a space in the visitors' lot between a big Mercedes and a small Toyota. They might offer membership to the Mercedes owner some day, but the Toyota driver didn't have a chance.

I took the path that led to the outside pools and the docks.

Unlike the island, the place was maintained as well as a naval vessel anticipating an inspection. I remembered some very good times at the club, and I knew I had had some very good times there that I didn't remember.

I hoped I wouldn't run into anyone who knew me then.

There were four large docks that jutted out into the man-made harbor. Not all the boats were yet in their berths. It was early and I knew that some of them were probably being sailed up from their winter homes in Florida or the Caribbean. The biggest yachts were moored at Main Dock.

The docks were spotless, each adorned with antique lampposts that would rival Venice.

It was nice. I could hear the slap of lines and the sound that boats make and smell the fragrance of the river itself. Gulls wheeled above.

Across, on the Detroit side, were other marinas, so the shore appeared pleasant. Only a Detroiter would know that just beyond that seascape an area existed that would rival anything offered in the worst Third World slum, and fully as dangerous. But if you were at the Fountain, you didn't think about things like that.

Somewhere, back at the main building, a small combo was playing Cole Porter.

Suddenly I missed drinking so I hurried along the dock, past several dock boys, college kids hired as much for looks as ability, and toward the big boat at the end.

The *Sirocco* was moored with the stern in. It was enormous, or seemed so, the kind of racy yacht you see in movies or with Robin Leach standing on the deck gushing on about the wealth of some sultan or arms dealer.

Several people, in their best casual wear and sipping drinks, were standing on the aft deck, an area as large as some houses.

"Charley!"

Cat Palmer came rushing down the gangplank. She was

dressed in a stark white sailor outfit, only no sailor ever looked like that. It was bright and tight, and while chaste, it really wasn't. She had let her hair down, literally, and the total effect was erotic.

She could see that in my eyes. "Like me?" she asked softly.

"Who wouldn't?"

"Come on, I'll introduce you around." She looked down at my shoes.

I knew what she was thinking. I lifted a foot to show the sole. "Docksiders," I said. "I used to belong here. I know how touchy boat people can be about marks."

She laughed. "Especially my father. Come on. Let me show you off a bit."

It was a typical law school collection, professors who were minor gods to their students and who had taken on divine airs. It made no difference whether they were male or female, the sureness about the universe and their place in it was almost palpable. The wives and husbands were just a little easier to take.

Some of the professors knew about me, their eyes letting me know they knew the bad as well as the good.

One of them said he had tried a case against me years ago. I didn't remember him or the case, but I made a mental note to avoid him if I could, since he looked like he wanted an informal rematch.

I took a proffered orange juice from a young waiter and Cat offered to show me the boat.

Calling it a boat was like calling New York a village. The damn thing had staterooms below that were as big as the Ritz. Above, it was fitted with more electronic gadgets than the Concorde. Everything was top of the line and looked it.

I made the appropriate oohs and ahhs.

Cat led me to the prow and we sat down with our feet dangling over.

It was a warm evening, warm enough to be pleasant. She sipped wine while I nursed the orange juice.

We sat silently for a while, looking around at the other boats, enjoying the quiet, listening to some more strains of Cole Porter.

"Nice," I said.

She nodded. "I was practically raised here at the club. It's like home in a way. Of course, it's the center of my father's life."

She pointed up at a short mast near the radar. "See that?"

"The flag?"

"It shows that Daddy is a former commodore of the club. I think he's prouder of that than being on the bench. He's also chairman of the trustees now. For all practical purposes, he runs the club."

She sipped her wine. "Oh, there's a club director who does the actual day-to-day stuff, the hiring and firing, but he reports to my father." She giggled. "Daddy says this is his country and he's king."

"It sounds like he is."

"Whatever, he loves it. Whenever he visits another club, here or in Florida, it's like visiting royalty come to call. He pretends he's above it all, but he isn't. He eats it up."

"Does he ever take this vessel out?"

"Not often anymore, just special occasions like the start of the Mackinac race, that sort of thing. He can do it himself, with a crew, of course, but he uses a captain now. He has a man on call when he needs him."

"Slightly expensive, from the looks of things."

"You bet, but he's made careful investments and this is how he likes to spend the money. Nothing wrong with that, is there?"

"Guess not. It's his money."

We sat again in silence.

"I like you, Charley," she said quietly.

"I like you too. I liked you when you were a little kid."

"I'm not a kid anymore."

"So I've noticed."

She smiled and gazed off at a row of moored sailboats. "Times have changed, Charley. A grown woman no longer has to bat her eyelashes hoping that a man'll ask her out."

"So?"

"So, will we see each other again?"

I took a sip from my glass, but the orange juice was gone. "Boy, girl, you mean?"

"I prefer man, woman, but yes."

She was looking directly at me now.

"Cat, I've got an important case coming up before your father, as you know. Next week, as a matter of fact. After that, I don't know how long the panel might take to come down with a decision. I don't think it would look kosher if I were romancing the judge's daughter, at least under those circumstances, would it?"

"I'm surprised. After all this time, you really don't know my father very well. Something like that wouldn't affect his decision one way or the other."

"I wonder. For openers, there's a considerable difference in our ages."

"He likes you, Charley. But, as I say, even that wouldn't affect him."

"Maybe not, Cat. But it wouldn't look good to some others perhaps."

"Are you saying we can't go out until your damn case is over and done?"

"Exactly."

She glanced away and said nothing for a moment.

"Afterward?" she asked.

"Why not?"

She studied the sailboats again. "I usually get what I go

after, Charley. It seems only fair to warn you."

We rejoined the others on the fantail. As I thought, my old opponent wanted to reargue the old case he said we had tried. He was hitting the wine pretty hard and his wife looked alarmed. I managed to wiggle away, and after a time I told Cat I was leaving.

She walked me to my car.

She kissed me good-bye with surprising passion, then stepped back.

"The minute the decision comes off press," she said quietly, "I'm coming after you."

She wasn't smiling.

I drove off the island thinking that maybe ending up with a rich man's daughter wouldn't be the worst fate in the world.

I just wondered how the rich man might feel about that.

7

ickey Monk had begun to call on a daily basis as
the date for argument approached. There was no
point to the calls, he had no last-minute instruc-
tions, nor did he urge me to even greater efforts.
Mostly it was like a form of prayer, and drunken
prayers at that. Mickey's rate of drinking was
accelerating alarmingly. Sometimes I could hardly understand him. Usually those were the calls that came late at
night.

I tried to reassure him, but I didn't think I was doing
a very good job.

To his credit, I think Mickey's primary concern was
really Will McHugh and what was going to happen to
him if the appeal was lost. Mickey's own desperate
plight was in second place, although it looked like a
close second.

If the case was lost, McHugh would exist in a kind of nightmare, a helpless creature encapsulated in an aging trailer, incapable even of the option to kill himself.

Mickey Monk would be thrown into bankruptcy; his office would close, and with no inclination to stop drinking, he would most likely lose his license and look forward, if he lasted that long, to a life on the streets.

But nothing would happen to me.

Oddly, I didn't find that thought as consoling as it might have been.

So I put in a little more effort than usual. For the few days before the court date, I adjourned everything so I could concentrate on my research to ensure that no matter what the judges might ask I would be able to answer and, I hoped, persuade them.

I felt ready and I should have been confident. But whether it was my mental picture of McHugh, or Mickey's drunken calls, I was becoming increasingly anxious.

A nervous lawyer is not a good thing to be, not for the lawyer, and especially not for the client.

The afternoon before the hearing I called the court. Sometimes there are, for any number of reasons, last-minute adjournments. Judges get sick, or something else unexpected happens. The courts, especially appellate courts, are tough about granting adjournments, but sometimes it does happen upon showing extreme emergency.

It wasn't happening with the McHugh appeal. Everything was on schedule.

I should have been pleased and eager. But I wasn't.

I again wished I hadn't taken the case, my reluctance still rooted in a kind of nameless dread.

I doubted I could get an adjournment by pleading nameless dread as an extreme emergency, so I accepted my fate and restudied my notes.

THE COURT OF APPEALS had scheduled three cases for argument. The McHugh case was number two. The court started, at least this panel did, at nine o'clock. Each side in each case, where oral argument is requested, is entitled to thirty minutes each. So, if everything went according to plan, the first case would take an hour. In theory, then, I could arrive there at a leisurely ten o'clock. But in the law, nothing ever goes entirely according to plan.

The first case might even be settled and withdrawn, right there, without warning, the so-called courthouse-steps settlement. If that happened, the judges wouldn't want to sit around with nothing to do for an hour, so they expected—more, they ordered—all attorneys on the calendar call to be there at nine o'clock, no matter how many cases might be scheduled before theirs, just in case.

That arrangement might be inconvenient for the lawyers, but not for the judges, and since the judges set the rules, it was their convenience that mattered.

I got up earlier than usual, showered, had coffee and toast for breakfast, although I had no appetite. My briefcase contained everything I needed, carefully catalogued and classified. But what I needed most was in my head. And that seemed weirdly unclassified, although I knew, from experience, it would come flowing out when it was needed. It always had. Still, there was the niggling fear that this might be that dreaded first time.

I put such thoughts behind me and drove to Detroit. Some people I suppose go to battle with bands and martial music. I listened to a tape of the Beach Boys.

By the time I encountered the rush-hour traffic into downtown Detroit, I was almost relaxed.

Parking is no great problem in Detroit, but choosing a

parking lot is. I paid a premium rate to park in a garage where the probability was high that my car might still be there when I got out. No guarantee, just a fond hope.

The Michigan Court of Appeals hears cases in various cities. In Detroit, usually, the cases are heard in the First Federal Building, a modern high-rise set at the corner of Michigan Avenue and Woodward, a location that once was the very center, the heart of Detroit, where all the major streets intersected, about a quarter mile up from the river, the hub of all the major department stores and fine shops.

The river is still there, but the department stores—those still standing—are boarded up, and the fine shops are only a distant memory. The streets still intersect, but the main traffic is out on the interstates now and the shopping has moved to the suburban malls.

What once was the throbbing core of the city now looks forlorn and desolate, as if an enemy army had marched through and sacked the place.

For anyone who remembers how it used to be, there is a sadness, like seeing your favorite uncle, once so robust, now frail and dying.

But entering the First Federal Building is, in contrast to the main street outside, like stepping into Oz. It's clean; bank cops patrol the sparkling lobby. People smile, laugh, move with a sense of purpose. The problems outside are just that, the problems outside.

I took the elevator up to the ninth floor, got off, registered as being present for battle, then went into the court's main hearing room.

COURTROOMS, THE KIND the public attends, are designed with an air of the theatrical. Especially the ornate old courtrooms with their dark woods and polished carvings. Even the modern ones, stark as they may be, still are artfully crafted to be places where public dramas will be enacted on a daily basis.

I always thought the underlying intention was to give the audience their tax money's worth. If judges looked like shoe clerks and courtrooms somebody's basement, it would be difficult to persuade the citizens that what goes on was worth the salaries and the cost. So, the more important the court, usually, the more important the trappings.

But not appellate courts, not the kind where the only people in attendance will be lawyers, usually. Everybody knows the score, so there's no need to make the place look like the Gaiety Theater.

The hearing room where we would argue was like that. Very nice, very comfortable, but very plain.

The judges' three chairs are arranged behind a dais that puts them only slightly above eye level with the lawyers. In some trial courts a lawyer can get a serious whiplash by having to strain his neck to see the judge sitting so high above him. But not here.

Set just in front of the judges' bench is a simple wooden lectern, the kind politicians speak at, complete with a gooseneck microphone. On each side of the lectern, tables are placed where the lawyers called up to argue their case can sit, arrange their papers, or take notes while they listen to their opponent spread lies to the three-man court.

The spectator section seems more like an airport waiting area, although the chairs, an upgrade on the standard theater seats, are wide and comfortable, but not so much as to lull anyone to sleep. Snoring is against court rules.

The Ford attorneys were already there when I arrived. I had met with two of them before, eager young men, with that lean and hungry look Shakespeare warned about. The third I knew by reputation. Craig Gordon was their firm's leading appellate specialist, a man who probably knew the judges better than the law, but was no slouch on the law either. I didn't have to be told he would be the one presenting the appeal to the court. This was his specialty. He was as relaxed as an ambassador in a friendly country.

I introduced myself to Gordon. We exchanged the usual lawyerlike pleasantries, like casual friends meeting outside a theater, not talking about the case but chatting about the weather, the sports teams, anything that might be commerce for light conversation.

Both of us, of course, were taking measure of the other's probable abilities. We shook hands. He joined the two lean and hungry associates on one side of the room and I selected a chair on the opposite side.

I looked around to see if there were any familiar faces. The only other people there were two especially young lawyers: a long-haired white man, very thin; and a black woman, about twice his girth. Both were grim faced and clearly nervous. The first case on the docket was a criminal appeal, and I guessed they were going to argue the thing. I wondered which one was the prosecutor.

The only other people in the court were two somber elderly men who sat together and chatted softly with no evident expression, like two men waiting for a bus. I recognized them both, although I had never tried any cases against either of them. Both were senior partners in large Detroit firms. I presumed each represented a side in the last case of the morning, an appeal in which one large bank was suing another.

That was it. None of the cases merited enough interest for any of the media to be present. So it would be strictly business, the nuts and bolts of the law, quietly conducted by fewer than twelve lawyers, counting the judges.

Having once clerked for the court for a year, I had the advantage of knowing what was going on backstage, so to speak. By now the judges were robed and going over the case memorandum for the first docketed case.

That short memo was all-important, the keystone really of each and every appeal. I used to prepare them, giving a brief statement of fact, the issues raised by the briefs, some of the legal cases involved, and a tentative suggestion as to how the case might be decided.

It would be the controlling document through the hearing, sometimes the decision itself, and often the basis for the language found in the ultimate printed report of that decision.

Some judges relied upon that memo, with minimal input from their clerks, as the final word, and considered little else. Others used it as a launching pad for their own intensive study. These were judges who were scholars at everything they did. No hair was too fine to split. Mostly, the others were a mix, some a trifle lazy, some too diligent, but all of them trying to do justice and move the docket as best they could.

But it was that little memo, very secret, that got everything moving.

With some exceptions, the judges discussed the memo briefly before hearing each case. Immediately after the hearing, they sat down again and felt one another out on how they might go. If no immediate decision could be reached, they agreed to more discussion in the future. Usually, even with no agreement, one of the three judges was selected to write the decision if it looked as if his viewpoint might prevail, or if he or she seemed particularly interested.

The others, the easy cases, were decided right then, right after the hearing, with one of the judges elected to write the decision. Which, when translated, meant that the judge's main clerk had been designated to write it, and the judicial process moved quickly on.

I guessed they had just finished looking at the memo.

A bored court officer appeared, looked out at the handful of lawyers as if we might suddenly turn into an unruly mob, then he banged the gavel and announced the entrance of the appellate judges.

We all stood up.

THEY CAME OUT IN SINGLE FILE, each judge taking his designated place before a chair. They remained standing. As always, the judge who had been selected as the chief judge for the panel took the place in the middle. It was his job to run the court.

Franklin Palmer was the chief judge. He looked around the room, his eyes meeting mine for a moment but without even a hint of recognition.

The gavel sounded and we all sat down.

Judge Palmer began a recitation of the basic rules. Each side had one half hour for oral argument. At the beginning of the presentation, each lawyer could reserve part of that time for rebuttal, if he wished. He warned the lawyers that a two-minute warning would be given as their deadline approached, and even if in midsentence, that final deadline would be strictly observed, with no exceptions.

I noticed a few of the clerks had quietly come in and taken chairs near the front of the courtroom. They knew they'd probably have to do the work, so they were getting in at the beginning.

As Judge Palmer went over the ground rules I studied each of the other two judges.

I knew Judge Robert Chene. He had been a circuit court judge before winning election to the higher court. I had tried a number of circuit cases before him. He was about sixty, I thought, very thin, and although he looked like Hollywood's idea of a hangman, he had the reputation of being a soft touch. He had been a plaintiff's lawyer before becoming a judge. I hoped he still looked at the world from those same eyes, eyes that would have seen a lot of Will McHughs.

The other judge I had seen around but had never worked with before. Short, compact but with a jowly face, he was only forty, but his advanced baldness made him look older. I knew he had come from an insurance defense firm, before being appointed by the governor, and the word was out that he still carried with him the negative attitude insurance lawyers seem to develop or are born with. He didn't come down often on the side of the plaintiffs in injury appeals. His name was Phillip Noonan. There was a Phillip Noonan, a cousin, on the circuit bench. Lawyers, who love to bestow nicknames, called the one on the circuit bench Sweet Noonan. This judge had been tagged as Mean Noonan.

Franklin Palmer, on the other hand, looked as if central casting had chosen him to play a judge. A handsome man with even features, his light blue eyes suggested there was very little they missed seeing. He was deeply tanned, tall and square shouldered, little changed from the time, years ago, when he had been my criminal law professor. His hair had turned a handsome white about his ears, but other than that, he seemed ageless.

I could see in him a suggestion of Caitlin, his daughter.

The first case, the criminal appeal, was called.

The side that brings the appeal argues first. A man by the name of McDougal had been caught with stolen property in his car, property that had been taken from a house a mile and a few minutes away from where the police stopped McDougal. He had later been convicted.

The young man with the long hair was McDougal's attorney. I guessed he was a public defender, and judging from his state of near collapse, I also guessed that this was his first appellate case.

He placed his briefcase and notes on one table while his opponent, the young black woman, went to the table on the other side and did the same. She pretended as if she did this every day of the week, but I noticed her hands were shaking. She was young for an assistant prosecutor and this, too, was probably her first case on appeal.

The fear of the unknown is always the worst fear, they say. And they are right.

The young man adjusted the microphone and spoke into it, his lips as close as if he were underwater and the microphone was his air hose. His shaky words boomed through the room like trembling thunder. He jumped back as if by electric shock.

"It's a delicate instrument," Judge Palmer said, smiling slightly. "You don't need to get right on top of it. It will pick up quite nicely. Now, sir, you may proceed."

The young man took a deep breath and began. "If the court please I represent Melvin McDougal who was convicted of possession of stolen property. It is our contention that—"

"It is customary to introduce yourself, counsel," Judge Palmer said, again in a quiet and friendly voice.

"Oh, yes, of course. I'm sorry. My name is Melvin Swartz. I represent Mr. McDougal, as I said, and it is our—"

"Do you wish to reserve any of your time, Mr. Swartz, for rebuttal? You don't have to, of course, but it must be done now or not at all." Judge Palmer smiled.

"Rebuttal?" The spoken word rose almost to a high C.

Judge Palmer's expression was still kindly. I noticed Judge Chene was amused while Judge Noonan grimaced in irritation.

"In case your worthy opponent says something that you feel should be answered, it is usually best to reserve a few minutes, even if eventually you decide not to use them," Judge Palmer said softly. I heard one of the young Ford lawyers snicker.

A glance from Palmer silenced the offender immediately.

"Ah, if the court please, I'm new to this," the young man half whispered. "What's a usual time?"

Judge Noonan threw his arms down in exasperation.

Judge Palmer smiled. "Five minutes, two minutes. It depends."

"I'll take the five minutes," the young man said, sounding like a contestant on a game show.

Judge Chene laughed.

"Let the record show that Mr. Swartz has informed the court that he wishes to reserve five minutes of his allotted time for rebuttal," Judge Palmer said. He smiled at the nervous young lawyer. "You may proceed, sir."

Every lawyer there was remembering first times and the pain of embarrassment. Suddenly there was absolute quiet.

Once again the young man visibly steeled himself and then began to speak. "My client, Mr. McDougal, was driving a friend's car east on Adair Street when for no reason—"

"He was there at three in the morning, right?" Judge Noonan demanded.

"That's his right, your honor. It's a public street. Anyway, he was driving—"

"The policemen say he was speeding," Noonan persisted.

The young man shook his head. "That's what they testified, but Mr. McDougal has denied it, from arrest right through to …" He hesitated.

"To conviction by a jury of his peers, right?" Noonan smiled, but it wasn't warm.

It was a bad sign. For whatever reason, Mean Noonan was on the muscle. I hoped he might vent it all on the poor kid, but I suspected he would save some for the rest of us.

Of course, young Mr. Swartz didn't have a chance. All lawyers have been in that uncomfortable position, of having to argue something, anything, for a client who is so obviously guilty or negligent that even the appearance of a chorus of angels singing on behalf of the client wouldn't do a bit of good.

Eventually all the judges started shooting tough questions. Toward the end, Swartz began to give back as good as he got, with respect, but with a growing fire in his belly. I smiled. Steel needed time in the fire to become something really special. I thought that one day Mr. Swartz would turn out to be very good indeed.

They all took him on, even kindly Judge Palmer, firing questions as if he was the person accused.

Judging by the tone of those questions, Mr. McDougal—who was relying on an illegal search as a defense—could look forward to serving out his very long sentence. But by his own fault, not his lawyer's. Young Mr. Swartz had done everything but organize a jailbreak.

I felt almost more sorry for the young woman prosecutor. By the time Swartz had finished, the judges were no longer interested. Their minds were made up. She had prepared for this important career moment for weeks, maybe months. There probably wasn't a search and seizure case decided in the last hundred years that she didn't know by heart. Her dress looked new. It was her moment in the sun. But they weren't interested, and not one of them asked even a single question.

Judge Palmer advised her that her time was almost up. She was shaken and her voice had lost some of its original vivacity. She stopped right there. "Thank you for your kind attention," she said quickly, and sat down.

"Mr. Swartz, you have your five minutes for rebuttal. If you choose to use them," Judge Palmer said.

Swartz stood up and walked to the lectern. "Mr. McDougal, my client, asks for nothing more than any other American," he said with surprising forcefulness. "Justice."

Swartz stood there, his thin back ramrod stiff.

And that was, as they say, that.

Judge Palmer merely nodded.

"All rise," the court officer called.

We stood and the three judges trooped off. They would be back in a few minutes, after the brief conference, then it would be my turn.

Swartz walked by me on the way out.

"First time?" I asked.

He looked at me, his face slightly flushed.

"I suppose it showed."

"It did. But you did a good job."

For a minute I thought he might lick my hand, then he nodded and walked on.

His opponent, the stout black young woman, also walked by me.

"Nice job," I said.

"My ass." She smiled. "I don't care though. I won the case, and that's what goes into the record books."

She looked down at me. "You're Charley Sloan, right?"

"That's right."

"They still talk about you back at Recorder's Court."

"Good or bad?"

She grinned. "Mixed. You up next?"

I nodded.

"Give 'em hell, Charley. We warmed them up for you."

8

While the judges were out, my opposing counsel and myself took over our spots at the tables by the lectern.

Craig Gordon, my opponent, was so smooth it looked as if you might be able to skate on him. He smiled as I approached. It was the kind of smile Muhammad Ali used to give lesser opponents just before the bell rang.

"This shouldn't take too long," he said. "The issue is rather simple, I think."

"The verdict was for five million, more now with interest. How would you like to save a couple million?"

He raised an eyebrow. "Split the difference?"

"Something like that."

"Look, if it were up to me, I'd probably try to work something out. Perhaps not that fat, but something.

However, Charley—may I call you Charley—it's not up to me. Those two young tigers behind me have the ear of our corporate client. It's all or nothing as far as they're concerned." He shrugged again. "So, I guess any compromise between reasonable men is out of the question."

"I understand. Then, how about just agreeing to take it easy on me?"

He chuckled. "I like you, Charley. If this were a boxing match, you're the kind of fighter who'd tell me my shoelaces were undone and then hit me when I looked. I promise I will take it as easy on you as I know you will on me. Fair?"

I laughed. I couldn't help but like him. "Fair."

I went back to my chair at the table. I tried to keep the picture of Will McHugh out of my mind, but I couldn't. I tried to think only of the legal issues, but I kept hearing the terror in the echo of Mickey Monk's voice.

Now it would be all up to me.

"All rise," the court officer called as the three judges came trooping back in.

"Good morning, Mr. Gordon," Judge Palmer said as Gordon took his position at the lectern. "It's always a pleasure to see you here."

In my imagination I suddenly saw a vision of Mickey Monk ambling down a dark alley looking for bottles, a ruined homeless man. Will McHugh's fate was too horrible even to contemplate. Gordon smiled at the three judges and they smiled warmly back.

"With the court's kind permission I should like to reserve five minutes of my allotted time for rebuttal." He smiled again. They smiled again.

He did a lot of appeals and obviously did them well. He had earned their respect, and I think they actually looked forward to what he was going to say.

It wasn't an old-boy network in the usual sense, but

Craig Gordon obviously had an edge over someone like me.

"As the court knows, this is basically a product liability case. Let me begin by saying that no one, not my client, not myself, are any more distressed by the terrible injuries suffered by the plaintiff. We don't dispute the extent of those injuries and our hearts go out to the plaintiff and his family."

All three judges nodded sympathetically.

"And, believe me, if my client were responsible for those injuries, this case would not be here. We would have gladly paid for any wrong we might have done."

He paused. "But this is the crux of the matter—we haven't done any wrong. We—"

"Just a minute, Mr. Gordon," Judge Chene interrupted. "Are you saying you have no quarrel with the amount the jury awarded, if, let's say, we determine your client was the cause of the injuries?"

I suddenly felt a warm spot for Judge Chene.

Gordon paused, then nodded. "I will show that my client is blameless. However, the amount awarded by the jury is not being contested."

Judge Chene made a note.

Gordon then continued. He had a good voice and an easy manner. "This case turns on a small mechanical device. The plaintiff alleges that it was improperly made and designed, and that it resulted in the sudden acceleration that allegedly caused the accident that is the subject of this lawsuit. This, I submit, was never proven at trial, and—"

"The jury seemed to think that it was, Mr. Gordon," Judge Chene said softly.

He paused, almost like a clergyman about to deliver a telling piece of scripture. "All of us here, you distinguished judges, my learned colleague, and myself are lawyers who have known hundreds of jury cases. Juries are comprised of human beings, not machines. Sometimes, and I submit this is one of those times, they let their human sympathy get in the way of pure reason. What they saw in court was a fellow human, bound to a wheelchair for life. Against that specter they saw a small, well-designed piece of metal. They let their hearts rule their heads, I'm afraid. But we are men of the law, gentlemen, and as such, we must follow what is right, no matter what the circumstances."

"McHugh, by his own admission was drinking, isn't that so?" Judge Noonan queried, his voice a harsh rasp.

"That is the testimony," Gordon agreed, almost reluctantly, as though McHugh were his best buddy and he hated to admit human error.

This guy was good, very good.

Gordon continued his argument, which was interrupted by numerous questions from the judges, a standard and expected circumstance. Chene probed with quiet questions about the device we alleged had caused the acceleration. Noonan acted as if he were cocounsel with Gordon, asking questions in the form of one-liners demonstrating that he believed McHugh was drunk and the sole cause of his own troubles.

Judge Palmer asked very few questions. When he did, they revealed no hint as to which way he might be leaning.

Finally, Gordon ended on a clean point of law, citing several good cases on product liability. He ended with a quote that would have made Winston Churchill envious. He had done a good job, a competent job.

From my point of view, too damn good.

Craig Gordon thanked them for their attention, and then it was my turn.

I remember being in fistfights, some as a boy, others, later, in bars, but always the memories were disjointed recollections of fists thrown and received, snippets of combat, a collage of pain and effort, more dreamlike than documentary in the memory.

My argument before the court was a little like that. It seemed sudden, at times bordering on violent and over almost before it began, with memories of voices raised sometimes, sharp exchanges, but no actual blows, only verbal jousts.

Judge Chene, I remember, had seemed to have been on my side. He and Judge Noonan got into quite a brawl. Of course, not between themselves. I was the tennis ball in their match. Each man took on the other through questions to me. The action was fast, the emotions muted but furious.

I remembered being as eloquent as I could be in describing Will McHugh's plight—his diapering, the loss of the last vestige of dignity. Noonan had scoffed, but Chene had been my protector.

Oddly, I could not recall one question asked by my old mentor, Judge Palmer. I was conscious of his eyes, but I could read nothing in the expression.

And then I was done.

Gordon used his five minutes in a smooth statement of the law, in sharp contrast to my emotional pleas. It was very effective, I thought.

I had reserved time also, just in case.

"Mr. Sloan, any rebuttal?" Judge Palmer asked.

I got up and once again walked to the lectern.

I really didn't know what I might say. I took a moment to look at each judge. Noonan looked away.

"This morning, in the first case before this panel, a young man represented a defendant in appeal. It was, he told me, his first case. He was nervous, as you may recall.

"He did not have the experience of the distinguished Mr. Gordon, or even myself. He was just a young lawyer trying very hard to say what he believed in. I thought he said it so perfectly, I'm going to borrow his rebuttal and make it my own."

Even Noonan was looking now. "Will McHugh asks for nothing more than any other American." I paused. "He asks for justice."

There was no applause, nor was there any other reaction. Except, once again, the three judges got up and exited the courtroom to conduct their short meeting.

The court officer rapped the gavel and it was all over, at least for Will McHugh.

I gathered up my papers and stuffed them into my briefcase.

Craig Gordon came over and offered his hand. "Nice job," he grinned. "Too bad it wasn't a jury."

"For juries I throw in tears and an occasional faint."

"I must come and see you in action. It sounds exciting."

He left in the company of the two young tigers. I gave them a few minutes to get clear of the building and then followed.

I wondered what I could possibly tell Mickey Monk.

IT ALL SEEMED SO ANTICLIMACTIC, this one brief hour to decide the fate of so many: McHugh, his wife, their children, and poor Mickey Monk. I was all alone in the elevator, and in my imagination it took forever to get down to the lobby level.

I decided I'd call Mickey Monk from a lobby phone.

"Charley!" The deep voice rumbled like a crack of thunder.

I turned to find myself confronted by Jeffrey Mallow, the former judge, towering over me, making me feel like I was being confronted by a bear.

"What brings you down here, Charley? Lonesome for the city?"

I shook my head. "I just argued a case upstairs."

"Which one? Not that product liability case you were telling me about?"

I nodded.

"C'mon, Charley, you must tell me all about it."

Once again he grabbed me with an enormous arm and half picked me up as he moved swiftly toward the building's rear entrance. "I'll buy you a coney island. That's something you can't get up in that little shit-kicker town of yours."

"I'd like to, but I have to make some calls."

"Nothing's more important than a coney island, Charley. Nothing. They have medicinal properties. The Greeks were the first physicians. This is what they used for medicine."

The only way I could get away was to call for a cop. But, he was right, there was only one place to get real coney islands, and it was just across the street in two fast-paced Greek restaurants that specialized in practically nothing else. Locally, they were famous and had been for fifty years.

And, surprisingly, I was hungry.

"Okay," I said, "but we'll have to make this fast."

He dragged me across Michigan Avenue and shoved open the door to one of the restaurants. The main lunch crowd had not yet arrived, so we had the place almost to ourselves.

"Let's grab a table," Mallow said. "I hate sitting at that damn counter."

We sat down and a young Greek waiter came for our order. He looked as if he had just stepped off the old "Saturday Night Live" Greek restaurant set. Only this place had been here long before that, and even before television.

Mallow ordered two coney islands and a beer.

I asked for one and a mug of coffee.

Our waiter shouted in Greek to the cook—stationed at the front of the place with his grill in full display—who shouted back in Greek.

"So how did it go, this product liability case of yours?" Mallow asked as the waiter slapped down the coffee and beer in front of us.

"Hard to say. Judge Chene seemed favorable."

Mallow snorted. "Don't let that fool you. Chene just likes to be everybody's friend. He could smile and shoot you in the ass at the very same time. I never really liked him much."

"Noonan seemed hostile to my side."

Mallow laughed. "He was born hostile. Mean Noonan, the name fits him like a glove. Besides, he almost always sides against injury plaintiffs. He can't help it. I think it's a habit with him."

He took a long pull at the beer directly from the bottle, eschewing the glass. "What about Frank Palmer? He was on that panel, right? How did you read him?"

"I couldn't. As far as I can tell, no one can."

Mallow chuckled. "On the bench we used to call him the Sphinx."

The waiter returned and again slapped down the dishes, as if to do otherwise would have been impolite. A kind of Greek cultural flourish.

A Detroit coney island, I'm told, is unique to the Motor City. It is a long hot dog in a bun, covered by a watery chili and enough chopped onions to ski on. All of this mixed with a river of strong mustard. There's no easy or dainty way to eat the things. One coney island requires at least a dozen napkins, and even then clothes and skin are stained almost forever.

In my opinion, it's all worth the sacrifice.

We attacked them in silence. There was no other way. Conversation was not possible. Trying to eat the sliding, sloppy concoctions required absolute concentration.

Finally, we were both done. A mountain of stained napkins lay between us. I sipped the coffee. It was almost as good as the hot dogs.

Mallow signaled for another beer. "Well, Charley, what's your gut hunch? Did you win?"

"Frankly, I don't know. I hope so, but you know how those things go. I won't know until the decision comes down."

Mallow gulped down half the new bottle of beer. "Tell you what. I've got to be up there later today. They want me to sit as a visiting judge in a month or two. Let me nose around and see what I can find out."

"I appreciate the thought, but that's not necessary."

He smiled broadly. "Hey, we St. Benedict boys have got to stick together." He stood up and looked down at me. "I used to run the joint, remember. I'll look into it."

"There's no need, really."

He shook his head, as if shaking away my protest.

"It's a favor, Charley. I do them all the time. I'll let you know what I find out."

Before I could protest further, he was gone.

Also, I noticed, I got stuck with the check.

I sipped the last of the good coffee. Jeffrey Mallow was probably just putting on a show for my benefit, a performance to remind me that once he was an important man.

If that's what it was, I felt sorry for him.

I paid the cashier and then went looking for a public phone.

MICKEY MONK SNAPPED UP the phone as soon as his secretary told him I was on the line.

"Jesus, what took so long?" he almost screamed at me.

I decided to lie a little, out of kindness. If I told him I had stopped for lunch, he would have thought I was a monster. "The first case took longer than expected, and the judges were out for a while after that. Anyway, it's finally over."

"Well, what happened?"

"It went according to plan, Mickey. There were no big surprises on either side, no miracles."

"You must have *some* idea of how it looks for us?" It was a question, but it sounded more like begging.

He had bet his whole life on the outcome. I knew I'd have to pick my words carefully so he wouldn't be crushed or falsely elated.

"I can't say for certain, but I think Chene bought our argument. Every question seemed to indicate he was on our side."

"God bless the little son of a bitch."

"On the other hand, Noonan sounded like the opposition attorney. He got rather nasty at times."

"He's a prick. Everybody knows that. What about Palmer?"

"He hardly asked a question, either way. I saw nothing that would even let me guess which way he might be leaning."

Monk chuckled softly, the way people do when they know a secret. "Hey, Charley, he's your buddy, hell, he's your mentor. He'll go along with us. I know it."

I almost wished he was right, but I knew he wasn't. "You don't know him, Mickey. He follows the law as he sees it. Even if it was his mother arguing the case, it wouldn't make any difference. We'll get no special advantage. He goes strictly according to the law. I told you that from the beginning."

"I know, I know. But, people, even judges, are human. You watch and see. We got just as much law on our side as they do. He'll go for us. I know he will."

I sighed. Mickey desperately wanted a world far more kindly than the one he presently occupied.

"Will you call the McHugh family, or should I?" I asked.

"I'll call them. They know me better."

"What are you going to tell them?"

"What do you mean?"

"Mickey, this thing is still a crap shoot."

He snorted. "Maybe. But what the hell, why not make them feel a little good about things for a while. What can it hurt?"

"It could hurt a lot if we end up losing."

There was a pause, and then he spoke quietly, without emotion. "Yeah, it could, and it will, if that happens. In the meantime, what can a little hope hurt, huh? Let them fantasize about spending the money, at least for a while."

"What are you going to tell them?"

There was another pause. "I'm going to tell Will McHugh you think you've won the case."

"But—"

"Fuck it, Charley. Even if it goes bad eventually, let's allow the poor fuck a few dreams before the world caves in on him."

"When will you call them?"

"In a half hour or so. I have to prepare. This is going to be a three-martini call. I feel real good, real optimistic after three quick ones. I should sound natural enough. At least I hope I will."

He paused. "Tell me the truth, did you do your best, Charley?"

"Of course I did."

"That's all anyone could ever ask."

9

Saturday came and I picked up Sue Gillis at her apartment. As far as floor plans went, her apartment was almost a duplicate of my own—two small bedrooms, a combination living-dining area and a compact kitchen. Her apartment complex bordered a local golf course; sliding doors that opened to a small balcony off her living room provided an unobstructed view of towering trees, manicured lawns, and hedges. It was like having a private park just beneath the front window.

My place looked out on a parking lot.

There were some other basic differences between our two apartments. Hers was an honest-to-god home, tastefully decorated, lots of plants and paintings, an inviting nest that suggested comfort and sanctuary.

Mine looked like a transient hotel, just a place to sleep and not much more.

I liked her place better.

Sue, dressed in tight jeans and a T-shirt with a printed photo of Elvis above a slogan saying he was alive and in Kalamazoo, looked even younger than usual. She wore no makeup, at least none that was apparent to me, and her ponytail swung with a life all its own. In short, although she was closing on forty, she not only looked like a healthy and vibrant teenaged cheerleader, she looked much more like my daughter than my date.

When she had inspected me at the door, I wasn't sure she liked what she saw.

"You look uncomfortable without a suit and tie, Charley. Are you?"

I nodded. "I even wear them to bed. It saves money on pajamas."

Actually, I thought I looked pretty snazzy. My summer slacks, a nice deep tan, were pressed. My shirt, a pullover, also tan but lighter, fit reasonably well, and I wore my docksiders with tan socks. But, not even in the wildest imagination, might I be mistaken for a cheerleader.

Sue had prepared a tray of exotic cheeses and even more exotic crackers. I drank a highly spiced iced tea; I wasn't sure what she had in her glass, and it seemed impolite to ask.

The sliding doors were open and a gentle breeze was as relaxing as a cloud of Valium. I hated to think about having to leave.

"I could only get lawn seats," Sue said. "But I go to a lot of concerts out at Pine Knob and I kind of like that better than being jammed into the pavilion seats. I prefer lying out on the grass, watching the night sky, and listening to the music."

"If it doesn't rain."

She laughed. "Should I bring an umbrella, Charley? Are you one of those?"

"Those?"

"Rigid people. Everything has to be planned, every contingency envisioned. Schedules kept, clothes hung on numbered hangers. Are you one of those?"

"Jeez, I hadn't thought about numbered hangers. What a great idea."

"I packed a picnic lunch," she said. "We can dine under the stars, if that suits you?"

I grinned. "Fancy French things?"

"Baloney sandwiches."

"Let me warn you. I'm sort of the Craig Claiborne of baloney sandwiches. As a critic, I'm merciless. They had better be good. Shall we go?"

PINE KNOB, NORTH OF DETROIT, is like a lot of other outdoor summer pavilions on the fringes of big cities throughout the country, booking big name entertainers, and, mostly, selling all available space to thousands who pay a healthy price to see and hear the star attractions.

Ushers guided all of us motorists, whose vehicles were kicking up clouds of dust in the unpaved fields used as parking lots. It went smoothly enough. Then we joined the others, and like an army of ants, we all trudged toward the entrance, moving through checkpoints, showing tickets and allowing search of all hampers so that no guns, hard liquor, or antitank missiles might be brought in that could possibly later cause temptation among the less disciplined.

The show was good. Merle Haggard hypnotized the crowd, which moved and danced to his thundering songs of broken barroom loves and homesick prisoners. His act and his band were professionally slick, but they appeared really to get into it just as much as the crowd.

Sue got into it as much as anyone, jumping up, dancing to the rhythms, moving with the agile grace of youth. I watched, first amused, then, aroused. Even the baloney sandwiches failed to curb my fired-up imagination. It was seldom that I lusted after cops, but this was one of those exceptions.

After the performance we found our car and waited in a river of other cars as the thousands slowly began the trip back home.

Sue, still on a high from the music, found a country and western radio station to continue her mood.

"Did you have a good time, Charley?" she asked as we inched slowly toward the highway.

"Sure."

"Really? You didn't look it. Mildly amused, that's how you looked."

"More than that, Sue. I enjoyed the music, but I think I enjoyed watching the people more. Some of those folks looked like they'd just stumbled out of the backwoods. Others looked like they had come from a country club. Dogpatch and debutantes. It's a fascinating mix."

"So that's all it was for you, people watching? Didn't you at some point want to stand up and dance?"

I glanced over at her, but she was smiling.

"Sue, to tell you the truth, I haven't got up and danced around since the day I got discharged from the army. It's not my style."

"I guess you thought I was a bit ditzy."

"Oh, I already knew that. Everybody in Pickeral Point knows that."

She laughed. We finally reached the interstate, and traffic began to move along at the usual suicidal rate.

But while the speed picked up, conversation didn't. One of those uncomfortable long pauses happened, and it was still an hour's drive back to Pickeral Point. I hoped it wouldn't be driven in silence. Finally, she spoke. "What made you want to become a lawyer, Charley? A childhood dream?"

"I never really thought about being a lawyer. I didn't know what I wanted to be. I got a liberal arts degree and still had no idea what I wanted to do."

I laughed. "I worked in a couple of factories, did some construction, that sort of thing, while I was going through college. I did learn, though, that hard, sweaty work didn't call out to me as a life's occupation."

"So, then what happened?"

"I was giving serious thought to becoming a dentist."

"You've got to be kidding me. There's nothing wrong with that, obviously, it's just that you don't seem like the type, frankly."

A big semi went barreling by. "A friend of mine had enrolled in dental school." I glanced over at her and smiled. "Listen, if you've earned your money digging ditches as I did, the idea of wiggling a little tool around in someone's mouth and getting big bucks for it sounded like a pretty good idea. I could get into dental school. My grades weren't good enough for medical school, but I had a shot at the other."

"What changed your mind?"

It was as if I could still remember every detail. "I went down to St. Benedict's to register for dental school. In those days St. Benedict's had a law school and a dental school and they were in the same building. I saw someone there I knew, and he said he was in law school. He said he liked it and suggested I give it a try. He made it sound more interesting than teeth, and perhaps even easier work.

"So I went to the law office and got the paperwork to register there."

"No aptitude test or anything?"

"Not in those days. At least nothing I couldn't handle. I think they were more interested in whether you could scratch up the tuition. I could, so they took me in."

"And so began a great career."

"Not right away. Oh, I passed everything the first year,

but I was just getting by. Then the second year I took criminal law."

"And you liked that?"

"A lot. I think the main reason was the professor. He was, and is, a judge, and he was a tremendous teacher."

"Would I know him?"

"Maybe. He's on the court of appeals. Judge Franklin Palmer."

"I've heard the name or read it," she said. "Does he know that he was such a big influence in your life?"

I nodded. "For some reason, I really don't know why, he took a liking to me. The criminal law course then numbered about a hundred students, give or take. Anyway, he seemed to pick me out. He arranged for a clerk's job in a law firm for me during school, and later, after graduation, as a clerk to another appellate judge."

"He was, as we cops say, your rabbi."

I nodded. "Later, I got pretty successful in trial law in Detroit and we sort of drifted apart. Also, I was getting pretty successful as a drunk, and that may have had something to do with it too.

"But when they were about to disbar me, I asked him for help and he helped arrange it so that I only got a year's suspension."

"He sounds like a favorite uncle. Do you see him much?"

"I never did, really. It was never a social relationship. To this day I don't know why he helped me.

"In fact, I argued a case before the appellate court this week and he was the presiding judge. He never gave an indication he had ever seen me before."

"Well, it sounds like you'll get his vote no matter what."

I shook my head. "Palmer isn't like that. He'll decide the case on the issues and the law. I'll get no special preference."

She was quiet for a moment. "He sounds like a strange bird to me."

"Maybe. But if it wasn't for him, I'd be back selling shoes, or real estate."

"Shoes?"

"While I was suspended from practice I sold shoes. And I did some real estate work."

"Men's and ladies' shoes?"

"Yup."

She giggled. "Charley, tell me the truth. Did you ever peek up the ladies' skirts?"

I looked at her for a moment before I answered. "Only if they asked me, officer."

I SUPPOSE WE BOTH KNEW it was going to happen. We were adults, free, and not without experience. That so thoroughly modern condition.

But despite that, it came as kind of a surprise to me. I was invited up for coffee, and that led to more conversation; and then, as if following a mutual script, we had ended up in bed.

We made love, not like strangers but as if we had spent years together, an easy and satisfying time.

I awoke on Sunday in her bed, awakened by the aroma of toasted muffins and fresh coffee.

Breakfast was followed by more explorations of our mutual lives and likes, and then more soft and satisfying love.

Sue Gillis's sense of humor made her fun to be with.

We spent the entire day in bed.

Reluctantly, I finally went home to my own place, an apartment that seemed as empty as an abandoned cave.

I opened a ginger ale and sat in the dark, sipping it slowly and thinking.

I wondered if I might be falling in love.

I wondered if I even knew what love was.

■ ■ ■

MONDAY I GOT UP LATE, still thinking, and when I finally wandered into my office I encountered the silent wrath of Mrs. Fenton. It was a good thing she worked for me and not the other way around, because from the fire in her eye I knew if things were reversed I would have been fired instantly.

"You've missed some phone calls," she snapped, thrusting the messages at me. "One was a judge." She said it with an icy tone that implied my tardiness had probably just ended what little career I had left.

The message was from Jeffrey Mallow.

"He's a former judge," I told her. "The title is only honorary."

She seemed disappointed.

The other message was from Sue Gillis. She was at work.

I called her immediately.

"It's me," I said when she answered.

"Hi," she said. "I suppose you find this call something of a surprise."

"A pleasant one. Official?"

"No."

"Good."

She giggled. "I'm embarrassed. I shouldn't have called, but I've spent all night thinking about you. Are you flattered?"

"Who is this again?" I said.

There was an intake of breath and then she laughed. "You can go straight to hell, Charley."

"Before I go there, how about dinner tonight? Or is that rushing things?"

"Not from my point of view. But I can't. The sheriff is

sending me to Lansing to work with a state police team up there on a case where we think there might be a local connection. I should be back Wednesday."

"How about dinner Wednesday then?"

"Okay." She paused. "Will you miss me?"

"Who is this again?"

She laughed and hung up.

To my surprise, I realized, as a matter of fact, how much I would miss her.

I called the number Mallow had left.

"Slatmore and Mallow," a nasal-sounding woman said, pronouncing the names like a conductor announcing the next train stop.

"Mr. Mallow, please?"

"*Judge* Mallow," she corrected me. "Who shall I say is calling?"

"Charley Sloan."

"Has this to do with a case?" she asked. "Are you a client?"

I guessed she was charged with screening out creditors and other nuisances.

"I'm a lawyer," I said. "I'm returning the judge's call."

"Please hold," she said, her tone indicating that she didn't believe me for a minute.

I was patched into recorded music and listened to Johnny Mathis telling me how my chances might be until he was cut short in midcroon.

"Just a moment for Judge Mallow," the woman said. It was not a request, it was a command.

Finally he came on the line. "Charley," he boomed. "By god, you country lawyers keep cushy hours. How are you?"

"Fine, for a Monday. What's up, Judge?"

"As I told you, I looked into that matter we discussed. I think I have a little information that might prove useful."

"Good. What is it?"

"Well, I have to run now. Will you be here in Detroit in the next couple days?"

"I have to attend a sentencing in Recorder's Court tomorrow morning."

"Ah, lost a case, did you?" His tone was jocular but there was a nastiness just under the surface.

"Pleaded to a lesser offense. Everybody's happy. Especially my client. Anyway, I'll be there in the morning."

"We should talk," he said. "Unfortunately, I'm booked for lunch. I have a deposition to take at an office in the Ren Cen in the morning." He was talking of the huge riverfront complex that had become the new centerpiece of Detroit. "Tell you what. When you get through with Recorder's Court, meet me at that bookstore. You know, that big chain place in the middle of the lobby just off Jefferson."

"What time?"

"Whenever you get there. You may be first, or I may. It's not a bad place to kill a little time in case we don't connect immediately. I'll see you there tomorrow."

"Well, maybe some other day might be more convenient. We could have lunch—"

"No, Charley. No. This really won't keep. I'll see you tomorrow."

He hung up before I could even reply.

10

Recorder's Court, Detroit's criminal court, once was my second home, the place where I had made my reputation—and my fortune. Subsequently, I had lost both, of course, but even for old times' sake I had never really wanted to go back to that judicial factory where it had all begun for me.

It wasn't the kind of place that inspired nostalgia any more than a rectal thermometer evoked happy memories for an overworked nurse.

The court was something like a thermometer of the community's health, rectal or otherwise. The docket reflected a violent society cannibalizing itself, where stories of cruelty and horror were so commonplace they attracted no special notice unless there was some unusual novelty connected with the atrocity.

I went to the line of lawyers showing their credentials.

All others had to pass through airportlike metal detectors. I jammed my way into an elevator with other lawyers, prosecutors, muggers, murderers, and thieves, the usual morning collection of participants in the American judicial system.

The judge, an old law school chum, was running through the sentences like St. Peter after a worldwide epidemic. There were just too damn many and not enough time.

My man got probation and a fine for something that would have put him in prison for a decade twenty years ago. Before I could even say thank you on the record, the next customer was being sentenced.

Detroit was the place where the assembly line had been invented. Old habits are hard to break.

The whole thing had taken only minutes. I regretted telling Mallow I would meet with him. Waiting around seemed like a complete waste of time.

In the old days, of course, it wouldn't have been. I would have located a friendly tavern, struck up several acquaintances and struck down a number of ounces of expensive liquor and hardly minded the wait.

Those were, I hope, the old days. Now killing time was healthier but not nearly as much fun.

I walked south, taking a stroll through what Detroiters call Greektown, a block-long stretch of Greek restaurants and stores, one of the few tourist attractions left in the old city.

It was a pleasant morning, not too hot, not too cool, like Goldilocks's porridge, just about right. I decided to leave my car where I had parked it, a city parking structure, next to a church. There were other reasons for locating the structure there, but I suppose it didn't hurt that you could duck in and say a prayer that your car would be there when you got back.

I walked toward the Renaissance Center. It was a duplicate of the huge glass towers in Atlanta, sticking up into the sky like a challenge to God. God apparently wasn't impressed, since the place had been losing money from the first day it opened.

Still, it looked good.

Approaching the towers from Jefferson was like coming up on an enemy fort. It had walls just like a fort, except there were no cannons mounted on top. The explanation was that building electrical equipment, heating plants were all housed in those forbidding walls. It might have been true. But no one really believed it.

Detroit had been under a number of flags—French, English, American—and each time an enemy force approached, history tells us that Detroit promptly surrendered.

The current rumor was that the mayor was hoping for an enemy force so he could finally get rid of the place. The fortresslike walls would provide a picturesque place to hand over the sword. But there wasn't much hope anybody could be suckered into accepting.

I walked up the incline through the walls and entered the main tower of the Ren Cen.

I like bookstores, I always have. I prefer the old-fashioned kind where the owner knows you and sets aside books he knows you'll like, but though such stores still exist they are growing increasingly rare.

Chains, albeit impersonal, offer a good selection of whatever subject grabs your interest.

I actually looked forward to spending an hour or so just nosing through the books, but he was already there, waiting for me.

"Charley," he said, this time almost in a whisper, an attitude very different from his usual barked-out greeting.

He hurried out of the bookstalls and grasped my hand. "I'm glad you could make it."

I thought his hand felt slightly sweaty.

"That damn deposition fell through," he said, gripping my elbow and steering me toward the exit to the street. "But that happens, doesn't it? Annoying, but something we all have to live with, eh?"

It was the kind of question that required no answer.

He continued to steer me past the walls, down Jefferson, past Mariner's Church and toward the riverfront plaza.

"I love to walk, Charley," he said. "God knows, I hardly have time for it anymore, but it is one of life's true pleasures, don't you agree?"

"What did you want to see me about, Judge?"

He smiled as we walked past the Dodge Fountain toward the river. "Oh, many things, Charley, many things."

He gestured toward Canada on the other side of the river. "Beautiful, isn't it? I come here often. It's peaceful."

A ragged man had been eyeing us. Finally, he made up his mind and approached.

"Say, could you gentlemen help a fellow out?" he asked, his jagged smile exhibiting missing teeth.

Judge Mallow smiled back. "Get the fuck outta here," he said in a conversational voice.

I think the man was more surprised than offended. He shrugged, said something under his breath, and shuffled off.

Mallow didn't even notice. "A foreign country, right on our doorstep," he said, gesturing across the river as if he had just discovered Canada. "A peaceful border. No cannons, no soldiers, just friends."

I said nothing. I realized he was waiting for a young couple who had been standing at the river railing to move away. Finally they did.

"As I promised," he said very quietly, "I looked into your McHugh case."

"You didn't have to."

"I know." He turned so that his back was against the river railing. He looked directly at me. "Frankly, it doesn't look too good for your side of things, Charley."

"Oh?"

He paused. "You're not stupid, Charley. You realize that as a former chief judge of that court I still have a lot of power there."

Actually, the opposite was true. Mallow had been in trouble, and trouble was something other politicians moved away from like baskets of snakes. He was almost without friends now, but apparently reluctant to admit, or perhaps even acknowledge, this brutal truth to himself.

"I can still make things happen over there," he said, sounding like he really thought he could.

"Judge, what are you trying to tell me?"

He studied me for a moment, then looked around. We were alone.

"You were a clerk over there once, Charley. You know about the hearing memo, right?"

I nodded.

"Secret, right?"

I nodded again.

"Only the judges on the hearing panel, their chief clerks, and the clerk who prepared the memo have access, am I right?"

"Yes."

He smiled. "If that document was given out to someone who wasn't entitled to see it, such an indiscretion would result not only in discharge but probable disbarment, correct?"

He didn't wait for me to answer. "If the attorneys could get their hands on the memo they would know when to settle and when not to settle. It would destroy the purpose of the appeal, would it not?"

"Okay, Judge, you've made your point. I know all this as well as you do."

This time there was no smile. He reached into his inside coat pocket and extracted a folded piece of paper and handed it to me.

"Read it," he said, "but quickly."

The wind off the river had picked up; the paper danced in my hands as I unfolded it. It was a photocopy of the hearing memo in the McHugh case.

"Interesting, eh?" he said.

The memo was standard. I had written enough of them myself to know it was genuine. The facts were brief, but accurate. The law was set forth in an evenhanded way, citing the strongest cases for both sides.

The recommendation was to overrule the jury verdict and decide the case on the law and against Will McHugh.

I read it twice and then looked up at Mallow.

He snatched the paper from my hands and carefully began to tear it up into small pieces, letting the wind pick up each piece and wing it into the choppy river water where it floated for a moment and then sank.

He said nothing, merely looked at me without blinking.

"So, I presume this means I lost," I said.

"As I said. It doesn't look good."

I thought about Will McHugh. I could almost see his haunted eyes looking at me. And I thought about poor Mickey Monk.

"Why did you show this to me?"

For a moment he didn't reply. Then his face grew stern. "I may be able to help you, Charley."

"What do you mean?"

"Would you like to win, Charley? Despite that memo?"

"The court doesn't always follow those memos."

"True."

"Judge, what are you trying to say?"

He looked around, and then across the river at Canada. "Beautiful," he said. "So peaceful."

He smiled; it was a soft, secret expression, as if he knew something but wasn't ready yet to say what it was.

"I may be able to help," he said quietly. "There's a lot of money involved here, and that always means there's elbow room. I'm glad you agree to my help. Stay here, Charley, and enjoy the view. I'll be in touch later."

He ambled away quickly before I could reply. I watched him go.

It seemed to me that the Honorable Jeffrey Mallow was starting to put together some kind of shakedown.

Maybe the case had already been won and decided. Perhaps Mallow was looking to take credit for something that had already happened. He would want to cut himself in for a big slice of the fee. It would be raw theft. For whatever reasons, he was a desperate man.

I wondered what the next step might be.

I looked down at the roiling river water. It was twenty-five feet deep there, murky with swirling currents. It was dangerous.

From my point of view, it wasn't the only thing that was dangerous.

I WALKED BACK SLOWLY to where my car was parked. And I took my time, for a change, driving back to Pickeral Point.

I needed to think. I wasn't even sure that the conversation had been the opening gambit to solicit a bribe. Jeffrey Mallow was a peculiar man in a number of ways. Perhaps stealing that secret memo was some kind of demonstration that he still had clout at the court where once he reigned. For all his bluster, I began to sense the pathetic man beneath the noise. A failed man. A man who once had power and a degree of fame, and now no longer had it. Maybe this was no more than a demeaning act to solicit someone to look upon him with respect one more time.

He had mentioned money but only in an oblique way.

Perhaps he was like the old ragged man he had so roughly rebuffed. Maybe this was his way of asking for a handout.

I thought of Mickey Monk telling me that rumor had it some of the judges were for sale.

I again wished I had never heard of the damn McHugh case.

My small ship was sailing into very dangerous waters.

A lawyer, who did nothing wrong, except perhaps to fail to report a bribe, could lose his license, or even go to jail.

Especially a lawyer with a past like mine.

11

When I got back to the office I decided to skip lunch. It wasn't any attempt at a diet, or even the press of business. I just didn't feel like eating. Mrs. Fenton, who apparently didn't wish to join in my unofficial fast, went off to lunch at her regular hour.

There was nothing particularly interesting in the mail, not even a catalogue of note, nothing to take my mind off Mallow's strange conversation.

I was watching a big freighter coming up the river when I heard the office door open. Even the sound was tentative.

I got up to take a look.

He was young, early twenties, dressed in working clothes with the Harwell logo, which meant he was employed in the local boat building plant. The Harwell name always gave me a jolt, even though that case was well behind me now.

He was short, stocky, and had the thick hands of a workman. His sandy hair was worn long to hide jug ears that stuck out like side porches. It only made things worse. I recalled the ears but nothing else.

"Do you remember me, Mr. Sloan?"

I nodded and smiled as if I did.

"You handled the deal when we bought our house a couple of years back. My name's Ed Ravell. My wife is Mary." I remembered them.

Ed Ravell's face was the bland, innocent kind that they use to sell soap. A nice face, nothing much behind it maybe, but honest. And well scrubbed.

"I'm sorry I didn't call for an appointment. I'm on my break, and I was hoping you could fit me in for a few minutes."

"Sure, Ed. Come in."

I sat behind the desk and he took a seat opposite me. I remembered the wife, too. They had one small child who ran all over the bank's closing office and Mary Ravell had been very pregnant with another close on the way. I remember thinking that she was probably a very pretty woman when not frazzled and had time to attend to herself. She was the obvious boss of the family and handled all the details at the real estate closing.

"How are the children, Ed?" I made it sound as if I had been the family lawyer since the arrival of the first Ravell in Kerry County.

"They're fine," he said quickly, obviously anxious to get on to the business that brought him in.

"What can I do for you, Ed?"

He had a complexion that colored easily. Suddenly he looked like a ripening cherry.

"My wife is seeing someone." He blurted out the words quickly, as if just the physical act of saying them was painful.

"How do you know?"

"She told me."

"She did?"

"Well, more or less."

I sat back in my rickety chair and studied him for a minute. "More or less?"

"I want a divorce," he said. "How much will one cost?"

"Depends. Michigan is a no-fault divorce state. If you want one, you get one, that's the simple part. What isn't so simple is things like alimony, custody, and child support. People tend to fight about those things and that runs up the legal bills. Does your wife want a divorce too?"

He looked surprised. "I don't know. We didn't talk about it."

I took out a legal pad so it would look like I had some purpose and then looked back at him.

"How did all this come about, Ed? Just tell me the story as you know it."

In a way it was difficult to keep from laughing, the story was so mundane. But it would have been like laughing at a dying man who lay writhing in pain.

The Ravells had joined a card club in the neighborhood after moving in. It wasn't much, just four couples who played cards every other Saturday night. Pickeral Point is not a hub of show biz activity on weekends.

Without Ed noticing, his wife became attracted to one of the male players, a man much different than Ed, outgoing, exuberant, fun loving. And, I guessed, his ears were probably not as prominent as Ed's.

I got the impression that Ed was the type who wouldn't notice much unless it was brought forcefully to his attention.

The other couple moved away, and it was then that Mary told Ed that she had engaged in what she described as heavy petting with the other card player. She said it had never gone beyond *that*, although the affair had gone on to last several months. She said she was filled with guilt and remorse and desperately needed forgiveness from her husband.

Ed figured she had screwed the daylights out of the guy each and every day of those several months.

So did I, although I didn't say it.

"So," he said, his lips tightly compressed, "that's why I want a divorce."

I tossed the pencil across the desk in a show of disbelief.

"It never happened," I said.

"What do you mean? She said it did."

"Ed, women are funny sometimes. Different from you and me, you know?"

"Hormones?"

I nodded, as if that was the true meaning of life.

"They have different needs than we do. I think Mary invented this whole thing just to get your attention. I see a lot of this kind of thing, Ed. All lawyers do. Women get desperate. They'll say the goddamnest things, even if they aren't true."

"But …"

"You said you noticed nothing, right? If she hadn't 'confessed' this great sin, you saw nothing to even make you suspicious. Right?"

"Yeah, but—"

"No buts. You have some marital problems, Ed, but not the kind you think you have. You and Mary had better start seeing a marriage counselor, so she won't have to cook up crap like this to get your attention."

"They cost money."

I nodded. "They do. Depends on who you see. I'll give you some names. They might see you a half-dozen times at say fifty to seventy-five bucks a visit."

"Jesus!"

"Well, it's well worth it. If you should get a divorce, even if the legal fees didn't get too high, you'd still be paying support for almost eighteen years for two children. We're talking maybe sixty thousand dollars, maybe more."

His mouth flopped open but nothing came out.

"So you see, a small investment now in keeping a happy marriage will add up over the years."

His cherry complexion had gone dead white.

"Anyway, Ed, she invented all that crap just to see if you're still really interested." I wrote out two names of counselors, although I knew he probably wouldn't see either one.

I handed him the paper. "These are good people," I said.

He was still in shock. With some people, money really talks. Ed Ravell was one of those.

"What do I owe you?" he asked, obviously afraid of the answer.

I glanced at my watch. "I charge a hundred an hour," I said. "We've been here about half of that. Fifty bucks should cover it."

"You didn't used to be so expensive," he said.

I smiled. "You know how it is, Ed. The price of everything is always going up."

"I don't have that much on me."

I escorted him to the door. "Send it to me."

Mrs. Fenton came back as Ed Ravell was going down the stairs.

"Who was that?" she asked. "A client?"

"That was a man who came seeking justice and instead found faith."

"Pardon me?"

"Think nothing of it," I said as I walked back into my office. I could almost hear her fume.

MICKEY MONK CALLED ME just after I got home. Mickey was drunk, but I had come to expect that. He had two kinds of drunk—one, the best, was happy and cheerful. The other, the worst, was morose and whining.

Tonight it was number two. I let him ramble on about a number of subjects, his wife, his children, a small-time case that had found its way into his office, all kinds of cheerless patter. I thought he was about to wrap up the nightly report, and then he asked if I had heard anything about the McHugh case.

I told him no. If I had even suggested that Jeffrey Mallow had showed me the secret court memo, Monk would explode the case, himself, and me.

I asked him where he was.

He was in a bar on Detroit's west side. I knew it well, it was a dump. It was one of those places where the atmosphere is a mix of stale beer and urine, and at times the urine was the least offensive aroma. It was not the kind of place you'd take your mother, unless Mom happened to be a drunken stevedore.

I suggested Mickey take a cab home.

He resented the implication and declared that he was in full possession of his faculties. He wished me a frosty farewell and hung up.

It was a quiet evening after that, at least for a while. I watched the cable news and then a documentary.

My daughter, Lisa, called from school. I understood it was one of those duty calls. School was good, she was working hard, she was seeing a new guy. Lisa had dropped some weight and had apparently joined a boy-of-the-month club. Anyway, this month's sounded like he was half-human, which was an improvement over last month's boy.

I asked if she needed money. She said she didn't but it was one of those slow, reluctant refusals. There were a few expenses she hadn't anticipated. The income from her part-time job wasn't stretching quite as far as she thought it should. I huffed and puffed, she expected it, and said a check would be in the mail tomorrow.

She told me she loved me and I told her I loved her, and that was that, the duty on both sides discharged, until the next time. Still, it made me happy to talk to her, duty or not.

I turned off my apartment lights and looked out on my scenic parking lot while I sipped an iced ginger ale. I knew I would have trouble sleeping. I tried to think of good things, like Sue Gillis, but my mind kept returning to the riverside meeting with Jeffrey Mallow.

I could still see, as if it had been recorded on film, the sight of those little pieces of torn memo paper fluttering down to the surface of the water, floating for a moment and then sinking slowly, one by one, dreamlike, a fairy paper trail disappearing forever.

The more I thought about the conversation, the worse it became. Trying to figure out what Mallow was up to was like trying to work out a chess problem. No matter what piece you mentally moved or where, you created a new problem for yourself, a new threat.

I was almost relieved when the phone rang.

I didn't bother to turn on the light, there was adequate illumination from the parking lot. My watch's shining dial said it was just past eleven o'clock.

"Yes," I said, expecting a wrong number at this hour.

"Mr. Sloan?" The woman's voice was shaking. "Mr. Charles Sloan?"

"Yes, this is Charley Sloan."

"I need your help, Mr. Sloan," she said and then started to cry.

I figured it was a wife whose husband had just walked out the door.

"That's what I'm here for. Help. Who is this?"

There was some more sniffling, it sounded genuine, then she spoke as best she could. "You may not remember me."

"Try me."

"I'm Rebecca Harris."

"Becky Harris," I said. "Sure, Becky, I remember you. What's up?" I presumed Howard Wordley, her sometime lover, had probably smashed her around again. "Is it Howard Wordley?"

"Can you come over to my house?" she asked, again in a voice that trembled so badly her words were almost inaudible.

"It's late, Becky. Frankly, I'm in bed. Let's meet at my office first thing in the morning." Then I thought about the earlier problem. "Are you hurt, Becky? Did he hurt you?"

All I got was tears.

"These matters are usually best handled by the police, Becky. I know that may sound a little odd, given your recent experience, but …"

"Oh, God …" It was a wail of pain, more spiritual than physical, but nevertheless real.

I flicked on the light. "Where do you live, Becky?"

She gave me the address. I knew the area, a fringe neighborhood not too far physically from the gold coast mansions on the river but economically on the other side of the moon. It was a place of transients, people hanging on to their lives by their fingernails. "I'll get dressed and be there as quickly as I can."

It was impossible to get anything more from Becky Harris. She was crying too hard.

IT WAS A NICE CLEAR NIGHT, a little nippy for the end of May, but pleasant. Out on the river a freighter signaled, sounding like a distant train. It was answered a moment later by another big boat. In the still night, both boats sounded lost and lonesome.

Pickeral Point had gone to bed, or so it looked. I passed only one other car on the main street. Nothing stirred on the side streets.

I found Becky Harris's place easily enough. It was at the end of a block of very old, poorly maintained houses. Two houses were boarded up and one had obviously burned, leaving only a ghostly shell. Those who lived here lived close to the bone, and the mailman and government checks were the only touch these citizens had with the people who ran their lives.

Close up, you could almost smell poverty's breath.

Becky's place was a small single-story house set well back from the street. It looked a bit better kept, even in the dark. There was a small porch in the front. A single light was on inside, but nothing else showed. I eased the Chrysler into the rutted driveway.

A battered old car, older than the one I used to drive, was parked on one side of the porch. I could see it reflected in lights from a nearby house.

On the other side of the porch, parked in close, as if trying to hide, was the stern of a big, new Mercedes. My headlights caught it, and the gleaming gray steel seemed somehow obscene and out of place. I quickly killed my headlights.

Up until I saw the Mercedes I had been relaxed. Relaxation vanished as quickly as my headlights.

I walked up on the old porch. The wood creaked with every step. I tapped lightly on the screen door. The main door was already open.

"Mr. Sloan?" Her voice was just above a whisper.

"Yes," I whispered back, and felt ridiculous for doing it.

She appeared, but the inside light was behind her so I really couldn't see her face very well. She was nicely dressed, dark slacks and a fashionably baggy sweater.

She opened the door and I stepped in.

She grabbed me and hung on as if she would drown if she let me go. Her entire body trembled with small, continuous spasms.

"There," I said, trying to soothe her. "Everything's going to be all right."

I looked over her shoulder into the small living room. It was tiny, just a couch and a chair separated by a worn coffee table. Nothing matched. A small color television was set on the coffee table.

But I could see that everything was not going to be all right.

Howard Wordley sat in the old overstuffed chair. He looked like he might have sat there often. The old chair held him like a glove. He was slouched a bit so that his head was supported by his rather large stomach. He was looking directly at me. He was fully clothed. Expensive stuff, from his sports jacket to his tasseled polished loafers.

His small round hands were perched along the top of his belly.

I didn't say hello. There wasn't much point. He was dead.

He had a small caliber bullet hole the size of a thin pencil just above his right eyebrow, and another just below it. There was little blood at either wound. His dark jacket looked a trifle too dark in several spots, and I presumed bullets had entered there too.

If he was a suicide, he had been extremely clumsy about it.

"Help me." Her voice was like an echo from somewhere inside my chest. The shaking was getting worse.

I guided her past the awful sight in her living room into a small kitchen and sat her down on a kitchen chair.

"Listen to me," I said sharply. "I can't tell you what to

say, and I can't build a story for you to tell the police. Do you understand that?"

She nodded.

"If you shot him," I said, speaking slowly so she would understand me, "there are several defenses. One, self-defense. If he was trying to kill you, or you thought he was, and based on past experience with him that doesn't seem too unlikely. If that was the way it was and you shot him to save your own life, that's called self-defense.

"Another defense is mistake. If you mistook him for a burglar, probably not too plausible seeing how well you knew him, but if it was a mistake and you did think he was a burglar, that is a legitimate defense. I can't tell you what to say, but I can tell you your legal rights." I was telling her what to say, but it was called the lecture and a protection against an obstruction of justice charge.

"Mr. Sloan," she interrupted me.

"Becky, I'm a lawyer, not an accomplice. I have to report this and I have to do it now. There's a record of when you made that call to me. They'll check everything. I can't do you much good if I'm in jail too."

"Mr. Sloan. This is a nightmare. I didn't mean to do it."

"Okay, let's make this very quick. Tell me exactly what happened. If it was self-defense maybe there is something I can do."

She tried to light a cigarette but her hands were shaking too badly.

"Lately, Howard's been coming over here to"—she looked away—"to see me. It's been, well, fine. You know, comfortable.

"But his visits started getting less and less." She looked at me again. "He said it was business." The word *business* was spoken with sharp bitterness.

"Tonight he came over unannounced. Usually he tells me if he's coming and I get in some wine and cold cuts, that sort of thing."

"Go on," I said, conscious of the passage of time.

"Tonight he came over. He sat down"—she nodded toward the living room—"and told me everything was over between us."

"Because of his wife?"

She shook her head slowly. A sob preceded her next word. "His sales manager. A woman, a young woman, who looks like a cheap whore. He said he had started seeing her."

She looked at me, tears flowing like little rivers. "He said he wanted a younger woman."

"And suddenly you don't remember anything after that," I prompted.

She shook her head. "I remember everything. I went to my night table, got my gun, it's a small pistol I keep for protection. This can be a dangerous neighborhood. I came out and shot him. First in the face and then in the stomach."

"How many times?"

"Six, I think. The gun has a six-round clip. I fired until it was empty."

"Did he say anything when he saw you with the gun? Was there a struggle?"

"No. He didn't have a chance, really. I just started shooting."

"How long after that did you call me?"

She paused, thinking. "Minutes, I guess. I was so upset. I loved him. I didn't mean to kill him, or even hurt him. It was just so …" She started to cry again.

"Where's the gun now?"

She reached into her slacks.

I shook my head. "No. Keep it there. Give it to the police when they come."

"Mr. Sloan, what will I do?"

I sighed. "First, you refuse to make any statements to the police unless I'm there with you. This is important. Do you understand?"

She nodded.

"They will have you seen by doctors. You will refuse to discuss any aspect of what happened here unless I'm right there with you."

"But—"

"Please, Becky. I don't know what I can do for you under these circumstances, but whatever I can do legally, I will."

"Thank you."

"And don't talk to any fellow prisoners in the jail about what happened here. That's a favorite device, a sweet, kind cellmate, full of sympathy, who later turns out to be a cop."

She nodded, then paused. "Mr. Sloan, I don't have much money. The most valuable thing I have is the diamond ring Howard gave me."

I figured, given Howard's reputation for honesty, that the ring was probably glass, not even cubic zirconia.

"We'll work it out," I said.

I walked out to the living room. Wordley was just as relaxed as before. I gingerly picked up the telephone and dialed the police.

12

They came quickly enough, at least the first scout car did, arriving in only a matter of minutes. Then came the detectives covering the night shift, who seemed annoyed. Not that a murder had been committed, but that someone had been so inconsiderate as to do it on their shift.

The Kerry County medical examiner, Dr. Ernesto Rey, was at a convention, so the police had to borrow a pathologist from Oakland County, a man I knew well, a good doctor, careful, intelligent, and, unfortunately for defense lawyers like me, an excellent and skilled witness.

Finally, Stash Olesky made his appearance. His deep-set eyes were swollen with sleep, his blond hair uncombed, making him look more like an overage paperboy than Kerry County's leading murder prosecutor.

When fully awake, Olesky's wide cheekbones gave those eyes a certain quiet menace, like a Polish aristocrat thinking about killing the czar. Now he looked like he was thinking nothing more sinister than going back to bed.

Olesky was good, the best trial man on the prosecutor's staff. He had a reputation of being absolutely fair. Plus, he was a hell of a workman. He would have made an excellent judge, or just about anything else connected with the law, but he liked criminal trial work, and he particularly liked trying murders.

I liked him a lot, and if that wasn't entirely mutual, I think he did respect me. It was always a little hard to tell what Stash might be thinking behind those expressionless but penetrating Polish eyes.

We did the expected legal dance. He tried to wheedle me into allowing them to take a statement from my client. "Just to clear up a few small things," he said.

I said since there was no proof that my client had done anything illegal, she should be released in my custody.

It was like two roosters in the henhouse, flapping their wings at each other. It was meaningless, but expected.

They took poor Becky away, first to have nitrate tests done to show if she had fired a weapon, then fingerprints, and then to the county hospital to discover any injuries, or lack thereof, that might later influence the case.

Stash assured me Becky would be inviolate from questioning unless I was present. His word, I knew, was good.

The medical examiner didn't spend much time on the body. He didn't have to.

He pulled off his latex gloves and smiled at me.

"You're getting faster, Charley. You didn't used to beat the cops to the scene in the old days."

"New management techniques. Computers. They work wonders."

He chuckled, then looked at Stash. "Is there someplace we can talk?"

Stash smiled, or what passed for a smile. "Go ahead. Charley probably knows more than we do anyway."

The doctor shrugged. "Six shots, six hits. At a carnival she would have won a prize."

"When you say 'she' I presume you're just picking a convenient pronoun out of the air?" I asked.

"C'mon, Charley, this isn't a courtroom. I looked at the weapon. It's an old purse gun, .25 caliber, six shot clip. The old ladies' gun, as they used to call it. Hardly better than a BB gun."

"It did the trick, though," Stash said.

The doctor nodded. "Yeah. I won't know for certain until I cut him up but I think that one of those shots just over the right eye probably did the killing. Based on the angle, I think that puny little slug just flew right past the occipital cavity and blew out his brain stem. That's just a guess, but I'll find out."

"The other five shots were for insurance," Stash said, taking out a cigarette.

"Whatever. In any event, he's dead. I'll do the autopsy in the morning and fax a copy. The lab work will take longer. Any hurry on this one?"

"Not on my part," Stash said, looking at me.

I shook my head. The doctor waved good-bye.

The detectives and the evidence men continued working as Stash guided me into the small kitchen.

He finally lit the cigarette and exhaled a cloud of smoke. "What's the background here, Charley? There's no reason to hold back. I'll know everything by morning."

He was right. I pulled out a chair and sat down.

"Did you recognize her, Stash?"

"Sure. She's a waitress up at the inn. Lovely person." He grinned. "And a hell of a good shot, too."

"Howard Wordley, you obviously know."

He nodded. "He's a fixture. I should say, was. I haven't gone to a benefit or a public party since I got up here that he wasn't glad-handing the people. He sold a lot of cars that way."

"Did you like him?"

Olesky shrugged. "Hey, he immediately knew I couldn't afford a Mercedes or any of his other fancy wagons so I became a nonperson. That's probably why I didn't burst into tears when I first saw him there dead in the chair."

"Remarkable restraint."

The meat wagon crew carried out their cargo, and most of the detectives, except a handful of technicians, had gone.

"So, Charley? Tell."

"A few weeks ago Becky Harris came to my office. She wanted me to check on a complaint she had made to the police against Wordley. She claimed rape."

Those eyes of his became a little less sleepy.

"You'll see the pictures, Stash. Wordley goddamn twisted her head off. Came within an inch of killing her. That's not my opinion, that came directly from your police doctors."

"Who was the officer in charge?"

"Sue Gillis."

"Sue's very good, very competent. What happened?"

I sighed. "Like most cases, there were a few flies in the ointment."

"Like what?"

"Becky Harris was Wordley's lover. At first, he was taking her up to Port Huron, buying her dinner, and getting some good old motel passion in exchange for the turf 'n' surf."

"Then?"

"Then old Howard decided that doing all that was a waste of time and money, so he insisted on a nice quick economical oral act of love in the inn's parking lot. No mess. No unnecessary time loss."

"Ah, I admire an organized man. Then?"

"One night Becky somehow sensed that the romance had gone out of their relationship. She refused the usual service."

"And that's when he twisted her head off?"

"Right."

"She made a formal complaint?"

"She did. Wordley retained the famous Victor Trembly, the Clarence Darrow of Port Huron."

"Getting him as your lawyer is an admission of guilt right there." Olesky smiled.

"Anyway, after consulting with Trembly, Wordley said Becky was a prostitute and that he paid her twenty dollars for each service performed. He said, on the night of the injury, she wanted more money and that when he refused she came at him with a knife and that he strangled her to save his own life."

"Had he been cut?"

"No."

"No knife produced?"

"None."

"So?"

"By the way, Becky had been arrested and convicted for accosting and soliciting in Cleveland ten years ago. She said it was a mistake and I believe her."

He chuckled. "You would."

"We went to consult with your new boss."

"That asshole. If he even lasts until election, it'll be a miracle. What did that master intellect have to say?"

"Despite the photos and the rest of it, he would not issue a warrant, even for assault."

"How come you didn't go to the papers, Charley, and take that asshole's skin right off?"

"I didn't need to. I painted a picture of every feminist in the county carrying cards and marching, coming down to the office to perform ritual castration."

"They'd never find anything to cut, but go on."

"He then agreed to prosecute, at least on assault."

"So?"

"Wordley, coached by Trembly, sought out Becky and persuaded her—even gave her a ring—that he truly loved only her, and soon, he didn't say how soon, he would jettison the current Mrs. Wordley and then the two of them could drive through blissful life together in his always-newest model Mercedes."

"And she believed him?"

"Must have. She dropped all charges."

"Did you talk to her after that?"

"No."

Olesky watched the last technicians pack up and leave. We were alone in the small house. Only a scout car and two bored officers sat watch outside. Someone had removed Wordley's Mercedes. A few people, even though it was late and the action was over, still hung around, watching from porches.

"What do you think happened here tonight, Charley? I mean, off-the-record?"

"Just two lawyers schmoozing, or are you trying to see what kind of a defense I might come up with?"

"A little of both."

There was no harm in it, since I had no defense. Maybe talking might help me think up one.

"We both know that new lovey-dovey relationships, especially those inspired to keep one party out of jail, never work, generally, right?"

He nodded slowly.

"My guess is that things were coming apart and old Howard wanted to go back to the quick blow job routine."

"So?"

"Tonight she said no, and remembering what happened the last time, she was afraid that this time she would really be killed. As a precaution she stuck the old gun in her pocket, just in case. And, like a nightmare, it did start happening all over again. He spoke the same threatening words to her, and when he started to get out of the chair and come after her, she fired."

"Did she tell you that?"

"No, as a matter of fact, she was too upset to really tell me what happened. This is strictly what I'm surmising happened."

He walked into the little living room. There were a few bloodstains in the chair, the usual chalk marks and police tape, but everything else was just as it was. Of course, Wordley was gone, too.

"Let me give you my guess, okay?"

"Go ahead."

He gestured at the room. "Hey, admit it. No signs of a struggle, no knife or other weapon laying on the floor or anything like that, right?"

He walked to the chair. "Wordley, as fat as Santa, you recall, was wedged into this old overstuffed chair. Except that he was dead, he looked happy as a clam to me. His little feet dangled, they didn't even quite touch the floor. I'm on the short side myself, so I notice things like that. In other words, Charley, he didn't exactly look like he was in midattack."

He sighed, looking down at the chair. "Look, Becky Harris is a nice woman, aging but she still has that big dream, the dream of holding hands in the sunset with someone who loves her and takes care of her. Nothing wrong with that. A lot of women have that dream. Men too. Her problem is she hooks up with Wordley, who's a world-class user. But even knowing that, she tries to keep the dream alive. It happens all the time, Charley, we both know that."

He slowly shook his head. "Even after he hurts her physically, she can't let go of that dream. So she goes on seeing him, hoping somehow it will still all come true."

He looked at the chair as if he could still see Wordley sitting there. "The way I see it, this little prick picks tonight to end the romance. He waltzes in here, sits right there and tells her they're through."

Stash seemed almost lost in himself. "She probably would have accepted that, given time. If he said he was going back to his wife, or something like that. The dream would have been damaged but not destroyed, not crushed."

He turned and looked at me. "I figure, and it's only a guess, that Wordley had another babe and that he announced this charming piece of news tonight. Probably a younger woman. Becky might even know her. Women who dream, at Becky's age, Charley, can turn dangerous no matter how soft or tender they might be inside. Getting tossed over is one thing, getting tossed over for a younger woman, that's the spark that ignites the dynamite."

He looked again at the chair. "My guess is that she blew. No words, no tears, just fucking pure animal rage. She went to the bedroom, fished out the gun, and came back in here and blew his philandering ass away. She probably didn't say a word while she did it, just kept working the trigger."

I laughed. I hoped it sounded genuine. "It's time you come out of the prosecutor's office and join us on the other side of the table. We're the story weavers, Stash. But frankly, for your sake, I hope you come up with something better than that by the time of the trial."

He shrugged. "As I said, just a guess."

It was as if he had talked to Becky Harris directly.

I was impressed. I hoped I didn't show it.

He walked me out.

"Nice night," he said. "I'd invite you for a beer, Charley, except I know you don't drink."

"How about coffee?"

He shook his head. "Not at this hour. I don't sleep so good as it is."

The two scout car cops were watching us.

"Doesn't that bother you, Stash?"

"What?"

"Being seen talking with the opposition?"

"I'm honest, Charley. People know that. Judges, lawyers, most everybody. When you earn a reputation like that, it's like a shield. I can do things, talk to people, go places, and nobody even questions it."

"You sure?"

He smiled. "Goddamn right, or I wouldn't do it."

"What are you going to charge Becky with?"

"I won't know until later. Right now, it looks like first degree."

"But—"

"If it's like I think it is and she stepped into the next room to get the gun, that's premeditation." He smiled. "Anyway, it is for starters."

He got in his car and started it.

"Keep your shield up, Stash."

"It's always there."

"Tell me, Stash, do I have a similar shield?"

He looked at me closely and then spoke.

"With me, you do. But, frankly, Charley, given your reputation, I'm in the minority."

FIRE ALARM, SHIP SINKING, AIR RAID. I couldn't tell which until I woke up. The ringing, of course, was my bedside phone. I glanced at my watch. It was just eight o'clock.

I lay there for a moment wondering if I had dreamed the whole thing. Perhaps Howard Wordley was on his lot selling the latest BMW to some Port Huron fat cat.

Maybe Becky Harris was working the morning shift at the inn, serving up tons of bacon and eggs. Life, like coffee, perhaps was percolating right along for them both.

If it had been a dream it had been very real.

I picked up the phone.

"Yeah?"

"Charley, this is Sue. I just got into the office. My God, what a terrible thing to have happen. The report says you were the first one on the scene."

It was, obviously, no dream.

"Charley, they want to assign me to the case." She sounded frightened.

"You work sex crimes," I said, coming awake, "not homicides. Why?"

"Because of the previous case, the one Becky Harris dropped. They want me to work with Morgan and Maguire."

I thought of the two old detectives, both retired from Detroit homicide, both looking and sounding like kindly grandpas, but both with the hunting instincts of cobras.

"I talked to Stash Olesky last night. I presume he's in charge of the case for the prosecutor?"

"Yes."

"They're all good people, Sue. What's the problem?"

"I would think that was obvious."

"In what way?"

There was the kind of pause that's often called pregnant.

"If you can't see the way, perhaps there isn't a problem," she said sharply.

Although I knew it would offend her, I laughed. I couldn't help it.

"Look, it may be funny to you—"

I cut her off. "We are seeing each other, Sue. As long as everyone connected with the case knows that, I see no problem. Is that what you mean?"

"Of course, that's what I mean. And you may see no problem, but others might."

"Like who?"

"Like my bosses, the new prosecutor, maybe even the judges. A few insignificant people like that. Maybe even the newspapers."

I sighed. "Tell them to assign someone else to the case. Tell them just like you told me."

She paused. "I did."

"And?"

"They said that isn't an excuse. They suggested we stop seeing each other until after the case is over."

"Ah, come on?"

"Well, Parkman, the new prosecutor did. And, failing that, he said that I wasn't to discuss the case with you, not even to mention it."

"Is that Olesky's position?"

"No."

"What did he say?"

I heard what sounded like the beginning of a giggle. "He said that the only way I could help you on this case is to shoot the woman out of jail. He told me to quit worrying."

"He's right."

"But the newspapers, Charley, what—"

"Today will be the only time the papers will be interested. Look, Wordley is a Port Huron car dealer, big fish, small pond. His lady love blows him away and that's good for a few paragraphs, but there's no mystery, no money, nothing that would make it anything more than local news."

"What about the sex?"

"Hey, a seventy-year-old merchant is banging a fifty-year-old waitress, but not often. If that's your idea of the kind of hot sex that sells papers or lights up the six o'clock news I'm glad you became a cop instead of a journalist. You would have starved."

I rolled over and sat up. "Now, given that, would the fact that the waitress's lawyer has a romantic interest in one of the lady cops assigned to the case be the kind of thing that *The Washington Post* might jump on?"

"No, not when you put it that way."

I looked at my watch again. I figured I had had four hours of sleep total. It wasn't enough, but I could catch up later.

"Besides," I said, "she didn't kill him."

"What!"

"As far as I'm concerned, a Mazda dealer, an Oriental-looking fellow seen lurking around her house, snuck in the back door, stole the little pistol, and blew away his main business rival."

"Charley, have you gone nuts?"

"No. But I do have to come up with a defense. That's the one I shall be working on until I consult with my client later this morning. I presume you people plan to arraign her?"

She laughed. "We have to take her before the judge, Charley. It's the law."

"Sue, I'll see you later then. But in the meantime will you do me a favor?"

"Sure, if I can."

"Start looking for suspicious Japanese car dealers. It's the break in the case you people desperately need."

She laughed and hung up.

I replaced the phone.

Funny, I didn't feel like laughing.

13

I stopped by my office for a moment before going to court. We would have to go through the ritual of having Becky Harris booked on an open charge of murder. There would be no possibility of bond, not yet, if ever. It would be like a Kabuki drama. Prosecutor, defense, judge: we all knew our parts and would perform them even if what we said had no substantial effect. At least Kabuki is entertaining.

Mrs. Fenton, who seemed unusually impressed by judges, told me I had another message from Jeffrey Mallow. His secretary had said it was urgent and commanded that I should call at once.

I told Mrs. Fenton it could wait.

Sue Gillis tried not to look at me in court, but that only made her peek at me all the more. If she hadn't told everyone about our situation they would have easily guessed. Becky Harris went through it all as silently as I had instructed her. She reminded me of one of those old stone figures carved above graves, staring down, no emotion showing. There was an emptiness in her eyes, as if she had glimpsed the future and no longer wanted to look.

I asked Stash Olesky if I could have a few minutes with Becky before they took her back to jail. The court had no other business for a while, so they let us sit at the counsel table. A court officer sitting in the witness box was the only guard. He was reading the paper and was far away enough not to hear anything we said unless we shouted.

The *Free Press* had a small item on page three about the case, nothing much, since there wasn't much, and besides, the paper's deadline had just about matched Howard Wordley's.

I asked her if she needed anything, probably the silliest question in the world. What could a woman in her situation need, except perhaps a pardon or a file and an escape map.

She asked for some toiletry items from her home, and I said I would bring them.

Finally, we got down to business.

"Becky, please understand I can't lie for you. I can't invent a defense. All I can work with is what you give me. Do you understand that?"

She nodded.

"Last night you told me Howard said he was tossing you over for a younger woman, his sales manager. You said you stepped into your bedroom and took out the gun, already loaded, went back into the living room and fired it into him six times. Is that about what you told me last night, more or less?"

She nodded again.

"Last night you were in shock. Anyone would have

been. You may have told me things that weren't so. People, sometimes, if they feel very bad, very guilty, will do that. In effect, lie about what happened, almost as a way to punish themselves. Now—"

"What I said happened is what did happen, Mr. Sloan."

I sighed. "Becky, you aren't cutting me much slack here. I have to form a legal defense."

"I don't want one."

"They haven't yet set the degree of murder they're planning to charge." I gave her my usual lecture on the degrees of murder in Michigan. Life behind bars with no parole for first degree; a chance for parole with second degree; and time or even probation for manslaughter, given the circumstances.

She nodded, but I didn't think she was listening closely. I decided there was no point in discussing plea bargains, at least not yet.

"Where did you get that gun, Becky?" I thought maybe changing the subject might help improve communication.

"Cleveland," she said. "Years ago. Ten, maybe fifteen."

"Did you buy it?"

"No. A boyfriend gave it to me. For protection."

"How about the bullets? Are they the original bullets?" A small bullet that ancient probably wouldn't have enough kick left in it to dent someone, let alone kill.

She shook her head. "No. Those didn't come with the gun."

"When did you get them?"

"A couple of weeks ago."

"Weeks?" It was the kind of rhetorical question asked by a diligent prosecutor. Same disbelieving inflection, too.

"Howard got them for me," she said.

"He bought you a box of bullets?"

"No. He just brought over six and loaded them for me. He said old ammunition wasn't trustworthy. He said there was no point in having a gun if it couldn't do the job."

He had been right about that.

"Where did he get the bullets?"

She looked up at me. "From his wife."

"Pardon me?"

"Howard said his wife has the same kind of gun. She keeps hers next to the bed too." She stopped. "Of course, they haven't slept together in years, but he knew she kept it there."

"He took the bullets out of her gun?"

"No. She has a box of bullets. He got them from there."

I didn't know what use, if any, I might be able to make out of the information, but I had so little that even a meager scrap seemed to possess enormous potential.

I warned Becky again about talking to anyone else about the case and promised to bring what she'd asked for to the jail. I told her the various legal steps that would lead eventually to trial.

"I don't want a trial," she said firmly.

"I know," I said. "Let's just take things one day at a time, okay?"

"Where will they have Howard laid out?" she asked.

"What?"

"Has a funeral home been selected?"

"I don't know, Becky. I don't know when or where the funeral will be."

She looked up at me, her eyes filled with tears. "I hope they dress him in a blue suit. He looks so nice in blue."

MRS. FENTON WAS SCOWLING, even more than usual, when I got back to the office. "*Judge* Mallow called again," she scolded. "He called, not his secretary. He said it was very important."

"If he calls again," I said, "tell him I haven't come back from court."

"But he said it was important."

Ordinarily, I am the soul of tact, but her manner provoked a minor explosion.

I turned and glared at her. "Is there something wrong with your hearing?" I snapped. "Do what I tell you. Understand?"

In all the months we had been together it was the first time I had even raised my voice to her. If I had grabbed her hair and punched her nose I probably wouldn't have been able to equal the hurt I saw in her widening eyes.

I felt like a louse, but it was necessary. If I was a louse, it was one who didn't want to get any deeper into the game that Jeffrey Mallow seemed intent upon playing.

I closed my office door and flopped down in my chair. In a moment I planned to go out and apologize.

Wimps are not made, they are born.

The mail was stacked in a neat pile on my desk. I leafed through it, mostly a collection of bills and solicitations on the latest multivolume sets offered by competing law book companies.

One caught my eye. It was five volumes, leather bound, covering everything about space law that could interest attorneys in that field. The space they were referring to was outer space, and, judging from the brochure, nothing was left uncovered. Water rights on planets, if water was present, mineral rights, and mining law were presented in thousands of pages of print reproducing proposed agreements and old earthbound lawsuits. So, if suddenly we decided to colonize Mars, an attorney owning these books could hop the next space shuttle, open an office, and make a million overnight. The books cost a mere $695 for the set, and annual updates—not to be missed—would cost another $200 a year.

I tossed the brochure, wondering not only who would buy the set but who had taken the time to reproduce and project old mining claims and ancient ranching disputes. I didn't think the company would find a ready market, but it was their business so maybe I was wrong.

Among other wonders was a postcard from Key West. It showed a red ball, presumably the sun, sinking into dark water, presumably the Gulf of Mexico.

The note on the back wasn't much, not even a wish you were here, just a scrawled sentence saying Miles Stewart was returning to Michigan. The postmark showed the card had apparently been delayed even more than usual. Doctor Death, according to the date on the card, had arrived yesterday.

He was another one I didn't wish to talk to if I could avoid it.

But he had been in my thoughts, or at least his case had been. *The New York Times* on the weekend had carried an excerpt from a *Harvard Law Journal* concerning assisted suicide. It was in the form of an essay, but I thought it might be worth reading in case it raised cases or issues I didn't know about. I had forgotten to do anything about it and the postcard jogged my memory.

I called St. Benedict's law library. The issue I wanted was there, just in. I asked the kid to put it aside for me and said that I would be there tomorrow, as usual, prior to my Thursday meeting of the club.

He was only a law student but he was learning fast. The idea of doing anything for free had already sounded repugnant to him, although he did agree reluctantly to hold the article for me.

I tried apologizing to Mrs. Fenton as I left but she had climbed deep within herself and stared out at me from two hostile eyes. I figured she would eventually relent.

I went to Becky Harris's house. It was still under guard. A bored Pickeral Point policeman sat in a car out in front. I knew him and there was no problem with being admitted to the house.

He came in and stayed with me the entire time as I gathered up the things Becky had asked for. I didn't know if he was following orders or if he was just lonesome.

His name was Cecil Anderson, a stout man who had avoided trouble for all of his thirty years on the little police force. He was more gossip than cop. He loved to talk, and he did, incessantly, as I went about my business. But he was a decent man, his gossip was more gentle than vicious. I got the feeling that after thirty years at a boring job Cecil needed stimulation, if only that of his own voice.

"Becky's a nice lady," he said. "Some of those women who work up at the inn get the idea that they're better than other people. I think they believe some of the glitz of those rich customers rubs off on them or something, but not Becky. She always had a nice word for everybody." He paused. "Do you think she's got any chance at all?"

"Do you?" It was clear Cecil had an opinion on everything and would express it even if you really didn't want to hear it.

"You'd know better than me, but from what I read in the paper and from what I hear, God, I don't think she's got a prayer. But you never know," he said, and grinned at me. "Look at what you did in the Harwell case."

I had grown to hate that name but I tried not to show it.

"Did you know Howard Wordley?" I asked.

"Is this official?"

"What do you mean?"

"Mean? Shit, Charley, if you should stick me up on the witness stand as your main witness, there goes my job, my pension, and God knows what else."

"Look, Cecil, if you had information that would save an innocent person, wouldn't you come forward?"

"Sure."

"Then what's the problem?"

"Tricks, Charley. They say around town that you're full of tricks. I don't want to get my ass in the grinder because of some kind of lawyer trick."

"I won't trick you, Cecil. I promise."

He smiled an innocent, trusting smile. I almost felt bad about lying to him.

"Now, what about Howard Wordley?" I asked.

"Old Howard, he wasn't such a bad guy. Of course, I been here thirty years, and so was Howard." Cecil smiled. "Back then, way back, he could never keep that damn thing in his pants. There wasn't a lady in town, married or single, that Howard wouldn't take a shot at." He took off his cap and scratched what was left of reddish gray hair. "Of course, I thought he'd eventually slow down. Age gets to us all, doesn't it? But apparently not Howard. He was always trying." He put the cap back on. "Tried once too often, I guess, eh?"

"Looks that way. What about Mrs. Wordley? Do you know her?"

He nodded. "Real nice lady."

"Did she know about Howard's little hobby?"

"She had to. At least I think she did. They live together, or now I guess I should say lived. But they never went out together. She belongs to that fancy country club up here, Peach Creek. He does too, but I understand there was an agreement that it was her club and he was never to come unless invited."

Cecil sighed. "As a cop, you see a lot of those kinds of marriages. They live in the same house but they go their own way. A lot of people live like that, rich and poor."

I saw a gossipy gleam in his eye. "She's a Weaver you know."

"What's a Weaver?"

"One of the founding families up here. Her father, old Don Weaver, owned half the county. I understand he left most of it to his daughter. That's how Howard got the money for the car dealership. I hear she's the real owner, he's just the front man, always has been."

"A rich woman all on her own. I wonder why she didn't just dump Howard, or jerk him in on the golden leash?"

"Women, they are funny people, you know? I think she actually loved Howard. I don't know, of course, I don't run in them circles. I just hear things."

"How is she taking the death? Is that one of the things you hear?"

"Oh, sure. There isn't much to talk about up here, is there? They say she's taking it well, very sad, very calm, a real lady. She's making the arrangements herself. Howard's going to get a first-class send-off."

"Tell me, Cecil, was there ever any police trouble with the Wordleys?"

"You mean like family trouble runs? Black eyes, yelling, that sort of thing?"

"You should have been a detective."

He thought for a minute, then shook his head. "If there had been, I would have known. I'd remember something like that."

He walked me to my car.

"You going to see Becky?" he asked.

I nodded.

"Tell her Cecil said hello."

I DID SEE BECKY. She looked even more despondent than before. I wondered about the possibility of suicide, but the sheriff's people running the jail were two steps ahead of me. An informal suicide watch was already in place.

Since I was already in the neighborhood, I dropped into the prosecutor's office to see Stash Olesky.

He lived in a cubbyhole office jammed with dusty books and piles of yellowed reports. He cleared off a chair near his desk for me and then turned those Polish eyes on me.

"I saw those photos, by the way," he said, "the ones showing Wordley's handiwork on Becky Harris."

"In color?"

He nodded. "For once, you weren't exaggerating."

"I never exaggerate."

He merely smiled. "We traced the gun."

"And?"

"It was stolen in a burglary. Your little lady was in possession of a hot weapon."

"Bullshit."

He shook his head. "Nope. This is on the level. It belonged to some woman in Cleveland. They burglarized her house about ten years ago. It's the same gun, same serial number."

"Doesn't mean anything. Somebody gave her the gun."

"Still a hot gun, Charley. You know juries. God, how they hate those hot guns."

"So?"

"Those pictures don't mean anything legally, but I am impressed with the amount of damage old Howard inflicted on your lady. Still, she zinged him with a stolen gun. What I'm thinking about here is a plea."

"To what?"

"Just thinking, you understand, not offering. I have to check everything through the new asshole now. New rules. But for thinking purposes only, how does second-degree murder sound to you?"

"Recommended time?"

"No recommendation. It would be strictly up to the

judge. Ten chances to one he'll give her life. Hey, she does eight of that and is back out on the street. Not bad when you think about it."

I pretended to consider the offer. "How do you know she shot him?"

Stash's smile slowly spread across his broad Polish face. "Nitrate tests all show she fired the weapon. Her cute little prints, only hers, are on the gun and trigger. A video of her actually doing it would be better, but not much."

"What about the cartridges?"

"What about them?"

"You know what they are, don't you, Stash? Little metal things that hold the powder and the slug and when fired the powder explodes, the slug goes zip and in the kind of gun in this case the empty shell is ejected."

"Thank you for the lesson," he said sourly. "I had always wondered about how that worked."

"I presume you found her prints on the empties? I mean, to show she loaded the weapon and all?"

"Fuck you, Charley."

"Well?"

"The only fingerprints on the brass was Wordley's. Sometime or other he must have loaded the gun for her."

"How about that night maybe? Maybe he was trying to kill her, and his scheme went awry."

He sighed. "I presume you don't want to talk plea at this time?"

"We'll talk, Stash, but not now."

"Anytime, Charley. Just remember I'm under new rules. Everything I do or agree to has to be cleared with the new boss."

"I liked the offer or whatever it was you made, Stash, but if there is a plea, I think we can work out something much better than what you suggest."

He laughed. "When this is all said and done, Charley,

you'll have old Wordley committing suicide."

He grinned, then paused. "Hey, wasn't that the shit you used in the Harwell trial?"

AFTER STASH I popped in on Sue Gillis.

"Charley, this doesn't look good, you coming here to see me like this."

People were watching us, but I thought they seemed more amused by Sue's discomfort than the situation itself.

"How about I slip you some cash openly, then they won't think this is some kind of sexual bribe."

"Charley, please."

"Or tonight maybe, I could slip into dark clothing, grease my face, creep over the golf course, and then slither up to your balcony. Would that make you feel better?"

"Slither?"

"I'm good at it. I took lessons. But, in lieu of that, how about dinner tonight? We could sneak off to some far and exotic place like Mt. Clemens, that's if you really want mystery and seclusion."

"I can't tonight," she said.

"Everybody eats, Sue. What do you mean, can't? Do you have another date?"

"I should say yes, but it isn't that. I have to pound out reports on the work I did up in Lansing. It's important work, Charley, and I can't say more than that. I'll grab a quick sandwich here. How about tomorrow night?"

"I'll be in Detroit tomorrow night. I usually am on Thursdays."

She raised a quizzical eyebrow.

"I go to an AA meeting on Thursday nights. I've been going to the same one for years. I could skip, of course."

She shook her head quickly. "No. What about Friday?"

"Okay by me."

"Me too."

"Shall I pick you up at your place?"

"Seven?"

I grinned. "Done."

I got up to leave, then stopped. "Oh, by the way, could you bring along the Becky Harris file? That'll give us something to talk about."

"They have an asshole contest every Saturday over in Richmond, Charley. If you enter, I think you have an excellent chance at winning."

MRS. FENTON HAD GONE by the time I got back to the office. She left the telephone messages for the day on the corner of my desk. Mallow had called three more times. He left his home telephone number, and each message was marked either urgent or important.

I turned in my lopsided chair and watched the river.

An enormous ore carrier was gliding by, its majestic prow sending up a wave at least ten feet high. In the resulting wake, some damn fool in a small outboard was bouncing over the crests like a Honolulu surfer.

He drew ever closer to the stern of the big boat, and occasionally the great propeller could be glimpsed churning in the white water.

If the boater got much closer, that white water would be turned instantly crimson.

I wondered what prompted people to dance so close to obvious destruction.

I looked again at Mallow's messages and then pitched them into the circular file.

14

Thursday looked like an easy day, which in one way was fine, but easy days don't produce much profit for lawyers like myself, single practitioners, which was the price that lay on the other side of easy days. Mrs. Fenton didn't even say hello when I showed up at the office. Her thin lips were clamped tight as she thrust a telephone message at me.

Jeffrey Mallow was up early. She wrote down the message in quotation marks to convey his growing anger.

I smiled at Mrs. Fenton and wondered how much longer the silent treatment would be applied.

I didn't call Mallow back, hoping that by now he was getting the message that I wasn't going to participate in whatever scheme he had thought up.

All I had scheduled was a real estate closing in Mt.

Clemens. I represented the buyers. I dug out the file and drove to Mt. Clemens.

There are a number of interesting names of cities in Michigan. Bad Axe, Battle Creek, Grindstone and the like. But Mount Clemens was named after a mountain that never existed.

A fur trader named Clemens canoed up the Clinton River and established his camp on a high bank, ten or fifteen feet above the water. He traded there with the Indians and trappers for fur. He came every year and always pitched camp in the same place. The area is so flat you can shoot pool on it, but Clemens had a sense of humor and named his little lump on the water Mount Clemens. The Indians thought it was hilarious, but the mapmakers didn't know it was a joke, and its nonmountain became official.

While it had gone on to grow to be a fair-sized city, it was still just as flat.

I parked my car and went into the bank where the closing was to be held.

It turned out not to be easy. Everyone ended up screaming at everyone else. Deposits, set asides, taxes, there wasn't an item that wasn't contested. The sellers' attorney threatened suit. I threatened countersuit. The bank's attorney threatened to sue everybody. It was not a pleasant morning, and the pitched battle continued on into early afternoon.

The deed and the other papers finally got signed, but it was more like two bitter armies drawing temporary treaty lines than the happy buying of a home.

I didn't get out of there until three. My clients weren't speaking to anyone, not even me, although they got everything they had demanded.

Fortunately, I'd been paid in advance.

I grabbed a hamburger at a fast-food place and choked

it down, then drove on into Detroit and to St. Benedict's law school.

IT WAS ALMOST AS IF Caitlin Palmer had been waiting for me. She came up to me as I cleared the guard at the law school entrance.

"Well, how did it go, Charley?"

"What?"

She smiled. "The case you argued before my father. He said the case had been heard. Do you think you won?"

"I don't know. Did your father give you a hint?"

Caitlin's smile faded slowly, not out of offense, but more out of puzzlement. "He just said he thought you had done a very good job."

"How did my name happen to come up?"

She paused. "I told him I had seen you."

"At the boat?"

"Yes. I'm an adult, Charley. I told him I had invited you as my date."

"What kind of a reaction did that provoke?"

"Frankly?"

"Yeah."

She looked away and then spoke. "He said you were much too old for me."

"That's all?"

"Dad brought up all the other business."

"You mean, my drinking, marriages, and near disbarment?"

She still did not meet my gaze. "Something like that."

"In other words, he didn't approve."

Surprisingly, she laughed as she looked at me. "Let's say he wasn't wildly enthusiastic."

"There goes my case."

"Charley, my father would be fair no matter what.

He'll make up his mind on the law, nothing else. You don't have to worry about anything personal having a bearing on the outcome."

"But if he feels …"

She frowned. "He's my father and your judge. He will do both jobs to the best of his ability. And as far as my personal life is concerned, I make all the decisions."

"I wonder if anyone can be quite as fair as you say he is."

"Believe it. How about dinner tomorrow night?"

I smiled. "I thought we agreed that we wouldn't see each other socially until the decision comes out. Especially now, Cat."

She raised an eyebrow. "Charley, in some ways you're more of a puritan than he is."

"Still …"

"We'll see," she said as she turned and walked away.

I thought about things from her father's viewpoint. I wonder what I would do if my daughter, Lisa, said she was interested in a recovering drunk, a three-time loser in the marriage wars who had almost lost his law license once, a man who would be one drink away from destruction for the rest of his life. And a man twenty years older than my daughter, who, in addition to everything else, lived from fee to fee with no worldly goods to endow anyone with.

I doubt I'd be ecstatic.

I was absolutely sure Judge Franklin Palmer wouldn't be either.

Poor Will McHugh.

I FOUND A LITTLE CUBBYHOLE in the law library and was almost halfway through the assisted suicide essay when it seemed as if a mountain had blocked off my light.

I looked up into the florid face of Jeffrey Mallow. A very angry florid face.

"There you are," I said, whispering cheerfully. "I've been trying to get hold of you."

Lying is often an excellent defense, although I didn't think it was going to work this time.

"I want to see you," he snapped, teeth clenched. "Now."

I started to get up.

"Take your things," he commanded.

I shrugged, deciding to humor him. I slipped the article into my briefcase and snapped it shut.

This time there were no bear hugs. He moved ahead of me like a blocking back, so swiftly that I was having trouble keeping up. He exited the library and moved down the hall to a darkened classroom. He tried the door and opened it, motioning me to go inside. The only light was from the outside through the classroom windows, but it was sufficient, since a big gas station across the street was brighter than any moon.

"Sit," he said, tossing a one-armed student chair at me.

Anger can be contagious; now I began to feel the urge to respond in kind.

He half stood, half sat on an instructor's desk about five feet away.

"What the hell's the matter with you, Sloan? I'm breaking my ass trying to do you a big favor and you don't even have the courtesy to answer my phone calls?"

"It's been a busy time for me," I snapped.

His face was mostly in shadow, including his eyes, so I couldn't read any expression in them.

"Besides," I added, "I'm not looking for favors."

"You may not be looking for one, but, by God, you need one."

"You mean, in the McHugh case."

"I mean exactly that."

"What kind of favor are we talking about?"

He hiked himself up on the desk, hunching forward, his face closer, but still in darkness.

"You saw the memo?"

"Yes."

"It could go either way, but the memo indicated the court should favor the position of the other side."

"I saw what it said."

"There's a lot of money at stake here," he said. His voice had dropped to a near whisper. "A lot of money."

"So?"

"Money can talk, very loudly."

"Then I'm going to lose because Ford Motor has a hell of a lot more money than I do. If there's going to be an auction, I'm in no position to bid."

I wasn't able to see his reaction.

"What's the total fee here, one third of any award?"

"That's right. It's Mickey Monk's case. He won it at trial. I just argued it. If we win I get twenty percent of Monk's fee."

Mallow was silent. "A lot of money," he said, finally. "If the case is won, Monk makes—what—better than a million and a half?"

"We talked about this before," I said.

"So, given the interest growing during the appeal, you would see—what—maybe three hundred or four hundred thousand as your cut of the fee, right?"

I said nothing.

"A lot of money," he repeated softly.

"So?"

"Suppose someone could arrange it that you won?"

"Is this the favor you talked about?"

If he was smiling, I couldn't tell. For a moment, all I heard was the sound of his heavy breathing.

"How much would something like that be worth?" he asked.

"Well, for openers, probably five years in prison, disbarment, and God knows what else."

He didn't laugh, nor did he react in any other way.

"I know the law, probably one hell of a lot better than you. I've been at it longer. I'm talking money, and you know it."

"It wouldn't be worth a penny. I don't do business that way."

He laughed. "You think I'm wearing a wire, don't you?"

"No, I don't."

"Want to search me, Sloan?"

"No, I don't."

"I think a favor like that would be worth at least half your fee."

"Mine, or Monk's, too?"

"Just yours. We don't know Monk. We don't trust anyone we don't know well. We deal strictly with you. Only you. We're talking your cut, what, two hundred thousand, one and a half, something like that."

"What does this money buy?"

"A vote," he said softly. "Just one little vote. Of course, that's all you need anyway."

"What kind of scam are you trying to pull, Mallow?" I knew it always irritated him if someone refused to call him judge.

"Scam?"

"Shakedown, extortion, fraud, solicitation for a bribe, there's all kinds of terms to cover it, both in the law books and on the street."

"What are you going to do, report me?"

"It's a possibility, you keep this shit up."

Mallow snorted. "Oh, just think of it, Charley. You waltz into the feds, whatever, and say Judge Jeffrey Mallow, former chief judge of the Michigan Court of Appeals, tried to shake me down." He laughed. "Hey, they'd check. They have to, by law. It would be your word against mine, Charley. The word of a busted-down drunk lawyer versus one of the most important men in this state. This time they'd jerk your license forever."

To let it sink in, he paused. "And you know goddamn well I'm telling the truth, don't you?"

The problem was that I did.

"And suppose I pay you money and still lose? I'm in the same position, as I see it. No one would believe me."

"You won't lose. I guarantee that."

"Did you ever sell roofing material?"

He laughed. "No. Believe me, I'd see to it you were satisfied before one dollar was paid."

"Who gets the money?"

"I would think that was obvious."

"Noonan?"

"Noonan is too stupid to even let in on a thing like this."

"Chene?"

Mallow shook his head. "Chene is already in your corner."

"Oh, sweet Jesus, you're not trying to tell me Franklin Palmer can be bribed."

"Bribe is such an ugly word, Charley. I'd suggest we toss it from our vocabulary from this point on."

"I've known Palmer since law school. He's as straight as they come. I don't believe you."

He sighed. "Charley, everybody needs help sometimes. You needed help when they were trying to lift your goddamned license. Frank Palmer helped you then. Now, he needs some help. We all get in financial binds, eh? So, it's payback time, Charley."

"You're full of shit!"

He stood up and loomed over me. "We'll need an answer soon, Charley."

Mallow walked to the door, then stopped. "Think it over. It's a lot of money. You came in on it late, Charley. The other guy, Monk, did all the real work. It's really a windfall for you. Try to think about this, then, as a kind of sharing of the wealth."

Before I could even think of replying, he was gone.

15

You were pretty quiet tonight," Bob Williams said as he eyed me over the lip of his coffee cup. Only a few members of the club still lingered in the basement of St. Jude's church. Williams, like me, is a recovering alcoholic, and a psychiatrist. Beyond that, he is about as close as anybody comes to being my best friend.

We waved good night to the last few to leave. That left us with the task of cleaning up—emptying the ashtrays, cleaning the coffee urn, setting the chairs in order, and turning off the lights.

"Problems?" he asked.

I shrugged. "A few."

I was still shaken from my encounter with Mallow. I could think of nothing else. Somehow, I was frozen mentally, unable to conjure up alternatives, able only to replay the incident over and over and over again. I thought I might be going through something like shock, the same thing that happens to people after a serious accident.

The meeting had gone on without my conscious notice. My preoccupation must have showed.

"We're alone," Bob said. "Want to talk about it?"

"Your usual outrageous rates, I presume?"

"Depends. If it's something really dirty, I may just waive the fee."

"This is one I can't talk about, not even with you."

Bob Williams is as big as a small mountain and looks like a tackle for the pros. He wears his hair in a tight military cut, and his face could be the model for any painter or sculptor who wanted to depict a ferocious Indian. He was only part Native American, but he looked like Sitting Bull's kid. His appearance was forbidding, but he was much the opposite, a gentle man who cared about people, sometimes maybe too much. That had caused him to drink originally. The alcohol crutch was gone now, but not the concern.

"Charley, you're a lawyer. Let's do this on a patient-doctor relationship. That way my lips are sealed."

"Maybe they are, maybe they aren't. No offense, but this is something I don't want anyone to know about. There are reasons."

Williams frowned.

"It's a legal matter," I added quickly so he wouldn't feel offended. "I really can't talk about it."

"Are you in some kind of trouble?"

"It's possible."

"Did you do something wrong, Charley? Screw something up?"

I laughed. "Actually, quite the opposite. I didn't screw anything up, and I didn't do anything wrong. At least, not yet."

The place was a little spooky. The only light left on was

hanging just over us, shining down like a small spotlight on the two of us and the big coffee urn. Beyond the ring of light, the huge basement was as shadowy as a dark forest.

"The word *wrong* in our culture can mean many things, Charley," he said softly. "Going through a red light is wrong, even if you can see there's no traffic. Tossing an old lady down a staircase is also wrong. The word has many tints and shadings. What kind of wrong are we talking about here?"

"I haven't thrown any old people down stairs, so I guess that's one kind of wrong eliminated."

"This problem of yours," he asked, "does it mean hurting people, if say, it's merely technically wrong?"

If Mallow weren't merely running a scam and the proposed bribe was on the level, and paid, I thought about who would be hurt. Ford Motor would have to pay the judgment, but I honestly believed that they should, anyway. Even if the result was fixed, the end would still be just. If it went the other way, the fate of Will McHugh and Mickey Monk was almost unthinkable. And, in my judgment, unjust.

"Let's say no major damage would be caused anyone," I said. "But if discovered, the jail population could see a nice little statistical jump."

"Including you?"

I nodded.

"Well, in that case, it would seem the answer is obvious. Why risk it?"

I looked off into the darkness. "It isn't that easy."

Williams made no reply, just waited until I spoke again.

I didn't believe Mallow, but I wondered what I would do if he had been telling the truth about Palmer. It seemed impossible, but then, nothing ever was entirely impossible. Improbable, but not impossible.

"In the mood for a hypothetical question?" I asked.

"Best kind. Go on."

"Suppose you owed someone very big."

"Money?"

"No. Maybe something closer to life itself. Maybe your career."

"Okay."

"Now suppose that person asked you to do something that you could do, relatively easily, but was a felony, a big one. But no one would be really hurt if you did it."

"And if you refused?"

"A lot of people would be hurt, badly."

He played with his now-empty coffee cup. "If that isn't entirely hypothetical, you've got yourself one big problem. It sounds like something you might find on an ethics exam."

"Suppose it *was* an exam question, what would you answer?"

"I can't," he said bluntly. "I don't have enough facts to even consider an answer. You want to take this out of the hypothetical and tell me what's going on?"

"I just told you, at this point, I can't."

We sat in silence for what seemed like a very long minute.

"Obviously, I can't advise you, Charley. But it's this kind of thing that's dangerous for all of us alcoholics. You know that."

"What? Stress?"

He shook his head. "No. Indecision. I trust you still recall the serenity prayer." He said it with a sense of irony, since it was the cornerstone of much of the AA philosophy. Each of us knew every word of it by heart.

"God," he said quietly, repeating the prayer, "grant me the serenity to accept the things I cannot change, the courage to change the things I can, and the wisdom to know the difference."

"I don't know if any of that even applies in this case."

"It always applies, Charley. Use it. It'll keep you from trying to find a solution at the bottom of some bottle."

He got up, and we finished cleaning up. We walked out and locked up. The last person out always got the job.

Bob walked me to my car.

"If I can be of any help," he said, "let me know."

"Sure."

"And, if this is a legal problem, maybe you can find someone who can help you. A judge, an old friend, someone you can trust. There's usually somebody if you think hard enough."

I nodded.

"And, if it's something you can't change, accept it."

WHEN I GOT TO THE office Friday morning I half expected another message from Mallow, but he hadn't called. Mrs. Fenton broke the silence barrier, but her voice still carried the bitter tinge of lingering resentment.

She had prepared coffee. At least it was warm.

According to the previous day's obituary, Howard Wordley was being laid to his final rest even as I sat behind my desk. He had been laid out at P. J. Anderson's, bullet holes artfully concealed by deft cosmetology, for the public to express their sorrow.

Howard himself wasn't much of a draw. Car dealers who extracted the last dime from their customers seldom were, but Mrs. Claire Wordley brought out the crowds. I had heard the funeral home had been packed with numerous delegations from the charities she supported, the businesses she owned, and from fellow members of exclusive clubs to which she belonged.

P. J. Anderson's was handling the whole show, which meant Howard would be transported for his last ride not in a Mercedes but rather in a Cadillac hearse, since that was the only kind Anderson owned. It seemed like a final irony, being transported by the opposition company. Nearly on a par with being shot by a gun he himself had loaded.

I didn't attend. Lawyers defending people who are responsible for the funeral being held in the first place are seldom welcome. Anyway, I never did like Wordley.

I sipped my coffee and watched the river. It was funeral weather, heavy, gray clouds and a slight drizzle. The kind of weather that provokes somber thoughts.

It had been a bad night for me. I slept, but it seemed only in half-hour intervals. The Mallow problem curled through my mind like a twisting snake.

The more I thought about it, the more convinced I became that he had been lying. When he called again, I would tell him just that, as I had before, and turn down his bogus offer.

Still, the possibility loomed before me: maybe he wasn't lying.

I gulped down the coffee and got to work.

Stash Olesky called to inform me that his new leader had finally made a decision on what Becky was to be charged with. Olesky said it was to be second degree, since Becky had made no statement and they really couldn't show she had gone to get the gun as Stash had surmised.

That in and of itself was a victory of sorts. Becky, even if she pled guilty, was probably looking at eight years as a practical matter. The hope of eventual freedom beat no hope at all.

Stash asked about the examination.

In Michigan there are two ways to bring a person before the bar for trial. The first is by grand jury indictment. The second, and more popular, is by a charge by the prosecutor to be heard in open court at a hearing called a preliminary examination. A judge determines then if a crime has been committed and if there are reasonable grounds to believe the defendant may have done the dirty deed.

Holding a formal examination in Becky's case would serve no purpose. I already knew what kind of a case they had against her and I didn't want to give her a chance to plead guilty before I had a crack at dickering for a lesser plea or sentence.

"I'll waive the examination, Stash," I said. "I'll put it in writing and drop it off today, if you like."

"Monday's good enough," he said. "Look, Charley, my boss tells me I'm not to consider manslaughter. And, if a plea is offered, the term of punishment is to be left up to the judge. I will have no discretion. I wanted you to know that. Now, having been informed, do you still want to waive examination?"

"Suppose I got the widow to okay manslaughter?"

"He might change his mind. You should know that he changes his mind about every three minutes. Still, even then, I doubt he'd want to risk any criticism. He might be afraid the sentencing judge might have some unkind words."

"Suppose I got the judge to agree, too?"

He snorted. "I doubt that."

"Why?"

"Charley, the case will go to Evola. He's set up for the next major felony. It's the vacation season, after all. He's the only judge around."

"Damn."

"You should have been nicer to him in the Harwell trial."

"Fuck him."

He laughed. "If that's your thing, Charley. But what about the examination? Still want to waive?"

I couldn't think of a thing I could do for Becky by insisting on an examination.

"I'll still waive, Stash."

"Okay. To tell you the truth, Charley, I don't think you've got a chance at trial. I know you're good, but unless you've got one of your famous tricks up your sleeve, poor Becky is a goner."

"What, Stash, are you worried?"

"Not me, Charley. I got sleeves too."

I KEPT BUSY THE REST OF THE DAY, although most of it turned out to be make-work. Every time the phone rang, I kept thinking it would be Mallow. I had geared myself up to talk to him, to get it over with, but each time it was someone else.

I didn't call him because I figured he might interpret such a call as a hooded invitation to negotiate. I didn't want any ambiguity about what I planned to do.

Several times I considered calling Judge Palmer himself, to let him know how his name was being used. Once, I even looked up his number. But the haunting thought that he might actually be involved stopped me, although I was almost positive that couldn't be the case.

Almost was the key word.

I made up my mind to wait for Mallow.

Mrs. Fenton went home, as usual, precisely at five. I waited around until it was time to pick up Sue Gillis for our dinner date.

I took a couple of calls, people who wanted appointments. But no Mallow.

My anxiety level escalated with every call. I tried to think of the serenity prayer. It wasn't helping.

I took Sue to a small restaurant on Lake St. Clair. It was the kind of place that looked awful from the outside. A large shack, half of it hanging out over the water, held up by ancient and insecure piles. Peeling paint, warped wood, and rusting gutters only added to the negative impression.

Inside, it was better, but not much, with mismatched tables and old kitchen chairs.

Tourists took one look and drove on. The locals knew that when the cook wasn't drunk, the fish he prepared was probably the best in the world.

I had called to make reservations. It was done in two stages. First, I asked if Harry the cook was drinking. If he was, there would be lots of tables available. No local went there to eat when Harry was loaded. The girl on the phone sounded as though she were giving a weather report. I was told Harry was stone cold sober and it looked like that dry condition might just last at least into the early evening. There was one table left for eight o'clock; there had been a cancellation, so I grabbed it.

By the time we got there, Harry was nipping but still straight enough to prepare two perch dinners of a quality that would make the best cordon bleu chef resign from sheer envy.

The place was packed with locals. Everyone knew everyone else.

Sue had some former customers in attendance—a couple who ran a very successful sex therapy business until they were convicted of prostitution. Sue said the man was doing well as a boat salesman. His partner, a flashy and fleshy blonde who laughed a lot, was doing secretarial work. Sue wasn't entirely convinced that therapy sessions weren't still being offered to selected customers. But we were all out for a social evening, not business, so cordial waves of hello was how it went.

A man I had gotten a divorce for sent over drinks, a martini for Sue and an orange juice for me. He was with a hard-eyed woman half his age. The way she looked at him seemed to me like the way a Bedouin might look at a particularly promising camel. I figured there might be even additional divorce business sometime in the future. We saluted each other with raised glasses across the crowded room.

Harry came out of his kitchen to say hello. He was a steady client of mine. He no longer had a driver's license, no one could have saved that, not with the number of convictions he had accrued, but I had managed to keep him out of jail, except for a night or two, for assorted assaults and other numerous disturbances of the peace.

Harry's nipping was obviously increasing in frequency and amount, and I pitied the later diners who would come and find that Harry's culinary magic had floated away, lost in an alcoholic fog.

I had tried several times to get Harry into the club, but he wasn't interested. I suspected that one day he would topple over into a giant skillet, and there, amid bubbling butter and onions, he would sauté his soul into the hands of that great maître d' in the sky.

"Something's bothering you," Sue said after we had eaten and were sipping coffee.

"Why do you say that?"

"You're unusually quiet."

"Maybe you're seeing the real me, ever think of that?"

"If it's the Becky Harris case," she said, "I can't talk about it, you know that."

"It's not that."

"What then?"

"Nothing."

"A family problem? Your daughter?"

"No."

She raised the coffee cup to her lips, watching me.

I smiled, trying to look as though I hadn't a care in the world.

She just shook her head. "If you refuse to talk, I can take you back to my place and force it out of you."

"Blackjack and handcuffs?"

"You know, Charley, sometimes I wonder about you."

SHE DIDN'T USE ANY weapons or restraints, and we made love in the most gentle fashion. I had almost forgotten my problem, and she, thankfully, had forgotten to continue to pry.

My secret, such as it was, remained mine.

I spent the night, but Sue had to go to work Saturday morning, so after a quick cup of coffee with her I went back to my own place to clean up. It was raining softly and the air had the chill feel of another all-day drizzle.

The red light on my answering machine was blinking. I wondered if it might be Mallow.

I played back the messages. One was from a former client who wanted to get a divorce. Even on the short message tape, I could hear his wife screaming at him in the background. I thought the call was more for effect than a serious inquiry about my legal services. He said he would call my office on Monday.

The other was from an old friend, Jason Bishop, a judge who was lining up a St. Benedict alumni golf outing, who asked if I might be interested. He left his home phone number.

It was while I was taking my shower that I realized that Judge Bishop knew all the players in my little drama, and he knew them well. Including me. He was one of the centers in the so-called St. Benedict Mafia.

To his face, he was called Judge. To his close friends, Jase. But other than face-to-face encounters, he was known to bench, bar, and press as The Bishop.

It wasn't only because of his last name. He looked like a bishop, or at least Hollywood's idea of a British bishop. He was rotund, with a wisp of white hair that lay like a low halo around the back of his head. He wore tiny reading glasses that were perpetually perched near the tip of his nose. His face was forever solemn. A small, tight smile was the only expression he ever allowed himself, although, in fact, he had a wild sense of humor. He favored black suits, which contributed to the priestly look. It was as if he had been conjured up by the casting directors for Masterpiece Theatre. He had everything but the traditional gaiters.

Always, he spoke quietly—even in the midst of the most violent courtroom battle. But his words carried surprising force, empowered by a superior intellect, quick mind, and an uncanny knowledge of people in all walks of life. His gentle eyes, a blue as pale as milk glass, seemed to see more than any other eyes.

He had sent me to jail once for contempt when I got carried away in a trial before him. I sat in a cell for an hour, which, together with my apology, had constituted what he considered adequate punishment.

Over the years, even during my most turbulent times, he had become my friend, and later, one of my advisers.

He was as much a state political fixture as had been his father before him. The elder Bishop, a legendary state senator, had been one of the most powerful men in Michigan. His son, the judge, was the same. There wasn't anyone who held important office in the state whom he didn't know and who didn't know him.

They might kid about The Bishop, but I had never heard anyone speak of him with anything but respect.

He was a wise man.

Bob Williams had suggested that I might seek out someone, someone I could talk to, someone I could trust, someone I could talk to in confidence about my situation.

I toweled off.

Before I even had a chance to give it a second thought, I dialed The Bishop's number.

16

The last time I had seen The Bishop had been at his wife's funeral, almost a year before. Since then, he had moved from the big house in Grosse Pointe to a smaller condo only a few blocks away. He gave me the new address.

It was about an hour's drive from Pickeral Point, and he invited me for lunch. Saturday, he said, was customarily reserved for golf, but the rain had washed that plan away. He said his only other alternative was to sit around the golf club and play cards. He liked golf, but he didn't like cards, so he sounded genuinely glad to have something else to do.

I didn't give him a clue about why I had called.

The drive down wasn't bad, the rain wasn't that hard, although the mist thrown up by big trucks made passing hazardous.

I wondered if I was really doing the right thing.

In the shower, my looking for The Bishop's advice seemed like an inspiration. Now driving in an entirely different cascade of water, I wondered about the wisdom.

Jason Bishop had graduated from St. Benedict with Franklin Palmer, and was only a year or two ahead of Jeffrey Mallow. Bishop had been elected as a Wayne County Circuit judge almost before his law diploma was dry, thanks to his politician father. He had helped many others, including his old classmates, to attain high political office. I wondered if talking to him about Franklin Palmer and Jeffrey Mallow might turn out to be one of the biggest blunders of my life.

No question, he was an oddity. Judge Bishop could easily have gone up the judicial ladder but had turned down a federal judgeship as well as a nomination to the state supreme court. He liked what he did and where he did it. If power and influence were money, he would be a very rich man. But The Bishop lived comfortably, quite content on his judicial salary. For him, wealth, like ambition, apparently held little allure.

His condo was a luxury row house built during the 1930s, the units looking like something you'd see in the older, more elegant streets of Philadelphia or Baltimore.

I located his number, parked the car, and jogged through the rain toward the front door.

There he was, opening the door, before I even got there.

From the waist on up, he looked more like a bishop than ever, wearing a gray pullover with a white collar buttoned at the neck. The impression was definitely clerical.

But from the waist down, things were different.

He wore garish plaid trousers, golfing attire, I presumed. The plaid was woven of sickly reds and decaying greens. If an animal looked like that, a vet would have put the poor thing to sleep.

I'm of average height, more or less, and The Bishop was several inches shorter.

He shook my hand solemnly and led me through his rather sparse living room into a small kitchen, a room that had the look and feel of where he did most of his living.

"You've saved me from a fate worse than death, Charley," he said in his surprisingly soft voice. "I faced a day of pinochle with dullards who don't understand the game."

He gestured to a kitchen chair. "I've prepared sandwiches, complete with pickles and fixings. Now what to drink, eh? I have coffee, tea, soft drinks, beer, liquor, even bottled water. That's courtesy of my daughter, who thinks tap water is poisonous and designer water is just like being in heaven."

"Coffee's fine, Judge."

"Still in the program, I take it, Charles?"

I nodded.

"Good. Would it bother you if I had a beer?"

"Not at all."

He had gone to some trouble with the sandwiches. Apparently from living alone he was learning about kitchens and cooking. The coffee was a special blend, imported, and tasted like it.

"I called a number of the St. Benedict crowd about the golf outing, Charley. But you're the only one who responded immediately. Have you become a devotee of the game, by any chance?"

"I don't play anymore. It frustrates me, frankly."

He nodded, as though I had just said something terribly profound.

"The game was created by God to teach man humility," he said. "If you're not here as a golfer, Charley, may I inquire what dark need my phone call unearthed?"

I watched as he sipped his beer. Suddenly I felt the need to drink. I looked away.

"I need some advice," I said.

"Advice is like flatulence, Charley. I'm full of it." He stood up, poured out the beer, and in its place, took coffee.

"You didn't have to do that," I said.

"I know. Now, Charley, let's hear your problem."

Looking into those soft blue eyes had a hypnotic effect on me. I began awkwardly, but soon, soothed into comfort, I told my story, beginning with Mickey Monk's request through my latest conversation with Jeffrey Mallow.

He listened as though we were in court, nodding occasionally, asking a few questions, but otherwise evidencing no discernible reaction.

Finally, I was finished.

He poured fresh coffee for us both, then sat down and studied me for a moment before speaking.

"I was a senior in law school when Jeff Mallow was a freshman. We go back a long way."

My heart sank. Maybe I had managed to pick the wrong wise man.

"In those days, Charley, after admission to the bar, the law practice was a lot tougher to get into. Most of our boys went into work as insurance adjusters, things like that, something to bring in a steady income while they ran around like mad dogs trying to dig up clients. Some made it, some didn't. Darwin didn't have to travel all the way to the Galapagos Islands. He could have studied one of St. Benedict's old graduating classes. He would have learned all he needed to know about the survival of the fittest."

He got up. "How about a cigar, Charley?"

I shook my head. "That's something I gave up, too."

"You'll be sprouting white wings any day now. It's my last vice, and I cling to it, despite my doctor and my children. I limit myself to two cigars a day."

He produced a cigar that was long enough to lift a truck. It was the equal of three normal cigars. He lit it with a kitchen match, then turned on the blower over his kitchen range. The cloud of smoke was sucked up, but the pungent aroma still permeated the small room.

He studied the glowing tip as a doctor might inspect a lab specimen. Satisfied, he drew again on the cigar, blew out the smoke, and continued.

"I was lucky, of course. My father got me a job with the prosecutor and then had me appointed to this job when old Judge Herbert got caught with a lady—not his wife—and resigned."

He smiled at the memory. "The old man rigged the thing. He didn't frame Herbert, but as soon as it happened, he saw a way he could provide a lifetime job for his son, and he did."

He laughed. "He had a vote the governor needed. Badly. Very badly. Cynics might call it selling out. Even extortion. In any event, I got the job, and I have had it now for forty-two years."

He fondled the cigar. "We were a tight group, those of us who survived old St. Benedict. I used my new position and power to help my classmates and friends. Frank Palmer was one. Jeff Mallow was another."

"Judge, I'm sorry if I've …"

The Bishop shook his head, indicating that I should remain silent.

"Frank Palmer got a job as criminal law professor at the school. They do that now with nationwide searches when they need a professor. Then, it didn't pay much, and it was considered a part-time job for one of us who needed it. Frank did, and he got it.

"Later, as you know, he was appointed to the appellate bench. I had something to do with that, not a lot, but I helped."

As he drew in another long puff, the cigar tip glowed an oddly vibrant red. "Jeff Mallow followed the same career track, more or less.

"You have to understand, Charley, we were all Detroit boys, mostly from the working class, and we didn't have many friends besides ourselves. We tended to cling together, a sort of ragtag, self-help society, if you will."

I nodded. The same thing had applied to my own graduating class.

"Jeff Mallow was always a little brash, but likable. Did you know why he quit as chief judge of the appellate court?"

"To join Armstead Meade, so the papers said."

The Bishop nodded. "True enough—Armstead, Meade, Slocum and Herman, the biggest law firm in the state, and the most expensive. They took him on as a full partner, too. Of course, he was bringing something to that firm far more valuable than his former judicial title."

"Oh?"

"Jeff had managed to persuade our most famous and most affluent alumnus, Jacques Mease, the wizard of Wall Street, to sign aboard as his client. Obviously, Mease's business would mean millions of dollars in future legal fees, so Armstead Meade grabbed Jeff Mallow like a hungry cat might go after a big fat fish."

He chuckled, but there was a sadness in that sound. "Unfortunately for all concerned, about a month later, the feds dropped the net on Mease. As you know, he turned in almost everyone but his mother. Did a year. Kept millions. Escaped to the South Seas."

"Mallow must have made some money before that happened," I interjected, "perhaps as a defense lawyer for Mease?"

The Bishop shook his head. "Not a penny. Mease made his own deals with the feds. Of course, having lost the fat fish as a client, Armstead Meade showed Jeffrey the door so fast he didn't know what hit him.

"He's been going downhill ever since. He talks like he

owns the world, but he's almost bankrupt. I understand he's about to file."

"So that's why he's so desperate for money?"

The Bishop nodded, then relit the cigar.

"Jeffrey," he said through the smoke, "has borrowed from every one of us, some more than others. He has, financially, hit the very bottom."

"Judge, what should I do? If I turn him in, it's his word against mine. Financial problems or no, I wouldn't be believed."

"You could turn him in and wear a wire."

For one long minute, I thought he had to be joking.

"That would eliminate the credibility problem," he said.

I shook my head. "No. I'm not a cop. The man's desperate. He's running a fraud. God, maybe if I were in his shoes I might do the same. I'll just tell him it's no deal, and let it go at that. Besides, lawyers who blow the whistle on judges, even ex-judges, aren't the most welcome people in court. It could hurt me worse than him. Anyway, there's no point in doing it."

"It's your decision to make, obviously." The Bishop nodded slowly, then spoke again, this time in an even softer voice. "Charley, I would appreciate it if you'd keep me advised on this." The last was spoken in a voice that was just above a whisper, but there was no question that the statement had the snap of a command.

"Sure. If you like. But, given what you've told me, there's no real problem. I'll just tell him to go to hell, and that's the end of it."

I got up. "Well, then, thanks for the lunch and the advice."

"Any time. Tea and sympathy, that's my true calling."

He walked me to the door. "Let me know as soon as you hear from Jeffrey."

"Any special reason?"

"Perhaps."

"Like what, if you don't mind telling?"

"I'm interested. Frank Palmer also has been borrowing heavily."

There it was again, the same quiet voice.

DRIVING BACK TO PICKERAL POINT, every bar I passed seemed to be blinking a special invitation just for me. I saw the cars parked in front of the places. I knew inside it would be cool, dark, and a baseball game would be on the television above the bar. A man could forget trouble there for a while. Just sip and watch the game, the mind out of gear, human intelligence coasting.

I could even conjure up the tart taste of a fresh, cold beer.

Thoughts like that were dangerous.

There were no Saturday AA meetings unless I drove all the way back into Detroit, and there were a lot of saloons to pass before I got there. Sue Gillis was staying overnight at her sister's in Toledo. Bob Williams was away at a medical seminar.

I had two choices. I could go to my office and watch the rain on the river, or I could go to my apartment and watch the rain on the parking lot.

I needed someone to talk to, and not the guy who happened to be sitting on the next bar stool.

So I drove to Herb Goldman's Marina.

Despite the rain, the parking lot was surprisingly almost full, although it looked as if most of the boats were still in their wells.

I jogged through the drizzle to Herb's office. It didn't look like an office, it looked more like a dumpster that needed emptying.

He was seated in an old chair staring out the window. His oil-stained clothing looked exactly the same. If he had more than one set, they all had to be identical. He turned and his yellow eyes inspected me suspiciously.

Uninvited, I stepped in and found another battered chair, cleared it of papers, and sat down.

"You see 'em out there?" he asked.

"The boat owners?"

He nodded. "They're all out there in their little bitty boats, snug and sipping beer or bourbon or whatever, telling each other they're having a helluva good time."

He sighed. "The problem is, they probably are."

He squinted. "What brings you here?"

"Thinking about people drinking."

He nodded slowly. "Maybe it's something in the air." He gestured toward the boats. "Usually, it doesn't bother me. Today it does."

I nodded my head in agreement.

"As I see it," he said, "you and I got two choices."

"And they are?"

"We can walk over to O'Hara's saloon, get blind, stinking drunk, ruin our lives, and end up as street bums."

"Sounds good. What's the other?"

He stood up. "We can go fishing."

"It's raining."

"It just so happens, I got rain gear in my boat."

Much of Herb Goldman's wealth comes from the water, so I presumed his boat would match both his affluence and his vocation.

I was wrong.

We climbed into an overlarge metal rowboat, badly dented, powered by an outboard engine that looked like the inventor's original model. I slipped into a rubberized poncho that smelled of oil and dead fish. Herb loaded on a bucket of minnows and a six-pack of diet Pepsi.

The engine sounded like an airplane, but the motor took us out into the river.

"Do you swim?" Herb asked.

"Not all that well."

He kicked a life preserver to me. "Put it on," he said. "I understand there's some kind of medal they give for drowning lawyers, but I'm too busy to go to the ceremony."

The rain became more intense and the wind was causing choppy waves.

Herb quickly and expertly rigged two trolling rods and gave one to me. The rods were the only equipment that looked as if someone cared. Well used, they had the feel of a loved and polished weapon.

We began to move very slowly parallel to the shoreline.

"Rain usually means good fishing," he said. "Besides, the great thing is that it keeps some of the assholes off the water."

Almost before the last word was out of his mouth, a kid in a huge cigarette boat, the kind they use on "Miami Vice," roared by, throwing an enormous wake. We bobbed up and down like a car on a roller coaster.

"I didn't say all, just some," Herb said. The rain pelted down on his bald head, making his simian features look even more animal-like. Suddenly he became alert and gave his rod a snap like a ringmaster. "Gotcha," he growled.

He reeled in a large walleye. It flopped at our feet.

"Three pounds, easy. You want it?" he asked. "If you do, you got to clean it."

"I don't want it," I said.

He gently grabbed the fish and eased it back into the water. "They say you can eat these fish. They say all those chemicals the Canadians kicked into the river are gone. And if you believe that, I'll tell you right now where Elvis lives."

I was about to ask about going back. The wind was becoming sharp, making the rain colder and stinging.

Then I saw what I thought was Franklin Palmer's yacht. It passed close enough for me to read the name on the stern. It was the *Cat's Paw* out of Algonac. It was a twin to Judge Palmer's boat.

"You see that?" I gestured toward the yacht.

"*Cat's Paw*," he said. "I did some work on its engines last year. Damn nice boat."

"Who owns it?"

"A guy who manufactures safety gadgets for cars. He has three plants across the country and enough money to buy anything he damn well wants."

"What would a boat like that cost, Herb?"

He looked at it again. "That's a sixty-foot Sheridan, handmade in Florida. Of course, a lot depends on what goes with it, power, and that sort of thing, but a boat like that would run maybe a million, maybe more."

"A million!"

He grinned, showing the spaces where his teeth used to be. "Yeah, new. Secondhand, the prices on those things drop off like a cliff. If you're interested, counselor, you can buy that one for maybe half a million, maybe a hair less. Depends on how bad the owner wants to get rid of it."

"What would it cost to keep and run one of those things?"

"Charley, like J. P. Morgan said, if you have to ask, you can't afford it. Just docking, upkeep, and the like would probably feed Yugoslavia for a year."

He squinted at me. "You're not thinking about boats, are you?"

"You mean, buying one?"

"Yeah."

"No."

He nodded. "That's good. Charley, take my word for it. A boat is a big hole in the water, a place for assholes to sit."

"Speaking of assholes sitting in boats, shall we spare the fish?"

"We just started."

"I'm soaked and cold. I think it's going to storm and this dinghy of yours might sink. But that aside, I'm having a wonderful time."

"Still need a drink?" he asked.

"Not in the least."

"Me either."

We both reeled in.

Herb turned the boat, revved up the old engine, and we went back up the river, throwing up mountains of spray from the crest of every wave we crossed. By the time we got back to his marina, I was adding seasickness to my list of complaints.

"Fun, eh?" Herb said, grinning at me.

THUNDER WAS BOOMING as I was driving back to my apartment. Whatever discomfort I had felt seemed well worth it. The urge to drink was gone.

It was another battle, fought and won. There would be others, probably for the rest of my life, but each victory added a little more inner strength, very important strength. Despite the fact that I was cold, wet, and smelled like a sewer, I felt good about myself.

As soon as I got inside my apartment I stripped to the skin, tossed the clothes into a garbage bag and then the dirty clothes hamper. My shoes were probably ruined, but I packed them with newspaper anyway.

I lingered in the shower, letting the hot water pour down, feeling the heat spreading through every part of me. It was a pleasantly sensual experience.

I dried off, slipped into my worn robe, and padded out toward the kitchen to make coffee.

It was then that I saw it.

My answering machine, the little red light blinking over and over, looking to me like the accusing eye of God.

I wondered if it was Mallow.

Despite my curiosity, I didn't hit the message button. I made coffee, on the strong side, laced it with milk and a touch of sugar.

I sat next to the telephone, looking at the blinking light and sipping.

Finally, I reached over and punched the button.

The machine whirred and the recorded tape played the message.

"This is Miles Stewart. It is Saturday afternoon, two o'clock," the familiar voice said, pronouncing the time with a sneer. "I will be here at my apartment until six. Call me. It is important."

I didn't know if I was elated or disappointed that the call had not come from Mallow. Facing him was one of those things that you want to have over with but aren't anxious to do.

Doctor Death I could handle.

I knew his home number and dialed.

"Miles Stewart," he said, sounding as though he were introducing himself to the peasants at large.

"Charley Sloan," I answered. "What's up?"

"Where were you?" he demanded.

"It's Saturday. I usually drop by a convent up here and have sex with the nuns. Now, why did you call?"

"I'm going away again, for a while."

"Where?"

"Pointe Aux Flam."

Pointe Aux Flam was once Michigan's Newport. Huge summer homes of the wealthy had been built at the turn of the century up on the tip of Michigan's Thumb. They weren't the palaces of Newport, but they were quite splendid Victorian mansions. The old owners had a colony and managed to hold on to the properties, passing them down like diamonds, generation to generation.

The places had been built along a cliff, and each had

long stairways going down to a magnificent Lake Huron beach.

Once, I had seen them from the water. It was something you never quite forget.

"Is this trip for pleasure, Doctor, or are you going up there to help some poor soul into the next life?"

"Have you been drinking?"

"No."

"Sounds like it to me," he snapped. "I'm going up as the house guest of the Cronin family."

"Like in Cronin lumber?"

"Yes. That family."

I sighed. "Look, at the risk of sounding repetitious, you realize that if an elderly or sick Cronin dies while you're up there, it'll tend to prove the state's case. Judges read newspapers, too, you know."

"I shall inform you when I return to the city," he said coolly. And then he hung up.

I replaced the receiver. The red eye of God was merely glowing, not blinking, showing that there were no other messages.

The Stewart appeal wouldn't be scheduled for some months. I didn't look forward to it, even though I felt sure I would win.

I didn't like Miles Stewart, almost as much as he didn't like me.

It was not an unusual lawyer-client relationship, but that didn't make me feel any better about it.

Sunday came and went. I called Sue Gillis several times during the day, but she didn't return to her apartment until just before midnight. I had almost given up. I suggested that I come over. She suggested I didn't. Apparently it hadn't been a happy visit with her sister.

When I arrived at my office Monday morning, Mrs. Fenton was at her desk. There were no messages waiting. Mallow still hadn't called.

Mrs. Fenton was reserved as usual, but the chill was gone, so I presumed I was back in her good graces.

I had coffee and began to plan my week. There wasn't much action, but enough to keep busy. A couple of court appearances and some real estate work. It looked like a break-even week.

And then Mrs. Fenton presented herself unannounced, an unusual circumstance.

"I have a friend who knows Mrs. Wordley," she said.

"So?"

"She went to the funeral. She said it was quite lovely. Very tasteful."

I wondered how the clergyman had evaded the manner and cause of death. Being blown away by one's mistress was a bit tough to cover up, even in the best biblical language. He must have been skilled if he had.

"Mrs. Wordley, Claire, donated all the flowers, there were a great many, to the hospital."

"Allergy ward?"

"Of course not."

She stood there in the doorway. Apparently there was more that she wanted me to know.

I waited.

"My friend tells me that Mrs. Wordley is going away for a while."

"Probably a good idea, given the circumstances. It'll give her a chance to get herself together."

"She's quite together," Mrs. Fenton snapped. Apparently Mrs. Wordley was one of her personal heroines.

"I'm glad to hear it."

Her frown deepened. "We represent that Harris woman."

"We do."

"You indicated you wanted to talk to Mrs. Wordley about obtaining a lesser plea." Her tone indicated her disapproval of such a course.

"I want to talk to her, but it can wait until she gets back."

Mrs. Fenton came as close to smiling as she ever did. "That may be some time. I understand she's going to Maine for the entire summer, and then to Europe. She may be back by Christmas, according to my friend."

"Damn! When's she leaving?"

I thought she paused for effect. I could see the malevolent glitter in her narrow eyes. "Tomorrow," she said.

MRS. HOWARD WORDLEY had an unlisted number. I called the dealership and told them I was her nephew from Toronto. I said a car accident on the way to the funeral had put me in a hospital. I had missed the funeral, but I felt I had to extend my sympathy to Aunt Claire. My personal phone book was lost in the accident, I explained to the girl on the other end of the phone. I said I couldn't remember the phone number because I was in such pain. My left leg and hip had been crushed and this was the first phone call I had been capable of making.

I went into a few more gruesome details in a quavering voice. She gave me the unlisted number without question.

A small victory, but I enjoyed it.

I dialed the home and got the maid. I figured the injured nephew ploy wouldn't work twice, so I took a risk and told the truth.

The maid, who had been so friendly, suddenly turned snappish, but she did agree to ask Mrs. Wordley if she would speak to me.

It was such a long wait, I wondered if the maid had just simply changed her mind.

Then I heard someone pick up the phone.

"This is Claire Wordley." The voice was cultured and without the slightest hint of emotion.

"Mrs. Wordley, my name is Charley Sloan. I represent Rebecca Harris."

"I know who you are, Mr. Sloan."

"Mrs. Wordley, I wouldn't have bothered you now except that I understand you're leaving on an extended trip."

"That's right."

I tried to phrase things so I wouldn't provoke anger or disgust.

"In criminal matters, Mrs. Wordley, it's common for the prosecution to ask the opinion of the family on what should be done. Usually, it's in relationship to sentencing, but sometimes the family is consulted if a lesser plea is offered."

"I would presume the prosecutor would talk to me, not you," she said evenly.

"Ordinarily, yes. But since you're planning to go away, I wonder if I might talk to you about this. I realize how you must feel, Mrs. Wordley, and I apologize for what must seem extreme thoughtlessness. But I do have a client to represent."

"I've read about you," she said. "And I've seen you on television."

"Look, if my reputation bothers you, I can bring along the prosecutor who's in charge of the case."

"That won't be necessary. How long will all this take? I'm in the middle of packing."

"Ten minutes, twenty minutes, not much longer."

She paused. "I could spare that at lunch, if you didn't mind talking then?"

"Fine."

"Do you know where Peach Creek Country Club is?"

"I've never been there, but I know where it is."

"I'll meet you there at noon, Mr. Sloan. I'll leave your name so they'll let you in. I'll meet you in the grill."

I was about to express my genuine appreciation when I

realized that Claire Wordley, widow of Howard Wordley, had hung up.

PEACH CREEK WAS FAMOUS. The championship course had been designed by Robert Trent Jones. The initiation fee, a secret, was said to be so high that only the very rich could even think about it. God must have loved the rich, he made so many of them. Word was that applications for Peach Creek were piled a mile high and by the time anyone was approved for membership they were too old to play golf anymore.

To get to it meant a long drive over a farm road. My Chrysler kicked up dust as I passed small farmhouses and well-tended fields. The sign was small but I saw it. I turned at a stand of trees and drove down a shaded country lane.

The lane ended at low-slung white buildings with roofs the color of ripe peaches. I pulled into a crushed stone drive and ended up at an entrance covered by a canopy.

An exceedingly polite young man wearing a blazer and slacks was waiting. I thought he was a member, but it turned out he was the valet. He took my car and sped quickly away.

Another young man, somewhat older, also in a blazer and slacks, but of a more expensive cut, came down the steps.

"Mr. Sloan." He said it with such warmth that anyone hearing would have thought I owned the club. I wondered how he even knew me. "Mrs. Wordley is in the grill. Please come with me."

I saw no guards, although I suspected a security system equal to Fort Knox probably existed. If it did, it existed out of sight.

Inside, Peach Creek was nothing special. It looked like an old country club, the kind that used to exist fifty years ago, quiet, comfortable, with an old-shoe feeling to it.

It was like turning the clock back to 1938.

The grill looked like a grill, all burnished wood, big tables, lots of room with a well-dressed and cheerful-looking staff moving competently about.

I was led to a table at the back.

Claire Wordley was a little thing. She was sitting, but I guessed she was no more than five feet tall and less than a hundred pounds. Her hair was stark white and worn in a kind of athletic pageboy. Her features were strong and the bone structure solid. She had been a beauty once. Age had brought her down to handsome. She was one of those outdoor women whose skin had been permanently darkened by wind and sun. She wore no glasses and her eyes, dark green, had a shrewd look. Her lips were thin but not severe.

My escort held a chair for me.

"You've put on some weight since the Harwell trial," she said in that same cultured, matter-of-fact voice. "I saw you on television then."

"I'm eating more regularly. The fee was substantial."

She laughed quietly, exposing perfect teeth, whether her own or her dentist's dream, it was impossible to say.

She was dressed in a fashionable tennis outfit, pure white with specks of red trim.

I wondered if this was considered standard mourning gear for Peach Creek widows.

As if by magic, a young waiter appeared.

"A drink, Mr. Sloan? I'm having a martini."

"Orange juice," I said.

She suggested we order. I got the impression that anything she suggested was converted immediately into law at Peach Creek.

She ordered a salad and, at her suggestion, I ordered something called the back-swing sandwich, a mix of meats, specially broiled.

The waiter must have possessed Olympic speed. He was back with the drinks before the olive had sunk to the bottom of Claire Wordley's martini.

She sipped, then put the glass down.

"Again, Mrs. Wordley, I must apologize for having to do this so soon after the funeral. If it wasn't that you were leaving …"

She held up a hand. "I understand the necessity. But let's make this as brief as possible."

"Of course."

"Please go on, Mr. Sloan."

"I represent Rebecca Harris."

"So you said."

"She's been charged with second-degree murder in connection with the death of your husband."

"Any question that she didn't do the shooting?"

"No."

"Self-defense, I suppose?"

I sighed. "That will be the defense."

There was a pause.

"You really are uncomfortable talking to me, aren't you, Mr. Sloan?"

"That's right. This is hardly the time, I know. And, obviously, this is a delicate situation."

She sipped the martini again. "Let me make this easier for you. I was married to Howard for more than forty years. Like many marriages, it was stormy. For the last ten or fifteen years it was a marriage in name only. I stayed because in my circle divorce just isn't done. I know what Howard was, and I know his weaknesses. There was no point in a divorce. I happen to own everything anyway. We stayed together for appearances, nothing more."

Her green eyes met mine. "But he was still my husband. He was murdered and I believe justice should take its course."

She played with the martini glass. "The police told me all about Howard's little fling with your client. I wasn't kept in the dark. I know what was going on between them."

"How about the rape?"

Her eyebrow raised slightly. "What rape?"

As quickly as I could, and as delicately, I ran down what had happened.

"These photographs," she said, "of the damage he did to the Harris woman. Do you have them?"

"They're in my briefcase."

"May I see them?"

"They aren't pretty, Mrs. Wordley."

"Let me see them." She spoke softly, but it was, nonetheless, a command.

I took them from my briefcase and handed the file to her. She thumbed through, showing no emotion, even when she studied the close-up of the neck injuries.

Then she handed them back.

"So, if this goes to trial, everyone will see these pictures?"

"They will be the basis of the self-defense claim."

"If it goes to trial and she's convicted, what will happen, as a practical matter?" She asked the question as though she were asking a sales clerk about the quality of an item of interest.

"The charge is second-degree murder. If convicted, Becky Harris would probably be sentenced to life. But, as you say, as a practical matter, that would mean she'd serve seven, maybe eight years, tops."

Those green eyes locked onto mine. "Hardly worth it, is it? A trial, I mean. The whole town would be abuzz, the whole sordid mess dragged out all over again. And"—she paused—"those pictures would become public. That certainly wouldn't do much for Howard's memory. Or, to be frank, for me."

She finished the martini. "I presume there's an alternative or you wouldn't be here."

"I'm going to offer a plea to manslaughter. That carries up to fifteen years. But the prosecutor won't even consider it unless you approve."

Our food was served, but neither of us touched it.

"Let me be candid, Mrs. Wordley. If the plea were accepted, I would try to get probation for her, if I can."

She shook her head. "I may not have been overly fond of Howard, but I think probation is quite out of the question. That is, if I have anything to say about it."

"You do."

She signaled for another martini. "I would insist that the woman do some time."

"How much?"

"Do I actually get to set the term?"

"No, but the judge will take your wishes into consideration."

She thought for a while. "I would think nothing less than six months. I feel the community would probably see that as sufficient punishment. That, plus the promise that she never return here to Pickeral Point. Does she have family here?"

"No. I'm sure there would be no problem that way."

She nodded. "Well, what happens now?"

"I'll notify Mr. Olesky, the prosecutor in charge, and tell him you have no objections to a manslaughter plea, providing Becky Harris serves at least six months and never comes back to Pickeral Point. He'll want to talk to you, perhaps even get that in writing."

"But there are no guarantees, are there?"

"No. I won't lie to you, Mrs. Wordley. The judge will also have to approve the plea and sentence."

"You didn't even touch your sandwich," she said.

"I'm really not hungry."

She nodded.

"How is she paying you?"

"Becky?"

"She was a waitress, I believe. I doubt she has much."

"The only asset she has is a ring your husband gave her."

"Howard gave her an expensive ring?"

"She thought it was. It turns out it's cubic zirconia."

She smiled. "And that's your fee? You certainly work cheap, Mr. Sloan."

"Maybe. But look at it this way. I'm taking everything she has."

She chuckled. "You are a villain, after all, aren't you? Do have your Mr. Olesky call me."

"Thank you," I said, standing.

She wasn't smiling. "Should I ever shoot anyone, Mr. Sloan, I shall hire you immediately. I like someone who'll work for zircons."

17

When I got back to my office, my sense of elation was tinged by a heavy echo of self-disgust at having coerced Claire Wordley. She had agreed not to oppose a lesser charge. But it was the threat of the trial, where the alleged rape and the photos would be made public, that did it. It wasn't extortion in the usual sense. No angry threats, no raised voices. We had both been civilized about the whole thing. Smooth or not, I preferred triumphs that didn't leave such a terrible taste in my mouth.

There still had been no message from Mallow.

I called Stash Olesky and told him what the Widow Wordley had agreed to.

"You're an amazing man, Charley," he chuckled. "How did you do that? Hold a gun on her, or did you show her pictures of her youthful self engaged in disgusting sex acts?"

"Photographs," I said. "I'm not much on guns. But she's leaving town tonight for the rest of the year. I'd appreciate it if you'd call her and confirm what she told me."

He sighed. "Well, tell you what I'm going to do. I'm going to grab a steno and hop right out there. Given the man I now work for, unless it's in writing, it won't count."

"I appreciate that, Stash."

"Glad to do it. It'll get me out of the office. Of course, that's only the first task, Mr. Hercules. Getting Judge Evola to agree is something I'll bet considerable money against. No ill wishes, Charley. But he's just waiting to stick it up your candy ass, and this seems like the first chance fate has been good enough to provide."

"I am a weaver of magic and spells," I said. "You might be surprised."

"No might about it. Anyway, I'll take care of Mrs. Wordley, if only to see what Evola eventually does to you."

"Fear not. Blessed are those who seek justice, for they will see heaven."

He laughed. "Fat fucking chance. But good luck anyway."

IT WAS GETTING TOWARD the end of the day when Mickey Monk called. He didn't sound drunk.

"How's it going, Charley?"

"Not bad. You?"

"I've seen better days. Obviously, there's nothing new on our case, right?"

"Nothing new." I didn't dare even hint about Mallow's offer. Mickey couldn't be trusted with that kind of information.

"I thought maybe you might have heard when a decision might come down. I mean, you know, from your friends over there."

"Nothing so far."

He paused. "I hope to Christ it won't be much longer." Again he paused, then continued in a more quiet voice. "The bank foreclosed on my house today."

"Jesus!"

"Well, it's just a legal paper at the moment. I still have the redemption period. If I'm lucky, we'll win our case before they actually evict."

"How much do you owe?"

"Big house, Charley." He laughed. "And a bigger mortgage. Even if I sold it now, with prices going down where I live, I'd still owe. Right now, I'm three months' payments behind, a little over six thousand."

"That's a big house."

"My wife has expensive tastes."

I thought of my bank account. Even with paying for my daughter's education, I had managed to squirrel away over $30,000. There had been some big fees after the Harwell case, but none recently, except for Dr. Death.

"I can loan you the six thousand, Mickey," I said.

"I appreciate that, Charley, but I couldn't pay it back if the McHugh case goes down the tubes. I'll stand pat."

"It's there if you need it."

He chuckled. "Hey, I'm a gambler. I've put everything on the McHugh case. It would be bad luck to hedge that bet now, not while we're so close. I'll let it all ride. Let luck decide the thing."

I wondered what he would say if he thought luck might have nothing to do with it. That his luck, perhaps, was a crooked ex-judge offering a deal.

Mickey wouldn't have hesitated. He would jump at the chance, even if it meant going to the wise guys to come up with the front money. At this point, he would be willing to toss his life onto the pile of things he had already wagered.

"If I hear anything, I'll let you know," I said.

"The whole thing is in your capable hands, Charley. I've got no worries."

Mickey Monk hung up, leaving me holding onto the telephone and at least a ton of guilt.

MRS. FENTON HAD GONE HOME when he called.

I picked it up before the machine issued the usual message. For whatever strange reason, somehow I hadn't expected the call. I thought he might have decided to drop the whole thing.

"Hello, Charley."

It was Mallow.

"I'm glad you called," I said. "This has gone far enough. I'm not in the market for what you suggest."

"Now, Charley, there you go, jumping to conclusions." He laughed. "How do you know this is even about the other thing?"

"Isn't it?"

He chuckled. "Well, in a way, I suppose it is."

"I told you I'm not interested."

"There've been some changes, Charley."

"I suppose the price has gone up."

He laughed. "My god, you've become a cynic. You have to develop a more tolerant attitude. You'll get an ulcer if you don't."

He paused, then spoke more softly. "We have some time here, as you know. As I said, there have been some changes. Changes, by the way, favorable to you. My friend and I have been having some serious discussions about the problem."

"How about I call your friend? I'll bet he hasn't the slightest idea of what you're trying to pull off here."

"I'm not trying to pull off anything, Charley."

"The hell you aren't. I've been asking around. You're up

to your eyeballs in debt, with no way to pay it off. If you think I'm a chump, and if you think I'm going to make a contribution, you're badly mistaken."

He paused, then replied. "You're wise to check things out, Charley, so long as it's done in a confidential manner. Obviously. But you're right, I am in some financial difficulty. It happens to all of us at times." He paused. "As I recall, it happened to you, and not so long ago."

"It did. But I sold shoes and real estate to get by. I never tried extortion."

He laughed, and that surprised me.

"Charley, you're losing your sense of humor. Believe me, this is strictly a business matter, nothing more."

"Take a trip to Jackson Prison, it's full of guys who tried the kind of business deal you're talking about. I don't know how I can make this any clearer, but the answer is no."

"I understand," he said quietly. "But please do me the courtesy of talking to me face-to-face."

"It won't change the answer."

"Perhaps not. But I think you owe it to us. If not me, then certainly to my friend."

"I don't owe you anything."

"That's probably true. But I don't think that applies to my friend, does it?"

"If you don't get off my back and drop this, I'll call him myself and let him deal with you."

"If you like. Do it." He sounded confident. Much too confident. "All I'm asking is to meet and talk this over. Then, if you still feel the same way, no harm's done."

"It won't—"

"I'll let you know the place and time."

He hung up.

I sat staring at the telephone. I decided that if he did call, I'd refuse the meeting.

What could he do to me?

Nothing.

As if that thought summoned up a ghost, in my mind I saw once again Will McHugh, tied to that dreadful chair, a prisoner in that equally dreadful trailer.

AS A COURTESY, I called Judge Bishop at his court-room. He had just heard a motion and was preparing to hear another, so he was in chambers and took my call.

"Good morning, Charley. I presume there have been developments?" Even over the phone, his quiet voice still had that odd force of command.

"Mallow called," I said. "I wouldn't disturb you, Judge, but you did say you wanted to be informed."

"You're not disturbing me, Charley. What did he say?"

"He said there had been some changes proposed. He wants a face-to-face meeting. When I told him no, he said I owed it to Judge Palmer."

"Did he use Palmer's name over the phone?"

"No. He referred to him as 'my friend,' but we both knew who he was talking about."

"What did you say?"

"I said I would call Palmer direct."

"And?"

"He said to go ahead if I liked."

"He wasn't upset?"

"Didn't seem to be."

There was a pause. "When is this meeting supposed to happen?"

"He didn't say. He said he'd let me know."

"Don't call Palmer," Bishop said.

"Why not?"

"Just a hunch, Charley. Let's see what happens."

"I don't intend to meet with Mallow."

There was another pause. "Let me know when he contacts you."

"This has gone far enough."

Now the voice grew even more soft, but ever more commanding. "I'd meet with him, Charley. Play this thing out. You never know what it might lead to."

"Supposes it leads to Judge Palmer? I'm not going to have any part in bringing him down."

"I understand that. But, so far, it's more curiosity than anything else, isn't it? Humor me on this, Charley. I'd consider it a favor."

"That's what Mallow says all this is, just a favor."

"Let's see." I heard someone speak to him. "I have to go now, Charley. Keep me advised."

I didn't have time to speculate on what The Bishop had in mind. Mrs. Fenton buzzed and advised me that I had two unscheduled visitors. Prospective clients. I told her to bring them in.

They were father and son, and looked it. I knew the father. He owned the local radio station and several other businesses in town. I had represented his chief talent in contract negotiations, a disc jockey who used the name River Rat. The negotiations had been amicable.

"Mr. Denton," I said, "it's good to see you again."

We shook hands.

"This is my son, Peter."

Sidney Denton was fifty-ish, with a square and heavy body, half-fat, half-muscle. He was blond. His white skin was freckled.

His kid was an absolute duplicate, only younger. I guessed about twenty.

Both men had exactly the same meaty and strong grip in their handshakes.

"Please sit down," I said. "Now, what can I do for you?"

Sidney Denton smiled. It was one of those board-of-commerce smiles, the smile of a confident businessman who expected to either sell you something or to buy, but at a bargain.

"Pete has gotten himself into a bit of trouble," he said. "I'd like you to represent him."

"What kind of trouble?" I looked at Pete, who seemed as supremely confident as his father.

"A kid prank," his father answered. "Pete is a junior at Central Michigan University. He was home for the weekend with a couple of his buddies, and they got into some trouble. They had something to drink, you know how college boys are."

"Go on."

"We just came from the jail. I posted bond for Pete."

"Bond? What's he charged with?"

"It's all a mistake," the father said.

"Could be, but what's the charge?"

"Armed robbery," Pete snapped.

His father glanced at him as if he disapproved of his choice of words.

"Tell me what happened," I said to Pete.

"Well, they were—" his father began.

I held up my hand to stop him. "Please. I'd like to hear this from your son."

Denton frowned.

Pete shrugged. His expression was neither friendly nor unfriendly. If anything it bordered on sullen.

"Me, Chris Baker, and Norris Child were here for the weekend. They were staying with me at my parents' place. It's on the river.

"Anyway, we went into Port Huron on Saturday and cruised around that big mall there for a while. There wasn't much to do. We came back to my house. My parents had gone to a party. We started drinking beer, you know, having our own party."

"I don't like Pete to drink and drive, so I allow him to

drink when he's home. We, my wife and I, entertain a great deal, so there's a fully stocked bar."

"The three of you started drinking, then what happened?" I asked Pete.

"We got into a discussion about crime. About robbery, mugging, and things like that."

"And?"

"Chris Baker said I wouldn't have the guts to commit something like that. Norris agreed. They were egging me on. Like I said, we were drinking."

"Go on."

"Finally we bet some money. I got one of my father's pistols."

"I'm a gun collector and a hunter," the older Denton interjected, defensively.

"We drove to the gas station at Main and Elm. It was the only thing open."

"I know the place," I said.

"They waited in the car and I went in with the gun. I stuck it up, just like I said I would, took the money from the till, and came back to the car."

"The police arrested them about a mile away," his father volunteered.

I sat back in my chair. "Did they tell you that you didn't have to make a statement?"

"Yeah, just like in the movies."

"Did you make a statement?"

He shrugged. "It was just a gag, just something to prove a bet. Yeah, I told them. Wouldn't have made any difference. Chris and Norris were so scared, they were blabbing and told them everything they wanted to know anyway."

"Were they charged, too?"

Young Denton nodded. "At first. But the cops dropped the charges on the promise they would testify against me. So much for good friends."

"Did the gas station attendant identify you?"

"Sure. I knew him. He knew me. We went to high school together. At first he thought it was a joke, that is, until I fired a shot into the ceiling. That scared the shit out of him."

I nodded. "Undoubtedly."

"It was a joke," his father said. "They didn't need the money. It was just a college-boy prank. It wasn't a robbery."

"After you fired the shot, did the attendant say anything?"

Pete half smiled. "He begged me not to shoot him. He always was a wimp, even in school."

"Have you ever been arrested before, Pete?"

He shrugged again, it was becoming an irritating gesture. "Speeding, a couple of times. Fighting once."

"Assault?"

"At a football game. I got a fine and probation, that was all."

"Are you on probation now?"

His father cleared his throat. "He is. It's up next month. But on this other thing, I think when this is all explained, just some college boys out for fun, it'll help clear things up. Of course, what happened was serious, Pete knows that now. I was thinking that you might get the charge reduced. A fine, probation, public service. Pete is prepared to do whatever he must. He knows he's stepped over the line."

I looked into his father's eyes and I saw the prayer there. He wanted some reassuring words, something that would let him know his son would be all right, that nothing serious was going to happen to him.

"Let me explain what Pete faces here. The charge is robbery armed. In Michigan, that calls for a sentence up to life in prison. Also, I'm sure they charged him with the possession of a firearm during the commission of a crime."

Pete nodded. "They said something like that."

"That charge, unless there's a plea bargain, calls for a mandatory two years in prison, all on its own. Mandatory. The word means you have to do the time, all of it."

Sidney Denton paled. Pete showed no reaction.

"Even if it was just as Pete says, to win a bet, it's still an armed robbery plus an assault on the attendant. A pistol was used, fired, and money was taken."

I looked at the kid. "You do drugs, Pete?"

"No."

His father frowned. "He smoked some pot in high school and got in trouble for it. As far as I know, Pete doesn't use anything now."

"When the cops arrested you, did they run a Breathalyzer on you?"

He nodded.

"Did they say you were drunk?"

The half smile returned. "It showed I was drinking, but I wasn't legally drunk." He said it with a kind of smirking pride.

"If you had been drunk, it might have been a defense, not a good one, maybe, but one that would show that you were too stiff to form the necessary intent." I paused. "And you're sure you weren't high on something else? A little cocaine, maybe?"

"Beer, man, that's all we had."

Sidney Denton looked even more pale. "What can you do for my son?"

I sat back and tried to form the words so that they wouldn't hurt too badly.

"If it's as Pete says, there isn't much anyone can do. He planned an armed robbery and carried it out. He used a loaded gun and fired it, even if it was only to make a point. His two companions will testify against him, saying they never thought he would actually go through with it. Pete confessed to the police after they read him his rights. In other words, they have an ironclad case of armed robbery, plus the weapon charge I just spoke about."

"But it was a prank. A judge would take that into consideration."

I nodded. "He would. Also, Pete's a college boy, comes from a good family, and the judge would also take all that into consideration. But Pete's on probation now. That's another crime, violation of probation. So, for openers, you've got the robbery armed, the gun charge, plus the violation of probation."

"What exactly are you saying?" his father asked.

"My guess, and it's only that, is that even if a lesser plea could be worked out, Pete is looking at one to two years in prison."

"Bullshit," Pete snapped. "I've read about murderers getting probation."

I nodded as I thought of Becky Harris. That was exactly what I was trying to work out for her. "That does happen sometimes. Usually, it's in Detroit, where murder is a kind of hobby. But this is Pickeral Point, and they look at things a bit differently in these parts."

"I know all the judges here," Sidney Denton said. "They know me, they know my family. Surely something can be worked out?"

"Maybe. Six months in prison, the rest in a halfway house. It would depend on the judge and would also depend on luck."

"What about a jury trial?" the kid asked. "That's why we came here. They say you can get anyone off."

"That would be nice, if true. And if it were true, you would have had to wait in line. I do my best, but that's all I can do. I doubt a jury would look on a college boy sticking up a gas station as amusing. You stand a better chance if you can get the right judge and a plea bargain."

"Probation?" his father asked.

"Anything's possible, but I'm afraid Pete's looking at more than that."

"You said this guy was good," Pete snapped at his father. "He's a fucking asshole."

I smiled. "He'd do well in front of a jury," I said to his father. "Tell you what. Just like the doctors, why don't you get a second opinion?"

Sidney Denton nodded.

"And, then, if you want to come back, I'll do everything I can for Pete."

"How much do I owe you?" Sidney Denton asked, his voice deep with defeat.

"If you decide to come back, we'll work out a fee for services."

The kid smirked, got up, and swaggered out the door. He was, like his old man, half-fat, half-muscle, but there wasn't enough muscle to protect him from what would happen to him where he was going.

Pete Denton was about to get an education that would be unobtainable in any college.

I felt sorrier for his father.

Justice sometimes wreaked havoc on the wrong people.

18

Sue Gillis prepared dinner at her place. She made pasta with Italian sausage, having added oils and spices that made everything speckled with green and red. When I first looked at the heaping bowl, I thought I might be able to nibble a forkful or two, if only to be polite. Hamburgers are usually as fancy as I get. Of course, on the first mouthful I found the kind of delight usually associated with sex. I ate until I was near bursting.

Much to her amusement, I had to pass on dessert.

"You don't run into too many cops who can cook," I said, sipping coffee.

"I have many talents, Charley. You've barely scratched the surface."

"So it would seem."

Sue had laced her coffee with brandy. She had done it

so I couldn't see, but a recovering drunk has the nose of a hunting dog when it comes to alcohol. I said nothing.

"So, Charley, have you solved your mysterious problem?" she asked.

"Not yet."

"Want to talk about it?"

"I wish I could, Sue, but I can't. Especially not with an officer of the law."

"Turning criminal, are you?"

"I'm trying not to."

She frowned. "That serious?"

"Well, not really, just a touch sensitive. I'll tell you about it when I can. It's a little like the Becky Harris case. You can't discuss that, right?"

She made a face. "I'm not supposed to. Stash Olesky says you got Mrs. Wordley to agree to a lesser plea. How'd you do that?"

"I slept with her."

"Charley, I don't like those kind of jokes."

"I didn't really. I just let her think I would. Old women are funny like that. They'll believe anything."

"According to Stash, you won't be able to get Evola to agree."

"Probably not. All I can do is try."

She sipped her coffee. I could sense she was thinking about something else. She had that quizzical look in her eyes.

"Charley, how many times have you been married?"

"I've already told you. Three. Each was a unique human experience, not unlike being in a plane wreck or having been a prisoner of war."

She didn't smile. "That bad?"

I sighed, wishing I could loosen my trousers without looking like a dolt. "Worse in some ways. There are things alcoholics can do to each other in a marriage that would turn the stomach of a Gestapo officer. Frankly, it wasn't all a one-way street. I developed my own nasty brand of cruelty."

"I doubt that."

"Sober, I am as you see me. Drunk, I am something altogether different."

"So, I presume that means you would never marry again?"

There it was: It was *the* question. Eventually they all asked it. Even I asked it, but only of myself. I never got a clear answer, nor could I really give one.

"What's on your mind, Sue? Is this leading to a proposal?"

"No." She looked away. "I guess experience shapes how we see life."

"Usually."

"My marriage," she said quietly, "for as short as it was, was a beautiful experience. I never believed two people could be as close as we were, or share life so completely."

I said nothing in reply.

"I suppose I miss that sharing most of all. I have a good life here, Charley. I like my job. I have a ton of friends. I get out, and I do things. But that sharing is still missing."

"So you'd like to get married again someday?"

She nodded. "Yes, but it would have to be just as special as the first time."

"That's a tough order. You can never truly duplicate anything in this life, at least never the way it once was. Everything is a compromise, one way or the other."

"Don't you get lonely, Charley? I don't mean for sex, or even friendship, just to be close to someone, so close ..." Her words trailed off.

"I understand what you're saying, Sue, I really do. I get as lonely as the next person, perhaps more. But marriage hasn't worked for me, not in that way."

"Things have changed, Charley. You've changed."

"I'm sober. That's the biggest change." I looked at her.

The cheerleader vivacity seemed to have flown. There was something different in her eyes. A need I hadn't before seen.

"Sue, staying sober is my number one job. I haven't been off the stuff all that long. It takes a lot of energy, it really does. I don't know if I'd have enough left over to make a marriage work."

"Even with someone you loved?"

"Even with someone who loved me."

"So marriage is out, then?"

I shook my head. "Never say never. But at the moment, I'm not prepared to take the risk."

She paused, then spoke. "At least you're honest, Charley."

"Sometimes."

She smiled, but it was a sad smile. "More coffee?"

"Sure."

We sat quietly then, just talking. Various subjects, about family, old friends, schools, one subject leading easily to another.

But we didn't mention marriage again.

When the evening began, I had entertained carnal thoughts and expectations.

Now, it was late, and those thoughts and expectations had somehow evaporated.

I kissed her good night. It was a chaste kiss.

I drove home.

And I was lonely.

TUESDAY MORNING I had a drunk-driving trial. It wasn't anything out of the ordinary, no injuries, no damages, just my man clocked at eighty miles an hour on the wrong side of the road, right after the bars closed. He had had previous drunk-driving convictions. The policeman was professional on the stand, and the standard

Breathalyzer evidence stood up, despite all my efforts to discredit the machine.

I lost, which didn't surprise anyone, including my client. He would have pleaded guilty, but mainly he wanted to cause the police some inconvenience. He got a large fine and several weekends in the county jail. He would have received more, but he had a job and a family. His driver's license was now a memory. I tried to get a restricted license for him, one that would allow him to drive only to work and back. The judge merely shook his head.

My client seemed content. I tried to interest him in AA or some rehabilitation program, but he indignantly informed me, as I knew most drunks do, that he didn't have a drinking problem.

It had been a wasted morning, but I had been paid my fee up front, so that helped ease the frustration somewhat.

I grabbed a quick hamburger and then went back to my office.

Mrs. Fenton handed me my messages.

Mallow hadn't called.

There were other calls I would have to answer, but at the moment I didn't feel like doing so immediately.

I swung my chair around and watched the traffic on the river. It was a clear and sunny day. Boats, looking like water bugs, zipped up and down past fishermen who were trolling, moving but almost imperceptibly.

A large freighter was coming up the river, gray and weathered, looking as though it had come from the other side of the earth, which was probably exactly the case.

Mrs. Fenton buzzed the phone and I picked it up.

"There's a sheriff who wants to talk to you. He says his name is Miller."

"It probably is," I said. "Put him through."

I heard the click. "This is Charles Sloan," I said.

"Mr. Sloan, I'm Sheriff Miller. Cork Miller. I'm sheriff of Harbor Beach County."

"Right up there in the tip of the Thumb, right?"

"Michigan's thumbnail," he said. "That's what our chamber of commerce calls it."

"What can I do for you, Sheriff?"

"Got a man here who wants to talk to you. This is his one official phone call." He chuckled. "Long-distance, too. Hang on. Here he is."

"Get up here!" The words were spoken hysterically. "They have me in jail!"

I knew the voice, but I couldn't resist.

"Who is this?"

He yelled in response. "This is Doctor Miles Stewart!"

"Well, Doctor, why do they have you in jail?"

"They have accused me of murder."

Suddenly my amusement evaporated.

"Listen to me," I said, "and listen to me carefully. I don't want you talking to any policeman, prosecutor, or anyone else. I will get up there as fast as I can. It's about a three-hour drive." I glanced at my new diver's watch, a gift from a client. "I should be there about five."

"Can't you call someone and get me out on bail?"

"Not until a degree of murder is fixed by a judge."

"This is outrageous!"

"I'm sure it is. Would you ask Sheriff Miller if I can talk to him? Put him back on."

"He wants to talk to you," Stewart snapped. The good doctor wouldn't be making too many friends up there, not with his usual arrogance.

"Miller here."

"Sheriff, I will be representing Doctor Stewart. I should be up there in about three hours. I've instructed Stewart not to make any statements. I don't want him questioned unless I'm present."

"No problem, Mr. Sloan. We're a friendly bunch up here. Have you ever been to our jail?"

"No, I haven't."

"It's not much, not by big city standards. I'll see your man gets a private cell. That's the least we can do for a celebrity."

"Celebrity?"

"Hey, he's Doctor Death. We've all read about him. This is going to be a major event up here."

"Who is he accused of killing?"

"I suppose by all the rules I shouldn't be telling you anything, but you'll find out anyway. Your client is said to have put old Sean Cronin to sleep." He chuckled. "The big sleep."

The sheriff was apparently someone who liked to talk.

"How is he supposed to have done it?" I asked.

"Injection, just like they do down in Texas to those folks on death row. One little shot and out you go, no pain, no strain. Anyway, that's what's alleged. From what I've read, your client makes a habit of this sort of thing."

He laughed. "Jesus, he really didn't have to do it. Old Sean was eighty-eight and as sick as it's possible to get. Bad heart, bad lungs, bad kidneys, you name it, he had it."

"Is Cronin supposed to have requested the injection?" In every other case, that had evidently been the situation.

"Oh, no. The old man was real dotty, to boot. One of his daughters is supposed to have set things up." He stopped. "Well, it's a long story, and I guess the prosecutor will get bent out of shape if I tell you everything. Anyway, fact is, Cronin's dead. The prosecutor and Cronin's other daughter say your man did it."

"I'll be up as soon as I can."

"Don't worry about the doctor. Our jail isn't much, but it's clean. If one of our clients gots the money, we let them order in from a restaurant here in town. Damn good food. Otherwise, the menu is baloney sandwiches."

"Thanks."

"By the way, take your time getting here," he said, laughing. "We don't get much murder in this county, but we're tough as hell on speeders."

IT WAS A TWO-LANE HIGHWAY most of the way, but the drive up wasn't bad. There wasn't much traffic, and what there was moved along at a good clip.

Broken Axe, Michigan, served as the county seat for Harbor Beach County. It was a nice little town. Quaint, as if time had forgotten about it and nothing had changed in fifty years. The business section was about two blocks long and looked like it catered to farmers and their needs.

The courthouse and the jail were relics, two plain lime-stone buildings, and if Abe Lincoln himself had come walking out of either one of them, it wouldn't have been all that surprising.

Above the jail, giant oaks stirred in the breeze. There was a serenity about the place that you could inhale.

I took in a lungful, and went into the jail.

The wooden floor was worn, but other than that, every-thing was well kept. A sign saying OFFICE hung out over an open door.

I stepped in. There was a counter and several signs instructing people what to do to apply for various permits. A stout woman looked up from a computer ter-minal.

Her smile was engaging. "Can I help you?"

"I'm looking for Sheriff Miller. My name's Sloan."

The smile became a big grin. "Oh, you're here for Doctor Death." She turned and yelled at another inner door, also open. "Cork, Doctor Death's lawyer is here!"

He looked like an advertisement for beer, the kind where they show the good ole boys sitting around the local bar playing pool and acting like adolescents, all jokes and good humor.

His uniform was clean, but not pressed. He wore a black leather belt with the largest pistol I had ever seen, hanging off at an angle.

He looked about forty, maybe more. About six foot and fifty pounds too heavy, he wore a military haircut over an uneven head. His face was fat, and when he smiled, the face looked like it spread out over his collar. And he looked like he smiled a lot.

He came around the counter and took my hand in a grip that made it seem as though we were brothers who hadn't lain eyes on each other in years.

"Pleasure to meet you, Mr. Sloan," he said.

"Call me Charley. Everybody does."

"Good! We're real informal up here. If anyone called me anything but Cork, I'd think they were mad at me. Would you like to see your client?"

"I'd like to see the prosecutor who'll be handling the case first," I said.

"Just one guy, the main man. This is a small county. We couldn't afford two full-time prosecutors. His name is Eddie Rand. Young guy, got elected right out of law school. Hard worker, though. You'll like him. Come on."

He led me from the jail to the courthouse. "This doubles as our court and the county offices."

We entered an office marked PROSECUTOR. A young man sat behind a desk, his feet up on it, a telephone cradled in his ear. He wore faded jeans and a work shirt. Unlike the sheriff's, his hair was long. Skinny, with long legs and an angular face, he was a flashback to the sixties.

He nodded a greeting as he spoke into the phone. "Gotta go," he said, "looks like I got some customers who seek justice. Or whatever. I'll see you later, sweetie."

He got up lazily, extending his hand. "You gotta be Charles Sloan."

"Call him Charley," the sheriff said. "This here is the county's chief law enforcement officer, Charley. Edward M. Rand, Esquire."

Rand laughed. "How'd you like me to tell Charley here your real name, Cork?"

The sheriff guffawed. "You wouldn't, now, would you? Not while I'm carrying this gun."

"You're right. How about some coffee, Charley?"

"I wouldn't mind."

Eddie glanced at the sheriff. "Cork, call over to your jail and have three cups sent over." He looked at me. "Lousy jail, but the best coffee in the state. Now, Charley, what can I do for you?"

"For openers, how about letting my client go?"

Eddie might have looked like a teenager, but his manner was mature, assured.

"I would, Charley, if it was strictly up to me. Hell, keeping that man means I'm going to have to try him for murder. That's a lotta work for the pennies they pay me. Plus, it'll interfere with the important things in my life, like fishing and chasing women. But"—he smiled—"if I let him go, they'd let me go right after him, and work up here is hard to find. You got any easier requests?"

"Tell me what you know about the case. Frankly, I haven't talked to my client, and outside of the fact that somebody named Sean Cronin is no longer with us, I don't have any other details."

The stout woman from the sheriff's office brought over the coffee. I took a sip. As advertised, it was great coffee.

Eddie Rand went back to his usual place and once again put his long legs up on the desk.

"I'll tell you as much as I think is fair. Okay?"

"Good enough."

The sheriff brought up two chairs and we sat down.

"Pointe Aux Flam is a small community inhabited by some very big people. Old money people. They spend their winters in Florida and their summers up here with us common folk. Most of them are elderly, and there aren't many of them." He drank from his cup.

"Anyway, Sean Cronin is one of them, an old lumber baron, I'm told. Retired, and rich as hell. He has two daughters, women who you might call old maids. Unmarried, and not surprising, either, since these two are not the best-looking females to ever grace the planet. Donna and Doreen."

"Twins?"

"Ugly enough to be, but the fact is, one is a year older than the other."

Rand smiled. "The two women, both in their sixties, compete at everything, including taking care of Poppa. The old man should have been in a nursing home, but that would have put an end to the competition."

"You apparently know a lot about the family," I said.

"There's three things we do up here. We fish, we screw, and we gossip. The fishing isn't as good as it used to be, the screwing is dying out, but the gossip is our main source of entertainment. We know everything about everybody."

He grinned. "Anyway, Charley, Doreen decided it was time to end Daddy's suffering. She reads, like the rest of us, and she contacted your client. Donna didn't agree, by the way. Doreen paid your man two hundred thousand dollars—by check—for his services. He came up and Sean Cronin went down, so to speak."

"Autopsy?"

I thought I saw a gleam of triumph. "Given all the circumstances, I thought our regular man might be out of his depth, so I sent for Doctor Anderson from Lansing. You know him?"

Clyde Anderson was the best forensic pathologist in the state.

"We had the body shipped to Bay City, and he did the

autopsy there. The report's not back yet."

"So far, you haven't got a case."

"Well, I haven't given you one delicious detail. Miss Donna watched Doctor Stewart go into her Daddy's room, inject him, then sit there until he died. Not bad, eh?"

"What are you charging him with?"

"You tried that case in Detroit. That was what? Second-degree murder?"

"It's on appeal."

"Yeah. But this one's not an assisted suicide thing, Charley. Here's what this one is: one guy going into a room and killing another guy. No request. No nothing. And in front of a witness. We're going for first-degree murder."

"You'll never make it stick."

"Look, I'm a young guy. We don't get many murders up here. I'm just trying to get all the experience I can."

"Can I see my client?"

"You bet. No reason not to. Cork, take Charley over to the jail. Let him talk as long as he likes."

The sheriff walked me back to the jail. He grinned. "See, I told you he's a nice guy. I knew you'd like him right off. And I could tell he likes you. By God, this should turn out to be a lot of fun."

THEY LET ME INTO HIS CELL. No guards, no cameras. The sheriff merely locked the cell door and told me to yell when I wanted to come out.

Dr. Miles Stewart got up as I entered. He slipped into his suit jacket and busily began to put himself together, although he was without his tie. He didn't have a belt, or shoelaces, either.

"You took your time getting up here," he snapped at me.

"Were you planning on going somewhere?"

He stopped and glared. "Out, that's where I'm going. I presume you arranged bail?"

"There isn't going to be any bail. We are going before the district judge up here in a few minutes and the prosecutor is going to charge you with first-degree murder. Bail is not granted in those circumstances."

"You can't be serious?"

"I'm afraid so," I said. I sat on the cot, hard and lumpy as it was. "Well, you can't say I didn't warn you, can you? You've got yourself into a tub of trouble this time, Doctor. You better tell me your side of things before we go to court."

"Perhaps I had better get another lawyer."

"It might be a good idea. Sometimes a local man is best. He knows all the players. I can ask around, if you like."

He fumed for a moment, then shook his head. "Too late now. You're my lawyer and I'm stuck with you."

"Actually, I'm not your lawyer. I am indeed your attorney for the Detroit murder case wherein you are accused of killing Francis X. Milliard. You paid me twenty thousand dollars to defend you, including appeals, if necessary. For that case, I am your lawyer. But this is an entirely different matter."

"Just what are you saying?"

"If you want me to defend you on this charge that you killed Sean Cronin, I will require an additional fee. This time it's thirty thousand dollars for the trial only. Appeals, if necessary, will be extra."

"You are a goddamned bandit!"

"You can get a local lawyer here to do the job for a lot less, probably. It's up to you."

I was hoping he would be angry enough to get somebody else, although the money would buy a lot of tolerance for his infuriating arrogance.

His eyes narrowed. "You know all about me, all about the other cases. Someone new might not be as well prepared as you."

"There's something to be said for continuity, obviously. But if you're worried about offending me by selecting someone else, don't. I think I'll be able to live with the rejection."

His lips became one thin angry line. "All right, I'll hire you. But this time you had better win, goddamn it."

I smiled. I was enjoying his discomfort. "Results are not guaranteed, only effort."

"Bandit," he muttered as he sat next to me.

"Well, how about this—let's hear your version, Doctor?"

"This whole thing is outrageous. As I told you, I came up here as a house guest of the Cronin family. I called you to tell you that, if you remember."

"I remember."

"The Cronin estate, they call it a cottage, is quite splendid. The view of Lake Huron is extraordinary. The Cronins proved to be excellent hosts."

"Especially Sean? I presume you and he went grouse shooting or fishing or …"

"He was on life-support systems when I got there," he said defensively. "The man was barely alive. I looked in on him, of course. I am, after all, a doctor. He was quite critical. He was eighty-eight and every life system was beginning to fail."

"Was he conscious?"

He paused. "That depends on your definition. He was alert and talking, if that's what you mean. But he mistook me for someone out of his past, and the conversation was meaningless."

"He was dotty, in other words."

He sneered. "That's how a lawyer might look at it, I suppose."

"One of the sisters is supposed to have seen you injecting Sean Cronin. True?"

He smiled that infuriating smile that was nothing short of a superior grimace. "What, did I inject him, or did she see me?"

"Did you inject him?"

"No."

"Why would she say she saw you do it if it didn't happen?"

"I have no idea."

"Who invited you to be the Cronins' house guest?"

"Miss Doreen Cronin. A very pleasant and gracious woman."

I nodded. "The cops here say she paid you two hundred thousand dollars to do in the old man."

"That's ridiculous!"

"It might not be so ridiculous if they produce that check in court. Does it exist?"

"I cashed it. I mailed it to my bank. But it was for scientific research. She made it out to my foundation."

"What foundation?"

"The Miles Stewart Foundation. It's all legal, all registered by my accountants, if you're wondering."

"This foundation, how many people does it employ?"

"No one at the moment, just me."

"I presume the Cronins are old family friends?"

He arched an eyebrow. "There's no need to be sarcastic. I met them for the first time when I came up here."

"Why did they invite you?"

"Miss Doreen did. She had heard of my scientific accomplishments."

"I'll bet."

He frowned. "Think what you like."

"I think you were hired to come up and put old man Cronin away. How do you do it? Drugs? Strangulation?"

He smiled frostily. "No one has been able to show that

I caused death to occur, not here, not anywhere."

"This time they've got a witness."

"Miss Donna?"

"That's who they tell me."

"She's as dotty as her father was. You'll have no problem discrediting her on the stand."

"We'll see."

I stood up and yelled for the sheriff.

Cork Miller came lumbering along, grinning widely.

"Did Doctor Stewart have a checkbook in his possession when he was admitted to your little hotel?"

Miller nodded. "Oh yeah, wallet, checkbook, the works. He was all packed and ready to leave when we were called over there by Donna Cronin."

"Would you mind bringing the checkbook? The doctor here would like to retain an attorney."

Miller laughed. "Sure, Charley. Be back in a minute."

Stewart eyed me suspiciously. "He called you Charley."

"I make friends wherever I go."

After I got the doctor's reluctant check, Cork Miller walked me back to the courthouse.

"The district judge up here is a good guy," he said. "I think you'll like him."

Apparently Cork Miller knew no one evil or bad. It was an unusual and benevolent attitude in a sheriff.

"He used to be prosecutor, then he got elected to this judge job. Everybody loves him. He's got a good sense of humor and gets around—you know, weddings, funerals, that sort of thing. Outside of my own sweet self, I think Rudy Hathaway is the most popular man in this county."

"Rudyard K. Hathaway?"

"That's his proper name. But we all call him Rudy. Do you know him?"

I nodded, smiling. "I went to school with him."

"I'll be damned. Small world, as they say."

RUDYARD KIPLING HATHAWAY had been one of my study partners in law school. All law students form groups to help one another through the morass of the law. We had four in my group, and the least help and the most fun had been Rudy Hathaway.

His father, a rich beet farmer, had named him after his favorite author. But he didn't look anything like the original. If anything, he favored the old Mortimer Snerd puppet made famous by Edgar Bergen. He had unruly red hair, protruding front teeth, and practically no jaw. His laugh was high pitched and distinctive, like a falsetto machine gun, and it sounded often.

Rudy and I did much of our studying at rundown bars and only got serious when exams neared.

He was one of those school friends that you tell yourself you'll always be close to but never are. After graduation, he went up to Michigan's Thumb to practice law.

I saw him once, ten years or so ago, at a state bar convention in Grand Rapids. We both got spectacularly drunk and almost ended up in jail.

I got a Christmas card once after that, but we never got together as we had promised each other we would.

I wondered if he had changed.

Cork Miller walked ahead of me into the judge's chambers and announced me like an emcee introducing a comic at a club.

"Someone from your past, Rudy," he said before I came into view. "The one, the only, the famous Charley Sloan!"

He was sitting behind his desk in his robe, looking judicial as hell. He hadn't changed much. The red hair was graying, but that was about all.

"Well, Charley," he said, his face firm and solemn, "we've heard a great deal about what you've become.

You'll find, Sloan, that I run a tough courtroom here. No nonsense. I'm firm, but I'm fair. But let me make one thing clear, if you try anything fancy here, anything out of the ordinary, I will send you to jail." He glared at me. "You do understand, don't you?"

Before I could even think about replying, I was greeted with that machine-gun laugh.

"You ought to check his trousers, Cork," he said. "I think he shit." He grinned that front-tooth smile. "God, it's good to see you, Charley. You're looking wonderful, prosperous, and all that."

"You too."

He stood up and pulled off the robe. "This was just for effect." He held it out. "I think I should get this thing cleaned. It's getting a little rank."

He shook my hand. "Sit down, Charley. How about a drink?"

"I don't drink anymore, Rudy."

He nodded. "I heard, but I didn't believe. Me, too."

"AA?"

He laughed. "Nope, fucking ulcers. I miss it though."

"Me, too."

"Cork, go get the demon prosecutor, and we'll do a little business."

The sheriff left and we brought each other up to date on our personal histories.

"Then, I got elected to this job," Rudy said. "This kid Eddie Rand replaced me as prosecutor. Good lawyer, by the way. I'd be worried about him sniffing after my job except he's too busy laying half the broads around here, and the word is he smokes a little dope on the weekend. The people up here will tolerate that in a prosecutor, but not in a judge. He's no competition, so we get along splendidly."

He sighed and slipped into the robe once again. "Well, I'm going to grant the first-degree charge against your client, Charley, and bail is out of the question. I presume you'll want an examination?"

I smiled. "Absolutely."

He nodded. "Nine days from now. A week from Thursday. I'm open then. Time enough? I don't think Eddie would object if you wanted more time to prepare."

"Nine days is good."

He paused, and the smile became almost sad. "I suppose this has to be said. I love you like a brother, Charley, you know that. But you'll get no special breaks here. I'm not in the habit of doing business that way."

"That's a shame," I said.

His laugh sounded like it was carrying an echo.

Cork Miller returned with the young prosecutor.

"The first time I seen this prosecutor, Charley," Judge Hathaway said, putting an arm around Rand's shoulders, "I thought he was a dope dealer. Looks it, don't he?"

He didn't wait for Eddie Rand's reply. "Let's do some business. We'll arraign Doctor Death, no bond, and set examination."

"You do allow trials up here, I presume," I asked.

His smile grew large. "Yeah. Sometimes. If people ask real nice."

19

Before driving back I stopped in the only bookstore in Broken Axe and bought a half-dozen books, five technical and one Bible, to occupy Miles Stewart's mind. I knew the Bible would irritate him, so I couldn't resist. I delivered them to the jail.

On the other hand, Cork Miller was genuinely impressed by the Bible and assured me he would see the doctor got the books. I thought maybe old Cork might drop back to Stewart's cell for a nice religious chat, which would be a major irritant for the egomaniacal doctor. The prospect brightened my day.

The drive back was almost free of traffic, which left me plenty of time to think.

I thought of how I might possibly defend Doctor Death again. This time the case appeared much stronger.

This time they had an eyewitness. I had nine days until the examination. I planned to spend one or two days prior to that in Broken Axe. By that time, I would have the autopsy report and additional information. A day or two up there to prepare seemed adequate.

But during the three-hour drive, I mostly thought about what I would do if Mallow called.

It was a long drive and I came up with a number of possible answers. None of them seemed really to fit the situation.

IT WAS DARK by the time I arrived back at Pickeral Point. I decided to stop by the office before I went home. The outside stairway was lit, but I hardly needed it. A huge full moon, like a celestial spotlight making a full sweep, illuminated everything, including the river. I unlocked the office and flipped on the light.

Mrs. Fenton, as usual, had left everything as tidied as though we were expecting an inspection. I ignored the answering machine, which was blinking with the fury of a warning device.

My mail was in one perfect stack; my telephone messages in another.

The mail held no magic, nothing unusual or even interesting. But the telephone messages were another matter entirely.

Apparently the media had gotten word of Doctor Death's arrest about 3 P.M.; that was the time of the first message. There had been a flood after that: Detroit reporters, national newsmen, and television stations. Everyone wanted a callback. Everyone wanted an interview.

For a few days I would be a celebrity again. I wanted to feel that it was all annoying, but what I really felt was flattered, and I wondered if what I was doing was again growing a bit too fond of the spotlight. In the old days when I was drinking, I used to love that kind of attention.

Things had changed. I hoped I was one of them.

I hit the button for the phone messages. My machine could record up to twenty-five message units, and it looked from the number of blinks as if it had already gone to the limit.

Each message was preceded by an electronic blip, and then the taped words.

"Hi, Charley, this is Sherman Martelle of the *Free Press*. I called before. It's about your client Doctor Stewart. Please give me a call at the paper"—he carefully recited the number—"or at my home." Again, a slowly spoken number. "No problem with the hour. Anytime. Thanks."

The messages from media people followed, like soldiers, one after another. I did get one from a client who was having trouble with a neighbor. I jotted down his number to call in the morning.

I was almost at the end of the tape when the familiar voice spoke in that deep and commanding baritone.

"Charley, this is Judge Mallow. My friend and I believe you and I should get together. Don't ignore this call, Charley. Call me at my office tomorrow morning. I usually get in about ten."

I knew it was coming, so I shouldn't have felt so shaken, but I was.

The last message was from Mickey Monk. He was very drunk and apparently very jubilant. "Hey, Charley! Old Doctor Death handed you up another big one! We're on a roll here, pal, I can feel it. I can see the light at the end of the tunnel, Charley, I honest-to-god can! Luck is with us! We can't help but win. We are going …" The tape ran out.

It was like a message from my conscience. His life, as well as McHugh's, was in my hands.

I turned out the lights in the office and sat in my chair, turning to look at the river.

The lights on the Canadian shore looked like a string of Christmas decorations, with the moon silvering the river from shore to shore. A large freighter passed in front of my window, moving like a dark ghost, except that the running lights made me realize that the freighter and lights were real. It sounded its horn, signaling another boat somewhere down the river.

The horn sounded like the blast of that last horn on judgment day.

At least it sounded that way to me.

And, in a way, perhaps it was.

I SPENT AN HOUR OR TWO calling media people I thought might be important in launching a publicity campaign for my defense of Doctor Death.

I called Sherman Martelle at home.

"Thanks for calling, Charley," he said. In the background I could hear a television, which suddenly got turned off.

"Basically, what's your defense going to be this time?" Martelle asked.

"Same as before. He didn't do it."

"They say they have an eyewitness, one of the daughters of the deceased. They say she saw your man do the injection, and that death followed almost immediately."

"Who is *they*, Sherman?"

He laughed. "The prosecutor up there, a guy named Rand. I think he's getting a kick out of this. I asked him how many murders they had up there last year, and he said just two. Uncivilized place, apparently. Just two."

"Maybe modern culture will come creeping up to Harbor Beach County yet. What's my man supposed to have used?"

Sherman chuckled. "Didn't Doctor Stewart tell you?"

"He said he didn't do anything wrong."

"The prosecutor says he used potassium. Stopped the old guy's heart like hitting the brakes on a car."

"There's no way he can prove that."

"He says he can. What's your position, Charley? I still have time to call it in. It'll help offset what the prosecutor told us. You'll at least get your innings in for tomorrow's edition."

"Miles Stewart was invited up there as a friend of the Cronin family. He did not treat or touch Sean Cronin. The old man died in his sleep of natural causes. He was very ill. Apparently there is a problem between the two daughters, the only children of the deceased. These kids, by the way, are in their sixties, Sherm."

"Toddlers. Go on."

"One of the sisters trumped up this entire thing to gain advantage in the coming fight for the old man's estate. She knew of my client's problems and used that as an excuse to try to get an edge on her dear sister. Miles Stewart is innocent, Sherman, and we are fully prepared to prove it."

"Sounds good, Charley. Won't fly, of course. But it sure does sound nice. By the way, how's old Doctor Death taking this?"

"Off the record, he's pissed to beat all holy hell. On the record, he is heartsick that someone would use him in such a cruel way."

"I love it, Charley. You do know, of course, that your guy was paid two hundred thousand dollars for the hit?"

"That was a contribution to a research foundation run by Doctor Stewart."

"Charlie, do you honest-to-god believe that?"

"Of course."

He laughed. "Those people up in the Thumb, Charlie, are all old farmers. They are practical people. Your standard bag of tricks won't work up there. The only kind of bullshit they go for is the kind they can spread on their fields. They won't buy any of your usual sleight-of-hand stuff. A jury of those hayseeds will knock your big-city ass off."

"I plan to wear overalls, Sherman, and a straw hat."

"This is one trial I gotta see."

The other phone calls were similar. Doctor Death's nonculpability and my credibility were obviously quite suspect. No one was hostile, just disbelieving.

And so was I.

THE PROBLEMS OF MILES Stewart, M.D., occupied my mind sufficiently enough that I didn't think of Jeffrey Mallow, and my sleep was undisturbed.

But when I awoke, I knew I would have to do something about Mallow, and the old feeling of anxiety returned.

At the office, Mrs. Fenton seemed to be enjoying the attention of the press even more than I. She was as excited as I had ever seen her, which wasn't much, but was more than normal. Phone messages were coming in by the minute.

There was no use in putting it off, so I dialed Mallow's office number and even asked for him by his old title, avoiding another skirmish with his secretary.

"Good morning, Charley," he said, coming on the line almost immediately. "I see your old client has been up to his usual line of work."

"That's what's alleged. What can I do for you, Judge?"

"A meeting, Charley. How about this evening?"

"I'm pretty busy. Besides, you already know my answer."

"Then think of it as a courtesy. I belong to a health club downtown here. The Riverside Club. Do you know it?"

"No, I don't."

"It's small, but quite charming. Exercise room, sauna, and a large pool. It's part of the Riverside Hotel complex, right near where the old stove works used to be."

I did know the hotel.

"I'll meet you there at say, six. We'll have a nice swim."

"Look, Judge—"

"Be there, Charley. I'll leave word that you are my guest. There's parking right next to the place."

"This is a waste of my time and yours."

"It's an obligation. That's how I feel. More important, that's how my friend feels. I'll see you at six."

"Look, this is getting out of hand—" I abruptly stopped when I realized he had hung up.

The balance of the morning was taken up with talking to the media. I made several appointments for television interviews, although I wouldn't permit anyone direct access to my client.

Two minutes on television and a lynch mob would come after the arrogant Dr. Stewart, innocent or not. I would have to be the front man, just as before. Whether it would do any good or not remained to be seen.

At noon I called Judge Bishop. He had just come off the bench. I reported on Mallow's request for a meeting.

"The Riverside Club. I don't know it. It must be new," he said.

"He wants a swim and a talk," I said.

"Well, Charley, that can't hurt, can it? As I say, it might be interesting to see just how far he means to carry this thing. I'm certainly curious, even if you aren't."

"It won't change my answer. I already told him that."

There was a pause. "No harm done then, eh? Meet with him, Charley, then let me know what happened."

"Judge, if I dance with him much longer it might look like I'm a part of what he has in mind. People still go to jail for criminal conspiracy, you know."

He chuckled. "That's only if they agree to something illegal. You say you won't, so you have nothing to worry about. Isn't that right?"

Judge Bishop hung up.

It seemed to me that recently people were hanging up on me a lot.

I didn't have time for lunch. I gave an interview to a crew from a Detroit television station. They didn't like the lighting in my office so we did the interview out on the river boardwalk.

A small crowd gathered as the woman reporter asked me inane questions about Miles Stewart and the charge against him. My answers were probably as inane as her questions, but I hoped they would sound positive, if not entirely rational, when shown on the evening news broadcast. I also knew my shot would be about seven seconds long. No great harm or help can be done in seven seconds. I felt safe enough.

After they left, I went back to the office. Mrs. Fenton was on the phone constantly now, sounding like an efficient bookie just before race time.

She screened the calls and I took those I thought might do some good. Others, the so-called tabloids and tabloid-like television shows, I ducked.

At first it was fun, but then I began to tire of talking about Dr. Miles Stewart and the late Sean Cronin. It was like playing the same phonograph record over and over.

Mrs. Fenton stepped into my office. "I have a man on the phone who says he is an old friend of yours."

"What's his name?"

"He wouldn't give it."

"It's probably one of those tabloid people. Just take a message."

"I tried that. He said he had no connection with the press. He appears to be quite insistent."

This is a fact of life: publicity always draws kooks. So

far we hadn't attracted any, but I thought the streak was about to end.

"Put him on," I said. "I'll get rid of him."

She went back to her desk and my phone rang.

"Sloan," I said curtly.

There was a short pause, and then he spoke. "Well, Charles. It's been a while. How have you been?"

It was like an electric shock. I did know the voice, and I knew it very well.

"I see you're once again in the newspapers. It must be terribly exciting."

"Look—"

"No names, Charles. Not over the phone. You know who this is." He chuckled. "Just being prudent, you might say."

My free hand was shaking. I was talking to Judge Franklin Palmer.

"You're meeting with our mutual friend today, Charles. He relayed your concerns that you think he might be acting entirely on his own." He paused. "The purpose of this call is to assure you that he speaks directly for me. Do you understand that?"

"I do, but I can't believe it."

"Well, please do. We go way back, you and I, Charles. This is as embarrassing for me as I'm sure it is for you. However, I've done some favors in the past for you. Now, you get the chance to do one for me."

"Judge—"

"Charles. No names, no titles. Everything that needs to be said will be said by our mutual friend."

"But—"

"Please meet with him. Oh, there is one other thing. Something of a personal matter."

"What's that?"

"My daughter, Charles. No offense, but she is less than half your age. I think it would be wise if you and she broke off anything that might be starting. She's young, and the whole world is ahead of her. I like you, Charles, but I don't think you're quite suitable for my daughter."

"Nor do I, frankly."

"Good. Unpleasant business, but it had to be said." He paused. "Good-bye, Charles."

I held the phone in my hand long after the connection had been severed.

I knew his voice the way I knew my own. There was no possibility that the call was faked.

I felt like crying.

Much worse, I felt like I needed a drink.

Which made me, of course, rush out of the office.

"Where are you going?" Mrs. Fenton called after me.

"For a walk," I yelled back. "A long walk."

20

The walk had been very long, and by the end of it that sudden urge to plunge into a bottle had mostly gone. Not entirely. If it didn't completely let up, I knew I could find a meeting somewhere later.

I got in my car and headed for Detroit. I had tried to reach Judge Bishop, but he was gone for the day and there was no answer at his home.

I was completely on my own.

I took the expressway exit that would get me to Jefferson, one of the few main streets in Detroit that didn't look as if a terrible battle had been recently fought there.

There was new development down along the river. Some old warehouses and breweries had been turned into trendy hotels and apartments, complete with a sprinkling of high-end restaurants. Most of the complexes were in foreclosure, and the restaurants existed in the shadow of the neighborhood crime, relying on valet parking and their own private police to lure customers with the sometimes tenuous promise of security.

The early evening traffic was heavy and I wiggled my way over to the right-hand lane.

Once, in the area just before the bridge to Belle Isle, there had been two huge factories, a rubber plant that made the tires for all of Detroit's many makes of cars, and a stove works that had existed before the turn of the century, making a brand of cast-iron stove that was standard in kitchens from one coast to the other.

But it became more economical to make the tires elsewhere, and the stoves. Rubber was out, as was cast iron. Like old trees, the plants died, and were vacant for years. Then the bulldozers came, leveling the huge old structures and leaving behind a mass of crumbled bricks. And a lot of memories.

The factories had been located on the river so that the raw materials could be brought in by boat; the razed land became prime riverfront, or as prime as it gets in Detroit.

The Riverside Hotel now occupied the site of the old stove works, looking like a mountain of glass and steel girders. It was almost new, just a year or two old, but had been around long enough not to draw sufficient customers for the optimistic developers to pay the bank note. Now the bank owned it.

I found the health club. It was a one-story building standing just across from the hotel's main entrance. It was all brick, with windows set high up near the top of the roof. The architect had tried to make it blend with the hotel, but somehow he had missed. It looked like an orphan cub, discarded and pushed aside by its hulking and embarrassed mother.

The parking lot was attended, so I felt reasonably safe in leaving the car.

When I got inside, I found a small counter and a bored woman doing a crossword puzzle. She deigned to look up when I entered.

"My name is Sloan, Charles Sloan. I'm looking for Judge Jeffrey Mallow."

She blinked a couple of times as if I was speaking a foreign language. "Oh, yeah," she said finally. "He said you'd be here."

She shoved an open book at me. "Just sign the register, there, as a guest."

I did as instructed and she bent over and came up with several large towels, a small swimsuit, and an elastic wristband with a key attached.

She handed them to me. "The judge is in the members' lounge. That door over there. He's waiting for you."

"Thanks."

I walked past several stationary bicycles and through the door she indicated. It was like a small hotel lobby, mostly leather furniture. He was sitting in a large chair reading *The Wall Street Journal.*

"You're late," he said in that deep voice.

"Traffic. It's a long drive from Pickeral Point."

He didn't seem impressed.

"Ever been here before?" he asked.

"No, never."

"I'll give you the twenty-five-cent tour."

I wasn't allowed an option. He led the way up several stairs to an exercise room. It was all chrome and pulleys and looked like a space-age torture chamber.

"They got every goddamned exercise machine known to man here. You can build up every part of your body except your dick, and I suppose that's next. C'mon."

Mallow was wearing a dark blue jacket and gray trousers. I followed, clutching my towels and equipment.

"This is why I'm a member," he said, leading me into a sparkling shower room. "Here." He pulled open a door and cedar-laden air poured out. Steam, but it smelled like a forest.

"This is the best damned sauna in the city. Unlike you, Charley, I still drink a bit. If I drink too much, I come over here, take a steam and a few laps in the pool, and I'm as good as new."

He led the way through an open door. "These are the lockers. Your key has a number, use that one." He threw open a narrow locker and began to undress. He did it with purpose, not hurriedly, but as something he wanted to get done.

I located my locker and did the same.

As I disrobed, I was aware that he was looking at me. Mallow—who seemed even larger out of his clothes—was mostly fat and hair, with thighs that were thick and clogged and calves that were riddled with ribs. He stood there naked.

I slipped out of my shorts.

"Turn around, Charley," he said.

"What?"

"Turn around. I want to take a look."

"You haven't started batting from the other side of the plate, have you, Judge?"

He chuckled. "No. I'm just checking for wires. You're clean. Now you look."

He slowly turned, then slipped into black swim trunks. I did the same.

"You going to wear your watch?" he asked.

I held it up for inspection. "It's a diver's watch," I said. "Waterproof to three hundred feet."

He studied it. "Cheap."

"I don't know. It was a gift from a client. I didn't ask."

He smiled. "That model runs about a hundred and a half." He held up his wrist. "This is what you want,

Charley. A Rolex Submariner. It's good to a thousand feet."

"I seldom get down that far," I said.

He laughed, becoming more of his booming, self-assured self.

"C'mon, I'll show you the pool."

I followed him through yet another door and up two tiled steps. The pool was Olympic size. A large round Jacuzzi occupied one part of the huge vaulted room. Enormous windows looked out on the hotel.

"Why are we the only ones here?" I asked.

"This place isn't a grand success. Once in a while the hotel guests use the place, and sometimes some succulent young members show up, but usually you have the place to yourself."

He ambled toward the pool. "If you want to join, now's the time. They've cut their rates to practically nothing. Interested?"

"It's too far for me," I said.

He hopped into the pool. At this end, it was about waist level. "It's like bathwater. Come on in."

I hoped he was right, and he was.

"We could use the Jacuzzi over there, but the goddamn bubbles make it hard to hear. This suit you?"

I nodded.

"Want to do a lap or two?"

"You go ahead. I'm not much of a swimmer."

"Suit yourself."

Despite his large size, he moved easily through the water with a powerful stroke. He swam up and back twice, and then stopped. He shook his hair and then shook off the water from his face.

"I tell you, it makes you feel like a million bucks."

We were standing almost shoulder to shoulder. He leaned back against the pool and let himself down until only his head was out of the water. He smiled up at me.

"Frank called you, right?"

"He did."

The smile became a grin. "See, you thought I was pulling something. I'm surprised you didn't trust me, Charley. But at least now you know this isn't a one-man operation."

I nodded. "Yes."

"Surprised, weren't you?"

"Yes."

He laughed. "The world is full of surprises, Charley. Now here's the deal."

"I don't want the deal, whatever it is."

"Have the courtesy to at least listen."

"Go on."

"Frank and I discussed this very carefully. Your fee, as you said, should run somewhere around three hundred thousand. Frank said the original deal we offered was unfair to you, since you would have to pay taxes on the entire amount."

"Thoughtful of him."

"Don't be a smart-ass, Charley. Just listen." His voice seemed to echo off the surface of the water, only inches away from his mouth. "Frank figures that after taxes you would have roughly two hundred thousand. We split that. You get one hundred thousand and we get one hundred thousand."

"Look—"

He shook his head. "Wait, I'm not through. That's a lot of money up front, both Frank and I realize that. What we need from you is fifty thousand in cash now, and the rest when the decision comes down. We trust you, and that arrangement is fair."

"It's bribery."

He smiled up at me. "I look on it as a kind of insurance premium."

I slowly shook my head. "I want no part of this. If you

want to make a deal, I'll step out of the case and you can talk to Mickey Monk directly." I didn't want Mickey or McHugh on my conscience.

"No way, Charley. We deal only with you. We trust you, both Frank and me. Like I told you, Monk isn't a part of this. Monk isn't one of us, Charley, he isn't one of the old St. Benedict crowd. We take care of each other. Besides, Monk's got a big mouth on him and he's a drunk. We only deal with people we know are discreet."

"So I'm not the first?"

He eyed me. "It's a tough world. No, you're not the first."

"You'll get caught. Eventually. You know that, don't you?"

"No. We are extremely careful. We have far too much to lose." He ducked his head beneath the water, then came up and snorted out water. "Here's the deal. For the money, you get to write the opinion yourself. Frank will put it into his own words of course, but you'll be the author. Chene will vote with Frank, so the decision will be two to one. It'll look better that way."

"It's still no deal."

He paused and looked down at the other side of the pool. "You owe Franklin Palmer a lot, Charley. He got you your job on the court. He saved your fucking law license. What kind of a price would you put on what he's done for you over the years? It would be a hell of a lot more than a mere one hundred thousand, and you know it."

"Maybe, but—"

"He's the one who needs the help now. So do I, for that matter. Look, no injustice is being done in this case, is there? Ford has deep pockets. No one gets hurt."

"Why does Judge Palmer need the money? I've seen his boat."

Mallow laughed. The sound reverberated over the

pool's smooth surface. "That's part of his problem, the goddamned boat."

"Oh?"

He sighed. "It's a long story and none of your god-damned business but I'm going to tell you anyway. You remember our famous alumnus Jacques Mease, the fucking financier, right?"

"Of course."

"Well, Franklin and I made the mistake of getting too close to that rotten son of a bitch. I didn't invest with him, but Franklin did. Made money, too, a truckload of it, at least on paper."

He appeared to be looking at something only he could see. "Franklin is a smart man, but not too smart in this case. He bet the ranch, so to speak. It looked good, I have to admit that. He used the paper profit to finance the boat and the life-style that goes along with it. He loves that yacht club crap, always has."

He sighed again. "Franklin was like the rest of us, a poor boy to begin with. He really gets into those clubs and those honors. Becoming commodore was a much bigger thing to him than becoming judge. The big boat was part of it. He finally went all the way out on a limb and bought the thing he has now.

"When Mease took the fall on the insider trading, Franklin was clean of any criminal charges but he lost every goddamned cent. The boat is mortgaged for more than its worth."

He looked up at me. "Commodores don't go bankrupt, Charley. It's a matter of pride with Franklin. He's going to work his way out of this. He retires in three years. I know what he's going to do. He'll unload the boat, when he can afford to, buy a place in Florida and live out his life like a make-believe nautical king, prancing around those fancy clubs, commodore flag, rank, and all. All he'll need down there is his pension and a little extra."

"That explains him. What about you?"

He stood up and towered over me. "You probably already know what happened. I quit the court to be Mease's private attorney. The firm that hired me tossed me out the second he was indicted. And, I've had a few other problems. I need some money, too, Charley. Badly, as a matter of fact."

He looked down at me. "We wouldn't do this, Franklin and I, unless it was absolutely necessary."

I wondered what Caitlin Palmer would think of her father if she found out he was soliciting bribes to fix cases.

"Charley, look at it this way. You can probably get the entire fifty thousand from Doctor Death. Jesus, that guy must be a nut case, but he's got money. Again, no one gets hurt. Right?"

"If I did decide to go along, and I'm not saying that I will, when would you need the money?"

He laughed; it was a laugh that reverberated throughout the pool, the water, the strange circumstances of this meeting. "Jesus, don't you listen? We're in desperate trouble here, Charley. We need the money like yesterday."

I thought about Will McHugh. I wondered what he was watching on his blurry television set. I wondered where Mickey Monk might be. Probably at some bar and well on his tortured road to oblivion.

Monk and McHugh. They had gambled everything on me.

"Just so you know where you stand, Charley. This isn't a bluff. Franklin said to tell you just that. No money and you lose the case."

"A nice sense of justice."

"Also," Mallow growled, "in case you're thinking of blowing the whistle, it's just your word against mine. They'll think you're up to something. Franklin and I will both be sure you get nailed, if only to protect ourselves. Clear?"

"Very."

"We might have to do that anyway, if you don't agree. It's a tough world, Charley. We have to protect ourselves."

I needed to talk to Bishop, or to someone. I did owe Judge Palmer a great deal. And, as Mallow had said, no one would be hurt.

Except maybe me. I wouldn't be a criminal lawyer anymore.

I would be a criminal.

"I'll let you know," I said, climbing out of the pool.

"You go ahead, Charley. I'm going to swim some more."

I went in, back to the locker rooms.

I showered. I dressed.

But I felt dirty.

21

The urge to drink had returned full force. I tried not to think about it. I drove to Judge Bishop's home without stopping to call. Most pay telephones are located in establishments that serve liquor. I didn't need any extra temptation.

He wasn't home. A light was on, but that was the only sign of life. I rang the bell and I could hear the empty echo inside.

I needed a meeting the way a storm-tossed boat needs a harbor. Like most members of AA, I know most of the locations and times without having to check. There was a regular meeting in Grosse Pointe only a few blocks away, in a school. I would be late. It would already be in progress, but that made no difference. I was just glad of someplace to go; I knew I could go there.

I went but I didn't participate. You don't have to if you don't want to. I sat next to a well-dressed man who was obviously drunk. No one looked askance, we all had walked in those shoes.

He seemed to be trying very hard to pay attention. I noticed that because I wasn't.

There is a physical calm to just being at an AA meeting, even if your mind is somewhere else. I found that calm now and relished it, but my thoughts were full of Mallow and Palmer and what I might be able to do to escape the situation, if there was an escape.

The drunk got up and made a little speech. It was a nice speech, although the logic was about as off as he was. No one laughed. It was too much like looking in a mirror.

I left before the formal part of the meeting was over. I saw a lawyer I knew sitting in the back row. We both nodded and smiled, like members of any other exclusive club might do. AA was exclusive. You had to be a drunk to get in.

I drove to Bishop's house and tried again, but he still wasn't there so I slowly drove back to Pickeral Point.

WHEN I GOT HOME I thought about calling Sue Gillis. But I knew I would be using her to get over a rough patch, and that didn't seem fair. She deserved better than that. I couldn't tell her about my problem. She was, despite everything else, a cop.

My problem was whether or not I was about to be in the position of becoming a criminal. It wasn't the kind of thing to be discussed with a police officer, or anyone else for that matter, except perhaps a wise counselor, someone like Judge Bishop.

It wasn't as if I couldn't raise the money. I had my

thirty thousand plus the thirty thousand retainer Dr. Death had given me. Getting the fifty thousand was merely a trip to the bank.

Back at my apartment, I sipped a Coke and watched some old reruns on television. I tuned in to an old "Dragnet" episode. There, everything was crystal clear. It was a black-and-white show, both literally and in terms of issues. Sergeant Joe Friday knew right from wrong, and there was no in-between for him, or for the people who wrote the teleplay, or for that matter, the vast audience that once watched "Dragnet."

I had cut a few corners in my career, every trial lawyer has. But there was an ethical line, sometimes hard to see, but it was there, and I had never crossed it. I had never bribed anyone or attempted to fix a case. I was repulsed by lawyers and judges who did, and I felt nothing but contempt for them.

I wondered now whether it was my ethical sense or the sense of self-preservation that stayed my hand the few times in the past when I could have easily stepped over that line.

The law protected itself. Like cancer, corruption was slashed away when it was found. And, also like cancer, sometimes it was buried deeply. But a judge or a lawyer who took or extended a bribe, when caught and convicted, always did time. There was never any probation, or any sentencing break of that kind. Prison was a certainty for anyone who was caught doing what was being asked of me.

When I had been a prosecutor, and during those times when I was trying a defendant who might have inspired pity in the jury, I always told them this: men are not hung for stealing horses, they are hung so that other men don't steal horses. In the old West, I told those juries, a man's life depended on his horse. To let a horse thief off easy was to encourage others to try their hand at the same thing. No mercy could be shown. Rough justice. But real justice, nevertheless.

The life of the court system depended on its being free of taint, so while hanging might be reserved for horse thieves, prison terms awaited judges and lawyers who corrupted the system. The same rule applied. It was done without mercy, so that other lawyers and judges wouldn't be tempted to try the same thing.

The people who wrote "Dragnet" understood that.

Everything was black and white.

I wished I was back selling shoes.

IT HAD NEVER OCCURRED to me that Judge Bishop might have been out visiting a lady friend. It should have. He seemed embarrassed when I told him over the phone that I had stopped by his place the night before and hadn't found him in.

He might look like a bishop, but he was a widower, and he was as human as the next man. But if he was flustered, it didn't last long.

"So you met with him," he said.

"Yes."

"And?"

I briefly filled him in on what happened. I worried that his court phone might be tapped. It happens—and for sometimes innocent reasons—but I went ahead and gave him the details of the meeting anyway. My risk priorities were changing daily.

"You got a problem, Charley," he said when I had finished.

"You're telling me."

He paused for a moment. "If you don't go along, do you really think they'd accuse you of anything?"

"Mallow said they would. He said it would be self-defense. He sounded like he meant it. He said they were both desperate men."

"Sounds that way," Judge Bishop said. "I need some time to think about this, Charley. Maybe a day or two."

"They said they want a fast answer."

"Stall them, if it comes to that. Let me put my thinking cap on and see what I can come up with. Then, you and I can sit down and thrash this thing out. Okay?"

"Fine. I appreciate your help, Judge, I really do."

"Don't be foolish. Glad to do it. Sit tight, Charley, and I'll get back to you. And don't worry."

It was like being told not to breathe.

STASH OLESKY PHONED almost on the heels of my conversation with Judge Bishop.

"What can I do for you, Stash?"

"When did you plan to run the Becky Harris plea past Evola?"

"I don't know. There's no real hurry."

He grunted. "That depends. Look, you know I handle the major felony trials for this office, right?"

"Yeah. So?"

"Well, the citizens have been more active than usual and I'm looking at a long list of trials. Some murders, some robberies, and the occasional rape. Some will plead, some not. Frankly, I'm trying to get rid of the possible pleas so I can arrange my schedule."

"Efficient."

"Yeah. Besides, my new employer wants all major cases moved along fast so he can go to the voters with a record of accomplishment, a nice long list of convictions."

"I'd rather put off facing Evola," I said. "I don't expect to gain any ground with him. In fact, it might be a little painful for me."

"So's a dentist, but it's best to get it over with. Do you think the passage of time will help your position?"

"I suppose not. He's lurking over there in the courthouse, waiting for me to show myself."

Stash chuckled. "Yeah. This might be fun to watch."

"Just so we understand each other, the plea I offer will be manslaughter with the provision that she serve no more than six months."

"Plus she never comes back here. That's what Mrs. Wordley wanted," Olesky added.

"That would be part of the deal. Have you talked it over with your boss?"

"I did. He said to go along only if Evola approves every detail. My worthy employer has the fighting spirit of an inchworm."

"They can be fierce if cornered."

"Sure. Well, what about it? You want to go to the dentist or not?"

"Would you count it as a personal favor?"

"I would."

"Would that get me special consideration in the future?"

"No, but you would have the warm glow associated with helping your fellow man."

"If Evola doesn't go along, I'm going to trial, Stash."

"Look at it this way. He gets to do it to you one way or the other. Might as well put your toe in the water now and see what happens."

"How do you want to work it?" I asked.

"I can call and set up a meeting. Or you can."

"It would be best, Stash, if you did it."

"You going to be there at your office for a while?"

"Yeah."

"I'll call and see what I can do. I'll get back to you one way or the other."

It didn't take long. Stash called almost immediately.

"He'll see us tomorrow afternoon. Two o'clock, sharp."

"Did you talk to Evola?"

"Yeah."

"How did he sound?"

Stash laughed. "Like a tiger being told someone was bringing him a nice fat antelope."

"Oh, great."

"I'll see you tomorrow, Charley. Wear a pie plate over your ass. You may need it."

AFTER LUNCH I WENT to the jail to see Becky Harris. She sat behind the glass and tried to smile. She looked as if every day she was getting older.

"How are you doing, Becky?"

"I'm all right."

"Are you being treated well?"

"Mostly, yes."

"Becky, tomorrow I'm going to see the judge who is assigned to your case, Judge Evola."

She nodded. "I know him. He used to be a regular customer at the inn."

"Yes. Well, I'm going to try to work out a plea."

"I told you I'll plead guilty. You don't need to work out anything."

"It's my job, Becky. If you approve, I'll offer a plea of guilty to manslaughter on the provision that you serve no more than six months."

"I don't care, one way or the other. Work out whatever you want."

"As part of the plea, you would have to promise never to return to Pickeral Point."

For the first time she showed some interest. "Why would that be?"

"It would be a condition."

"I understand that, but why?"

I wondered how best to approach the subject and decided head-on might be best. "Mrs. Wordley insists on it."

"Did you talk to her?"

"I had to. I couldn't work out the plea unless she agreed. It's still up to the judge, but she was the first hurdle."

"Does she hate me?"

"No. I don't think so. As you told me, it wasn't a happy marriage. I guess she just doesn't want to risk running into you when you get out."

In what looked like understanding, she nodded her head.

"Where would you go, Becky, if I can work this out?"

She thought for a moment. "Cleveland, I suppose. I have a sister still living there. I could probably get work as a waitress."

She seemed to brighten for the first time.

"Well, the probabilities are that the judge won't go along, so please don't get your hopes up. Please."

"Hopes." She shrugged. "There's no hope in a place like this."

"I'll be seeing the judge tomorrow. In the unlikely event he will agree, he may want to take the plea tomorrow afternoon."

She again tried something that looked like a smile. "I have no other appointments."

"If he takes the plea, he will ask you if you shot and killed Howard Wordley, and you will have to answer yes, without qualification. Do you understand?"

"Yes."

"Okay. We'll see what happens. If it's no, I'll stop back tomorrow and tell you."

I stood up. She looked at me with those haunted eyes. "You're doing a lot of work for me," she said. "I can't pay."

"The ring's plenty, Becky. Don't worry about it."

"It's probably not even a real diamond."

"It is," I lied. "I'm being well paid for my services, Becky. Don't worry."

"That makes me feel a whole lot better."

I WENT BACK TO MY OFFICE. Mrs. Fenton handed me the messages. Judge Bishop was not among the callers. Nor was Mallow.

I had some office work to do. Nothing particularly challenging, just some provisions for a will and a review of a real estate case.

"I'm expecting a call from a Judge Bishop," I said to Mrs. Fenton. "If he calls, put him right through."

There were some calls to be made to clients, and I did that. There were some calls to be made to media people, and I did a few of those, but only ones that I thought might be helpful to Miles Stewart, M.D.

The will provisions were easy, and I dictated them to Mrs. Fenton. She would fire up the computer and insert them into our standard language. When printed out, it would look like I had spent three months slaving over getting just the right words. It helped justify the fee.

The real estate problem required not a lot of work, and I did that without having really to think about it.

The day passed quickly enough and Mrs. Fenton went home, which gave me the opportunity of sitting around the office with the lights out, watching the river.

There were a few calls. I listened to the answering machine take the messages, in case The Bishop called. But he didn't.

Finally, I packed it in, grabbed a quick sandwich at my favorite local restaurant, and then headed to Detroit for the usual Thursday night meeting.

I was tempted to count the Grosse Pointe meeting as a substitute, but I was in parlous waters, and I knew it would help my general state of anxiety if I went again.

And this one was with people whom I knew and liked.

Tomorrow I would have to face Judge Mark Evola. It wouldn't be pleasant. A big shot of courage was needed, and the AA meeting was just the place to get it.

FRIDAY CAME AND I WENT to the office. Perhaps if the sun had been shining I might have felt better. But it was dark, drizzling, and grim. If I had something scheduled in court it would have helped pass the time, but nothing was on my docket.

Judge Bishop was notable by his telephonic absence.

Time was running and Mallow would want an answer.

My anxiety was running, too, so I left the office, grabbed a quick lunch, and killed some minutes over coffee until it was time to go to court.

Usually, Friday mornings were set aside for motions in our circuit court. Mornings were hectic. But judges tried to dispose of most business so they could sneak out early and get a head start on the weekend.

Evola must have swept things clean quickly. I got up to his courtroom a few minutes before two o'clock and found I was the only customer in the deserted courtroom.

The clerk glanced up at me.

"We're closed," he growled.

"I'm waiting for Stash Olesky. We have an appointment with the judge."

He frowned. He knew me. He had been the clerk to a succession of judges. For whatever reason, he'd decided rudeness was the best defense against a hostile world and had developed it into an art form without parallel.

"Stupid time to see any judge, on a Friday," he growled again. "Stupid."

"The judge set it up," I said, smiling. "But you're right, it was stupid."

He didn't like that, and his deepening frown damn near drowned his eyes.

At that moment Stash came in carrying the Harris file.

"I'll let the judge know you're here," the clerk snapped and departed toward the judge's chambers.

"Got your pie plate in place?" Stash asked.

"Double strength," I replied.

The clerk returned. "The judge will see you now. Go right on in."

MARK EVOLA HADN'T CHANGED MUCH since he'd become a judge. He was nearing forty, but he looked much younger. His blond hair and blue eyes made his smooth face look babylike. He didn't stand when we came in, just sat there in shirtsleeves behind his large desk. Had he stood, he would have towered above both of us. At six foot six, Judge Evola was probably the tallest judge in the state.

His chambers had been decorated with the same photos he used to have on his walls when he had been prosecutor. They showed him during his basketball days as a star at Michigan State University. He looked exactly the same, except the teeth he had now were made by a dentist, the originals having been left in a number of famous elbows under the basket. The other photos were of Evola with politicians, living and dead. The walls were full of grinning faces.

Evola smiled warmly at Olesky, flashing his perfectly constructed teeth. When he looked at me, the smile was there, but then it diminished, like a light slowly going out.

"Sit down," he said, nodding toward chairs just in front of his desk. "What can I do for you boys?"

Stash opened the file. "It's about the Becky Harris case."

"So you said on the phone," Evola replied. "What do you have in mind?"

"As you know," Stash said, "the Harris woman has been charged with second-degree murder in the death of Howard Wordley."

"Right."

"Mr. Sloan has offered to plead Ms. Harris guilty to manslaughter, if he can be assured that she will serve no more than six months. Also, as a condition, Ms. Harris agrees not to return to Pickeral Point after being released."

"How's the widow feel about that?" Evola asked.

"She's agreed to it. I have it in writing."

"Let me see it."

Stash gave the document to the judge, who studied it for a moment, and then handed it back.

"And how does your boss, my successor, feel about accepting this offered plea?" Evola asked Olesky.

"It's okay with him if it's okay with you."

Evola looked at me. "And your client?"

"She'll plead under those conditions."

"I'll bet," Evola said.

We waited while Evola studied the ceiling. "Becky Harris used to wait on me on many occasions when she was working at the inn. I remember her as a quiet, decent person." He looked at Olesky. "Does she have a record?"

"One arrest and conviction. In Cleveland. A misdemeanor, accosting and soliciting."

"A mistake," I said.

Evola looked at me. "Oh? It's still on the record though, is it not?"

I nodded.

"I knew Howard Wordley, too," Evola went on. "He was always trying to sell me one of his fancy cars. He'd talk to me and hot eye my wife while he was doing it. I wasn't exactly fond of him. Still, shooting car dealers is a crime, although some may think it shouldn't be."

Olesky laughed, but he was only being polite. Lawyers are always quick with polite laughter for judges who are in the market.

"What's your opinion, Stash? You used to work for me. Give it to me just like you used to do, hair and all."

Olesky nodded. "I recommend the plea. Looking at it from all angles, justice is served. Becky Harris isn't likely to shoot anyone ever again. A long prison term would serve no real purpose, given all the circumstances."

Evola nodded. Then he looked at me. "I'll tell you what I'll do. If your client will plead guilty to manslaughter, I'll sentence her to one to fifteen years. If she doesn't get in trouble, she'll be out in six months. That suit you?"

"How about allowing her to serve the time in a halfway house. Like Stash says, she really isn't a criminal in the usual sense."

Evola shook his head. "I'll do this. I'll recommend that after three months she be considered for a halfway house. It will be up to the prison boys, but they'll probably go along. They usually do. Also, I'll make it a condition that when she's released she can't return to Pickeral Point. Now, that's probably illegal, but if no one has any objection, it should be no problem."

He studied me for a moment. "Well, Charley?" It was the first time he had used my name. "Is that agreeable?"

"Yes."

He nodded. "Good. Stash, run out and have the sheriff bring Ms. Harris over here. Tell my clerk to hunt up a court reporter. We'll take the plea now. I'll put all the conditions on record. I'll have to wait for a probation report before actually sentencing her, but that'll be just a formality."

"Okay, Judge." Stash got up.

I did too, but Evola called me back.

"Close the door on your way out," he called to Olesky.

For what seemed like a very long time, we sat in silence.

"You thought I was going to give you a hard time, didn't you, Charley?"

"It had crossed my mind."

"Because of the Harwell trial," he smiled, those big teeth smiling, taking over the room. But his eyes weren't smiling.

"I was thinking about you yesterday, Charley, and that trial. You know, if I had won that thing, I'd be in Congress now. I mean it, I would have won easily if it wasn't for the egg you left on my face."

"It was a fair trial."

"Bullshit. You pulled every dirty trick in the book, and a few the book didn't even know about. I wouldn't have minded losing so much if it had been fair."

"It was fair."

"Anyway, I was thinking about you. I heard on the grapevine that our junior senator has cancer. Terminal, I'm told. He won't be running again. You know what that means?"

"Outside of what you've just said, no."

"It means that if I were in Congress now I would have a real shot at that Senate seat, Charley. A real shot. And, if I got in, God knows how far I might have gone."

"You can't blame me—"

"Oh, but I can, and I do. You know what I'm going to be doing tonight, Charley?"

"I have no idea."

"I'm going to the Marina City Knights of Columbus for the Friday night fish fry. This judgeship is an elected job, Charley, and I have to spend most of my nights shaking hands with the voters. Tonight it's the fish fry. Tomorrow, I have to go to two Polish weddings."

"So?"

"If I were a congressman, I'd be in Washington, probably attending embassy parties, shaking hands with the people who rule the world. Quite a difference, wouldn't you say?"

"And you blame it all on me?"

"You bet I do. This is a good job, being a judge. I'll be doing it for the rest of my life. That's a lot of fish fries, Charley. No ambassadors, no kings—just a lot of fish and a lot of polka. All because of your dirty tricks, Charley."

"If you feel that way, why are you going along with this plea?"

The smile became almost evil. "I'm going to get you, Charley, and I'm going to get you good. And it's not going to be over some little murder case that means nothing to you. I'm going to wait until it's something where your fucking career hangs in the fucking balance, and then I'm going to nail your ass once and for all."

The smile had gone and I was looking into two very angry blue eyes.

"Good of you to warn me."

"You knew it anyway. This is just confirmation of what any idiot would know. I'm a patient man, Charley, and I can wait. But someday it'll happen. And it'll pay me back for every fucking bite of greasy fish I will have to endure for the rest of my life."

Before I could reply, Olesky was back. He didn't knock, he just walked right in. I don't know what he expected to find. Maybe my throat in the judge's hands.

He seemed relieved when he found us where he had left us.

"The defendant is here," Olesky said "So is the court reporter. We're all ready to go."

Evola nodded. "Okay, you fellows go on in. I'll be there in a moment."

I had just enough time to explain the one- to fifteen-year sentence to Becky.

Evola came out in his robe. It wasn't exactly a crowd.

There was Becky and the two matrons who had brought her over. The clerk still looked annoyed. The court reporter and Olesky and myself were the only other people in the courtroom.

Evola did a quick and efficient job, explaining Becky's rights to her and telling her what could happen if she were going to plead guilty.

He did ask her if she shot and killed Howard Wordley.

She sobbed softly as she admitted the crime.

Formal sentencing was set. Evola put the plea agreement on the record, and Becky was escorted away, tears still streaming down her very tired face.

The court reporter packed in her machine.

Evola stood up and started to leave the bench. Then he stopped for a moment and looked at me. A great toothy smile animated his face. "I trust you won't forget what I said, Mr. Sloan." He paused, as if for dramatic effect.

"Jeez, I'm sorry, Judge. What was it again?"

The smile blew out like a cut electrical line and Evola stalked back to his chambers.

"A couple of old friends," Olesky said, "meeting once again."

"Ah, let's hear it for nostalgia. May I buy you a coffee, Mr. Olesky?"

"And a sweet roll?"

"Anything your heart desires."

"A bribe, is it?"

Suddenly, it was a word that killed all the fun I was having.

took a walk before I went back to the office. Along the river there is a long boardwalk built by the city of Pickeral Point. It's big and wide and long and peaceful. It was built for the tourists, but the locals use it just as much.

It was still cloudy, and there was a feel of rain in the air that kept most sensible people away, except for a few fishermen, who leaned against the railing, looking off into the distance. It was a distance only they could see.

Sometimes when I feel the need for a drink, the walk along the river helps ease the urge. I didn't feel that urge now, thankfully, but I did need a dose of inner peace. I put my mind in neutral and walked.

Finally I decided I had to face the world once again. I got in my car and went back to my office.

Mrs. Fenton frowned a silent inquiry.

I knew she wanted desperately to know what happened in the Harris case, but she wasn't going to give me the satisfaction of asking.

"Looks like rain," I said.

She couldn't help it. Her face was strained as she spoke. "Did everything go all right in court?"

"You mean with Becky Harris?"

"Yes." The word was snapped out like a whip.

"Pretty well, yes."

Her eyes widened in annoyance. "What happened?"

"With Becky Harris?"

"Of course!"

It was kind of fun to rile her, but you could overdo things like that sometimes.

"Becky pled guilty to manslaughter. The judge will give her one to fifteen, but as a practical matter, she'll be out in six months."

"Six months! Claire Wordley will be furious!"

"Mrs. Wordley approved the sentence before she left."

"She did!"

"Oh yes. She didn't really care, of course. As you probably know, Mrs. Wordley has run off to Europe with a male stripper."

I went into my office without looking back. I could imagine the expressions, as much as she allowed herself, ranging from shock, disbelief, and then outrage at me.

I would have liked to look, but I didn't.

The mail and messages were, as usual, neatly piled.

Most of the messages were from the media, opposition attorneys, and court clerks. But two stood out like neon on a dark night.

Sue Gillis had called.

And so had Judge Bishop.

I called The Bishop first.

His secretary said he was just coming off the bench, so I held on. He must have come off slowly because my arm was beginning to cramp when he finally picked up the phone.

"Hello, Charles," he said with that distinctive even voice. "Sorry to keep you waiting. There was an attorney out there who wanted something signed. He finally took no for an answer. Fridays are always hectic around here."

"I remember."

"Hang on a minute, Charles, I want to close my door."

I waited.

"Charles, the reason I called is that I think I may have a solution to the problem you spoke to me about."

"That would be wonderful."

"How's your schedule tomorrow?"

"Fine. I'm clear."

"Could you meet me at my home? Say, about noon?"

"Of course. But Saturday's your golfing day. I wouldn't want to put you out."

"Oh, I think I can skip golf for a day. It looks like it might rain anyway. Noon, then?"

"I'll be there."

I sat quietly for a moment, enjoying the relief surging through me. I didn't know what kind of a solution he might offer, but it had to be better than none. It was a good feeling, like having your big brother offer to walk you past the bully at school.

Then I called Sue Gillis.

"Gillis," she said in her cop voice.

"It's me. Charley," I said.

"I was wondering if you'd call."

"Why wouldn't I?"

"I thought you might be frightened."

"Why?"

She sighed. "I had the temerity to speak the word *mar-*

riage. It was like a magician saying 'shazam,' suddenly you disappeared."

"I didn't disappear. I'm sure you've been reading about my favorite doctor. I got suddenly busy."

"Sure."

"It's true."

She didn't reply.

"Look, Sue, how about dinner tonight? We'll go to the inn. Would that make amends?"

"I can't tonight."

"Now who's disappearing?"

"It's not like that, Charley. One of the women here is having a birthday. We're taking her out to dinner."

"Okay. How about tomorrow night?"

"I didn't call to dragoon you into taking me out."

"I know that. Well, is tomorrow night okay?"

She paused. "I have some things to do, I wouldn't be ready until seven."

"Seven's fine. I'll pick you up at your place."

"Charley, you don't have to—"

"You're right, I don't. But I want to. I'll be at your apartment at seven on the dot."

This time I was the one who hung up.

I LISTENED TO A JIMMY BUFFETT TAPE on the way in, and by the time I got to the judge's street in Grosse Pointe I was completely relaxed and at ease.

It was like going to a doctor you knew for certain could cure you.

I rang the bell, and for a moment I wondered if he might have forgotten and gone out. It seemed a long time before he finally opened the door.

He was dressed almost formally, except he wore no tie. His dark blazer looked priestly enough, set against the high-collared white shirt.

"You're right on time, Charles. Come in."

"Thanks, Judge."

"Let's go down to the basement. It was built as a recre-ation room but I've converted it into a kind of office."

"Sure."

I followed him down a flight of narrow stairs.

It was a big room, paneled, with a fireplace at the far end. The only furniture consisted of some bookcases, sev-eral chairs, a desk, and a big sofa.

But it was a sofa that wasn't empty. On it sat two men who were watching as we descended.

My sense of ease and relaxation exploded like an atom bomb.

"Charles, I believe you know Harry Sabin, the chief of the attorney general's criminal division."

Sabin got up and we shook hands.

"And this is Captain Lucas Hagan of the state police."

Hagan stood up and also shook hands. I noticed that neither man had smiled.

My heart was suddenly beating at a trip wire beat.

"Sit down, gentlemen," Judge Bishop said, taking a seat behind the desk.

Harry Sabin was an old trial lawyer who had spent most of his career with the attorney general. He was short, stocky, and almost completely bald. He looked at the world from behind wire-rimmed glasses. I knew him. I had tried cases with him. He was the walking personifi-cation of the phrase "killer instinct." With gray, unblink-ing eyes, Harry didn't know what it was to retreat.

If they had dressed Lucas Hagan up as a nun, he wouldn't have fooled anyone. He was one of those men who probably looked like a cop in grade school. Big, well over six feet tall, trim and with cold brown eyes that seemed devoid of expression. At least they were as they were fixed on me.

"Charles, as I said I would, I have taken some steps to

help you out of your present difficulty. As you know, I used to be a member of the state's judicial tenure commission. I spoke to the attorney general and enlisted his help. Mr. Sabin and Captain Hagan are here today to fulfill that function."

No one, especially me, was smiling.

"I have told these gentlemen what you told me. Of course, that's obviously secondhand and they are here today to get it from the horse's mouth, as it were."

"Judge, I thought ..."

Bishop smiled that tight and small smile. "You thought, Charles, that we would meet here today, just the two of us, and I would have some magic formula for extricating you from this rather sordid business."

"That's right."

"Well, it would come to this anyway, wouldn't it? We could beat around the bush, but eventually it would become a police matter. This little meeting will save time and energy."

"Charley," Harry Sabin said, "would you mind if I taped this?"

I was still shocked. My initial reaction was to object, but given the circumstances, that seemed a little silly.

"If you wish," I said.

Lucas the cop was looking at me as if he suspected I was fooling around with his wife. His eyes were like agates.

Sabin gave the date, place, and who was present, speaking into his hand-held recorder. Then he placed it on the arm of the sofa, the one near me.

"Your name is Charles Sloan and you are an attorney at law," he said.

"Is this under oath?"

He shook his head. "No. This is just for my file." For the first time he allowed himself the ghost of a smile. "You'll notice, Charley, that I didn't read you your rights.

This is quite informal. I'm just used to doing it in the old Q-and-A form. I suppose it's the habit of a lifetime."

"I'm Charles Sloan," I said.

"You are the attorney of record in the case of McHugh versus—"

"I was hired to argue the appeal. Michael Monk is the attorney of record. He handled the trial in circuit court, which he won, by the way, and he was the author of the appellate brief."

"Why didn't he argue the case?" Sabin asked.

"Mickey bet everything he had on professional witnesses and other costs. He said he was too nervous to defend the verdict and he asked me to do it."

"You say hired? What was the agreement?"

I looked at Sabin. Those gray eyes were unblinking.

"Mickey has the case on a contingent basis. He is to get one-third of the amount of the verdict."

Sabin cut me off. "That verdict was for five million, right?"

"With interest, it comes to that, maybe a little more."

"So Monk will get at least a million and a half."

Sabin had spent most of his career with the government. State attorneys might complain about a lot of things, but overpayment wasn't one of them. Long-time government lawyers had a built-in resentment of the big fees sometimes collected by private lawyers.

"Mickey worked for years on that case. As I say, he spent every nickel he had on it and borrowed more."

"And what was the fee agreement between Monk and you?"

"Twenty percent of whatever he got."

"That would figure out to at least three hundred thousand, right?"

"Yes."

"That's a lot of money," Sabin said.

"It is."

"And your only duty was to argue the case in the court of appeals?"

"That was the agreement."

"That's not a bad wage for an hour's work, wouldn't you say?"

"Like Mickey's fee, it's payable only on winning." I looked at him. "You've argued in that court, haven't you, Harry?"

Sabin arched an eyebrow. "Hundreds of times."

"Then you know the hour spent in front of the judges requires weeks, maybe months of preparation. You have to be ready for whatever they ask."

Sabin's smile was far from warm. "So you're saying what little you did was worth the fee agreed upon."

"That's one way of looking at it."

Sabin nodded, but it wasn't a gesture of agreement. It just indicated he was changing the subject.

"All right, when did you first contact Jeffrey Mallow in relation to this matter?"

"I didn't contact him. He sought me out in St. Benedict's law library. He mentioned the case, but not by name, just that he had heard I was the lawyer on a possible big winner."

"Why did you think he brought it up?"

"Frankly, at the time I thought he might try to muscle me off of the case and try to take over himself. He is, after all, the former chief judge there."

"And you were worried about losing the possibility of all that money, right?"

"Maybe. The fee, by the way, wasn't like money in the bank. The McHugh case is one of those matters that could easily go either way on appeal."

Sabin nodded. "I know. I read the briefs before coming here. When did you next have contact with Mallow?"

I went over each step carefully, giving details as precisely as I could. Sabin asked few questions. But he did seem unusually interested in the secret court memo Mallow showed me and subsequently destroyed. Judge Bishop sat behind his desk listening, but saying nothing. The big cop asked no questions until I got to the part about the meeting at the health club.

"Give me that again, when you were stripped in the locker room, about the watches," he said, his tone not especially friendly.

"I was wearing this." I held up my wrist and showed my gift watch. "It's waterproof. Mallow said it was cheap and showed me his Rolex. His is a diver's watch."

"And you both wore your watches into the pool?" Captain Hagan asked.

"Yes, that's right."

"Did you swim?"

"No. I just stood in the pool at the shallow end. Mallow did a couple of laps before he got down to business."

"So you never got your watch wet?"

"I don't know. I don't think so."

"But he definitely dunked the fancy Rolex?"

"Yes. He wore it all the time he was swimming."

"And nobody was around?"

"No one. The only person I saw there was the woman who gave me the towels."

"So nobody was in or near the pool while you two were in it, right?"

His accusatory manner was beginning to annoy me.

"Right."

Sabin took over. "Let's go back to the phone call. You're absolutely sure it was Judge Palmer?"

"Yes."

"It might have been someone who sounded like him, someone Mallow put up to calling. Did you think of that?"

"I know Palmer's voice."

"You were his clerk, correct, in the court of appeals?"

"No. I wasn't assigned to him. But he did get me the job."

"Why?"

"I don't know. I think I impressed him. I was his student. He taught criminal law. Why I impressed him, I don't know. Anyway, I was grateful for what he did for me."

Sabin nodded. "You taught that course yourself as I understand?"

"I did. Judge Palmer got pneumonia. I taught the course for him."

"For a few weeks?"

"For the entire year he was off. At the time, he was very ill."

"Did you socialize with him?" Sabin asked.

"I was invited for dinner a few times. I saw him at law school functions. Other than that, no."

"Have you ever argued any cases, besides McHugh, before panels upon which he served?"

"A number of times."

"Win?" The word was spoken with an almost whispered suggestion, a nasty suggestion.

"I won a few. I lost a few. They were mostly criminal appeals. I was doing a lot of criminal work."

"That was before you were disbarred?" the cop asked, but it was more like an accusation.

"I was never disbarred," I said. "I was suspended from practice for a year. My license was never taken away."

"But disbarment proceedings were brought, were they not?" Sabin asked.

"Yes."

Sabin's smile was icy. "Would it be fair to say, Charley, that you escaped disbarment by the skin of your teeth?"

"That's one way of looking at it."

"But you had friends who went to bat for you," Sabin said.

"Yes. The root cause of my problems was alcohol, frankly. People who knew me knew that. The year suspension was to give me time to get a handle on my problem."

"One of the people who spoke for you was Judge Palmer," Sabin said.

"That's right."

"So did I," Judge Bishop interjected. "A number of judges did. For all his difficulty, Charley was known as a good lawyer."

"You went into a rehabilitation program."

"A drunk tank. Yes. I've been in Alcoholics Anonymous since."

"No drinking, not even one?" Sabin smiled.

"No." There had been one time, but it hadn't been voluntary, and I didn't count it as a slip, the term AA people use when we fall off the wagon.

"You were in serious financial difficulty when you were suspended," Sabin said.

"I had managed to drink away every penny I had."

"Did you go bankrupt?"

"No. I paid my debts. It took a while, but I did it."

"What did you do for that suspension year?"

"I sold shoes for a while, at a store in a mall. Then I sold real estate."

"Make money?"

"I barely survived, frankly."

"And now you're back on your feet."

"I'm getting there. Or I like to think I am. I support a daughter at college and run a one-man office. Sometimes it's a squeak, but I manage to get by."

"So, money is very important to you," Sabin asked, not smiling.

"Sure is. Isn't it for you, Harry? Or has the attorney general gotten open-handed with you people?"

Harry laughed, but didn't answer.

"Mallow said he and Palmer needed money," the cop said. "Did you believe him?"

"No reason not to," I replied. "I told you what he said."

"When it became apparent a bribe was being solicited, Charley, why didn't you contact the police yourself?"

I hesitated for a moment. "It's complicated. My primary duty is to my client. It's up to me to do everything possible, and legal, to win for him. To be candid, I didn't know exactly what to do."

"So you thought about paying the bribe," said Hagan.

"Maybe, not for long, though."

"Why?" Captain Hagan's eyes seemed even colder.

"The obvious answer is that to do so is a felony. But it goes beyond that. Maybe it's the way I was raised, or maybe it's how I think, but it's something I can't do. It may not be on the same level as being a child molester, but in my mind it comes close. Any judge or lawyer who does it is rotten. I think that way now, and I've always thought that way.

"Look, I've done favors and I've had favors done for me in courts and cases, but never for money. Corruption is like a disease. If you touch it, you got it. And, eventually, you'll die of it."

Sabin forced his mouth to do something that approximated a smile. "A pretty speech, Charley. But this isn't a courtroom, is it? And there's no jury present. So why did you contact Judge Bishop instead of us?"

"Frankly, I was trying to figure a way out so there would be no bribe and yet the case would not be lost."

"What did you think Judge Bishop might be able to do?"

"I don't know. I was hoping he might be able to do something."

The smile had vanished entirely from Sabin's face. "Like what? Call Palmer and tell him to back off, to pay the case?"

"I had no definite idea. I thought the judge might find a way to help."

Judge Bishop's face was a mask.

"And suppose he didn't call us in?" Sabin asked. "Would you have?"

"You want an honest answer?"

"That's what we're here for."

"I don't know what I would have done, finally. Mallow said if I didn't go through with the deal as they proposed, they would say I offered a bribe, to defend against anything I might say."

"I presume then you contemplated contacting us, given those circumstances?"

"If there was no other way, yes."

Captain Hagan stirred. "But you didn't do it, did you?"

"No, I didn't."

"How is this fifty thousand to be paid?" Sabin asked.

"I presume in cash. Mallow didn't spell out the details."

"Well, although you didn't contact us yourself, Charley, we're talking now, so that counts for something." Sabin's smile flickered off and on, this time it seemed a trifle more friendly.

"We'll go on from here. You set up the details with Mallow. We'll supply the money, marked of course. And at this next meeting you will wear a wire. I imagine they trust you now. Mallow won't suspect a thing. Maybe you can work it so Palmer is there."

"I'm not going to wear a wire."

Sabin's eyebrow raised slightly. "Oh? Why not?"

"For one thing, I'm not a cop. I've told you everything I know. I've reported what happened. You people can take it from here."

"You're in it pretty deep, Charley."

"No, I'm not. I've refused their offer. I'm not a coconspirator. I'm not in this at all."

"Without your cooperation, Charley, we don't have a chance of making a case. You're a lawyer, you know that."

"If that's the way it is, that's the way it is."

"We might consider this obstruction of justice, Charley. Have you thought of that?"

Judge Bishop shifted in his chair and studied me for a moment before speaking. "Why won't you wear a wire, Charley?"

"Look, Judge Palmer has done a number of things for me in my life. He's in a mess and I feel sorry for him. I'm not a Judas. They made a mistake when they approached me. Palmer should have known better. But I'm not about to give him the Judas kiss. It's like giving a bribe, it's corrupt, it's something criminals do when they want to make a deal. I won't wear a wire. I find it abhorrent, and I will not do it."

Sabin and Hagan exchanged glances, and then Sabin spoke. "I would urge you to rethink this, Charley. You're in considerable danger if you don't."

"From you people?"

"It's a possibility, isn't it? But Palmer and Mallow are the ones who can hang you, and, without our helping you, they probably will."

"It's a risk I'll have to take."

Sabin pursed his lips. "You know we can't just walk away from this, don't you, Charley? We have to act on the information you've just given us. That means we have to talk to Palmer and to Mallow."

A chill ran through me. I knew what was coming.

"What do you suppose Mallow will say? It's just your word against his. He is the former chief judge of that court, isn't he? He'll say you proposed a bribe. He'll say he didn't report it because he felt sorry for you, a drunk, or former drunk. That's what he'll say, Charley, and you know it."

There was a wistful look in Sabin's eyes. "And Palmer.

He'll say he never heard anything. Nothing from you. Nothing from Mallow. He'll point out that he helped you through a crisis once. He'll be properly hurt that you would make such an accusation. Am I right?"

I said nothing. He was right.

"And then we'll have to come after you, Charley."

"Oh yeah? I told you what I know. Why the hell would I even bring something like this up? What would I possibly have to gain?"

The big cop stirred again. "You saw that secret memo that said you were going to lose the case," he said.

"The one Mallow showed me and then destroyed."

"We only have your word on that," Hagan said. "You used to clerk at that court. It's not impossible that you could have gotten a copy on your own. And this might be an elaborate setup to either force the court to go your way, or to get a new hearing."

"That's insane," I said.

"You do have a reputation, Charley, for being a little devious now and then," Sabin said. "Maybe this is one of those now and thens."

"It isn't."

"Then wear the wire," the cop snapped.

"No."

Judge Bishop held up a hand and spoke in that soft voice of his. "They have a point, Charley. The case can't be made without your cooperation. You've asked my advice, and this is it. Wear the wire. If Mallow and Palmer did what you say, they don't deserve any consideration."

"I'm sorry, Judge. I can't. And I won't."

Sabin sighed. "Well, this puts a whole different light on it, doesn't it? Charley, let me give you your rights now. You have the right to remain silent, you have the right to be represented by an attorney, if—"

"Are you arresting me?" I asked Sabin.

He shook his head. "Not now."

"Not yet," Captain Hagan snapped. "I presume you have no pressing travel plans?"

"I'm going to Broken Axe next Tuesday or Wednesday. I represent a defendant there and examination is set for Thursday. I should be back Friday, at my office, if that answers your question."

"Doctor Death," Sabin said. "We know all about that."

"It's been page-one news. If you read, you should." This time it was I who was doing the snapping.

"Charley," Judge Bishop said. "Reconsider what these gentlemen ask. Otherwise ..."

The word hung there like an unspoken jail sentence.

"I'm sorry, Judge, I can't."

I stood up. "I'm an officer of the court. I've received a solicitation for a bribe and I have reported it. Unless that's a new crime and you plan to arrest me, I'm leaving."

"That's a stupid attitude, Charley," Sabin said, "and you're not a stupid man. Work with us. At this point we're the only friends you have."

"You're dead meat, Sloan," Captain Hagan said, his smile genuine for what seemed like the first time. It was the kind of smile an executioner gives his intended victim. "You won't wear a wire because none of this happened. Whatever little scheme you cooked up has backfired."

"Like they say in court, prove it."

I left them there, went up the narrow stairs, and let myself out.

The tree-lined street was as peaceful as when I had gone in.

But I wasn't.

23

I didn't take the expressway back. Instead, I drove slowly along the shore of Lake St. Clair, passing the little towns that hugged the rim of the big, shallow lake. I didn't play a tape or listen to the radio. I wanted to think. But I found I couldn't, not really, with the scene in The Bishop's basement playing itself over and over again in my mind.

I knew they wouldn't be able to understand my decision. For twenty years I had defended people who stood accused by sleazy "friends," friends who were usually worse criminals than my clients but who were in the position to make a deal, "friends" who were anxious to wear a nifty little recording device so they could escape punishment themselves.

Informer. For me, it was a chilling word, a word that spelled evil.

I had committed no crime. I had done nothing except try to save my client's case in an honorable way. I couldn't bring myself to be Judge Palmer's "friend," to stand close enough so his voice could be picked up by what was strapped under my shirt, all the time looking into his eyes, knowing that the man who had helped me so often would be destroyed by what I was doing.

But what Sabin had said was true enough. My word against theirs was not good enough.

Obstruction of justice was a possible charge against me. Filing a false felony report was another. Conviction on either charge would result in instant and permanent disbarment.

The saloons along the way seemed to beckon. A few stiff bourbons would help ease my anxiety. I could drift off into another world, a happier place.

No cops.

No Palmers.

No future.

I put the pedal to the floor and tried not to think of using that as a way out.

By the time I got back to my office it was midafternoon, a Saturday. I sat and watched the river. The day was overcast but otherwise pleasant, and an army of small pleasure boats boiled the waters, ignoring the occasional passage of a huge ship. It looked like everyone was having a good time. Fishermen trolled, water-skiers bobbed behind speeding tow boats, and big-time yachts moved majestically along, most of them with people partying and enjoying the trip, drinking and taking in the view.

I envied them, they looked so carefree.

I watched in the way a prisoner might watch traffic passing below his cell. They were free, I was not.

The Bishop was right. Mallow and Palmer were crooks now, and what they might have been before was forfeited. He said they deserved no consideration. They had crossed the line. I wondered at my own decision. I couldn't blame anyone else for the trouble I was in. I had brought it on myself, yet honor demanded that I act the way I did.

Honor. It was a word, a sound, a symbol. I turned from the river and picked up my dictionary.

Honor: it ran down most of a page and had many meanings. It meant high rank or position of distinction, a title given to officials, such as judges. Like the Honorable Jeffrey Mallow, or His Honor, Franklin Palmer. In that use it implied respect.

Honor also meant a keen sense of right and wrong; adherence to action or principles considered right; integrity.

Well, my license was in jeopardy, but my honor was intact.

I thought of all the people in the past who were famous for their integrity. Saints, mostly, either butchered, burned, or buried alive.

It was not a consoling thought.

A trial lawyer tries to conjure up what might come up, how the opposition will proceed, what is likely to happen.

I thought now of how Harry Sabin would probably handle the situation. He would wait until Monday morning to call Mallow. He would ask for an appointment. He and the state police captain would go to Mallow's office. Harry was devious, he wouldn't just blurt out what I had told him. He would work around to it gently, hoping to surprise Mallow with the accusation.

But Mallow would be ready for them. He was no fool. There would be only one reason that the head of the attorney general's criminal division would want to see him.

Sabin was right. Mallow would say I tried to enlist him in a scheme to bribe the court. He would be generous, saying he knew of my personal problems. He would say that he had merely rebuffed me. He would say how sad he was that I had sunk to such a personal low.

I could almost write the script.

That would probably happen Monday afternoon. By that time, Mallow would have checked with Palmer, and the stories would be solid and in place.

Harry Sabin would approach Palmer the way any working attorney approached a sitting judge, like an explosive that might easily go off. Harry Sabin knew that in the future he would be arguing attorney general cases before Palmer. It would be almost a formality.

I figured that meeting might be Tuesday afternoon.

Both interviews would be taped. Harry was that kind of lawyer.

He would prepare a written report for the attorney general and request a conference. An accusation about court corruption was a serious matter, one that wouldn't be put off for long.

My guess was that Harry and the cop would meet with their boss on Wednesday up in Lansing. The attorney general was an elected politician and would take no action before he had looked at everything from every possible angle.

He would call the chief justice of the state supreme court and the chief justice of the court of appeals and ask for a conference. That was his usual way of operating. Depending on their schedules, that might happen on Thursday, the day when I would be defending Miles Stewart at his examination in Broken Axe.

They would agree that my charge was unsubstantiated. Then they would decide to have the matter investigated by a panel. A panel that would find Palmer blameless. A panel that would recommend my disbarment.

They would do all this to avoid scandal and unfortunate publicity. The court's integrity had been questioned. It would be found intact, and the accuser punished. Especially an accuser who had been punished once before, one who had had his license suspended.

McHugh's case might even be reheard by another panel, but he would lose. Anything else would look bad.

They might even end up bringing criminal charges against me, just to show that they took this matter very seriously.

For a minute I thought about calling up Judge Bishop and telling him I'd changed my mind, I would wear the wire, I would make a case on Judge Palmer.

But I didn't.

Honor is a funny thing. Maybe even fatal.

I just turned again and watched the river.

I KEPT ON WATCHING, PUTTING MY MIND in a kind of neutral, and time passed. I almost forgot about my date with Sue Gillis.

I didn't feel like dinner, and I didn't feel like talking. But I went anyway.

When she opened her apartment door, I saw that she was dressed to kill, wearing a short black dinner dress, her hair and accessories perfect. She looked like a princess ready to go to the ball.

Apparently I didn't look like a prince.

"Charley, what's wrong? You look like you just lost your best friend."

She stood aside and allowed me in.

I made a feeble attempt at a smile. "It's been a difficult day."

"If you were anyone else," she said, "I'd offer you a drink."

"How about an orange juice, or soda, if you have it."

"Sit down."

She went to the kitchen and returned with a tall glass

full of juice and ice cubes. I closed my eyes and sipped, remembering something stronger.

"What happened?" she asked.

"It's a long story. Boring, too."

"Try me. I'm not easily bored."

I shook my head. "It would ruin your dinner, I think."

She studied me for a minute. "You really don't want to go out to dinner, do you?"

"Sure. We have to eat."

"I'm not hungry, Charley."

"You're just saying that."

"No. If we get hungry, we can send out for a pizza."

"You're all dressed up, Sue. You look terrific, by the way."

"Thanks. Wait a minute, okay?"

"Sure."

She went into her bedroom and closed the door. I walked over to the windows and looked out on the golf course. I could see a distant cart and several golfers. I thought of The Bishop. I wondered if he was on some course now.

In a few minutes Sue came back wearing a robe; the party clothes were gone.

"I wanted to get comfortable," she said.

"You didn't have to do that, Sue."

"I know I didn't." She waited until I came back and sat down, then she sat opposite me.

"So tell me, Charley. Something's been bothering you for some time. Is this it?"

I nodded.

"This isn't something that I'll have to arrest you for, is it?"

I laughed. "You'll have to stand in line."

"Oh, God, Charley, what have you done?"

It made no difference if I told her now. Everything would soon be a matter of public record.

I sipped the juice. "What I've done is I've been honest. And, this side of skydiving with no parachute, that's about as dangerous a thing a person can do, as it turns out."

"Go on, Charley."

"Do you remember me talking about the McHugh case? The big appeal case I argued?"

"The paralyzed man."

"That's him."

"So?"

I began to tell her the story, starting from the beginning, the first meeting with Mickey Monk, and as I talked it became easier.

She didn't ask questions, merely nodded her head. I realized I was like a soldier debriefing after a battle. Once I began, it was difficult to shut me up.

She didn't try.

I described the meeting at Bishop's house.

"He didn't tell you the police would be there?"

I shook my head. "To say the least, it was a very big surprise."

"This Judge Bishop," she said, "tell me more about him. How come you trust him as much as you obviously do?"

I had finished the juice and she got me another.

"It's hard to explain. Everyone calls him The Bishop. He looks the part. Over the years, he's been like the guru to everyone who ever came out of St. Benedict's law school. If you were in a spot, or needed advice, it seemed natural to go to him." I sighed. "He's like everyone's grandfather, after a fashion."

"You said he was a classmate of this Judge Palmer?"

"Yeah. And Jeffrey Mallow was a year or two behind them."

She shook her head slowly.

I raised an eyebrow in silent question.

"Charley, how come you have this reputation as being a smart attorney?"

I laughed. "It's a question I ask myself often."

"You were set up, I hope you realize that?"

"What do you mean?"

She looked away from me. "I'm a cop, Charley. I think a pretty good one, too."

"I agree."

"What you did was like going to the head fox to try to protect the chickens. Jesus, you said the bunch of you are like—"

"The mafia," I said. "They call us the St. Benedict mafia."

"Exactly. So you went to the don to try to turn in his capos."

"The Bishop isn't crooked."

"Probably not. But he's going to be looking out for his own people."

"I'm one of those people."

"Junior grade, Charley. The others are like him, judges, and powerful."

"I don't think you understand, Sue."

"I understand better than you do. The Bishop's the one who told you to play along, right?"

"Not to do the deal, just to see how far they would carry it out."

"Sure."

"C'mon, Sue, I'm not that stupid. I trust The Bishop."

"Charley, do you know why he had the cops there today?"

"To start the investigation of Mallow and Palmer."

She shook her head.

"Do you realize why they were so insistent that you wear a wire?"

"To make the case against Mallow, and Palmer, if possible."

"No."

"No?"

"They wanted you to wear that wire to set you up, Charley. You'd go to Mallow and he'd deny ever having made any kind of an offer. Think about it. That way, they'd have you on tape, caught in your own lie. Mallow would have been briefed and ready for you. They'd have a nice little case on a crooked lawyer, wrapped up real pretty like a Christmas package with a big, fat bow. You'd have been arrested and charged without a hiccup of publicity, or not much anyway, just another crooked lawyer caught."

"But that's paranoid!"

"Is it?"

"I think it is. I know Harry Sabin. He's as straight as an arrow. He'd have no part of anything like that."

"He wouldn't have to know, would he?"

"What?"

"Your friend, The Bishop, would have set everything up like a pie recipe. The attorney general's man would act like a normal prosecutor making a case. They'd expect that. No, the only people in this thing are your good friends, The Bishop, Palmer, and Mallow."

"The Bishop's no crook."

"You thought that about Palmer, too, you said you did."

I nodded in agreement.

"Maybe I'm wrong, Charley, but I think what you did was like going to Nixon to tell him about the Watergate burglary."

"God, I hope you're wrong."

"So do I, Charley. So do I."

We sat silently for a while.

"Should I order out for pizza?" she asked.

"I'm not hungry."

"Neither am I."

She got up and came over and sat beside me. She smelled good as she put a comforting arm around me.

"Maybe it'll work out," she said.

"Maybe."

"Miracles do happen, Charley."

I looked at her. "Do you really believe that?"

She didn't reply.

I laughed. "Well, if a miracle happens, it'd better happen by Friday. I think that's all the time I have left."

"Friday's a long way off," she said.

She got up and led me to her bed. We lay there in our clothes, not making love, just wrapped in each other's arms.

As I drifted off to sleep, I remembered thinking that at least this was consoling.

24

I awoke first on Sunday morning. Sue lay next to me, her breathing even and peaceful. I lay there, grateful to be with her. There are some benefits to living alone, but in times of trouble, it's reassuring to feel the presence of someone else close by.

And trouble was what I was in. I tried not to think of what had happened, but that was impossible. Like remembering an old movie, some scenes from the past few days relentlessly played over and over again in my mind.

To escape my own thoughts I carefully got out of bed, still dressed, and tiptoed into Sue's kitchen. I found the makings for coffee; her coffee maker was much like my own, so I soon had a good pot brewing, the aroma filling the apartment like pungent perfume.

It was the aroma that woke Sue, who seemed surprised

to find me sitting there at her kitchen table until she apparently remembered we'd spent the night together.

She was not a morning person. Her usual peppy personality didn't appear until she was halfway through her second cup of coffee. Then, as a good hostess, she made us both a huge breakfast of eggs and bacon and a ton of toast.

Since we hadn't eaten dinner, we both fell on the food like wolves.

"My sister's coming over today," she said. "I'm taking her out to lunch. You're welcome to come, Charley, if you like."

It was one of those polite invitations, made with a certain lack of sincerity. I suspect she didn't want to have to explain me to her sister.

"I'll take a pass," I said. "I have a million things to do at the office today, but thanks for inviting me."

She nodded.

What I'd said wasn't true, it was just a nice politic explanation that satisfied both of us.

After breakfast, we read the Sunday paper like an old married couple, exchanging sections and comments on what we read.

It had an old-shoe feeling about it.

When I'd finished the paper, I kissed her on the cheek. "I had better be going. Your sister will be here soon."

"If I can help, Charley, in any way, just say the word," she said, squeezing my hand.

"A ticket to Brazil, maybe, if I don't think of something else."

"You will," she said, but she didn't sound all that confident.

I went back to my own place, showered, shaved, and changed clothes. The light on my answering machine was blinking. I avoided it for a while, then decided I couldn't put it off any longer.

I hit the message button and they came marching forward like little recorded soldiers. None of them had to do with The Bishop, Palmer, or anything connected with my present situation. None of them were urgent. All of them would keep.

The messages had just finished, the button had gone back to an unblinking red light when the phone rang.

I debated letting it ring, but then decided to pick it up.

"Mr. Sloan?" a man's voice asked.

"Yeah."

"Mr. Sloan, you may not remember me. My name is Ray Panar. You were our lawyer when we bought our house last year."

At first I didn't remember, and then it clicked. He was a young guy with a pudgy wife and two howling little kids.

"I remember you, Mr. Panar. What's up?"

"I need your help."

"In what way?"

"I've been arrested."

"Are you in jail now?"

"Oh, no. They let me out on a hundred-dollar cash bond last night. My trial comes up tomorrow morning. I'm calling from a gas station near my house."

"What's the charge?"

"I'm ashamed to say."

"I have to know."

He paused, then spoke in a whisper. "Accosting and soliciting."

"Where were you arrested? A men's room?"

"Hey! I'm not that kind of person. The police say I asked a woman for sex in a bar."

"If that's a crime, the jails will soon be full."

"They said I offered her money. She turned out to be a policewoman."

"If true, that's a misdemeanor, Mr. Panar. Have you ever been arrested or convicted before?"

"Never. Not even a traffic ticket."

"A first offense is usually just a fine. You don't have too much to worry about."

"But I do! They confiscated my car! I told my wife I had been in a minor accident but if they take my car …" His voice trailed off.

"Okay. Can you come to my office this afternoon?"

"I can come now. I told my wife I was just going out for cigarettes. I'm using her car. I can't be away too long. She's mad as it is about me coming in so late last night."

"I'll meet you at my office in five minutes. You remember where it is?"

"Yeah, right by the river."

"Five minutes," I said.

HE WAS WAITING FOR ME when I got there. The wife's car was an ancient rusting station wagon. He was as I remembered him, a small compact man, beginning to bald, which made him look older than his thirty or so years. He was, I recalled, a tool and die maker, and although he made good money, his single income didn't stretch very far. He had watched every penny when he had gone over the accounting at the real estate closing.

Ray Panar was dressed in wrinkled slacks and an old pullover.

We shook hands, and I led him up the outside stairs to my office.

He sat opposite me across the desk, his jaw tense with worry.

"Can I smoke?" he asked.

"Sure." I shoved an ashtray over to him.

His hands shook as he lit a cigarette.

"What's the usual fee for this sort of thing?" he asked, nervously expelling smoke.

"Depends. If it's just a judge, trial is usually five hundred dollars. If it's a jury, it runs more. Usually, this kind of thing isn't a jury matter."

His eyes widened at the amount. "I don't have five hundred on me."

"Well, it's customary for a fee in a criminal case to be paid before the case is heard. Can you have it in the morning?"

He nodded. "Do you take checks?"

"Sure."

He seemed relieved. "I can just cover that then."

"Suppose we start from the beginning, Mr. Panar. Tell me what happened last night. Don't leave anything out, it might be important legally."

He nodded and inhaled deeply.

I was glad to have my mind occupied by something besides my own brand of troubles. As a diversion, Panar's would do nicely.

"Well, none of this should have happened," he said. "I mean, I didn't intend for anything like this. I got off work and had a few beers with some of the people I work with. I usually do of a Saturday night when I've put in a day of overtime."

"Go on."

"If I had just stopped there, it would have been all right, but I decided to have a few more beers on my own. You know, kind of get away from things for a while."

"Where did you go?"

"A couple of places. You know the Glisten Inn?"

It was a run-down old restaurant that employed run-down old go-go dancers on weekends. I had represented the run-down old owner several times in brushes with the law.

"I know the place," I said.

He nodded, coloring slightly. "I don't usually go to places like that, but, like I say, I just wanted to get away from things for a while."

He tried to smile. "Do you have children, Mr. Sloan? Young children?"

"I have a grown daughter."

"Well then, you probably remember how hectic things can get around a house with little kids running around. The wife most times is angry about this or that. It's always something. Anyway, I was going home, but I just didn't want to go home just then. You know what I mean?"

I nodded. My daughter had been raised by her mother after the divorce. I remember only the good things about a little girl, but then memory can be handily selective.

"Was this policewoman at the Glisten Inn?"

He shook his head. "No. I had a couple of more beers there. They have dancers there, you know."

"I know."

"I left there and decided to have just one more beer before going home. Do you know that little bar up by Morad Road, the Sand's Point?"

"I've driven past it. It looks like a dump from the outside."

"It is. I was never there before. There were only a couple of people in the place even though it was a Saturday night."

"One of them was the policewoman?"

He nodded. "You couldn't help but notice her. She was very pretty, sitting up there at one end of the bar, sort of sexy like. Well, very sexy like, actually. I sat at the other end of the bar and had another beer."

"Go on."

As he talked, he became more embarrassed, his cheeks pinking up like underdone pork chops.

"Anyway, she kept smiling at me and I had the bartender buy her a drink. I had a couple of hundred in cash on me. Where I work Friday's payday. She motioned for me to come and sit by her, and I did."

"Who spoke first?"

He frowned. "I don't remember. Maybe she did, or I did. I don't have much experience in that sort of thing." The pink got pinker. "This was, well, the first time, if you get my drift."

"I do. Go on."

"She said I was a good-looking fellow and that I was probably more of a man than my wife could handle."

"And that led to just how much of a man you were, I presume?"

"Yeah, it went like that. I was a little tipsy to be frank about it and I was sort of having a good time. Anyway, she says she can help me out, you know, with my sexual problems."

"Who mentioned money?"

He raised his eyebrows in surprise, as if I were Sherlock Holmes himself. "Well, I guess I did. She was sort of hinting around, you know. Finally, I asked if it was going to be free."

"And?"

"She just laughed and shook her head."

"But she didn't say anything?"

"No. I asked what I'd get for twenty dollars, and she said nothing."

The pink was becoming red. "So I asked what I'd get for fifty and she said a certain sex act."

"A certain sex act?"

By now he was as red as a sunset. "You know, oral sex."

"Is that how she said it, oral sex?"

He shook his head. "She said a blow job. My wife doesn't do that kind of thing ..." His voice trailed off.

"So you agreed?"

He nodded.

"Then what happened?"

"She said she would do it in my car. We went out to the parking lot. I was just getting into my side when she flashed this badge out of her purse and said I was under arrest."

He looked away. "Two big cops, in plainclothes, came out of another car and put handcuffs on me. Pretty soon a scout car came and they took me to jail."

"Did the lady cop go with you to the jail?"

"No. She went back in the bar."

"What about the plainclothes men?"

"They went back to their car. They sort of were kidding around with her."

"About what?"

"About having a good night, something like that. Setting a record, or something. They seemed to think it was very funny."

"I take it you made bail out of the money you had on you?"

"Yes. But they kept my car. Can they do that?"

I nodded. "If it's used in connection with prostitution, they can."

"Permanently!"

I nodded again. "That's right."

"Oh my God! It's an almost new Chrysler. If my wife finds out ... I don't even have it near paid for."

The red had receded to pink and then to chalky white. "Can you help me?"

"I'll give it my best shot. Meet me at the courthouse at eight tomorrow morning."

"Will any of this be in the papers? My boss is a strict Christian. I might lose my job if he gets wind of any of this. And, if my wife ..." He stopped, as if the thought was just too painful to express.

"Probably none of this will make any newspaper. This isn't exactly an axe murder. I wouldn't worry about publicity. Just meet me at Judge Mulhern's court tomorrow. He's the judge who hears this kind of case."

"Can you get my car back?"

"I'll do my best."

He got up and we shook hands. "I don't know what you must think of me, but I've never done anything like this before."

"I believe you," I said.

He walked to the door. "My wife wouldn't, if she ever finds out ..."

And then he was gone.

I took a minute and looked up entrapment in my law books, jotting down a few cases.

It was great not having to think of bribes, corruption, and self-destruction.

I should be the one paying the fee, I thought. My anxiety about myself was markedly lessened, at least for the moment. Worrying about somebody else was a lot better than seeing a therapist.

MONDAY MORNING CAME and I was ready. Ray Panar met me, this time dressed in a plain suit and tie. He looked uncomfortable. Obviously, ties and suits were something he seldom wore. His face had the haunted look you sometimes see at funerals.

He reluctantly handed me the five-hundred-dollar check. His eyes followed it as I tucked it away in my wallet.

Then we headed to the courtroom of the Honorable Thomas Mulhern. Mulhern, as the local district judge, had jurisdiction over criminal misdemeanors.

It was early, but the courtroom was already filled nearly to capacity.

"Do you see the policewoman?" I asked Panar.

He nodded. "She's over there, the woman in the tan suit. She sure looks different."

She was a pretty woman with dark hair tied back. She

wore no makeup, she really didn't need to. The suit was cut well, but you could tell there was one hell of a body underneath. She looked like one of those television pitch-women who ask you to switch banks, all business but with a suggestion of subtle sex.

"What's different about her?"

"The clothes for one. Lord, on Saturday night she damn near didn't have anything on. She had a teeny little skirt hiked way up, a see-through blouse, and a little black bra. Also, she wore her hair different, you know, combed full out."

"Makeup?"

"Hell, she was painted up like a fire engine."

Tommy Mulhern came out and court started. Tommy, a drinker, looked like he had had a particularly tough weekend. I remember when I looked like that on Mondays. His eyes viewed the world through a sea of pain.

It was not a good time to make the Honorable Thomas Mulhern angry.

The drunks came first, lined up one after another. Each had disturbed someone's peace or had passed out in an inconvenient place. They had the same kind of eyes as the judge, but he found no common bond. He worked through them quickly.

The young prosecutor, a new boy, midtwenties, made the mistake of objecting to something Mulhern said. It was a foolish objection, completely unnecessary, and it worked on Mulhern the same way a red cape works on a bull.

I could see it in Mulhern's squinty eyes. Before the day was over, the young man was going to get gored. As a les-son in manners, if nothing else.

Two prostitutes were brought up one after the other, worn-looking women who had been working in front of a mall on the far side of the county. In the light of day they

334 ■ WILLIAM J. COUGHLIN

were about as desirable as fungus. At night, and after a few drinks, apparently they could make a living off the visually impaired.

Tommy found each guilty and fined each fifty dollars or thirty days.

Then Ray Panar's case was called.

I walked with my client to the front of the bench. The policewoman stood to my left.

I pleaded not guilty for Panar.

The young prosecutor questioned the policewoman. She said she was working as a decoy in a bar where prostitution had become a nuisance. She said my client had approached her, bought her a drink, and had offered her fifty dollars to perform an act of oral sex in his car out in the parking lot. She had gone to the car, identified herself as a police officer, and had placed my client under arrest.

The prosecutor looked pleased.

Her name was Flynn. Carol Flynn. That had prompted a titter in the courtroom when she gave her name.

Now it was my turn.

"Have you been with the Pickeral Point police department long, Officer Flynn?" I asked.

"Objection," the prosecutor snapped. "That's not relevant."

"I'll take the answer," the judge said in a quiet voice. It was the same kind of voice like when a movie villain says "Go for your gun." The kid didn't recognize the threat.

"I've been here two weeks," she said. "Assigned to vice work."

"Did you arrest any other men, in addition to my client, on Saturday night, in or around the Sand's Point Bar?"

"Objection. This is—"

"Overruled. Answer the question," Mulhern growled.

"Yes," she said primly. We were standing shoulder to shoulder. Her perfume was expensive.

"How many?"

"Objection!"

"Shut up!" Mulhern glowered at the prosecutor, then those pained eyes sought the policewoman. "How many?" he asked her himself.

She hesitated for just a moment, then answered in a voice just a little bit softer. "Seven."

"Seven?" the judge said. "All men? All out of that one little bar?"

"Yes."

"Are these cases to be heard before me this morning?"

She nodded. "I believe so. Yes."

"Officer Flynn, are the clothes you have on the same clothes you were wearing Saturday night?" I asked.

"No. But about the same. A skirt and blouse. No jacket."

I looked up into the tortured eyes of the judge.

"Your honor, our defense is based upon entrapment. I can produce witnesses who will testify to what this officer was wearing. But seeing is better than hearing. I would respectfully request this court to order the officer to dress as she was when she arrested my client."

"Objection," said the prosecutor. "This is just harassment—"

Mulhern glared at him. "One more objection and you're going to join the parade to the holding cell. You got that?"

They had never told the young man in law school about judges like Thomas Mulhern. His eyes were wide with newfound knowledge.

Mulhern looked at his watch, then at the policewoman.

"I'll give you an hour. Go home, or to the station house, whatever, and come back here dressed exactly as you were in that bar."

"I'm not sure the clothes—" she said.

"One hour," he growled. "We'll try all your cases then."

The young prosecutor started to speak but the instinct for self-preservation stopped him, even though he managed to let go with a killer frown.

They called the case of a petty thief, so Panar and I sat down with the other spectators again.

The cases went along quickly. Mulhern was a fair man, usually, and his sentences were a bit on the soft side. Lawyers seldom make a fuss in those circumstances. Everything went clipping along until a collective gasp was heard coming from the back of the courtroom.

She still wore no makeup and her hair was still pulled back, but that was the last thing you noticed.

The skirt was so tight it looked like a wide belt and it came down only to her hips. She had the kind of legs that got Rockettes the job at Radio City Music Hall. They were long, lean, encased in black stockings and ending in very high heels. Her blouse was as see-through as smoke from a cigarette, and her ample breasts strained against a thin black bra that looked about to burst.

She moved through the courtroom, her head held high, ignoring the stares.

"Okay," Mulhern said as he found a thief guilty. "Let's all get back to the Sand's Point Bar. Are you ready, Sloan?"

I nodded and came forward with my client. Once again the officer and I stood shoulder to shoulder. "Doing anything after work?" I whispered so only she could hear.

Her lips tightened into a thin line.

The young prosecutor was in love. A bird could have flown in and out of his gaping mouth without his notice.

"Is that the outfit you wore Saturday night, Officer Flynn?" I asked politely.

"Yes, it is."

"And dressed like that you were approached by my client and six other men, one after another, that night, correct?"

"I said I was acting as a decoy," she snapped, coloring visibly.

"And you discussed sexual topics with my client, as well as the other men, that is, before the offer you said was made."

"We talked about things. Sex was one of them."

I looked up at the judge. "Usually, your honor, entrapment means that the police started the action that resulted in the commission of a crime. Basically, the cases say that if it wasn't for the action of the police, no crime would have been committed. That is the essence of the entrapment defense, that the defendant wouldn't have done anything illegal if he hadn't been trapped into it. Most of the cases concern spoken statements by police officers, but I submit the unspoken statement can be just as entrapping. I think the way this officer is dressed would provoke most men into at least thinking about commiting the crime charged here."

"I object," the prosecutor began, but he spoke with his eyes still fixed on the sexy cop.

"He's making an argument to the court," Mulhern snapped. "Has the Constitution been repealed and I wasn't told? It is his right."

"But—"

"Miss Flynn, do you fish?" the judge inquired.

"No, I don't."

"Pity. It's a wonderful sport. You throw out a bait and you hope a fish will come by and bite it. Not that much different from what you were doing at the Sand's Point Bar. More or less."

She frowned at him.

"But a fisherman has to be fair. He has to obey the rules of the sport. He can't spear the fish and he can't use dynamite. The bait has to be legal. Do you see what I mean?"

"No, I don't," she snapped.

"Well, let me put it this way. The bait you were using, dressed as you are, was like using dynamite to catch perch. If the pope had dropped into the Sand's Point Bar last Saturday night he might be up here before me this morning. I doubt if the pope hangs out around that kind of establishment, but if he did, even he might be tempted to think of carnal sin, given the way you were presenting yourself."

"I was supposed to look like a prostitute," she protested. "That's why I dressed this way. I was a *decoy*."

Mulhern smiled. "No, not a decoy. That implies a degree of sporting fairness. Your outfit is equal to dynamite and perhaps even illegal. I should find you guilty of fishing without a license, but I won't."

Despite what was undoubtedly a major hangover, I could tell he was enjoying himself. "I find that this nice young officer, with the best of intentions, entrapped Mr. Sloan's client. I also, without even bothering to hear the cases, find the same defense applies to every other man you arrested that night. This case, and the others, are dismissed."

"I'll appeal," the prosecutor squeaked.

Mulhern smiled. "That is your right, young man. I rather doubt you'll be successful, however. But you can always try."

The prosecutor lost interest as the policewoman walked from the court. He followed her every movement with rapt attention.

"Penny for your thoughts," the judge said, a small smile playing on his lips. His next words were a lot more harsh. "Call the next case," he barked at his clerk.

I walked out into the crowded hallway with my client.

"What happened?" he asked.

"You won your case. You'll get your bond money back and your car."

"Oh, thank God. How can I ever thank you?"

I tapped the place where I had my wallet. "You already have."

I walked Panar to the door. "If the police try to give you a hard time about the car or the bond, give me a call, okay?"

He nodded and left, heading across the square to the local police headquarters.

"That was quite a little skin show you put on back there, Sloan."

I turned and faced Victor Trembly, who had been the late Howard Wordley's lawyer.

Trembly was a Port Huron lawyer who did mostly criminal work. He looked the part. His suit was expensive but flashy. His glasses sparkled with what apparently were diamond chips embedded in their wide frames. He was about my height, about average, and slightly plump. He wore a diamond ring on each hand and a gold Rolex flashed below his monogrammed shirt cuff.

I cringed to think I used to dress very like Trembly, perhaps not as cheap but just as flashy. Trembly looked like a jerk, I thought. I reasoned that I must have looked that way too, and not so long ago.

"I'd like to give that little bitch a pop," Trembly said, leering. "That's the defense lawyer's dream, isn't it, to fuck a cop?"

"Try the Sand's Point Bar, Victor. A distinguished man like you can't help but score."

He grinned. "I picked up the client you lost," he said.

"What client?"

"The Denton kid, the one who stuck up the gas station. The college boy out for kicks."

"Are you going to work out a plea?"

"Why, for God's sake?"

I smiled. "Well, he was caught with the loot, he confessed, and the eyewitness knows him. How are you going to get around that?"

"Who cares?"

"What do you mean?"

"How do you make any money in the business, Sloan? I'm going to a jury with the kid."

"You'll lose."

The grin became wider. "I know that."

"So, what's the point?"

Trembly moved his hand so his diamonds would catch the light. "After the jury convicts, we go the appeal route."

"You'll lose there too."

"I know that."

We were beginning to sound like a vaudeville act.

"So?"

"Old man Denton owns the radio station. He's putting up everything he has to defend his college boy. By the time the kid is up in Jackson Prison and losing his virginity, I'll own the radio station."

"You are a sweet and caring human being, Victor."

"I'm also rich. Too bad you lost the client, Sloan. It would be fun owning your own radio station."

"You know any of those nasty lawyer jokes, Victor?" I asked. "You know the ones. Like, what do you call twelve dead lawyers? A start. That kind of joke?"

"I love them. Why, you got one?"

"I'm talking to one," I said, and walked away.

"Fuck you too, Sloan. You'll never be allowed to advertise on my radio station."

He laughed.

I hated the sound.

It seemed so unfair. An unethical slime like Victor Trembly was walking around without a care in the world while I was the one who was in trouble.

Justice, they say, is blind. I wondered if she might be just a little bit nuts too.

25

went back to my office after having defeated the nearly nude forces of law and order. There were messages, handed to me by Mrs. Fenton, but none from Judge Bishop, Harry Sabin, or Mallow.

According to my timetable, Sabin might be meeting with Mallow now. If it went the way I expected, Mallow might at this very moment be dropping the net that would spell disbarment or prison for me.

A surge of regret flowed through me. I wished for a moment I had agreed to wear the wire, repugnant or not. It would all have been so simple. The awful anxiety that gripped me would never have existed.

Then all I would have had to bear was guilt, and the feeling of having betrayed not only Franklin Palmer but also myself.

It was a strange trade-off, anxiety versus guilt. But my choice had been made.

It was too late to change things now.

I wondered how they would eventually come at me. Criminal charges meant exposing everything to public scrutiny. If I was arrested and tried, all my charges against Palmer and Mallow would become front-page news.

But a disbarment proceeding was never as sexy as a good juicy jury trial. It would be reported, but they could keep a nice lid on the allegations of corruption. After all, what would you expect from a crooked lawyer, one who had already once lost his right to practice?

I was willing to bet they would choose the disbarment route.

How they came at me would dictate which lawyer I would get to defend me.

At the moment, the best criminal defense lawyers in Detroit, not counting me, were Sylvester Drake and Wally Figer. The saying among Detroit street people was: if you're innocent, get Drake, if you're guilty, get Figer. I was innocent, but I would look very, very guilty. I decided if they did arrest me I would retain Wally Figer.

But if it came to disbarment, then I would select Henry Sheridan, who had once worked as the chief prosecutor for the agency charged with nailing crooked or incompetent lawyers. He was good, a hungry tiger on a rampage. As soon as he had established that reputation, he quit and went over to the other side of the table where the money was, the money of crooked or incompetent lawyers.

If they came after my license, Henry Sheridan would be my lawyer.

I might not win, but I would go down swinging.

THE REST OF MONDAY seemed to move along but at a snail's pace. I saw clients, made necessary phone calls, and dictated a few letters. I tried to keep busy so that dark and dreadful thoughts would be kept at bay.

It didn't work too well.

I took Sue Gillis to dinner. Nothing fancy, just hamburgers at the local greasy spoon, my restaurant of choice.

She was trying her best to be bright and cheery. The story of my antics at the examination were being woven into one of those cop legends. The way she was telling what she'd heard, I could see that in a few days the poor policewoman would be reported as being topless, at the very least.

She asked if I had heard from anyone.

I knew what she meant. I said no.

We both tried to make conversation but there were long and painful pauses, silences neither of us knew how to fill.

"When are you going up to Broken Axe?" she asked.

"Tomorrow night."

"Tuesday? The examination isn't until Thursday, right?"

"I want to have all Wednesday free up there. There's a lot of things I have to do."

"Like what?"

"I have to take a look at the official autopsy report. If I'm not satisfied or need to know something, I can call a doctor here or see one up there."

"Why?"

"Because I'm not a doctor. I gathered a lot of knowledge at Doctor Stewart's first trial, but I may need some background on the more technical findings, if it's new, the blood work and so forth. Besides, I may want to question some of the prosecution's witnesses."

"Will they allow that?"

"Probably. They're pretty confident. And, I have to talk to my client."

"I thought you didn't like him."

I smiled. "I don't like him. He doesn't like me. But that's not important. I've taken a job and I'll do my best. You'd be surprised at some of the people I've defended in the past."

"You mean people you didn't like?"

"Actually, I liked most of them. You know, when a burglar's not climbing through a window he can be as charming as the next guy."

"But not Doctor Death?"

"Charming is not a word that would pop into my mind when asked for a word association with the good doctor."

"Will you win, Charley?"

"I don't think so. Apparently, this time they really have a case. I'll give it my best shot, but I expect he'll be bound over for trial."

"First-degree murder?"

"Maybe. I might be able to get it down a notch, but it all depends on how their witnesses do on the stand. The judge is an old law school buddy, he might give me a small gift, but the coin could fall either way."

"St. Benedict?"

"Yes."

She frowned. "Like The Bishop, Palmer, and Mallow."

"Younger, but yeah, a graduate, like them. And me."

"Do you suppose he might …"

"What?"

The frown deepened. "This Bishop apparently has a long arm, Charley. Maybe you shouldn't take anything up there for granted."

"That's really paranoid."

"Is it?"

"Yes, I think so."

"Judges, like cops or doctors, stick together, Charley. I'm just saying you should know that and you should be careful."

We finished and then had coffee at her apartment.

Again, conversation was strained, and sex was obviously out of the question.

I kissed her good night and left.

As I drove home, I began to think that maybe this paranoia thing might be contagious.

I began to wonder if she might just be right.

I would be careful. Very careful.

I MADE A STAB at doing some work on Tuesday, but my mind was on other things. When I wasn't thinking of my own situation, I was thinking of how I could best defend Miles Stewart.

Finally, after lunch, I gave up. I told Mrs. Fenton I was going and wouldn't be back until Friday. I didn't tell her I might be spending Friday night in some jail. I thought she just might enjoy that image too much.

I went to my apartment and packed. Then I drove up to Broken Axe. Again, there wasn't much traffic on the two-lane state road going up.

It gave me ample time to think, which this time out wasn't relaxing at all.

It was Tuesday. According to my imaginary and projected timetable, Harry Sabin would be taking Judge Franklin Palmer's statement. Palmer would sink me, if by some chance Mallow hadn't.

There was no way I could stop it, nor could I interfere. It was at this point only an investigation in progress. One that I had caused, and one that I felt would come back at me like a wronged woman.

I tried to think of other things. Even the Buffett tapes didn't help.

It was a long three hours before I pulled into the small Michigan town. It had one hotel, called the Broken Axe Inn, a red brick building that had been there for over a hundred years according to the date carved above its entrance. It was an old railroad hotel; long ago the railroad had closed, but the hotel apparently served some purpose. It looked as inviting as a jail.

I drove through the small town and saw an old motel. It was a museum piece. It consisted of the owners' home and office and ten small units, one next to another, like rabbit warrens. Despite that, it looked better than the brick antique in town.

The vacancy sign was lit, although the middle letters didn't fully work.

I parked and went into the office. It wasn't much, just a battered counter and a couple of dingy plastic chairs, well worn and cracked.

I could hear the sound of television from somewhere inside. There was no door, just a single-sheeted curtain covering the source of the televised noise.

One of those old-fashioned hand bells, the kind you hit on top with the touch of a button, sat on the counter. I hit it twice.

At first there was no sign that I had been heard, then the sound of grumbling was mixed in with the noise of the television. I recognized the program as a game show. Apparently, amusement in Broken Axe was hard to come by.

A little old man, dressed in an undershirt, slacks, and slippers, shuffled out from behind the curtain. He poked his thick glasses up and stared at me.

"What's ya want?"

"A room," I said.

"You alone?"

"Yes."

He looked out at the car, as if trying to see where I was hiding the woman.

"There's two rates," he said. "Single is twenty-five dollars a night. A double is thirty-five dollars. If you bring a woman in, that counts as a double."

I smiled. "That's okay, I'm alone."

"One night." It was a statement, rather than a question.

"I'll be here at least to Thursday. I may stay over Thursday night. I won't know until then."

"I can only let you have a room for one night. They've been booked for the rest of the week. We got a big court thing up here and the newspaper people have booked all the rooms."

"That's why I'm here," I said, "the big court thing. My name is Sloan. I'm Doctor Miles Stewart's lawyer."

The old eyes widened, and then he grinned. I was looking at store-bought teeth. "Death's lawyer?"

"Well, we prefer his regular god-given name, but yes."

"Jeez, that would be something, I mean, you staying here at my place." The smile vanished. "But I got no room."

"Suppose you made a mistake," I said. "Airlines do that all the time. They overbook. You could call one of the people and say you had miscounted. You know, tell them they would have to get another room someplace else. I wouldn't suggest that, but if all the rooms here in town are taken, it would make it very inconvenient if I had to go to Bay City or someplace to sleep every night."

"That makes sense, but—"

"Suppose I paid you double double?"

"What do you mean?"

"A double is thirty-five dollars. I'd be willing to pay seventy dollars and guarantee you three nights, even if I didn't stay Thursday."

Money was as important in Broken Axe as it is in New York. Probably more, a whole lot more.

His eyes narrowed conspiratorily. "Up front?"

"I'll give you the money now."

"I don't know. Who would I bump?"

"Let me see your list."

He handed me a scrawled list of reservations. They

gave the name and the affiliation. Most of them were television people. A couple were Detroit reporters. One was Sherman Martelle of the *Free Press*. I liked Sherman. He would stay on the list.

But Connie Shine of the *News* was also on the list, the last name on it. Connie, a short loud Irishwoman, thought of herself as the last real reporter. Most of her stories centered on herself. If the pronoun *I* were ever eliminated from the English language, Connie would no longer be able to write, or speak for that matter.

"This woman," I said to my host, pointing at Connie's name, "is a horrible drunk and troublemaker. She's a walking disaster. If I were you that's the one I'd notify."

"All drunks are trouble," he said, not knowing he was talking to a former champion, "but a drunken bimbo is hell on wheels. I know. I married two of them."

He grinned his plastic grin. "You got yourself a room."

I paid the money by credit card and wrote out the registration form.

He looked at it with obvious satisfaction.

"Imagine! Death's lawyer, and staying with me!"

I was assigned the last unit, number 10. My host explained that way I'd only have to listen to the noise from one neighbor.

The room, like the motel, was a museum piece, a permanent musty odor being part of its charm. The linoleum floor tiles were curling up in places, and above, the ceiling panels were marked by various stains, all old and unidentifiable. The furniture was mismatched. The small bath had a shower, a tin box with a spigot, and the toilet seat was cracked. The wash basin was rusted in places.

But it was home. At least for the next few days.

My bed sagged a bit but was comfortable enough.

I lay down and looked up at the ceiling.

A truck rumbled by on the highway. The place seemed to shake. Somewhere I could hear distant music. I couldn't tell what was being played but I could catch a few notes of a saxophone sounding very lonely.

Old motel rooms held a kind of fascination for me. I wondered what had happened in this place over the years. Love, hate, despair, the little room had probably been the stage for all kinds of human dramas. Adultery and every other kind of human sexual behavior would have taken place here. Women would have cried here, men would have cursed. A parade of drunks had probably passed out on this bed.

Suicides too. Motels were always popular for that. Maybe even murder, but given the tranquil nature of this small town, probably not. Here, murder would be an occasion, not just a statistic.

All kinds of people before me had stared up at the ceiling. Most of them probably wondered what the future held for them.

Beneath the musty air I thought I detected the lingering odor of fear.

It was the last thought I had before I fell asleep.

26

Several times during the night, dreams awakened me. Anxiety dreams. I was being chased, threatened, put at peril by one thing or another. Each time I was jolted awake, I took a minute to figure out where I was. When I did, I realized I had enough real anxiety in my life to fuel a year or two of nightmares.

But each time I went back to sleep, so that when morning came, announced by passing trucks that sounded as if they were in the room with me, I was well rested.

The old shower had two kinds of water, red hot and ice cold, with nothing in between. I managed to get clean and still keep my skin on.

I dressed and found a little restaurant in town. A cluster of trucks was parked outside the place, usually a sign of good food. The drivers learned on their routes which places were good and which bad.

My order of eggs, bacon, and toast came and in a quantity sufficient to feed a platoon. The coffee was excellent and the young waitress seemed to think her existence depended on keeping my cup full.

I had bought a *Free Press* at the door. My case was on the front page, lower left-hand corner. Sherman Martelle had the byline. It was a kind of overview of the history of Dr. Miles Stewart and his brushes with the law. Martelle used the piece as a curtain raiser for what was yet to come in the courthouse at Broken Axe. I got a few good mentions, although I was characterized as "the sometimes controversial defense lawyer." I chose to think that meant a fighter for truth and justice. Another reader might think it was a way of calling me devious and possibly crooked. Like beauty, different people would see it in different ways.

The bill wasn't much. Prices up here were much different than downstate. I paid and left a generous tip for my hovering waitress.

I stepped out of the restaurant, took a deep breath, and began the first step in my defense of the very famous Doctor Death.

I drove to the courthouse. I wanted to talk to the prosecutor and get a copy of the autopsy report. I parked and was walking toward the entrance when I was intercepted by a very thin, very disreputable-looking man, about forty. He had the kind of evil face usually associated with child molesters. When he grinned, the effect was heightened.

"The great Charley Sloan," he said, extending a bony hand. He wasn't tall, and a shock of reddish hair stood out on his head like a wild brush. His accent was so Australian that he made Crocodile Dundee sound Polish.

His grip was strong but disgustingly wet.

"What can I do for you?"

"If you recognize me, you know what I want," he said, in that throw-another-shrimp-on-the-barbee voice.

"I'm afraid I don't recognize you."

If he was offended, he didn't show it. "I'm Reggie O'Malley. I'm on television."

"Australian television?" I wondered if Dr. Stewart's reputation had spread to the other side of the globe.

"No, mate. Right here, the good old United States of America. I'm with 'Inside Eye.'"

I had heard of the program, although I had never seen it. It competed with a number of exposé shows that did half-hour daily stories of prison rapes and child mutilations. None of the shows were likely to win a Peabody Award for excellence, but people in great numbers watched them. I had read that "Inside Eye" was the worst of a bad bunch.

"This case is going to turn into a real circus, Charley," he said. "You and your client are going to get knocked about by the press. I can help you."

"How?"

"Let my camera follow your every step, so to speak. Ours is a national show, good ratings. You'll get the chance to put your point across with us. We'll be on your side."

"Did you ever do any selling, Mr. O'Malley?"

The grin widened. "That's how I started out, mate. That's what this television thing is all about, isn't it? Salesmanship?"

I noticed out of the corner of my eye that we were being filmed by a burly cameraman holding a professional camcorder.

"Well, go somewhere else and sell something. I appreciate the offer, but what you suggest would be a breach of ethics."

The smile grew into a leer. "Hoo, Charley boy, when were you ever concerned about ethics? We hear you're a right nasty piece of work, even for a lawyer."

"G'day, mate," I said, walking past him and up the courthouse steps.

"It can go the other way, too, Sloan," he snarled. "We can make you out a perfect ass!"

I was going to say I did a pretty good job of that on my own, but I didn't. It would have looked bad and sounded worse on their tape.

I just waved, holding one finger slightly raised above the others. I wondered if that gesture was understood in Australian.

It had begun, the greatest show on earth. Doctor Death was becoming as well known as a rock star.

So was I. But maybe not in the context I wished.

EDDIE RAND SEEMED less laid back, but the young prosecutor was just as friendly as before. I thought he might be having a case of preshow nerves.

He gave me the autopsy report without the slightest hesitancy.

Dr. Clyde Anderson had a national reputation. He was a fair-minded man as well as being a good pathologist. I read the report carefully, including the toxology reports concerning the blood levels. I had had a master's course in the first Stewart trial, and it paid off now. I understood almost everything in the report, including the basis for the finding of felonious homicide.

"Pretty bad for your side," Rand said.

"More or less. Who do you plan on calling as witnesses tomorrow?"

"The deputy who went out to the Cronin place. The private duty nurse who was there when Stewart killed him."

"Did she see it done?"

"No. Your man isn't stupid. He said he'd look after Cronin while she took a coffee break. But she can testify to the old man being alive when your man came into the room, and being very dead shortly thereafter." Despite himself, he allowed a grin.

"Who else?"

"The treating physician."

"Why?"

"Again, to show Sean Cronin's condition before your man arrived."

"When did this treating physician last see the patient?"

"That morning. That was before Stewart arrived."

"Anybody else?"

Now he seemed distressed. "I suppose I have to call Miss Donna. She was there in the doorway when Stewart gave him the deadly dose."

"You suppose?"

He smiled sadly. "She's such a nice lady, I hate to put her through all this. But I guess there's no other way."

"And that's it?"

"Well, for the examination anyway. I might add some witnesses when we go to trial on this thing."

"So you think you'll win tomorrow?"

"Pride goeth before a fall, I know that. But if you can get this guy off tomorrow, Charley, I'll shave my head and follow you around as your first disciple."

"Only if you wear a saffron robe. What's the name of the treating physician?"

"Dr. Kim S. A. Kim. Everybody up here calls him Sam. He's the only doctor we've got. A little Korean guy, but everybody loves him."

"I want to talk to Donna Cronin."

He frowned. "Do you have to?"

I nodded. "That a problem?"

"Well, a little maybe. She may look ferocious, but

she's as shy and frightened as a barn owl."

"In that case, come with me."

"To keep you honest?"

"That, too, but also maybe to help ease her anxiety."

Eddie nodded slowly. "Do they do this sort of thing in the big city? You know, the prosecutor and the defense lawyer both interview the witnesses?"

"Sometimes."

"Okay, I'll call out there and let them know we're coming."

We drove in Eddie Rand's car, a Chevy sports model with racy lines and a motor that seemed to plead for exercise. It was a hunter's car, but only for two-legged game.

"You got to understand about the Cronin girls," he said as we sped along a dusty country road. "They're well liked up here. They aren't what you'd call pretty." He sighed. "They have the bodies of linebackers and the faces of bulldogs, frankly, but you won't find two nicer people. They contribute to everything, and not just a little. And they make pies and cakes for community things. They usually don't come. Too shy. If somebody gets sick or dies, they always send something over. Around here, they're considered minor-league saints."

"How about their father?"

"The opposite. A mean old bastard who didn't care a fig about this place. His girls doted on him, waited on him hand and foot. The people up here felt sorry for the daughters."

"So, no big turnout for the funeral then?"

He shook his head. "Huge. But everybody came out for Doreen and Donna's sake, not for his."

He nodded. "We're coming up now on the local gold coast."

I could see large Victorian homes set along a high ridge. Plenty of room between them, there they sat, separately, like decorative and elegant castles.

"Most of the owners only come up in the summer," Eddie said, "but the Cronins live here year-round. Like I say, they're very much a part of our community."

"Is that why you haven't charged Doreen Cronin with murder?"

He looked at me sharply, this time I saw nothing friendly. "Sloan, we're getting along real well here. There's no reason to bring that up."

"If things happened the way you say they did, Doreen contracted for her father's murder and paid for it. If that isn't murder, I don't know what is. Conspiracy to murder, accessory to murder. There are a barrel of charges to be brought."

"Are you going to bring this up in court?"

"Eddie, I'm the defense lawyer, remember? You can't have selective enforcement. Sure I'll bring it up. If not at the examination, then certainly at the trial. Anything less would be malpractice."

He looked troubled as he turned the car onto a paved road that led to the old wooden palaces.

"I suppose it's one of those bridges I'll have to cross when I get there."

"So you're not going to charge her?"

He smiled, but there was a sadness in it. "If I did, the people up here would lynch me."

He pulled into the driveway of one of the palaces, joining a number of other cars.

"This is it. I wonder what's going on?"

Reggie O'Malley and his cameraman were standing at the door. O'Malley was banging a slow cadence against the wood with his fist. The cameraman stood by at the ready. Several other people were nearby. I didn't recognize them, but I assumed they were also media people.

O'Malley stopped when he saw me. "Well, Sloan, what are you doing here? Going to put in the fix, are you?" He looked at Eddie. "Eh, this guy's the prosecutor, isn't he? I smell corruption here."

"Who the hell is this?" Eddie asked me.

"The press, my boy. The eyes and ears of the republic. This is just the tip of the iceberg. I imagine an army is at this moment descending."

Eddie grabbed O'Malley and tossed him away from the door. I noticed the cameraman was grinning as he filmed the action.

The door was opened by a wizened old lady, and Rand and I quickly stepped in. She bolted the door. O'Malley was shouting and again slowly banging at the door.

"Hi, Mrs. Legrand," Eddie said.

She smiled, crinkling her face into a million wrinkles. She reminded me of an ancient mummy.

She led the way through the enormous house.

"Who's she?" I whispered to Eddie.

"Mrs. Legrand, the maid."

"The maid?"

"In name only. She's too old for anything except serving tea. They have one of her granddaughters for the real work. They keep her on so she'll have some income in addition to Social Security. The Legrands are a big family up here and work is scarce. Her wages help out." He spoke in a normal voice, and then smiled. "Don't worry, Charley. Mrs. Legrand is almost stone deaf."

We were brought into a small sitting room in the interior of the house. I could see mighty Lake Huron beyond the windows.

Two women, both dressed identically in black, sat primly side by side on a couch that matched the house for age. They were not pleasant to look upon, more like two Chicago Bear tackles in drag. Eddie had described them as looking like two bulldogs. I had thought he was exaggerating.

He wasn't.

He introduced me, and we took two chairs opposite them.

"Charley here would like to ask you some questions, Miss Donna. I would prefer that he ask only you."

"Hey," I said.

He ignored me. "Why don't you leave the room, Miss Doreen. That way we can get this over quickly."

Before I could say a thing, she was up and gone.

"Who are those awful people out there?" The voice chirped like a small nervous bird. I looked around for a second before I realized it was Donna Cronin who was speaking.

"Just some trash from the television," Eddie said. "I'm going to call Cork and have them run off. Don't you worry about them, Miss Donna. Go ahead, Charley."

She looked nervous, perhaps even close to tears. It was unnerving, as if Dick Butkus were about to sob.

"Just a few questions," I said softly, trying to soothe her. "I'm told you saw Doctor Stewart inject your father. Is that true?"

She paused. "I saw him with the syringe."

"Well, start from the beginning and tell me what you did see, in your own words."

She was careful to protect her sister. She said that Dr. Stewart had been her sister's guest. She denied knowing that he had been paid any money. She said she had heard of his reputation. I asked her if her sister had wanted to end their father's suffering. She said it was true, but she, Donna, had said it was in God's hands.

I asked her if she knew Doreen had brought Dr. Stewart up to end their father's suffering. She evaded the question. For a shy person, she seemed to know how to answer so that her sister wouldn't be part of any conspiracy.

She said she had seen Dr. Stewart go into her father's

room. She denied that she had been watching him for just that reason. She said she saw him with his back to her, and when he turned he had a syringe in his hand. She said Stewart, mistaking her for her sister, had waved her away. She ran to get her sister and by the time they came back, Dr. Stewart told them Sean Cronin had died. She admitted she hadn't seen the actual injection.

Miss Donna said she had called the sheriff, that she had been angry when she had done so. She sounded as if she really regretted it now.

I didn't press. She was being truthful, except for the Miss Doreen part. I didn't want to expose any more of my hand by going further.

We thanked her and declined the offer of tea. Eddie called Sheriff Cork Miller, and within minutes two deputies came storming up and pushed the media people back to the road. The two officers took up positions blocking the drive entrance.

Eddie and I got back into his car.

As we drove out, Reggie O'Malley spat at us.

He missed.

27

The rest of Wednesday passed quickly. I was busy. I talked to the prospective witnesses, again with the benign help of the prosecutor, who began to act as my own personal ambassador.

Of course, he felt he had nothing to lose. In his mind Doctor Death was tried, convicted, and sentenced. All that remained was to go through the routine steps.

I had lunch with the sheriff and the prosecutor. Cork Miller was something of a cornpone comedian, an act that helped him at election time, and the lunch was filled as much with laughter as good food. For a while it seemed as if we were all on the same side. I think they felt a little sorry for me.

My last interview of the day was with my famous client.

The media army had rolled into town, and I found clusters of them wherever I went. Photographers snapped my picture as I entered the jail. I tried to look resolute and confident.

Hoping to provoke an angry response they might be able to use, a few of the reporters yelled hostile questions. I ignored them.

The few days in jail had done nothing to curb Dr. Miles Stewart's natural tendencies. I sat in the cell and listened to ten minutes of complaints. Some about the facilities, some about the legal system, some about me. There was nothing I could do but wait him out.

"And they have canceled my appellate bond," he snarled. "I suppose you know that?"

"It's what happens, Doctor, when you're on bond for one murder and they arrest you for another."

"So what happens if you get me out of this tomorrow? Do I go to prison?"

"You do until I can get the appellate court to reinstate the bond. That might take a day or two. It depends."

"Jesus! Have you any idea what you just said? I'm supposed to spend days in prison because of some halfwit bureaucratic system? That's absurd! I'm innocent until proven guilty."

I smiled. "Technically, you were found guilty of second-degree murder. The appellate bond is not an absolute matter of right."

"Goddamn lawyers!"

"Anyway, that's not our immediate concern, is it? If they bind you over on first-degree murder charges tomorrow, any bond is out of the question."

"You're paid to see that that doesn't happen."

"I'm paid to try my best."

He frowned. "You'd better do just that. Or face a malpractice suit."

I smiled. I knew that my smiling always irritated him. "Should the worst happen, there are a number of disbarred lawyers in prison who, for the price of cigarettes, will help you draft the pleadings."

It wasn't the response he expected and it stopped him cold. But only for a moment.

"What happens tomorrow?" he asked.

"You've been through it before, in the Milliard case. It's a preliminary examination. The prosecutor must show that a crime was committed and that there is reasonable cause to believe that you committed it. It's his show. He presents his witnesses. I get to cross-examine, but you don't take the stand, nor do I offer any witnesses."

"That's asinine."

"Could be. But this procedure is a safeguard against frivolous charges. The prosecutor has to show he has enough of a case to merit going to trial."

He was uncharacteristically silent for a moment, then he spoke. "What kind of a chance do I have tomorrow?"

"Doctor, I warned you what might happen if you decided to go back into the euthanasia business, didn't I? Well, they have the check from Miss Doreen. You say it was for research, the prosecutor says it was for services rendered. They have Miss Donna, who saw you with a syringe in your hand, standing over dear old dad, just before he breathed his last. And they have the autopsy report by one of the state's best pathologists. He says, on paper at least, that it was murder. You tell me? What kind of case do they have?"

Some of the arrogance drained out of him. Just some, not all. "Can you do anything tomorrow?"

"I'm going to try, Doctor."

"Will they be able to bring out ... the other things?"

"If you mean your conviction for murder, and the allegations that all this happened before, several times, the answer is no. Not formally. But you are a famous man.

Everyone in that courtroom tomorrow will have read about you and your little hobby. They don't have to say a word, you come in tarred with a very big brush."

"That's unfair."

"Probably. Fairness is sometimes a relative term."

"Goddamn lawyers."

I got up to go. Cork Miller answered my call.

"Try to look humble tomorrow," I said. "People like humble."

"Fuck you, Sloan," he snapped.

I presumed that humble was out of the question.

I HAD PUT OFF CALLING my office because I was afraid of the kind of message that might be waiting. But it had to be done. Just before five o'clock, the magic hour when Mrs. Fenton disappeared, I called.

It was Wednesday. According to my projected timetable, Sabin and the cops would have met with the attorney general to suggest that I be taken off the streets. Of course, that was my timetable, the one I was anticipating. Things might have been speeded up. Maybe they already wanted me to come in. Or maybe I would be arrested as I went to court in the morning.

Mrs. Fenton let me know she was irritated that I hadn't called until the last minute of the working day. Again, I thought she had mixed up in her mind who was the boss and who was the employee. But I let it go and listened to her recitation of the phone messages and the mail.

The *big* message hadn't come. Sabin hadn't called, nor had the cops, nor had The Bishop.

In a way I was relieved, but in another way what it meant was that it would be one more day of continuing suspense.

My motel was crawling with the media. There were several loud parties going on in several of the units. It was like a bunch of drunken alumni cutting up before the big homecoming football game.

And it was no place for me to be.

In fact, Broken Axe in general was no place for me to be, not if I didn't want to face the working press. I drove down to the nearest town, even smaller than Broken Axe, and had a quick dinner in a small restaurant. The food was good, and in this part of the farm world they believed a man worked best on a full belly, so the portions were good too.

After dinner I wanted to spend some quiet time preparing for tomorrow, but there was no place where I could do it. I knew the media people would have my room staked out, at least for a while. I drove back to Broken Axe, then followed the road to the lake and the gold coast homes.

I drove past the Cronin place. Lights were on in many rooms.

A sheriff's car was stationed at the entrance.

I kept driving until I came to a place where I could park and look out over the lake.

It was almost dark. Distant clouds, high above the lake, were washed in a soft red, a parting salute from the sun setting on the other side of the state.

A soft wind whipped up occasional whitecaps on the darkening lake below. Of course, it didn't look like a lake. It looked like an ocean, water stretching all the way to the far horizon. Canada was too far away to be visible. It was a freshwater sea holding in its depths just as many secrets as any ocean. It was a liquid graveyard, its waters concealing hundreds of wrecked ships, a last resting place for their crews.

It was deceptive.

Perhaps anyone driving by might look at me and see a man sitting peacefully in his car, watching the water, a tranquil man thinking tranquil thoughts, a man enjoying the final minutes of a good day. A man without care.

Also deceptive.

I tried to focus on the examination and what I might be able to do tomorrow. But like a radio station encountering interference, thoughts of my own plight kept intruding.

Dr. Miles Stewart, like him or not, was my client and entitled to my full concentration. Guilty or innocent, he was relying on me.

But I kept wondering if Sabin might have indeed met with his boss, and speculated on what they might have decided to do.

My thoughts bounced back and forth between Doctor Death and my own possible fate.

Finally I gave up. I started the engine and pushed a Jimmy Buffett tape into the slot. He sang a melancholy song about a man who wished he had been a pirate, a man who had no future and regretted that he had no meaningful past.

I turned on the lights and started back the way I had come.

The wistful song matched my mood exactly.

Being a pirate would have been far easier than being what I was. At least that's the way it seemed.

Maybe because the parties were still in full swing, I was able to sneak back into my motel room without being discovered.

I lay in the dark, listening to the mixture of sound: laughter, shouts, loud voices, singing, all blended into an alcoholic symphony. Several times people pounded on my door and called my name.

It would have been easy enough to get up and join them. But doing that would spell the end of myself and my career. It was almost worth it, just to end the suspense.

But I didn't.

I lay there. Listening. Thinking.

The parties died out around two o'clock. Shortly there-after I could hear the occupant in the next unit snoring, a big, loud alcoholic snore.

It must have been the up and down cadence of his lilt-ing nasal rhythm that did it. I drifted off as if I were lis-tening to soft music.

My little travel alarm woke me from a surprisingly deep sleep. If I had dreamt, I had no memory of it. For a moment I lay there, enjoying that wonderful lazy feeling you sometimes have in the morning, or at least you do until you remember what you have to do.

Thursday. Today I would try to help Doctor Death escape the clutches of the law. Also, today, if my projec-tions were correct, the law would finally get around to deciding which set of clutches would eventually grip me.

The lazy feeling blew away like smoke. I got up, danced in and out of the fiery hot shower, shaved, and prepared myself for the day.

They were waiting for me when I stepped out of the unit. They had been as quiet as hunters, but now with the game in sight they were shouting questions, thrusting microphones at me, and cameras were clicking away.

I smiled, nodded, and pushed my way to my car with-out saying anything but good morning. They tried to block the car but dodged out of the way as I slowly backed out.

Breakfast was out of the question. They would follow me like wolves after a stag, so I drove to the courthouse and encountered another group of media. It was a repeat performance except that the questions seemed sharper and more than a little insulting. O'Malley was with this pack, and his high-pitched voice dripped with venom as he accused me of everything but incest. I think he would have got around to that if I hadn't finally found the sanctuary of the courthouse. A deputy sheriff allowed me in and kept my pursuers out.

"The judge wants to see you, Mr. Sloan," he said, taking up a position at the door like Horatio at the bridge.

I went through the empty courtroom to the judge's chambers. The door was open.

"Hey, Charley! Come on in." Rudy Hathaway sat behind his desk, his feet up and looking as relaxed as if he was about to play a round of golf.

Eddie Rand sat on the judge's leather couch. He was dressed in a well-cut suit, and his long hair had been carefully brushed back. He looked like a hippie about to apply for a job in a bank.

"Have some coffee, Charley. And help yourself to the doughnuts. They're courtesy of Cork Miller. He's got a guy over there who's the greatest baker this side of Paris."

I poured coffee into a Styrofoam cup and gratefully bit into a doughnut. The judge was right. It was delicious.

I nodded my approval. "How come this guy works at the jail? He's really good."

Hathaway's rapid-fire cackle preceded his answer. "He doesn't work there, he's a resident. Every ninety days we let him out. He's good for about a week, then he gets drunk and beats up on his old lady. I put him back in for another ninety days. Boy, I miss those pies and cakes when he's free. But nothing's perfect, right?"

I helped myself to another doughnut.

"Charley, I'm delighted to see you, but I won't be sorry to see you go." Hathaway grinned. "I've had news people up the ass. One camera crew even came out to my place last night. I ordered them off—it's the folks' old farm, I got it when they passed on—and they still wouldn't go. Cork had to come out and run them off."

"A guy from Australia?"

"Yeah. Little runt, but with a big mouth. The whole gang of them are a bunch of pests. It's like having an invasion of locusts."

"They'll come up again, for the trial," Eddie Rand said,

sounding as if he didn't find them quite as annoying as the judge.

"Oh, shit. Don't remind me." The judge looked at me. "Listen, Charley, are you going to play things straight today or am I going to have to sit on you?"

"My reputation precedes me?"

"Something like that."

"Rudy, you can relax. This is going to be straight down the line, no tricks, no circus." I paused. "By the way, I expect to win."

Rand laughed. "Fat chance."

The judge frowned. "I thought you said no tricks. I'm not prejudging, but it sounds to me like they got your boy with the meat in his mouth, so to speak."

"Judge, I will be asking for no favors. Just a straight ruling on the law. A straight, fair decision is all I ask."

He cackled. "Shit, I haven't rendered one of those for years. Well, let's see what happens, shall we? You about ready, Charley?"

I nodded.

"How about you, Eddie? You got all your witnesses ready to go?"

"They're all waiting in my office."

Hathaway got up and slipped into his robe.

He grinned at both of us in turn.

"Showtime," he said. "It's showtime."

28

The courtroom quickly filled to capacity. One television crew, a pool camera, was set up at the side of the room to film the proceeding. The spectator section consisted of a mix of newsmen and locals all jammed together, eagerly waiting for the curtain to rise.

Judge Hathaway made a short statement about what was going to happen, with a warning that he expected the crowd to sit quietly and listen.

And then it began.

Eddie Rand called the deputy sheriff who had been first on the scene. He had interviewed Donna Cronin and had then arrested Dr. Miles Stewart.

I stood up when Rand was finished and announced I had no questions of the witness.

I heard an angry snort from my client, which wasn't hard to do, since he was sitting directly behind me.

The next witness was a state police detective who had come down on loan and was, in fact, the officer in charge of the case, if not officially.

He was a smart young cop, and Rand led him through the steps of his investigation quickly but carefully. I knew what he would say, since Rand had let me read his report.

This time I did have some questions.

"You said Doctor Stewart was already packed and about to leave when he was arrested, is that so?"

"Yes."

"Was his luggage searched?"

"The officers had reason to believe a murder had been committed. A legal search was done."

I didn't quarrel with legality. I think that surprised him.

"Did the officers find any medical supplies, drugs, syringes, that sort of thing?"

"No."

"That's all I have. Thank you."

Everybody looked surprised. The cop, Rand, the judge, and especially my client.

"What the *hell* are you doing?" Stewart whispered as I sat down.

I ignored him.

Rand then called Mrs. Legrand and her granddaughter, who had been at the Cronin home. Mrs. Legrand had to be helped into the witness stand and Rand had to shout his questions. Basically, she knew nothing except that Stewart had been a guest. The granddaughter's testimony was the same.

Again, I passed on questioning them. Behind me, I could sense Stewart's growing alarm.

Next Rand called the private nurse who had been on duty. She testified that Dr. Stewart had told her to take a break, that he would watch over the patient while she had a cup of coffee. The patient had been unconscious but alive when she left, she said. When she was called back, Sean Cronin was dead.

I asked her a few questions about the medicines given her patient but nothing more. As she quickly left the witness stand she looked grateful.

We took a short break. Rand and I went into chambers and had some more coffee with the judge. More doughnuts, too. Rudy Hathaway looked like he was enjoying himself.

"You off your feed today, Charley?" he asked.

"Just saving myself for later."

His high laugh must have been heard out in the courtroom.

"Well, I'm dying of curiosity. Let's go back at it, shall we?"

The crowd inside settled down quickly as Rand called Dr. Kim S. A. Kim to the stand. Doctor Kim testified that he had been treating Sean Cronin for practically everything that could go wrong with a person, from heart disease to kidney failure. He had seen Cronin the morning of the day he died. He said Cronin had been in bad shape but that he had seen him worse. He said that usually, on the request of the daughters, he saw Cronin once a day.

Rand turned him over to me.

"Doctor, did you expect Mr. Cronin to recover?"

He shook his head. "No. I had prepared his daughters. Mr. Cronin was very old and he was very sick. Frankly, he continued to surprise me by clinging to life."

"Doctor, were you treating Mr. Cronin with the drug Lasix?"

"Yes, among others. Lasix is standard when a kidney problem like Mr. Cronin's exists. Lasix helps the body get rid of excess water."

"This drug was given by the private nurses attending Mr. Cronin, I presume?"

"Yes. Under my directions."

"Did you direct that Mr. Cronin be given potassium chloride?"

He hesitated. "Yes. That's standard, in these conditions, to counter the effect of the Lasix. Lasix is a diuretic and in getting rid of fluid it tends to get rid of the potassium that the body requires in order to function."

"And the drug potassium chloride was there, in the house, for administration pursuant to your direction? Given, as a matter of fact, on a daily basis by the nurse. Is that correct?"

"Yes, it was."

"Thank you, Doctor."

Rand stood up for a moment, as if debating to continue questioning the doctor, then decided against it. "I have nothing further," he said.

"Thank you, Doctor." Rudy smiled from the bench. I guessed from the familiar warmth he exhibited that Kim was his doctor, too. "You're excused."

"I call Donna Cronin to the stand," Rand then announced in a loud voice.

She came forward as if going to her execution, her head down and her steps slow and uncertain. She took the witness chair and was sworn. Her answer to the oath given by the clerk was barely audible.

She was like a creature who lived in darkness suddenly pulled from that protection and shoved out into bright sunlight. I felt sorry for her. Physically, she might look like a professional wrestler, but that had been nature's nasty trick. Inside, judging from our first meeting, she was a shy girl, a sixty-year-old schoolgirl, afraid and without defenses.

Eddie Rand had to ask her several times to keep her voice up. It was a squeaky chirp and trembled at the edge of tears. Rand asked her about her father's last days and about his illness. Obviously, father had been the center of the Cronin universe. She told of his comas and periods of raving. A small tear trickled down slowly over her muscular cheek.

Rand tiptoed around questions that might involve her sister, but he did ask why Dr. Stewart had been invited.

Again, as she had in her home, she was careful to protect her sister, but she said a large amount of money had been paid to Dr. Stewart in the hope, as she put it, that her father's suffering could be brought to an end. She didn't expand on how that was to be accomplished, nor did Rand pursue it, except to ask her if it had been her idea. She said it hadn't been, and he dropped it right there.

Then her voice became a little stronger as she identified Miles Stewart and told of seeing him in her father's sickroom, syringe in hand. She said she had run to fetch her sister, and when they returned, Dr. Stewart told them Sean Cronin was dead.

"Do you believe that the defendant, Miles Stewart, killed your father?" Rand asked quickly.

Rudy Hathaway looked at me, expecting the usual objection. Conjecture was for experts only.

I merely shrugged and said nothing.

"Yes, I do," she said firmly.

Rand walked back, letting the answer hang in the air for effect and then he turned to me. "You may take the witness."

I stood up but didn't speak. She looked away. I could see her hands shaking in fright.

The courtroom was deathly quiet, waiting for what they thought would be fireworks.

I let them wait a minute and then I smiled at Donna Cronin. "No questions," I said, and sat down.

"What the *fuck* are you doing," Stewart hissed in my ear, "selling me down the fucking river!"

"Have faith," I whispered. I turned to smile at him. His face was flaming red.

"I call Doctor Clyde Anderson to the stand," Rand announced.

Clyde Anderson came forward—a tall, dignified man in his early sixties, looking more like a bank president than a pathologist. I had had him on a number of cases. He was an expert doctor and an expert witness, equally skillful in either role. I had studied his autopsy report until I felt I could recite it from memory.

"What is your name, please?" Rand asked.

"Clyde Anderson."

"And you are a physician licensed to practice medicine in the state of Michigan?"

Before he could answer, I stood up. "Doctor Anderson is well known to me. I will stipulate to his qualifications."

Rand seemed surprised, but then quickly continued.

"Did you perform an autopsy on the body of the late Sean Cronin?"

"I did."

Anderson calmly told of how the body was identified to him and how he had done his grisly work at the fine facilities of Humanic General Hospital in Bay City.

He went through the steps of weighing the organs, taking the blood and tissue samples, and then gave his opinion.

Sean Cronin, he said, had died from a lethal injection of potassium chloride, a drug that had caused instant cardiac arrest, which was the ultimate cause of death.

I stood up and glanced at my watch. "If the court please," I said, "I anticipate my cross-examination will be lengthy. I notice that it's close to lunchtime. I wonder if the court might consider taking the lunch break now?"

Rudy Hathaway scowled, pretending annoyance. "Are you trying to run my courtroom, Mr. Sloan?"

"I wouldn't think of it, Your Honor."

"What about you, Rand? You got any more witnesses, or is this it?"

"Subject to rebuttal, that's it," Rand answered.

"Well, despite counsel's rudeness"—he glared at me, but I knew he was acting—"we'll break now for lunch. We'll start again at one o'clock precisely."

He waited a beat. "I wish to see both counsel in my chambers," he snapped.

Rand and I followed him into chambers.

Taking off his robe, he addressed us. "How about I have Cork send over some sandwiches? We can eat here. No point in going out, not with that army of reporters waiting. Okay with you, Charley?"

"Sure."

"Mr. Prosecutor?"

"Fine by me."

He got on the phone and told Cork to have his excellent chef prepare sandwiches, all kinds and plenty of them. Then he put on water for coffee.

"What'cha got planned for the good doctor, Charley?" he asked as he spooned out the coffee grounds.

"I think you had better wait for that, Judge."

His high cackle reverberated throughout the room. "Good stuff, Charley?"

"I hope so."

"Hold on to your balls, Rand," the judge said. "I think we may yet find out how Charley here comes by his awesome reputation."

The sandwiches were just as good as the doughnuts.

And then it was time to start the examination again.

I was ready.

AT ONE O'CLOCK we trooped back out into the courtroom. It took a few minutes for everyone to settle down. Dr. Anderson once again took the witness stand.

"Doctor, in your report I notice that the lab report shows that Sean Cronin's potassium level was within normal range. Is that a misprint?"

"No, it is not."

"Did you discover a toxic level of potassium by some other means?"

"No, I did not."

"Yet you say that he died of a lethal dose of potassium. I did hear that correctly, did I not?"

He smiled. "You heard correctly, Mr. Sloan."

"Did you find, by physical examination, or lab reports concerning the tissues or blood, any substance in Mr. Sean Cronin that might be said to be at a toxic or deadly level?"

"No."

"As part of your examination did you investigate what medications were being given to Mr. Cronin, prior to his death?"

"I did."

"Was potassium chloride one of the prescribed medications?"

"Yes. Dr. Kim testified to that earlier today. He said, quite correctly, that the drug is given to offset the effects of a diuretic."

"Would that be standard procedure for someone like Mr. Cronin?"

"Yes, it would be. Given the condition of his kidneys and heart."

"How is that drug, potassium, given, Doctor?"

"Potassium is produced naturally by the body. It's necessary to life. It has a number of beneficial effects on the heart, kidneys, and other functioning organs of the body. When a sufficient amount is not produced naturally, when more is needed, it is prescribed. Too much is fatal."

"I understand that. But how is the drug usually administered?"

Dr. Anderson showed no signs of nervousness. He spoke as a teacher might to a somewhat slow pupil. "It can be given orally. In this case, Mr. Cronin was on an intravenous drip, glucose and water, and the drug was administered by injecting it directly into that IV drip. Potassium cannot be given by an intermuscular injection, the ones doctors usually give in their offices, because it's too painful. Even on an IV injection, it can be unpleasant. Sometimes liquid Valium is injected first."

"Did you find Valium in the blood?"

"No. I'm informed Mr. Cronin was unconscious much of the time. It probably wasn't needed, given that circumstance."

"Judging from your autopsy report, Mr. Cronin was in very bad physical condition, correct?"

He nodded. "Yes. He was of advanced age. To put it in layman's language, his heart had deteriorated to the point that it was more like a bag than a pump. The kidneys were almost useless. He was at the point of death from a number of causes."

"In your report, you make reference to Doctor Stewart's having been seen with a syringe, and you also refer to his reputation. Did that in any way contribute to your ultimate conclusion?"

"It did."

"I take it you accepted what you had been told as truthful?"

"Yes, I did. There was no reason to disbelieve what I was told. If it had been a gunshot wound and the defendant was said to have been seen with a smoking gun, I would have taken that into consideration as to whether it was murder or suicide."

"You equate the syringe with a smoking gun, so to speak?"

"I think most people would."

"Even doctors?"

He smiled. "Especially doctors."

"You conclude that the syringe held potassium?"

"I do. Given the deceased's condition, it wouldn't have taken much."

"But you found no toxic level of potassium in the body, isn't that right? How can you conclude it was potassium?"

"By a process of elimination."

"Oh? Can you explain this process to the court?"

He nodded. "If it had been any other kind of toxic substance it would have shown up in the lab work. Nothing was found. Potassium is natural to the body, as I said. Also, it dissipates quickly, especially in dying cells. The man died and I performed the autopsy approximately eight hours after death. By that time, even a toxic amount would have been dissipated, especially since a diuretic was being used."

"Have I got this right?" I asked. "You concluded it was potassium because you found no toxic amount of any substance?"

"Basically, yes."

"Even though the potassium level you did find was normal?"

"Something was in that syringe. Given the findings, it could only have been potassium. Anything else would have showed up."

I glanced up at Rudy Hathaway. He was following the testimony closely.

"Now, Doctor, let me propose to you a hypothetical question, if I may?"

He smiled.

"I will ask you to assume that a body, identical to Sean Cronin's, is brought to you for autopsy. But this time there is nothing in the record about Doctor Miles Stewart, his possible reputation, or any record of someone having seen a syringe, a smoking syringe. But, everything in the body is exactly the same physically. You perform the autopsy and find exactly what you found in

Mr. Cronin's body. What, in those circumstances, would have been the cause of death?"

Anderson looked at me. He smiled. I knew he would be fair.

"Cardiac arrest. The ravages of old age, basically."

"Death by natural causes?"

"Yes, exactly."

"Would it be fair then, Doctor, to say you found felonious death because of the reputation of the defendant and the circumstances reported to you, not because of the condition of the body in and of itself?"

He paused. Then he smiled. "A smoking syringe is hard to ignore, Mr. Sloan. Especially in some hands."

"Maybe. But you based your finding as to cause of death on what was told to you and not what you found physically, is that correct?"

"As I said, it was a process of elimination."

"But you found nothing toxic in the body, right?"

"That's correct. If you're going to kill someone, at least under these circumstances, potassium would be the vehicle of choice because, after an hour or two, it can't be detected."

"Like the little man who wasn't there? He wasn't there again today. Gee, I wish he'd go away?"

He laughed. "A bit more scientific than that, Mr. Sloan. It is a matter of deduction."

"Like Sherlock Holmes?"

"Without the assistance of Doctor Watson, but like that. The process of elimination."

"I have nothing further," I said.

Eddie Rand got up and made a show of going over some of the findings in the report. I could hear Miles Stewart's anxious breathing behind me.

"You are a fuck-up," he whispered in my ear.

Rand was going over the report again.

I stood up. "Objection. These questions have all been asked and answered before. The prosecutor is asking nothing new."

"Sustained," Judge Hathaway said.

Rand shrugged. "I have nothing more," he said.

"Any more witnesses?" the judge asked.

"No, Your Honor. The people ask that the defendant be bound over for trial on the charge of first-degree murder."

"Any argument, Mr. Rand, to back that up?"

Rand turned so that the camera in the back of the courtroom could catch his profile. Eddie, I thought, was in danger of going Hollywood, despite the rural setting.

"I don't believe any argument is necessary," he said. "We have shown that a crime was committed and that there is reasonable cause to believe the defendant committed it."

Rand sat down. He looked over at me and winked. It was the kind of wink a player makes to the other team after scoring the winning point.

"I presume you may have a word or two to say, Mr. Sloan?" The judge leaned back in his chair.

"Your Honor is entirely correct," I said, getting up and walking up to the bench.

"The prosecutor has stated exactly what he must prove for a defendant to be bound over for trial. He has to show a crime was committed. He has to show that reasonable cause exists to believe the defendant committed it."

The expression on Rudy Hathaway's face was unreadable. No one could tell what he was thinking.

"Let me address the last part first, if I may," I said. "I must agree with the prosecutor that he has shown reasonable cause to believe that the defendant's actions were criminal within the meaning of the charge."

"I want another lawyer!" Stewart shouted, standing up. The deputy behind him put a hand on his shoulder and pressed him back into his seat.

"It's a little late for that now, Doctor," the judge said. "Mr. Sloan is your lawyer and he is making an argument to the court on your behalf. I would advise you to be quiet. If not, the law allows us to gag defendants who tend to cause disruption in legal proceedings. I consider that fair warning, Doctor."

I looked back at Stewart. If he had a full syringe I knew who would get the needle at that moment. I nodded to him and smiled, then turned back and looked up at the judge.

"So, basically, I have no quarrel with the second part of the prosecutor's duty. It's the first part, the foundation, that I submit has not been met. He has not proven that a crime has been committed."

I could hear some exclamations behind me, but nothing more audible from Stewart.

I had memorized some Michigan cases and I now quoted them to the judge. He made a show of jotting down the citations.

"Basically, those cases, and others, say autopsy findings cannot be based on evidence outside the physical findings, no matter how persuasive they might otherwise be. In a murder case, a cause of death must be established, a felonious cause, an unnatural cause. That is not the case here. An old man died when his diseased heart stopped. I submit that is the only admissible cause of death shown. No matter how appealing conjecture might be, it can't be the ruling fact in an autopsy. You can call it process of elimination, deduction, or whatever else, but it boils down to guesswork, nothing more."

"The defendant was seen with the syringe just before the man died," the judge said. "That's not guesswork."

"Yes, it is. It may have been something he was looking at. Perhaps he was gauging the effect of medical care received, or the quality of the equipment used. We have no way of knowing if that syringe was full, empty, used, or new."

I met Rudy Hathaway's eyes. "Everyone presumes my client went up there to kill Sean Cronin, to put him out of his misery, whatever. Yet he brought nothing with him. Nothing was found on him or in his effects. He would have no way of knowing that a potential deadly drug was on hand. This whole case is based not on fact, but on suspicion."

Hathaway looked troubled.

"It can't be suspected that a man was killed," I continued. "It must be shown by medical evidence. The body was examined just hours after death. There was no attempt to hide anything. Nothing was found that would be toxic. Only suspicion. Suspicion can poison the mind, but it can't kill the body."

For effect, I waited for a minute. I was making a good argument, I thought, although I didn't expect to win. I expected Hathaway to duck the issue and bind Stewart over. I could take another shot when the trial came up. If, that is, I was Stewart's lawyer. Given my circumstances, by that time I might not be anyone's lawyer.

I looked at Rudy Hathaway. "They haven't proven a felonious cause of death," I said. "They haven't proven that a crime was committed. I ask that the charge be dismissed."

I returned to my seat.

"You're fired, you son of a backstabbing bitch!" Stewart rasped in my ear.

I ignored him.

The judge looked at Eddie Rand. "Any rebuttal, Mr. Rand?"

He stood up at his place. "None needed, your honor. The autopsy report says it all. Sean Cronin was murdered."

Then he sat down.

Rudy Hathaway appeared to be lost in thought, and

then he spoke as he stood up. "I want to see both lawyers in my chambers."

He stomped off the bench, and Rand and I followed him in.

Rudy left the robe on as he sat behind his desk. He fished out a short cigar, lit it, and puffed for a minute.

"I notice you said nothing about Miss Doreen all through this business, Charley. How come?"

"That had nothing to do with my point about the autopsy. Obviously, if you bind Stewart over, it's something that has to be brought out at trial. Justice may be blind, but she's not stupid. A jury has to know the full background. The prosecution can't play favorites, even up here."

"I can offer Miss Doreen immunity if she'll testify against Stewart," Rand said. "It'll be no problem, Judge."

Hathaway made no reply. He took out the cigar and studied it as if he had never seen it before.

"A trial won't be for just one day," he said. "It will be a media circus and it could last weeks."

"We don't get much live entertainment around here, Judge," Rand said. "I think the people will love it. A thing like this sure beats the county fair."

Hathaway did not laugh. "I was thinking of the Cronin girls," he said. "I don't think they'd love it. Did you see Miss Donna? God, it was a torture for her. I thought she might have a heart attack right there on the stand. And Charley didn't even ask a question."

"She'll be all right," Rand said, but he didn't sound as if he meant it.

"It would be a circus," the judge repeated. "Doctor Death. Mercy killing. It wouldn't be just a bunch of media jerks. A trial would bring up the wackos, the right-to-life bunch, the right-to-death bunch, and God knows who else." He looked at me. "Am I right, Charley?"

I nodded.

"What difference does that make?" Rand demanded, but without real fire. "There's been a murder here."

Hathaway puffed again on the cigar, emitting another puff of smoke.

Things seemed to be going my way, so I decided to keep my mouth shut.

The phone rang. Hathaway frowned. "Damn it, I told them to hold my calls."

He picked up the receiver. "What is it?" he snapped. "I'm a little busy here, in case you didn't notice." Then his face seemed to relax. "Oh, him! Sure, I'll talk to him. I always have time for that."

He smiled before he spoke again. "Hey, Judge, how are you doing?"

This was then followed by some grunts, some yeses, a few "un-huhs," but nothing much else. Then Hathaway did speak. "Yeah, we're just about done up here. I was just about to go out and give my Solomon-like decision."

There was another pause while he listened.

"Sure," he said. "He's right here. You want to talk with him?"

He looked up, grinned, and handed me the phone.

"Hello," I said, puzzled.

"Charles, this is Judge Bishop."

I almost dropped the phone.

"Rudy says you folks are just about through up there."

"That's right."

"Well, that's convenient. Charles, could you arrange to be in my chambers tomorrow morning? Say, eight o'clock?"

"What's the problem, Judge?"

"We can discuss that then. I trust I can count on you?"

"Should I bring an attorney?"

There was a pause. "At this point, Charles, I don't think it's necessary. I would appreciate seeing you alone."

"With Harry Sabin? Like the last time?"

"Please be here at eight o'clock, Charles. We can talk then."

He hung up and I handed the phone back to Hathaway.

"God, I just love that guy, don't you?" Hathaway beamed. "The Bishop. You can always count on him if you're in trouble. He's always ready to help a friend. Right, Charley?"

"Depends on the friend," I said, my heart beating at a trip wire pace.

Hathaway's look was confused. "Well, he's a great guy in my book." He took a final, big drag on his cigar. "I guess there's no reason to put this off. Let's go out and face the lions."

Rand and I walked out with the judge, then took our seats. The crowd in the courtroom quieted down. Even though Stewart was glaring at me, he said nothing.

"The court has carefully listened to the testimony given in this matter," Rudy Hathaway said in his professional judicial voice, stern and crisp. "And the court has carefully examined the autopsy report and listened to counsels' arguments."

He looked out in the direction of the camera. "The first function of a preliminary examination is the proof of a crime. The people must show that a crime actually happened. The test is not reasonable cause to believe it happened, but that it did happen. And that is a problem in this case."

I heard the rising murmur in the courtroom.

"I listened to Doctor Anderson. The crime of murder must first be established by evidence as to the cause of death. Here, a very old man, a very sick old man, died. He died in suspicious circumstances. However, there was nothing found in the body to show that he died of anything other than natural causes. He may have been poisoned by potassium chloride, but 'may have' doesn't answer the test imposed by the law. A murder may have been committed here, but again, 'may have' does not meet the standard imposed. It must be proved."

He paused. "In this case, it was not. On that basis, the charge of murder is dismissed."

Behind me the courtroom erupted. The judge left the bench and the clerk rapped unsuccessfully for order. Deputies kept the news people penned in the spectator section.

I turned and looked at Dr. Miles Stewart. To me, he appeared to be in shock.

"What does this mean?" he asked, almost in a whisper.

"The charge that you murdered Sean Cronin has been dropped."

"I'm free?"

"Of this charge, yes. You're still on appeal in the other matter. Your bond has been canceled, and as I told you, they'll send you to prison on the original conviction until a bond can be posted."

"How long?"

"Days, maybe weeks."

"You had better do it quicker than that."

"I'm not doing it at all."

"You're my lawyer!"

"You fired me."

His face grew red. "Then I want the fee I paid you back."

I shook my head. "Sorry. You paid to have me defend you on this case. I did, and I won. I earned the money, Doctor. On the other case, the appeal, let your new attorney contact me. We can come to some agreement on that fee."

"I don't want another attorney. You can't weasel out of this!"

I stood up and looked down at him. "You got by this

one by the skin of your teeth. If you do the potassium shuffle again, they'll get you one way or the other. You're out of business, Doctor."

"You're scum, Sloan, nothing but scum."

I smiled. "Say hello to the boys in your cell block for me, will you? Be sure to tell them you're a virgin. That way they'll be gentle."

His mouth worked but nothing came out. The deputies quickly took him away.

Eddie Rand was standing before the bench as though he were lost. I grabbed his arm and led him into the judge's chambers.

Hathaway, out of his robe and with his feet up, grinned at both of us.

"Surprised you, didn't I?" he asked, looking at me.

"You sure as hell did."

The judge looked at Rand. "Don't look so hurt, Eddie," he said. "You tried a nice case. It wasn't you. You just didn't have the medical. Anyway, this saves the Cronin girls and it saves the town. It might be a little unjust, but then, what isn't?"

He smiled at me. "Boy, I could sure use a drink. You sure you've sworn off, Charley?"

"Yes, Judge, I'm sure."

"Well, I suppose I'll have to stick to my guns too or end up bleeding again." He took out another small cigar. "Both you boys had better be prepared to meet the press out there."

He frowned at Eddie. "Be a little charitable in your remarks, Eddie, at least about me. I'd appreciate it. And I'll remember it." His high cackle sounded. "We do a lot of business, you and me. It's best to be friends."

He was right about the media. They were beginning to sound like an unruly mob, and it was a mob that had to be faced.

I stood up and started for the door.

"Did I hear you say you were seeing The Bishop tomorrow?" Hathaway asked me.

I nodded my head in agreement.

He beamed. "Be sure to say hello for me, Charley, will you? It pays to stay on the good side of a powerful man like The Bishop. Am I right, or am I right?"

29

knew they were only doing their job.

Still, that could have equally applied to the Mongols who swept into Europe burning and looting. It was a mix—newspaper people, magazine writers, free-lancers, television crews, both legitimate and of the O'Malley brand. In combination they resembled an angry-eyed, many-mouthed monster. Each had an angle to shoot, something different that would give them a slant or a lead that was unique.

And it was the story of the day, I had to admit that. The notorious Doctor Death had escaped the clutches of the law. Miles Stewart, M.D., had apparently committed murder and had gotten away with it. The rule so elo-quently stated by Fyodor Dostoyevsky, freely translated from the Russian, "Man, you do the crime, you gotta do the time," apparently didn't apply in Broken Axe, Michigan. They wanted to know why.

Cork Miller, in his usual efficient country way, had set up a press conference in the lobby of the jail. A bank of microphones and a lectern had been positioned facing what might easily have passed for a lynch mob.

Eddie Rand went first. He made a clean statement, saying he thought he had shown sufficient evidence to bind Stewart over for trial, but that he didn't quarrel with Judge Hathaway's decision. He said it was a close question legally and could have gone either way. He was being absolutely fair, but they went after him as if they had just discovered he had a new Swiss bank account paid for by Doctor Death.

He wasn't prepared for the barrage of questions that ranged from normal inquiry to allegations about his manhood and honesty. He was sweating, and the more they attacked, the more he began to shift from fair to ferocious. They were pushing him into making a statement that would play well on the evening news, film at eleven, a wild-eyed prosecutor yelling like a maniac.

I decided he had done me enough favors and that I owed him one back. I stepped up to the lectern and politely elbowed him aside declaring that I wanted my say.

Eddie had enough smarts to realize what I was doing. He looked at me the same way a puppy might who had just been saved from being gassed.

I insisted on making an opening statement, which was a repeat of the argument I had made to Judge Hathaway in court, calling into question the findings of the autopsy.

It sounded good to me.

Then I took the questions, smiling like a man running for office. They were all shouting, so I started pointing, like the president does at press conferences. That was something they understood, and pretty soon a measure of order was restored. I tried to pick people I knew and whom I thought wouldn't try to nail me upon a verbal cross.

O'Malley was jumping up and down with his hand up like a schoolboy who urgently had to go to the bathroom. His face was becoming as crimson as his hair.

To his surprise, I pointed at him. He opened his mouth but nothing came out. He had obviously forgotten what he wanted to ask. I smiled indulgently and pointed at another newsman. I could see humiliation mixed with hate in O'Malley's livid eyes.

I won some, I lost some, but overall I thought I came out even. I had said nothing that I would regret seeing later on television or reading in a paper or magazine.

They howled in protest when I thanked them for their kind attention and said it was late and that I had to return to my office downstate on urgent business.

Some of them followed me out to my car. I smiled and waved like President Reagan used to do, pointing to my ear as if I couldn't quite hear what they were shouting.

I returned to the motel and grabbed my bag. I thought they might be waiting for me, but they weren't.

Driving out of town, I felt like a prisoner making a successful escape.

It was a feeling that lasted for a few miles.

And then I remembered what awaited me.

The prisoner hadn't escaped after all.

THE THREE-HOUR DRIVE back seemed longer. It grew dark and started to rain, slowing most traffic but not all. A few idiots roared down the slick highway with suicidal abandon, passing recklessly in the face of oncoming traffic.

I stopped at a roadside restaurant for a hamburger and coffee. The hamburger was greasy and the coffee bitter, almost as bitter as my mood.

The victory back in the courtroom counted for nothing. My mind was occupied by what lay ahead for me. I had won other cases, over the years, but nothing would count tomorrow when I met with The Bishop.

It was Thursday, my usual meeting night, but it was too late now even to try to make the drive into Detroit, and so I drove back to Pickeral Point.

I didn't go to my office. Whatever waited for me there either in mail or messages seemed unimportant at the moment. I went to my small apartment.

I thought about calling Sue Gillis, maybe even dropping by her place, but I didn't feel like talking to anyone, even Sue. So I sat in my darkened apartment and watched the rain hit the parking lot below.

My mind was in neutral. I just watched the rain. I wondered what doomed prisoners thought on the last night before execution. I wondered if they might feel as I did, devoid of concrete thought, empty, just passing the time. Waiting.

Eventually I tired of the rain. I set the alarm for six. It was an hour's drive to Detroit and I had to be in Bishop's chambers at eight o'clock.

I really didn't expect to sleep, but somehow I did.

I awoke before the alarm went off, mechanically going through the routine of shaving and showering. I had some cereal although I didn't feel much like eating. And coffee.

I dressed carefully, not knowing whether I might be on camera, one way or the other, before the day was through. I made sure I had Wally Figer's telephone number, just in case I might have to make that one allowable phone call.

The drive was fast until I hit Mt. Clemens, but then the traffic on the expressway clogged up, and within a few minutes I was part of the rush-hour, slow march into Detroit.

I parked in a nearby lot and walked to Detroit's City-County Building, taking the elevator up to Judge Bishop's floor.

My timing was faultless, arriving as I did at exactly eight o'clock.

I walked across the courtroom, past the bench, and entered the judge's clerk's office. It too was empty.

The door to the judge's chambers was open. I looked in.

He was seated behind his desk in shirtsleeves. His head was down, his eyes fixed on the paperwork in his hand.

"Judge, you wanted to see me," I said.

He looked up, his eyes above the level of his reading glasses. That peculiar half smile flickered on his lips, the Mona Lisa smile, more enigmatic than welcoming.

He looked at his watch. "Charles. You're probably the only punctual attorney in practice today. Come in."

He indicated a chair in front of the desk.

"I've made fresh coffee. Want some?"

"No, thanks."

"Let me just finish this," he said, returning to the papers in front of him. As he read, he made a few notes in the margins.

It seemed a very long time. I could hear traffic noises creeping up from the streets below, muted but proof that there was life somewhere outside the deathly stillness of this deserted courtroom and offices.

Finally he finished. He stood up. "Sure you don't want some coffee?"

I shook my head.

He poured himself a mug from his coffee maker. Then he came back to the desk and sat down.

He sipped the coffee, smacked his lips, then put the cup down next to the papers he had been reading.

"I saw you on television last night," he said. "You're

amazing, Charles. How you got the doctor off must rank
with sawing a woman in half."

"They couldn't prove the deceased had died of anything
except natural causes," I said. "No magic tricks, I'm afraid,
just a matter of law."

That peculiar smile was refixed on his face again.
"Usually, on a close question, most judges will bind a
defendant over for trial and let a jury decide. Especially
someone as, well, famous as your client."

"Broken Axe is a small town. I think the media army
scared the hell out of everyone. They didn't want to think
of being invaded again. Besides, the main witnesses were
the deceased's daughters. I think Rudy Hathaway
thought going through a trial would be too hard on
them."

"Rudyard's a pretty fair judge. I'm surprised he'd let
something like that influence him."

"It wasn't a gift, believe me. The prosecutor didn't
have the proof. He knew my client did it. I knew my
client did it. Everybody knew my client did it, but they
couldn't prove it. It was a fair call."

"Justice triumphed, guilty or not, I take it?"

"The law triumphed. Procedure triumphed. Justice
may have taken a kick in the ass. It depends how you look
at it."

He sipped again at the coffee.

"Why did you want to see me, Judge?" I asked.

He studied me for a moment. "Can we put the answer
off for a while?"

"Why?"

"I'm going to ask you to indulge me, Charles. I wanted
you here with me for a purpose. Before the morning is
out you'll know why. Until then, unless you have strong
objection, I will ask you to stay here with me."

"There must be some explanation you can give me."

"Not at the moment, but soon." He chuckled. "I'm

going to ask you to trust me on this, Charles."

I wondered what other options I might have. I could think of none. I was in too deep now to object.

"But ..."

He held a finger to his lips. "I know this must seem somewhat juvenile, but let us speak of other things. At least for a while."

Again he sipped the coffee. "As I remember, you have a daughter. How is she doing?"

We talked. I bragged on Lisa for a while until the subject was exhausted. Then we talked about sports.

There was an unreal quality to the conversation, a lot like a condemned man chatting up the executioner. The axe was there, you just couldn't see it.

"I've adjourned my motions until this afternoon," he said. "I didn't want to be interrupted."

He glanced at his watch. "Funny, isn't it?" he said. "When you're waiting for something to happen, time always seems to move so slowly."

I didn't think it was funny at all.

THE JUDGE'S SECRETARY and clerk reported for work. They looked at me like an intruder, but said nothing.

We continued to sit there, the judge and I, trying to make small talk.

I felt like I was coming out of my skin.

Finally, his phone rang, and he quickly picked it up. He listened and then said, "Put him on."

Judge Bishop listened intently to whomever was speaking, silently nodding several times.

"Did he make a statement?" he asked.

Of course, I could not hear the answer. I just saw the judge move his head.

"Who's taking him up?" he asked. Again, he nodded in response.

"Everything go as you planned?"

He chuckled at whatever was said.

He looked at me. "Yes. He's here now. Sitting across the desk as we speak." He smiled. "I'll tell him."

He hung up and again studied me before speaking. He sipped the last of his coffee, then smiled again, this time just a trifle wider.

"You are, Charles, probably the luckiest man in the world."

Judge Bishop got up and now poured two cups of coffee. He handed me one without asking if I wanted it.

He sat down and looked at me.

"That was Harry Sabin," he said, "and that was the telephone call I was waiting for."

I was once again conscious of sounds. The secretary outside was typing something. Horns honked from somewhere below. A distant siren wailed. I was so aware I could have probably identified dust settling if I had thought about it.

"This would all have been so much easier, Charles, had you agreed to wear the wire as Harry asked. Although I understand your reasons, I must say I did not agree with them. However, that is all water under the bridge now."

His eyes met mine, and he continued.

"They just arrested Franklin Palmer."

"What?"

"They set him up rather cleverly, I think. He was arrested coming out of Jeffrey Mallow's office. He had fifty thousand dollars in marked money in his briefcase. Franklin has refused to make a statement, but the case is airtight. They are going to drive him up to Lansing to be arraigned privately up there. It's all been arranged. He'll be freed on personal bond. The press will not be informed until after the arraignment. Harry Sabin is scheduling a press conference for later this afternoon."

The Mona Lisa was smiling at me. "You took a terrible

risk, Charles, in not cooperating. Fortunately, for your sake, things have worked out, despite your reluctance."

"I don't understand."

He took out a key from his pocket and unlocked his desk. "When you met with Harry and Captain Hagan in my basement, Charles, you suspected we didn't believe you, isn't that right?"

"The thought had occurred to me."

He nodded, taking out a small tape for a microcassette recorder. "We had other knowledge, in addition to that which you offered. Both Franklin Palmer and Jeffrey Mallow were known to be in very dire financial straits. There was a persistent rumor that a judge, or judges, on the appellate court were corrupt. But nothing of a concrete nature presented itself until you came to me. As you know, I served on the judicial tenure commission and have continued to enjoy a certain unofficial relationship with the bar and police in cases where judicial corruption is suspected."

He opened the recorder and inserted the tape. "It was fortunate that you came to me. I was most flattered that you did."

He held up the small recorder. "Do you play poker, Charles?"

"On occasion."

"Then you know that sometimes a good player, lacking good cards, can still win if he's canny enough to run a convincing bluff."

"It happens."

"I could tell you what happened, but I think this recording—Harry Sabin gave me a copy—will explain more quickly and efficiently. No poker player ever ran a more successful bluff. By the way, it was all the idea of that state police officer, Lucas Hagan. You owe him a lot, Charles."

Before I could reply, he hit the play button and pushed

the tape recorder across the desk toward me.

I heard Harry Sabin's voice.

"Good morning, Judge Mallow," he said. His tone was not warm. "And this is Captain Lucas Hagan of the state police."

Jeffrey Mallow's deep voice boomed. "Good to meet you, Captain. And welcome to my office. Now, Harry, you sounded quite mysterious over the phone. What's up?" He sounded self-assured, congenial, but with just a touch of arrogance, the kind of condescension displayed by some people when they're meeting with those they consider to be a little bit lower on the social scale.

"A sad duty, Judge. You are under arrest for solicitation of a bribe, and—"

"What the hell is this?" Mallow demanded, his words cracking like a whip.

"I am required to give you your Miranda rights." Harry gave them in a singsong voice, despite being interrupted by Mallow, and he continued to the end.

"I know my goddamned rights," Mallow's voice was full of menace.

"Knowing that you don't have to answer any questions, do you wish to make a statement?"

"Hell, yes. I have nothing to hide, nothing." Mallow's tone was full of outrage.

"All of this is being recorded. Do you know an attorney by the name of Charles Sloan?"

"The drunk? Sure, I know him. Why?"

"He claims you—"

"Oh, let's cut out the shit!" It was Captain Hagan's rough voice. "We have the whole thing on tape, Mallow. We set you up and we got you." The cop's tone was nasty, malevolent.

"Bullshit," Mallow snapped back.

The cop's laugh was even nastier. "You thought you were being clever, didn't you, meeting him at that fancy health club, looking at his bare ass to make sure he wasn't wearing a wire."

"What do you mean?" This time Mallow's tone was a degree less arrogant.

"You're a stupid shit. What were you doing, playing James fucking Bond?" The cop's laugh was like a slap. "We had him wired, you pompous asshole. We had the wire in his watch."

"What?" The single word was barely above a whisper.

"Why did you think he didn't go for a swim? He couldn't get the watch wet." Now the laugh was like barbed wire. "You even looked at it. We damn near shit out in the truck when we heard that. But you didn't notice it wasn't working. It wasn't a watch, it was a microphone. Jesus, what a jerk."

Sabin's voice was low but strong. "He's right, Judge. We got it all on tape. Everything."

For a moment there was nothing but silence.

Then Mallow spoke, but this time there was no arrogance. "Look, perhaps we can work out something here."

"There's nothing to work out," Sabin said. "I'm sorry."

Mallow's voice had almost left him. "You don't understand. I was just a messenger boy."

"For who? Franklin Palmer?" Sabin asked. "Frankly, we don't think Palmer had anything to do with any of this. As far as we can see, this was a one-man operation. Yours."

"No, no, not at all," Mallow said. "This whole thing is Palmer's idea. I just told you, I was his messenger boy, nothing more."

"We don't have Palmer," the cop snapped, then laughed. "But we've got you, and that's enough."

"I can give you Palmer," Mallow said quietly, very quietly.

Again there was silence on the tape.

"What do you mean?" Sabin asked, just as quietly.

"He has nothing," the cop snapped. "He's just trying to wiggle off the hook."

"I can give you Palmer," Mallow repeated, his voice shaking.

"How?" Harry Sabin sounded doubtful.

"I can wear a wire. I'm the one who delivers the money. I can do that. You can use marked money."

Again there was a pause.

"And what would you want in return?" Sabin asked tentatively.

"Immunity."

"Fat chance," the cop growled.

"Look," Mallow said, close to whining. "Palmer set this whole operation up. I'm just his messenger. Oh, I get a commission, but a small one. It's Palmer's thing. I'm just a minnow here. Palmer's the fish you want."

"He's your friend," Sabin said.

"A business arrangement," Mallow replied shakily. "That's all, just a business arrangement."

"C'mon, Harry, let's arraign this asshole and get it over with," the cop said harshly.

There was a pause.

"I can't give you immunity," Harry Sabin said. "I'd have to talk to the attorney general."

"Talk to him," Mallow pleaded. "He'll want Palmer."

"I can't grant you immunity, Judge," Sabin continued, "and I'm not going to the attorney general unless you tell me everything right from the beginning. But remember, if immunity isn't given, it can all still be used against you. Knowing that, will you answer my questions?"

"Jesus," Mallow said. A peculiar sobbing sound reverberated through the tape.

"Well?" Harry asked softly. "Is that agreeable?"

"Oh, Jesus," Mallow repeated, but his voice sounded stronger. "Okay." The word caught in his throat. He paused for a moment and then sounded as if he had pulled himself together. "You see, none of this was my idea. But one day Palmer and I were talking—".

Bishop reached over and snapped off the tape recorder.

"Spilled his guts," he said, "as the saying goes. Of course, he put everything on Palmer, but that was to be expected."

"Did they grant him immunity?" I asked.

"They played with him a while, and then they did, on the condition that he cooperate fully. He did. He helped them make a hell of a case on Palmer."

Bishop sipped his coffee. "Of course, Mallow will be disbarred for life, obviously. It's a shame there won't be harsher punishment, but they couldn't have gotten Franklin Palmer without Mallow's help."

"Do they have him?"

He nodded. "They wired Mallow and set up a meeting. Mallow was instructed on what to say. Palmer walked into the trap without suspecting a thing. That was Tuesday. Today, they set up and taped another meeting, and Mallow passed the marked money to Palmer. Everything was recorded. Palmer was arrested as he left Mallow's office a few minutes ago."

"My God."

"It could have gone the other way, Charles. If Mallow hadn't gone for the bluff, they'd have only your unsubstantiated statement, nothing more. Mallow would have gone after you. Your license might well have been in jeopardy. Of course, you knew that."

I nodded.

"You have nerve, Charles. Guts, as they say in the street. I'm impressed."

"Now what happens?"

He leaned back in his chair. "As we speak, Captain Hagan is driving Franklin Palmer up to Lansing to be arraigned on the charges. It will be done privately.

Franklin will be released on personal bond. He will be allowed to drive back here on his own. Of course, everything will explode when Harry Sabin holds his press conference."

"When?"

"Today. Three o'clock. Up in Lansing. That's when you become a hero, Charles."

"What!"

He chuckled. "None of this would have happened, Charles, if it hadn't been for you. Harry Sabin is going to give you full credit."

"Jesus!"

"I take it that you're not pleased."

"You take that right. Look, I really didn't want anything to happen. I just wanted to do my job, try my case. All of this is like a nightmare. Now, it's going to look like I'm the prime whistle-blower in Middle America."

"Oh, Charles, people will know you are an honorable man. They'll respect that."

"People? What about judges? Jesus, every time I walk into a courtroom the judge will think I may be coming after him. It'll be like Jonah coming on board a ship. This is a personal disaster."

He smiled, a little warmly for the first time. "You did the right thing, Charles. Judges, lawyers, many others, will honor you for that. Many wouldn't have done what you did. Corruption is always so very easy. And opposing it is very difficult. Believe me, by the end of the day you will be a popular hero."

"What about Palmer and his family? You suppose I'll be a hero to them?"

"Franklin Palmer, whom I like, became a thief," Bishop said. "He did it voluntarily. He knew there would be a price if he were caught. He is going to pay that price now."

"Oh, my God."

Bishop got up. He came over and extended his hand. "For what it's worth, you have my respect."

He shook my hand, but it didn't make me feel any better. I wondered what Judge Palmer might be thinking as he was being driven up to Lansing. I wondered what he might be thinking about me.

"The press will have this at three o'clock, Charles. I suggest you make yourself available. It's always best to get these things over as quickly as possible."

I got up.

He chuckled. "This will make two nights running that I will be seeing you on television, Charles. You're going to be famous."

I had escaped the personal destruction that I had expected, but I didn't feel any better for it.

In fact, I felt worse.

30

drove back to Pickeral Point, staying in the right-hand lane and driving slowly. I was conscious that annoyed drivers were whipping past my slow-moving car, but I didn't care.

Franklin Palmer had been arrested in Detroit, accord ing to The Bishop, sometime around nine o'clock. Lansing was about two hours away from Detroit by car. The arraignment would take only minutes. Unless he stopped along the way, Franklin Palmer would drive back to Detroit and arrive somewhere around one or two o'clock. I wondered where he would go. I wondered if he would duck the press, go into hiding, or perhaps handle the charge defiantly.

I glanced at the car clock. If I was correct, Franklin Palmer would now be driving back from Lansing.

I wondered if he might also be driving slowly in the right-hand lane.

I wondered what he might be thinking.

I wondered if he thought about stopping and having a drink.

I know it was something I was thinking about.

THE STORM BROKE before the three o'clock news conference in Lansing, but only minutes before.

I was in my office, trying to organize my thoughts so that I could make a careful reply to the avalanche of reporters that I knew would soon descend upon me. I even made some notes.

Mrs. Fenton had been informed to hold all calls until after three, and to screen everything after that. I asked her to work late, and to my great surprise she agreed. She sensed something big was up and curiosity won out over established routine.

If Franklin Palmer didn't plead guilty I would be called as the main witness against him. I wondered how I would feel, sitting in the witness chair, his eyes on me, listening as I drove the final nails in the case against him.

I tried to put it out of my mind. Given the circumstances, I was sure he would plead guilty. Prison was certain, but maybe he could bargain for a shorter term.

"I know you don't want to talk to anyone," Mrs. Fenton said, peeking into my office, "but there's a state police captain on the phone, and he won't take no for an answer. His name is Hagan."

"I'll talk to him."

I picked up the receiver. "Hello, Captain."

"Harry Sabin asked me to call you," he said. His voice was professional, emotionless. It was a voice I knew well, the voice of a working cop.

"Are you in Lansing?" I asked.

"Yes. The Detroit police just called. Franklin Palmer has shot himself."

"What!"

"Apparently he drove directly from the court here to the boat he keeps at that yacht club on Belle Isle. Several people, the police say, talked to him but noticed nothing unusual. He seemed distant, but that was all. He went directly to his boat. He was the only one on it. A boat boy heard a noise and reported it. They found him in his cabin. He used a .38 caliber pistol, registered to himself, put it in his mouth, and blew the back of his head off."

"Oh, my God!"

"The police checked. He called no one that they know of. He left no note. At least none has been found. Harry Sabin said I should let you know immediately. This ends our case, of course, but it will just make the publicity that much more. The newspapers know he killed himself. In a few minutes, Harry will tell them why."

He paused. "Harry said you should know right away, to be prepared to handle the questions. He suggested you might want to prepare a written statement to hand out. He said that might take off some of the heat. Maybe he's right."

"Palmer's daughter. I presume she's been notified?"

"As far as I know." He paused again, and then spoke in a different tone, not quite so cold. "It wasn't your fault, Sloan," he said. "He brought it all down on himself."

"What he did doesn't carry the death penalty."

"He was a judge. Apparently, he thought it did. Anyway, it's done. He was a thief, a high-placed one, but he was still a thief. You did the right thing, Sloan. In fact, I kind of admired that you wouldn't wear a wire. I use finks all the time, but the fact is, I hate them. And I don't like lawyers as a general rule, but I might make an exception in your case.

"Anyway," he said, his voice reverting to his normal cop tone as he prepared to hang up. "He saved the state of Michigan the cost of a trial. You take care, Sloan."

MRS. FENTON LOOKED UP as I walked out.

"Where are you going?" she asked. "Are you coming back?"

I didn't reply.

I got in my car and drove to the inn.

The lunch crowd was gone and it was too early for dinner. Other than a few tourists, the place was almost empty. I walked past the reception desk to the bar.

I took a stool near the windows facing the river.

The bartender came over and smiled. "Yes, sir?"

"A double scotch, on the rocks," I said.

"You're Charley Sloan, the lawyer, right?"

"Yes."

"I saw you on television last night. Boy, you must be really good to have gotten that guy off."

"Just a journeyman doing his job." I was annoyed that he wasn't getting me my drink.

"I was just watching the television. They broke in with a bulletin about a Detroit judge shooting himself. Palmer, I think they said the name was. Did you know him?"

I nodded.

He shook his head as he moved down the bar and splashed a generous amount of scotch into a nice big glass. "It makes you wonder about people," he said, adding ice. "Man, there are sick people who would give a fortune for just a day or two more of normal life, and a guy like that blows it away, probably for nothing."

He put the drink on a paper napkin in front of me. I stared at it. The color was as beautiful as an autumn day.

"This guy did it with a gun," he went on. "I used to work in a hospital. Man, people would find the damnedest ways of killing themselves. They'd gas themselves, hang themselves, poison themselves. Human ingenuity." His laugh was big, at least as big as the scotch in the glass. "I suppose if you really want to do it, you'll find a way. Right?"

I looked at the beautiful scotch, and then up at him. He was still grinning.

"There are lots of ways," he said.

I got up and left a ten spot on the bar.

"Hey, your drink!" he called after me.

I didn't reply.

One suicide a day was enough.

AS EXPECTED, THEY CAME ON like the beginning of a rainstorm, just a few drops at first, and then the deluge.

The rest of the day went by in a blur. I gave an interview to Sherman Martelle of the *Free Press* and Danny Conroy of *The Detroit News*, plus a number of others, including the stringer for *The New York Times*. The newsmen piled up in my waiting room like patients waiting for a doctor during a flu epidemic. I handled them all. But I refused all on-camera interviews for television. They would have to rely on Harry Sabin's press conference for film clips. Even the best statement in the world could be made to look like something else with a little careful editing. I declined to take the risk that what I said might be turned into that something else.

Everyone, for a change, seemed friendly enough. There were a few hostile-sounding questions, but apparently they were going to treat me as a civic hero, just as The Bishop had predicted.

But that didn't make me feel any better.

I got rid of the last one about nine, and Mrs. Fenton departed, with enough stories and gossip to feed her lady friends for at least six months. She looked as happy as I had ever seen her, which wasn't very happy, but at least several steps up from her usual dour appearance.

I was alone when the phone rang. Without thinking I picked it up rather than let the machine take the call.

As soon as I recognized the voice, I regretted it.

It was Mickey Monk, but he didn't sound drunk. Not at all. Every word was spoken crisply with the snap of anger.

"You are a rotten son of a bitch, Sloan," he said. "You've blown the McHugh case. The poor bastard was relying on you. I was relying on you. He's done for, you miserable excuse for a lawyer. All you had to do was pay the fucking money. And even if you couldn't do that, you could've told me and I would have found a way to come up with it."

"Look, Mickey—"

"Don't give me that honesty bullshit. Your first duty was to McHugh, nobody else. I don't know what you expect to get out of this civic hero crap, but it better be good. It should be good enough to bury your fucking conscience so that you won't think about that poor bastard in his wheelchair. You fixed him for life, you sanctimonious prick."

"Mickey, there was nothing else I could do."

"We both know that isn't true."

"The case isn't over."

He snorted. "Jesus, I hope you don't think I believe that! You must think I'm stupid. It's over. They'll order a rehearing and then find for the company. Very quietly. They do that in this kind of circumstance. They'll kill the case like a fucking dying sheep. McHugh has no voice, no money. He had nobody but you, you prick. Now he has nothing."

"Mickey—"

"I never hated anyone in my life, never. Until now. I hope something really bad happens to you. You goddamn well deserve it."

"Mickey …"

I realized I was talking into a dead phone.

I hung up. The phone rang again almost instantly. But I had learned my lesson. The ringing stopped and my recorded voice was telling the caller a message should be left after the long beep.

I heard the beep, and then I heard the message.

"You are a murderer." The words were spoken in fury. For a minute I didn't recognize the voice, and then I knew it was Caitlin Palmer. "My father trusted you. He helped you. You killed him. I know you did, and you know you did. I hope to God your rotten soul burns in hell." She started to sob and then the message tape ended.

The machine made a small beeping noise, signifying it was ready to receive another message.

The little red light blinked at me like an accusing eye.

I almost ran from the office.

31

Sue Gillis was home when I got to her apartment. She didn't seem surprised to see me. She was dressed in jeans and a floppy shirt.

"I called you," she said. "Several times. But your secretary said you weren't taking phone calls."

"Mrs. Fenton has her good points. They escape me at the moment, but I'm sure she has them. Anyway, I should have told her you were on the A list."

She kissed me lightly. "I called you last night, too, but all I got was the machine."

Then she grinned.

"You've won, Charley. I thought in all honesty that they were framing you, but you won. The radio is full of what happened. You were a star on the six o'clock television news. They ran clips of everybody involved, including that judge, Palmer. They even showed his boat. It's a yacht."

"It was his love object." It came out flippantly, but I was saddened at the price he had paid to keep his boat and his commodore flag. Silly things in the general scheme, but he had been willing to risk dishonor and death to keep them.

"Have you eaten?"

"No. I've been too busy becoming a folk hero."

"How about I whip up some bacon and eggs?"

"Great."

She busied herself in the small kitchen. "You were terrific on television last night. Did you see it?"

"No."

"Of course, they twisted things a bit. They made it sound as if you had used some kind of trick to get that doctor off."

"That's show business."

"You looked great up there in front of all those microphones. I was very proud, Charley, despite what they seemed to be saying about using legal tricks."

"Thanks."

By the time I finished eating it was time for the eleven o'clock news. Sue switched on the set and each station— we switched around to see how they covered it—devoted almost the entire program to the story.

It was a natural. Every station had film clips in their library of everyone involved. I saw Franklin Palmer at a bar convention. I saw Jeffrey Mallow making a speech to businessmen. There was plenty of footage from the past to cover everyone. I saw myself. They didn't have to reach deep for me; they used my appearance before the microphones up at Broken Axe, only they cut my voice and the anchorman did a voice-over, giving some personal history about Charley Sloan, the lawyer. Flamboyant, was one adjective. Controversial, was another. He referred to my having had problems in the past with the bar, and the law. He did everything but call me a crook, stopping just short of that. His point was that the police had set a thief to catch a thief, although he didn't say it exactly that way. Almost.

It took a little gloss out of my status as hero. I imagined that the other media would take a similar tack.

We both sat quietly as the various news programs killed the last few minutes with sports results.

"You looked nice," Sue said quietly.

"And a little crooked. A dishonest man who turned honest for some secret reason known only to himself. Well, at least they got the name right."

"You're overreacting, Charley. It wasn't that bad."

"It'll be the lead story for a week. They'll do background pieces on Mallow and Palmer and me. They'll cover everything, including my license being suspended in the past. It can't be helped."

"Oh, Charley …"

"Then the editorials will call for a revamping of the courts, reform, that sort of thing. Then, you know what'll happen?"

"No."

"It'll all die away, like an old movie. People will remember feelings more than facts, if that. Six months from now most of the people glued to their sets tonight won't even be able to remember Palmer's name, or mine."

"Maybe it's better that way."

"Maybe it is."

She hesitated, almost shyly. "Would you like to stay the night, Charley?"

I looked up at her. "What, you think I'm easy?"

"There have been rumors."

I NOT ONLY SPENT THE NIGHT, I spent the whole weekend. We didn't go out except for a drive. Sue cooked, and I slept a great deal of the time. And we made love. Sue didn't mention marriage, but I found myself thinking about it. But that was a decision to be shelved for a less turbulent time.

For me the weekend was a time of healing. In my dreams I sometimes saw Franklin Palmer's accusing face, but during the waking hours I began to focus on the guilt that plagued me.

I felt bad that it had happened. But the state cop had been right: Franklin Palmer brought it all on himself.

He should have known better than to have Mallow approach me. Palmer did know me. He knew the man behind the sometimes questionable reputation. He should have known I was honest. But apparently he had forgotten the man and adopted the truth of the illusion.

Monday I went back to the office. The story was blowing out, but I still had newspeople calling. It was local. There didn't seem to be the kind of national interest generated by Doctor Death's case. Apparently crooked judges didn't spark a national taste. Maybe it was a familiar story elsewhere.

In any event, most of the calls were from local media people. Except one, just before eleven o'clock.

Mrs. Fenton was always impressed by judges. She was nearly swooning when she came into my office.

"The chief judge of the appellate court is on the line," she said, sounding as though she had just been conversing with God.

I nodded and picked up the receiver.

"Sloan," I said.

"Yes, Mr. Sloan. This is Judge Duckworth."

"What can I do for you, Judge?"

"This is all a terrible business for our court, as you can appreciate."

"Yes."

"Could you arrange to meet with me here in my

Detroit office about four? I've spoken to Craig Gordon, your opposite number on the McHugh case, and that's convenient for him."

I noted he had called the high-powered Gordon first.

"I can be there," I said. "What's the purpose of the meeting?"

"The death of Judge Palmer has thrown the court into turmoil at a number of levels. One, of course, is the situation in cases where he sat as a member of the panel and no decision has yet been made. The McHugh case is one of those, obviously, in addition to being the catalyst in all of this business."

He said it with a slight air of disgust.

"In any event, it is the disposition of that case that I would like to discuss with both of you."

"I'll be there," I said.

JUDGE DUCKWORTH'S OFFICE was large, befitting his title. He was a short and stout man. I had had cases before him and he had always been extremely serious. He was now as serious as a mortician as he faced Craig Gordon and me across his big desk.

Craig Gordon was as dignified and convivial as he had been when we had argued the McHugh case. He seemed to have a perpetual smile, a gambler's smile, a smile of a man who liked the cards he was holding.

Duckworth veered toward the emotional as he told us what a shock Palmer's death had been, and the circumstances. He said he had a duty to see the court wasn't dragged in the mud because one judge had violated his oath.

I nodded and Gordon smiled.

"It is in the interest of the court to dispose of the McHugh case in a fair and, one hopes, a speedy manner."

He shifted a bit uncomfortably. "There are two basic

ways we can proceed," the judge said. "The obvious way is to order a rehearing before an entirely new panel of judges. This, of course, would take quite some time. We are a busy court."

He looked at each of us. "The other way is to let the surviving two judges decide the case, as is."

Gordon sighed, then spoke. "My guess, and it's only that, is the two judges are split. One seemed to favor Mr. Sloan's view, and the other my own. In other words, a tie. As I understand the law, if the case turned out to be just that, a tie, the lower court ruling would be upheld. I would lose, and Mr. Sloan would win. Am I correct, Judge?"

Duckworth looked uncomfortable. "As usual, Mr. Gordon, you are quite correct."

Gordon's smile quickly disappeared. "May I ask you, frankly, if you've talked to the two judges?"

Duckworth colored slightly. "Everything in this case is unusual. I have never before polled any of my judges on how they might decide a case. But nothing like this has ever happened before. Yes, I talked to them."

Gordon nodded. "Is my presumption correct? It would be a tie?"

Duckworth nodded. "Yes."

Gordon pursed his lips. "I anticipated something like this when you called this morning. I talked at some length with executives at Ford about various possibilities."

He looked over at me and then back at the judge. "You know, Ford is completely innocent in this matter. It arises out of a business they acquired, and from a machine no longer produced. But it's the company name that's used in all the litigation, innocent or not."

The smile flashed back on. "I pointed out to the people I talked with that the case was a close one. I couldn't guarantee that we would win if it was reheard. You agree, Mr. Sloan?"

"That's my point of view, too."

Gordon went on. "If this case keeps on, it will always be associated with Judge Palmer's unfortunate death and the scandal surrounding it. There's a lot of money involved, but it's a drop in the bucket with the money spent by Ford to keep its good reputation in the market."

He paused. "I'm instructed, if a tie is probable, to agree to handle it that way. It's called public relations, or cutting your losses, but whatever, my client will agree to have the case decided by the two surviving judges."

For a moment I thought I had misheard him.

Duckworth looked at me. "I presume you have no objection?"

"Are you sure about the split?" I asked. "If that's a fact certain, of course, I agree."

Duckworth sighed. "This, gentlemen, can go no further than this office. I trust you both agree. The judges will issue opposing opinions. It is an exceptional solution to an exceptional circumstance. I hope to God I never find this court or myself in these circumstances ever again."

Gordon spoke. "I presume you'll want something in writing, agreeing that the case is to be decided by the surviving judges?"

"Yes," Duckworth said.

"I'll dictate something now, if you like?"

"That would be helpful," the judge said.

I still couldn't believe what was happening. "Of course, I will too," I said.

And we did, Gordon and myself.

With two signatures, the case was over in fact if not officially. According to Duckworth, that would be announced in a few weeks, after everything had blown over.

I had won the McHugh case after all.

CRAIG GORDON walked me out to the elevators.

"You must be feeling pretty good," he said.

"I feel good for McHugh. I feel bad that things had to happen this way."

"You're an interesting man, Mr. Sloan."

"Call me Charley."

He smiled. "Charley, you are a sole practitioner, are you not?"

"Yes. A one-man office up in Pickeral Point. It may not be glamorous, but it suits me. I make a living."

"I head up the litigation section at our firm," he said. "We engage in big-money cases mostly. I think we represent most of the large business interests in this part of the state."

I laughed. "That's nice for you."

"I have a number of lawyers working in the litigation section. Most of them have minimal experience at real trial work. Of course, we try to settle most matters before they ever see a courtroom."

"You should have settled McHugh."

"You're absolutely right. Hindsight is always best, of course. But our trial people, to be frank, did a very poor job before the jury. An appeal is usually only as good as the case it's founded upon."

"True."

"What I'm saying, Charley, in a somewhat roundabout way, is we need a good trial man, someone who isn't afraid to get into the fray and start swinging. I've talked to some of the others on the firm's governing committee and they agree with me."

"There are a lot of trial lawyers around," I said.

His smile broadened. "You're right, of course. How would you like to come with us?"

"Pardon me?"

"We are the premier firm in the state, Charley. You would be our principal trial lawyer. I'm authorized to offer a partnership. I think the income is considerably more than just a living."

I was stunned. "You know my reputation?"

"I've made it a point to know everything about you. I wouldn't make this offer unless I did."

"I wouldn't fit in," I said.

"Well, this isn't exactly a fraternity, Charley. If you did your job—"

"I'm flattered, believe me. But it isn't for me. I like what I do now, and the way I do it. I'm grateful, of course. But, believe me, there is an army of very good trial men out there if that's what you want."

"You're right. But you have one quality that can only be shown by demonstration. A quality that's of utmost importance to our firm."

"And that is?"

The elevator came and he stepped aboard.

"You're an honest man, Charley. These days, that's becoming a rare attribute."

I didn't get on, and the doors started to close.

"Think about it," he said. The last thing I saw was that famous Craig Gordon smile.

I CALLED MICKEY MONK. His office was only a few blocks away.

"What the fuck do you want?" he snarled into the phone.

"I want to talk to you. It's important."

"Bullshit, important. We got nothing to talk about."

"It's about the McHugh case. I just came from a meeting with Duckworth, the chief judge."

"What happened, as if I didn't know. What did you do, sell us out twice?"

"I want to talk to you, face-to-face," I said.

"If I see you I'm liable to punch your fucking lights out."

"I'll take the risk."

He paused. "All right. I'll meet you at Brown's Bar on Lafayette. You remember where that is, you sanctimonious—"

"I remember," I said, cutting him off.

"Five minutes," he snapped. "I'll be there in five minutes."

I hung up and walked to Brown's.

Most of the downtown bars had gone out of business, but Brown's had managed to survive. When I used to drink, it had been one of my regular hangouts. A small place, with a long bar and no tables, it was a place for people who were serious about their drinking.

When I got there and my eyes adjusted to the darkness I could see two people sitting at the far end of the bar. They sat staring beyond their glasses, looking at nothing. They were thin men, gaunt, and obviously intensely serious about their drinking.

I took a stool near the front.

I didn't recognize the bartender. Of course, it had been years since I'd been in the place.

"What'll it be?" he asked.

"Coke," I said.

"And what?" he asked.

"Just Coke."

He looked puzzled, as if no one had ever ordered just a soft drink before, then shrugged and went to get my order.

Mickey came in looking like a storm about to break. He scowled at me and took a seat two stools away, as if what I had might be catching.

"Double scotch, Fred," Mickey called to the bartender, and then looked at me. "All right, prick, say what you came to say."

"I met with Duckworth and Ford's lawyer, Craig Gordon."

"Why?" He took the drink from the bartender and gulped it in one swift motion, then signaled for another.

"Duckworth wanted to get rid of the McHugh case as quickly and quietly as possible."

"I'll bet he does. So, what did you do, take a job with Ford?"

I started to laugh but his face showed just how angry he was, so I stopped.

"Close, Mickey, but no cigar. Duckworth said there were two choices. One, we could have it heard again from scratch with a new panel. The other choice was to let the two surviving judges decide the case, as is."

"They should have contacted me. It's my case."

"I'm of record, Mickey, for the appeal."

"So, what was decided?"

"The Ford lawyer wants to distance the company from the case as quickly and quietly as he can."

He sneered. "What do they care? It wasn't their vehicle anyway. They bought the lawsuit."

"The public doesn't know that. The Ford lawyer figures that every time the case comes up it'll get a big replay because of what happened."

"What you made happen," Mickey snapped.

"Anyway, to make a long story short, they agreed to let the two judges decide it."

"A fix. I can smell it."

"One judge is for us, one judge will decide against us. Duckworth said so."

"So, it's a tie. Big fucking deal."

"If it's a tie, Mickey, the rules say the lower court judgment stands."

"Well, I …." His eyes grew larger as he realized what I had just said. "Tell me that again?"

"If the two judges don't agree, and these two don't, the lower court judgment stands. In other words, the jury's verdict decides the case."

"Ford didn't agree, knowing that."

"As I said, they want out. It wasn't their party to start with, and they'll pay the money just to avoid any association with the scandal."

"Charley, if this is some kind of joke—"

"Duckworth said they'd make it official in a couple of weeks as soon as everything died down. Craig Gordon, the attorney for the other side, and I agreed to that in writing."

"You mean we win?"

"Yeah, Mickey. The whole thing."

His face screwed up, and for a moment I thought he was going to cry. He looked away for a while and then again turned to me.

"I'm very sorry about what I said. About you."

"I can't blame you, given the circumstances. But I did what I had to do, Mickey. It turned out okay but I had no other options."

He laughed. It was a laugh that was almost hysterical. "Hey Fred, bring me two doubles, and buy everybody a drink on me. You too." Then he turned to me.

"You got to understand, Charley. I had bet everything on this case, everything."

"I do understand."

He giggled. "Jesus. You know, I can afford to quit this fucking business. I'm rich!"

"In a couple of weeks you will be."

"I can save my house. Everything." He took his drink from Fred and downed it. "Well, maybe not my marriage, but who cares? I'm going to have enough money to buy a boatload of women. Have a drink, Charley, a real drink. It's an occasion. We'll turn this into a victory party."

"I have to go." I stood up and shook hands with him. "Go easy on the hootch, Mickey. There's no use in having money if you aren't around to enjoy it."

"Jesus, Charley, how could I have ever doubted you? You are the slickest guy I've ever known. You managed to win the case and hang on to the hundred grand those two fucking crooks wanted. You really screwed them, Charley, you really did."

"I'll see you, Mickey."

I started to walk to the door.

"Charley!"

I turned.

Mickey raised his glass in a salute. "To the most devious son of a loving bitch I've ever known!"

He downed the drink and grinned.

I walked out into the sunlight.

I was new to the hero business and it seemed to me I wasn't going about it quite right.

■ ■ ■

William J. Coughlin was a prosecutor and defense attorney in Detroit for twenty years. At the time of his death in April 1992, he was Senior United States Administrative Law Judge. The father of six children and the author of fourteen previous novels, including the bestselling *Shadow of a Doubt*, he lived with his wife in Grosse Pointe, Michigan.

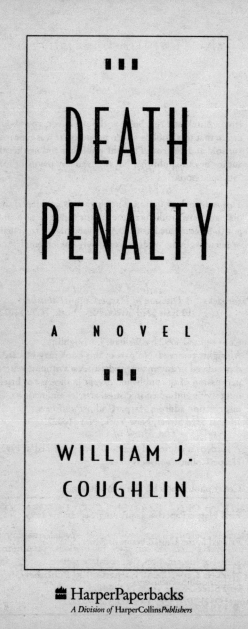

DEATH PENALTY

A NOVEL

WILLIAM J. COUGHLIN

HarperPaperbacks
A Division of HarperCollinsPublishers

This is a work of fiction. The characters, incidents, and dialogues are products of the author's imagination and are not to be construed as real. Any resemblance to actual events or persons, living or dead, is entirely coincidental.

HarperPaperbacks   *A Division of* HarperCollins*Publishers*
10 East 53rd Street, New York, N.Y. 10022

A hardcover edition of this book was published in 1992 by HarperCollins*Publishers*.

Cover photograph by Herman Estevez

First HarperPaperbacks printing: September 1993

Printed in the United States of America

HarperPaperbacks and colophon are trademarks of HarperCollins*Publishers*

❖ 10 9 8 7 6 5 4 3 2 1